# THE GATE OF VESSELS

# THE GATE OF VESSELS

Jacob Suarez

ISBN 979-8-218-50437-3

# Chapter 1

## THE THREE DAYS

ARCH SAGE THAYLUS STOOD at night outside the castle gates of Solace, the greatest kingdom in the realm of Khrine. The castle sat atop a high mountain overlooking the other six kingdoms in the distance, towers and villages illuminating windows and doorways. He took a deep breath, inhaling the cool night air.

A bright full moon lit up the kingdoms, all arrayed in a crescent shape along the edge of an immense plateau that comprised the realm. In the distance, he could see the kingdom of Nepheseer with its pointy towers made of black stone, flags swaying on spires. Farther off to the northwest, he gazed upon the kingdom of Wrethmire, its tall castle crowning Mount Atavis.

In the middle of the six kingdoms, a river ran from west to east, pouring over the edge of the plateau into the sea.

All of these kingdoms existed together, peacefully, all part of the realm of Khrine. But for how long? That he did not know.

The Arch Sage looked behind him at the castle of Solace, its towering stature taller and bigger than those of the other five kingdoms. And its library—incomparable.

Thaylus approached the closed front gate. His plight stabbed his consciousness like a knife.

The guard at the top of the wall came to the edge and made eye contact.

"It's the arch sage," the guard called out. "Open the gate!"

Through the gate, Thaylus saw two shirtless, muscular bald men rotate a crank that lifted the gate.

Thaylus strode through the gate and into the castle. In the main hall, polished marble floors gleamed, and pillars stood with golden fire mounts circling each. The pillars supported a vaulted ceiling four times as tall as any of the ceilings in the kingdoms below. From the ceilings hung chandeliers, crystals and emeralds sparkling in the firelight.

Thaylus cringed at the thought of the destruction of all this splendor—coming in just three days.

To his left, a gold encrusted silver door stood with a reflective sheen. Above it, in gold calligraphy, read "Treasure Vault." Thaylus had been inside more than a few times to assess and tally new valuable items added to the massive hold. He could clearly picture the chamber within, shelves eight feet high lining the vault walls. Chests of gold, wood, iron, and bronze filled the shelves.

No other kingdom compared to Solace's wealth.

A tall man in armor and a scarlet cloak neared Thaylus. They were the only two people within the great hall. The man had deep-set eyes framed with thin brows, and tonight, his eyes glittered like black pearls.

Thaylus nodded at him. "Greetings, General Everet. What keeps you up so late while everyone is fast asleep?" His voice echoed in the vast, empty chamber.

"Patrolling the castle. You have heard the rumors of thieves breaking in." General Everet tilted his head, his short, slicked raven-black hair unmoving. "How is my son doing?"

"Ethen is progressing well. Within two years he will be an official sage. He learns quickly."

"Good." Everet glanced at him, his square jaw tight. "Why are you awake?"

Thaylus tried to keep his face relaxed. "I am on my way to the archives."

"The archives? What is so urgent at this hour?"

Thaylus's breath caught. "I—I am entranced in a book, and I cannot think on anything else, even when I am lying in my bed."

Everet laughed. "My, it must be an excellent book. If only I shared your interest in knowledge." The general gave a wave. "I am retiring now. Good night, Arch Sage."

It wasn't an outright lie. Thaylus was indeed intent on a book, though it wasn't love of literature or history that kept him from his bed. It was the salvation of the realm—if that was even possible.

Thaylus watched him walk off, the general's heavy boots clacking against the smooth marble floors.

When the general was gone, Thaylus walked to the door and then to the spiraling staircase, which led down to the lower archive chamber.

A draft wafted through the stairway, causing the wall-mounted torches to flicker like dancing spirits. Each torch was bronze, with a snake winding around the handle, and the firelight made it look as if the snakes were twisting as he descended.

As he neared the bottom, Thaylus stopped and looked upward into the shadows, clenching his hands into fists. Was he wasting his time?

No. There was always a chance.

He took a seat at his desk in the arid gloomy space of the archives, deep beneath the castle of the kingdom of Solace.

His hands grew moist as he opened the book, eyes poring over the pages, searching for the answer. The book, titled simply Western Religion, was an ancient reference that spoke of the deities and customs long before the founding of whole realm of Khrine, long before Solace was even an idea. Maybe tonight he would find what he sought.

He read of a god named Elcore, said to have lived in the so-called realm of the gods before he was killed in a war with another god, Drahman, over the control of Khrine.

But it was all just folklore. Nothing more.

Thaylus took the book before him and slammed it shut.

"Nothing!"

His voice echoed in the chamber. He ran a palm down his face.

Even if the answer did lay in the archives, it would be lost in the enormous amounts of books and scrolls he had yet to examine. Thaylus slouched in his chair and gazed around the immense space illuminated by braziers—tall grey-bricked columns, shelves with myriads of books and scrolls, large tablets leaning against the base of the shelves.

He sighed and picked up another book, this one titled The Book of Durath.

A soft click sounded nearby, and Thaylus turned, then smiled.

A child with blond, curly hair and blue eyes in a small cloak appeared at the entrance to the archives. Prince Romous in his night garments.

"And what are you wanting tonight, young prince?" Thaylus beckoned.

This wasn't the first time Romous had snuck all the way to the archives. Thaylus was always impressed with Romous's stealth and quick eye, especially given that the child was only six years old. The last time he had come to the archives was three weeks ago, asking if he could take a book back to his room and read it.

Romous approached almost hesitantly. "Sage Thaylus, I had a bad dream.

May I stay with you for a while?"

Thaylus grinned and nodded. "Very well, Prince Romous. But only for a short time. Your father would upbraid me for letting you stay so late in the archives."

Romous pulled a chair so he could sit next to Thaylus and hopped onto the large leather-bound seat.

"What are you doing?" Romous asked, watching as Thaylus turned the pages of the book.

"Searching Romous, searching."

"For what?"

Thaylus patted Romous's head. "It is something you would not understand, little prince. Not yet."

Romous frowned. "I think I am smart enough."

Thaylus chuckled. "Perhaps, but it would trouble you."

"I can bear it."

"I am sorry, but no."

From the staircase came the clink of chain mail and boots, and Thaylus looked up to see a guard step into the torchlight.

Romous's eyes widened, and he gasped. He slipped of his seat and nestled next to Thaylus, looking up at the sage.

"Thaylus is letting me be here," the boy said.

"Is that true?" the guard asked.

Thaylus stood. "It is," he told the guard. "But now, my young friend, it is time for you to go to bed."

Gently, he nudged Romous forward.

Romous stepped to the guard reluctantly.

"Is everything in order, Arch Sage?" asked the guard.

"Yes."

The guard bowed. "Very well."

The guard and child disappeared again, up the stairs to the main castle level.

Thaylus returned to the task before him.

But again, as with the book before, he found nothing.

An hour later, he put yet another book aside. It didn't matter—book or one of the hundreds or even thousands of scrolls in the room, they all contained glorified folklore about worshipped pagan idols.

Thaylus rubbed his eyes and exhaled, then stood and trudged to the stairs.

His head pounded, his stomach knotted up, and his eyes burned from excessive reading. He needed rest from his mental plague.

But instead of his bed chamber, he headed for the sage's gardens.

He entered a semicircle colonnade of white marble. To his left, a mosaic floor of a long twisting dragon ran along narrow concourse with no roof or ceiling.

Thaylus walked through the garden, running his hand along the fence to his right. He went down a few marble steps leading to a wide area. Passing between two fountains shaped like blossoms, he came to a gate.

As he entered the cool space, Thaylus's mind returned to that night again—the night of his surreal, tormenting dream.

Swords that burned with black, smoky fire. Burning red eyes and dark, nebulous, shadow-like bodies. Dark foes. He saw it all in his mind's eye, the end of the whole realm. All of it to come to pass in three days' time.

He wished it were not so, but countless prophesies, from just a century to over a millennium ago, told of the dark entities coming. They were the Realm Dwellers—described just like in his dream.

Thaylus pushed away the recollection and opened the gate to the gardens. The full, bright moon cast a blue hue on the flowers, bushes, and trees.

To his surprise, Princess Athinia came around a cherry tree, the moon making her milky white face almost gleam.

She smiled at Thaylus. "Greetings Arch Sage. What keeps you up so late?"

"I would ask you the same question, Princess Athinia."

"I love the sage's gardens at night. The roses are beautiful in a full moon." Athinia tilted her head, her soft black hair swinging just so across her slender shoulders. "Are you worried about the Realm Dwellers' arrival in three days?"

Thaylus's throat went dry.

Athinia only laughed, putting a hand on Thaylus's shoulder. "There is no need for concern. The gods will deliver us."

His stomach clenched, her words like a punch. His dream was not a mockery—it was prophecy. The realm would not be saved by the gods, these dumb idols she and the rest of the kingdom believed in. They were created from the imagination of men! What could they do?

"I … I think I will retire for the night," Thaylus muttered. "I am tired."

"Of course, Thaylus. Good night," Athinia said with a smile.

Thaylus returned the way he came and headed for his room in the sage's wing. Walking past guards, he came to a small courtyard with a large brazier in the center. There, Thaylus warmed his hands.

As the heat relaxed his muscles, he let the tension go, sighing deeply.

What if there was a real answer to the dilemma the realm faced? Could there be real deity, one not dreamed up by men? One who had power to save the realm, to even be worthy of worship and reverence?

Thaylus pulled at his short, grey beard. If only.

With a grunt, he turned toward the corridor, in the direction his bed chamber. But as he walked, he glimpsed it again, yet another stone statue in the alcove. This one had the torso of an ape, the wings of a bat, and the face of a crow. And in the place of its eyes were two emeralds.

Thaylus felt his face redden. He could have spat upon the image.

This was why they were doomed. His people looked to dumb idols to save them.

When he reached his chamber, he collapsed onto his bed. His mind spun with thoughts of Realm Dwellers staining the ground with the blood of innocents, soldiers, and royalty.

Sleep came late. And that night, his nightmare returned once again. As he thrashed on his bed, his mind brought him to a small mound, watching as the dark foes lay siege on the armies of the realm of Khrine.

Thaylus smelled the salty, thick odor of blood, and the smoke from the black fire of the Realm Dwellers' swords burned his lungs. Their battle cries sounded like coals crackling hot and fierce as mind-searing screams came from women and children.

The horde of foes pouring into the castle of Solace looked like tar pouring into a stone-forged mold.

"No!" Thaylus cried, his throat raspy from the burning crops and houses. He fell to his knees, his hands gripping his grey hair. "No, no!"

And as he looked up, a Realm Dweller was swiveling toward him, lunging hard at Thaylus with sword raised.

Thaylus awoke in a hot sweat. He sat up, his legs tangled in the sheets and his breathing heavy. Just a nightmare, he told himself, his eyes darting everywhere. He was still in his room.

Morning sun glimmered through the window, and he swung his legs over the bed and onto the ground.

He dressed in his sage's mantle and made his way to the main chamber hall, his face a mask of gloom.

The mood of the hall was just the opposite. Inside, royalty, nobleman, and other esteemed retinue stood in groups, laughing. Warm smiles lit everyone's faces. Narrow stained-glass windows at the entrance wall caused sunlight patterns to dance on the ground. Hellos and good mornings echoed all around.

Thaylus kept his head down as he moved through the crowd all the way to the far wall of the immense rectangle, then through a wooden door and up a staircase to the highest tower.

At the top, he found King Trophimus and his son, Prince Romous, gazing at the orange-red sun as it rose over the Epoch Mountains in the east.

Even in his dark mood, Thaylus had to admit the view of the kingdom was stunning. Grey smoke rose from chimneys built atop thatched or stone roofs. Merchants set up shop in tents and kiosks. Fields of corn stalks grew where farmers doted upon crop fields. Beyond the kingdom boundaries, the wilderness lands of rolling hills and forests looked mysterious as a white mist snaked through them.

Thaylus's heart sank in despair. In two days all this splendor would be decimated. Only the destruction of the temples of the confounded gods raised his spirits.

Trophimus and his son watched in silence.

"Good morning, Your Majesty." Thaylus bowed his head in respect.

"Ah! Greetings, Arch Sage Thaylus! Is this not a beautiful day!"

The king's cheerfulness put a knot in Thaylus's gullet and a bitter taste in his mouth. If only Trophimus knew.

"Is not our kingdom the grandest in the realm?" the king asked.

"Yes, Lord, it is."

"And soon our most powerful foe will seek to destroy it in two days." The king narrowed his eyes and pursed his lips. "But our gods will surely crush them!"

"Father, what are Realm Dwellers?" asked Romous.

Thaylus and King Trophimus glanced at each other with a raised eyebrow.

"Allow me." Thaylus knelt and looked the prince in the eyes. "All you need to know is the Realm Dwellers are evil enemies with great and destructive power."

"Why do they want to hurt us?"

"It is their nature."

"Where do they come from?"

Thaylus and Trophimus exchanged another look.

"They live a place called the Abyss," Thaylus said. "It is not part of this world. That will have to suffice, young prince."

"What do they look like?"

Just then, the young prince's steward appeared and bowed to King Trophimus. "Sire, is your son still going on the tour in the woods with the rest of the stewards?"

The king looked down at Romous. "What about it, son? Do you still want to go?"

"Oh, yes, father!" the prince blurted as he followed the steward down the stairs of the tower.

"I truly wonder if Romous perceived anything you told him," Trophimus said. "You did as anyone could do though," he with a chuckle and a clasp on Thaylus's back.

Thaylus frowned, keeping his voice low. His relationship with the king was good, but the king was, after all, still king.

"My Lord, may I ask you … why have all our kingdoms in Khrine kept the coming of the Realm Dwellers such a secret from the people?"

Trophimus wrinkled his nose. "It would only vex the minds of our subjects. It would also distract them from their tasks."

"But what will happen when the Realm Dwellers do come? The people will be scared, my Lord."

"Any apprehension on their part will be quite brief, as I am certain the gods will destroy the Realm Dwellers promptly."

Thaylus wanted to grab the king, shake him by the shoulders, and scream the truth into him. What could make a sensible man worship wood, stone, and metal? If only another person had the same strange, burning, spiritual conviction he had since childhood to see the gods as they were—dumb idols!

"Thaylus, do you ever wonder how the Realm Dwellers came to be?" the king asked, gazing again at the kingdom below.

"They could have been on Khrine since man has."

"But why would the gods create such heinous beings?"

Thaylus shrugged. "It makes one wonder about the nature of the gods."

"What do you mean?"

Thaylus opened his mouth to speak then hesitated. "Perhaps there are evil gods—ones we do not know of. Who is to say these evil gods live in the Abyss as well? Maybe they live here, too."

Trophimus pulled at his chin. "Intriguing. But our gods are stronger even if there are evil gods. I am not afraid."

Thaylus felt powerless. A lump caught in his throat, and he turned away so the king could not see the emotion on his face. Placing his hands upon the stone balcony, he hung his head. What did it matter if the king saw his sadness or if the king asked why? The realm was doomed.

Was there some force that might save them? How could he find out? Could there be hope somewhere, anywhere?

Footsteps raced up the stairwell, and they turned to see a messenger breathing heavily with wide, glazed eyes.

"My Lord!" The messenger panted, bowing his head low. "The Western Kingdom has allied with the Realm Dwellers!"

Thaylus's and Trophimus's bodies jolted.

The king stared at the messenger hard. "Calm yourself. How do you know this?"

"One of our ambassadors heard two noblemen of the Western Kingdom speak of a pact with the Realm Dwellers."

"This is impossible!" the king roared. "They are still in the Abyss! It must be sorcery. We know of wizards who can change form."

"But why would they speak of something if it was not so?" Thaylus asked.

King Trophimus shook his head. "No. It must be necromancy! How could dozens of prophesies centuries old be wrong about the time of the Realm Dwellers coming?" Trophimus turned to address the messenger. "You are dismissed."

The messenger glanced at Thaylus then back to the king. "My Lord, what shall we do?"

"You are dismissed! I will tell you when I have thought on the matter."

The messenger bowed with glossy, wide eyes and scuttled down the stairs.

Thaylus's heart thumped like the steps of a raging buffalo. A force had arisen in the Western Kingdom. Perhaps this news could sway the king and others of the gods' fallacy.

# Chapter 2

## THE SCARLET LIGHT

BEFORE THAYLUS COULD UTTER another word, the king clutched his arm.

As they watched, a bright red light shot upward from the Western Kingdom castle.

A tremor of fear snaked down Thaylus's spine. He and the king stood still as statues as they stared at the light.

Trophimus backed away with glossy eyes and a gaping mouth. "That—that beam of light! Such evil!"

Thaylus shook himself, then took Trophimus's shoulders.

It took a few moments for the king to wrench his gaze from the light.

"Your Majesty, we must stay calm."

"But—this can't be true." Trophimus ran a hand through his hair. "It doesn't mean the Realm Dwellers have truly contacted the Western Kingdom. The gods are supposed to destroy the Realm Dwellers. The gods wouldn't let them exist on Khrine let alone aid the Western Kingdom. Moreover, the Realm Dwellers are to come in two more days, not today. Dozens of prophecies all point to that date. In two days!"

The king headed for the stairs.

"Where are you going, Lord?"

"I am sending messengers to the other five kingdoms to assemble at the royal court in the south wing." King Trophimus breathed heavily and shook his head. "The gods would not let anything overtake our kingdom. Everyone must feel horrified."

"My Lord, the light and the apparent betrayal of the Western Kingdom may be linked," Thaylus said as he followed the king down the stairs. "I should go to assess the matter immediately."

"No. I want you here for the meeting."

"But what if something important is transpiring there as we speak?"

"No." Trophimus stopped his descent, his expression hard. "I will send a scout."

"But my Lord!" Thaylus looked the king in the eyes. "None are more able than me to assess the matter, especially if it is sorcery or the Realm Dwellers. You know this."

The king looked at him a long moment, considering. Then he sighed. "Very well. Go."

Thaylus wiped a thin sheen of sweat from his forehead. "I will find what the light means."

Thaylus's heart raced. What power could do this? Could the work of potent magic have caused a glowing apparition? Or was it an early release of the Realm Dwellers from the Abyss?

In the main hall, the nobility surrounded them with wide doughy eyes.

"What does the red light signify?" demanded a stout man with grey hair. "Is it an omen of the Realm Dwellers?"

"Are we in danger?" asked a tall thin man, his lip jutting with the question.

"Our wise and able Arch Sage is on his way to see what it is," said the king. "In the meantime, stay calm."

Thaylus wanted to comfort them, but he, too, was horrified.

"Be vigilant," Thaylus said with as much authority as he could muster. "I will discover what or who is behind the light. Go about your regular tasks."

Only one man did not show panic. Instead, his eyes flickered with concern.

As the small crowd dispersed, Thaylus made a beeline for the man, Brythan.

"Do you think it's true?" Brythan asked quietly when they were alone.

He and Thaylus had been friends since Brythan was eighteen years old. Now, at age twenty-nine, he was the youngest nobleman to be ordained, partly due to the wisdom Thaylus had instilled in him. Thaylus thought him as a son to a degree. He was the sole recipient of Thaylus's deep admiration among the noblemen. Unlike the other noblemen, he didn't appear to feel the need to show off his wealth. He wore a humble gray cotton tunic covered by a brown mantle and a cloak.

"The pact? I do not know." Thaylus sighed. "But if the Realm Dwellers are already here, time is shorter than I imagined."

"How could King Nephaal stoop to such vileness?" Brythan shook his head. "He has always ruled the Western Kingdom with wisdom and honor."

"That is what I intend to discover. I am going now to the Western Kingdom to investigate the red light and the situation with the Realm Dweller."

Brythan lifted his chin. "I will join you."

Thaylus started to object, then held his tongue.

"Brythan, our friendship began when you were a young nobleman and only a teenager. I recall your days as an older teenager when you sought to learn from me the sagely ways." Thaylus paused, then finally gave a brief nod. "Now you are twenty-nine. I can think of no other than you to assess the pillar of light with me. I shall be glad for your company."

Brythan's jaw was tight. "I fear it is their portal to enter from. However, I do not think the Realm Dwellers have crossed over to our world yet. And there is something else."

Thaylus waited.

"I read about this, an omen of the Scarlet Light." Brythan's voice was low. "Only days ago. I found a tablet that speaks of the light—this very light that we now see above the Western Kingdom."

"What? How?" Thaylus almost couldn't believe it.

"I stumbled upon it in the temple of Areth, the one that burnt down decades ago. I'd heard from the priest that a tablet in Pyrithian became lost in the fire." Brythan's eyes were bright as he shared with the arch sage. "I thought maybe something about the prophecy could be found there, so I went looking and found it in a secret compartment behind the altar."

Thaylus's eyes widened. "Can you show me?"

"Quickly, follow me!"

Brythan darted away, his brown cloak swaying as Thaylus followed him between two rows of white marble pillars that upheld the vaulted ceiling.

At a small marble door with the crest of an eagle in the center, they entered, then proceeded down a narrow torch-lit hall toward the direction of the west wing.

The hall opened into to a large octagonal room, with doors set within all eight walls. Each door had the name of a nobleman engraved upon it.

Brythan opened the one with his name. Inside the room was tasteful but fine—a canopied bed, a small desk, and above it all a mural of the heavens painted with the most delicate of hands.

Brythan went directly to the desk and picked up a small dusty tablet with worn engravings.

"This is it. It's in the dead language of Pyrithia, so I cannot understand it all, but I was able to read enough."

Written upon the scroll they could both read the words:

> *An omen of scarlet light will reveal from where*
> *The beings of evil will usher in their siege on the foretold day.*
> *But the Lord and His Emissary from the Gate of Vessels*
> *Will subdue them....*

Thaylus tugged at his short beard. "The beam of light came true," he murmured, gazing at the ancient scroll. "And 'Gate of Vessels' and 'Lord and His emissary' may insinuate a deity. As for 'beings of evil'—"

Brythan's voice grew excited. "It seems like the Realm Dwellers, especially if rumor is true about one being spotted in the Western Kingdom."

Thaylus heart soared and his mind raced even as terror coursed through him. Could there truly be a being powerful enough to thwart the Realm Dwellers? Was there a benevolent spiritual entity involved with man's existence who might subdue these foes?

"We should leave now," Thaylus began. "I think—"

Just then, a loud crack split the air. The ground began to shake beneath their feet.

Thaylus and Brythan fell to their knees as the circular wall cracked and paintings hit the floor.

"We must get out!" Brythan clutched at Thaylus. "This quake is collapsing the whole room!"

"I cannot stand!"

"Crawl! The main chamber is reinforced by strong pillars. We'll be safe if we make it there!"

A piece of stone plummeted and struck Thaylus's calf.

"Thaylus!"

Brythan managed to rise on trembling legs. He seized Thaylus's arm and dragged him toward the door.

A slab of stone fell, blocking their exit.

"Our lives cannot end this way!" Thaylus cried, hands in fists. "My ultimate question has not been answered!"

All around them, the room was caving in upon itself.

"Arch Sage!" they heard from the blocked entrance.

Thaylus looked up to see six men using all their strength to bash the massive slab inward. With a last heave, the slab toppled.

Strong arms dragged Thaylus and Brythan out.

As they came to rest in the main chamber, the earthquake rumbled to a halt. The men who'd helped them, noblemen from their looks, staggered, their eyes wide.

"Thank you," Brythan managed after he caught his breath.

"It is a good thing we saw you enter," said a tall nobleman.

"And a good thing we were nearby," quipped another.

They all laughed wearily, gratitude at their escape washing over them.

Thaylus drew himself to his feet. His calf ached from the stone that had hit him, but he was not injured.

"We must see what has happened to the rest of the castle."

Brythan followed. They headed through the octagonal room and back to the main hall.

"I do not think it a coincidence the quake occurred this morning, so close to the time the red light appeared," Thaylus murmured to Brythan.

"What do you mean?"

"I fear to think of it. But I have a feeling we will find out. I need to get to the Western Kingdom."

When they reached the main hall, it was in shambles. Cracked pillars and fallen chandeliers littered the great space, causing a large fissure in the marble floor. Some people were being carried off on makeshift cots, while others tended to bruises or cuts.

Thaylus approached a physician. "Where is the king?"

"He wasn't hurt, thank the gods." The physician called over a helper. "Take Arch Sage Thaylus to the king."

When King Trophimus saw them, he rushed over. "Praise the gods you are safe!"

"I do not think there is coincidence between the red light and the earthquake." Thaylus shook his head in concern. "If you have no further use for us, I would like to set off at once. A singeing anxiousness compels me to go to the Western Kingdom, and quickly."

"That was no earthquake," muttered the king.

"What?"

Trophimus swallowed thickly. "A glowing red sphere came from the pillar of light and struck the base of the castle. That's what caused this."

"It must come from the Realm Dwellers," Brythan cried, then looked down. "Arch Sage, I must come with you."

"You are most welcome if His Majesty allows it." Thaylus embraced Brythan.

"You may go, Brythan," said the king. "It sounds like a good idea. I know Thaylus could use your help, not to mention your strong mind."

Brythan frowned. "It's not just that. It's Nephaal, rightful king of the Western Kingdom. We all know him to be an honorable man, full of integrity. I suspect another has taken the throne and made himself king in place of Nephaal."

King Trophimus's eyes flashed at the prospect. "In that case, you both should depart now on account of what just happened."

"It all comes from the Realm Dwellers," said Brythan. "I know this in my heart."

Anyone with a hint of education knew the stories. Thaylus recalled the oldest prophecy that confirmed the Realm Dwellers would be released on the appointed day, a prophecy he'd studied with Brythan not too many years ago. It was written on a tablet in the dead language of Pyrithia—the same language as the scroll they'd just been reading moments before the room caved in upon them.

Thaylus shuddered. Many prophetical scrolls and tablets from all seven kingdoms foretold the horrible day. Thaylus contemplated telling the Pyrithian prophecy to the king, but he knew Trophimus would have scorned anything relating to a sole supreme deity, even one spoken of in prophecy.

Trophimus pursed his lips. "We must trust in the gods. They gave us victory over the wizard King Vyprus during the old war. They will protect us now."

Thaylus could have screamed, or worse, struck the king. There was no supernatural intervention or hint of any divine power that ensured victory! He was so high, so regal, yet so foolish, just like everyone else who trusted in their daft gods.

Before leaving, they paid a visit to the armory. While weapons would probably prove little use against a Realm Dweller or a sorcerer, they did provide a degree of assurance.

Selecting two swords, the pair walked outside the front gate to Brythan's stalls.

"We need two fast horses to traverse to the Western Kingdom," Brythan told his stable keeper, a heavyset man in a dirty brown tunic.

By now it was close to noon, and the cool air brought the smell of hay and manure.

"You intend to go to that wretched beam of red light in the Western Kingdom, eh?"

Beneath the stable keeper's bushy eyebrows, Thaylus could see the dark expression in his eyes. "It kills my gut to say that evil light makes my flesh crawl. I have an itch the gods might not pull through against that vile sight."

The keeper's words sparked something, some hope, deep within Thaylus. Even just a hint of doubt in the gods appealed, even if it was motivated by fear.

"There are indeed some people who feel like you." Thaylus patted the man's arm reassuringly. "I think it is natural to think so. Don't feel guilty."

As they left, Brythan spoke in a low tone. "Why did you pacify his lack of faith? He does not have any other god to adhere to."

The sage did not know what to say. "I was only trying to comfort the man."

Brythan frowned. "Your heart is in the right place, but I think otherwise."

\* \* \*

An hour later, Thaylus and Brythan were riding through western Solace. The horses' hooves kicked up clumps of dirt as they passed through the wealthier section of the kingdom. Some had gardens with white porcelain fountains and luscious blossoms with small pillars surrounding verandas.

As they approached a cluster of homes, they could see a group of men gathered outside staring at the light, forgetting their hoeing, their selling of items, their wood working and any other daily labors. Children gripped their mother's hands. They all looked like statues as, mouths open, they gaped at the red light beyond the hills.

They could not tell them of the Realm Dwellers, Thaylus realized. It would frighten them, plus it would be disobeying King Trophimus. But he had to rid them of their fears somehow.

He felt dishonest, his heart heavy for the citizens.

"Brythan, I do not know what to tell them," Thaylus said with a stiff face.

"Allow me," Brythan said to Thaylus.

Brythan dismounted as the people slowly tugged their eyes from the light and toward him.

"Citizens of Solace," Brythan cried. "The evil essence of the light is a test from the gods to try our faith. Simply stand firm and wait for its passing. We are going to investigate."

An old man approached, his eyes flickering with anger. "You're hiding something from us! I can tell!"

A young woman went to the man's side and sneered. "He's right. You're lying!"

Suddenly, the attention was off the red light—and onto Brythan and Thaylus. The crowd pressed in, fists raised. Thaylus dismounted, thinking he could bring reason to the mob, but the moment his boots hit the ground, he knew it was the wrong idea.

"Tell us the truth!" a young man cried, pointing his pitchfork at the sage.

Another man grabbed the pitchfork, tossing it aside. "Put it down! You're assaulting a royal sage!"

"Calm yourselves!" Thaylus's bellow shook his ears, but it seemed the people could barely hear it above the clamor.

"Thaylus, look out." Brythan pulled the arch sage sideways, but it was too late.

A wild-eyed man with a cleaver cut through the masses and sliced down hard—right into Thaylus's leg.

A burn seared through his leg. Thaylus grasped the wound, his cry a sharp gasp.

But before anyone could react, chain-mailed guards in metal breeches swooped in, spears and swords brandished against the growing riot.

"Desist! Desist in the name of the king!" the guards hollered.

The mob dissipated, men and women hauled off in shackles. Those who remained sported bruises, bloody noses, and even worse, a stone-eyed glare indicating anger—and fear.

"My wound needs tending." Bright red seeped through the cloth Thaylus held tight against his leg.

An old woman in a blue dress and a bright face approached.

"I can help. I was a nurse during the old war."

She led them to a large stone house nearby and went quickly to work, wrapping his wound with green leaves and white bandages.

"These will soothe the cut." Her voice and hands were kind and swift.

"Thank you." Thaylus looked her in the eyes. "Please, I want you to have this." He ripped off a small, deep-blue gem embroidered upon his cloak. "A jewel is given to a sage when they do an exceedingly good deed. You're no sage, but this action is merit enough."

The woman flushed. "Thank you, but it is not necessary."

"Please, I insist."

"As you wish, my lord."

She smiled warmly, then ducked her head.

As they left, Thaylus smiled in return as she gave a gentle wave, then tucked the gem into the folds of her skirt and went back inside her house.

Thaylus watched her go. His heart moved with an inner stillness and a clear mind permeated his thoughts. It passed through his body like a cool mist—this woman, who could she be? Thaylus pulled at his beard, pondering.

Brythan led them back to their horses, where he addressed the head guard.

"What about the rest of the citizens?"

"I have posted men at all quarters of Solace. You have my word—no other riots will happen."

They rode on, past the wealthier farms and toward the lower-class region on the outskirts of the kingdom. Usually jovial and at ease, today the people were as solemn as prisoners, all eyes upon the red light. Even the children ceased playing with their wooden dolls, swords, and wicker balls, instead clinging to their parents.

"You come from the royal castle!" A middle-aged man with a downcast face called out as they approached the edge of the village. "I pray, what are you doing? Will you save us from it?"

"Be strong my friend," Brythan tried to reassure him. "All will be fine."

The companions rode on toward the wilderness, toward the red light.

# Chapter 3

## THE BEING OF POWER

THE CLOSER THEY GOT to the Western Kingdom, the faster Thaylus's heart pounded. Sweat trickled in a thick line down his back, and he squeezed the horse's reins hard.

Ahead, the blazing beam shot up to the clouds, themselves flickering and rumbling with red lighting.

"The evil from the light makes me shiver," Thaylus muttered.

Brythan nodded, his brows tight. "Whatever being resides there, we must not let fear keep us from our mission."

Ahead, Thaylus spotted movement. He slowed his horse. It was a person, walking toward them from a high hill.

Thaylus and Brythan eased their horses to a halt.

"Brythan, do you see? Who is that figure over there?"

Brythan rubbed his chin. "He approaches with his back toward the Western Kingdom. We should act with discretion."

Thaylus's stomach tightened. "If this person wields magic, weapons may prove useless."

"Perhaps he is simply a defector."

"Still, as you stated, we must use caution."

They dismounted, waiting for the approaching figure.

The figure came closer. Thaylus could see he was an old man, face pale and eyes bloodshot and bulging. Foam seeped from his mouth. The lines of his strained neck muscles made Thaylus cringe.

Slowly, the pair withdrew their swords, waiting. Watching.

Then, without warning, the old man lunged straight for Brythan.

His hands grasped Brythan by the throat.

Brythan's sword clattered to the ground, his face red with effort as he clawed at the old man's grip.

"Get off him!" Thaylus yanked at the old man's hands, but they were unnaturally strong.

Finally, the arch sage raised his sword, ready.

Before he could strike, the old man fell to the ground, still.

Brythan panted as the friends eyed each other.

"Is he dead?" Thaylus's eyes were wide.

The old man's body twitched. Then, as if he hadn't been deadly still a moment prior, the old man inched to his knees, took a deep breath, and attempted to stand.

"You there, stay on the ground! For what reason did you assault us? And who are you?" Brythan's voice was still raspy from the attack.

"H—how did I get here?" The old man took a few breaths, then clutched his head as if in agony. "My head is throbbing…"

"Answer me!" Brythan ordered.

"Remain cordial," Thaylus murmured to his friend. "I believe he no longer poses a threat. He doesn't know what happened."

Thaylus sheathed his sword, then offered a hand to the old man.

Gratefully, the man climbed to his feet. He clutched at Thaylus as if for balance.

"Do you have any clue where you are?" asked the sage.

"I … I'm not sure. The last thing I remember was fleeing for my life from this … this man."

"What man?" Brythan took a step closer. "Explain."

The old man caught his breath. "It occurred right in King Nephaal's throne room." He peered around, confused. "I thought it was just a moment ago, but from where I'm standing, I fear it's been some time. A man in a black cloak appeared before the throne, his presence coming in a swift flash of red light. He claimed to be a god, but none believed him for his human appearance. We knew he was a sorcerer…."

Thaylus watched as the old man tucked trembling hands closer to his chest.

"We feared his presence, and the king ordered the guards to apprehend this imposter. But then, with a mere wave of his hand, the guards went hurling into the air! Against the walls!"

Brythan and Thaylus exchanged glances.

"Do you know who created the beam of light?" Thaylus asked.

"What beam of light?" The old man turned to look, his gasp audible. "I had no idea!"

"What did the sorcerer want?" asked Thaylus.

Wide-eyed, the man just stared at the pillar of light rising from the Western Kingdom castle. A single tear trailed down his face.

"What occurred next?" Brythan took a step closer.

The stranger ran a palm down his face. "King Nephaal refused him at first, but the person threatened to harm women and children. His very presence instilled unspeakable fear. It was like a stark cold had filled the room."

His breath caught, and it was a moment before he could continue.

"I served as the king's chamberlain. I—I tried to escape, but he uttered strange words then something horrible came over me. A feeling, but it was almost like a cloak I couldn't get out from under. It was too hard to fight. I do not know what happened next or how I got here."

As they peered at the man, the bright day began to darken, as if a massive thundercloud had covered the sun.

"Look, there!" Brythan pointed.

Thaylus fought to hold steady as he watched three figures, in shadow-like dark, hooded cloaks, fly over the ground toward them.

"What manner of life is that?"

"Realm Dwellers!" Brythan exclaimed. "It must be. They have crossed over before their prophesied date of their coming!"

Thaylus and Brythan mounted their horses, then Brythan pulled the old man into the saddle behind him.

"Hold on tight!"

They fled in the opposite direction as fast as the horses could run, headed straight back to Solace. They didn't look back, just kept riding nonstop.

As they gained the top of a hill, Thaylus turned his head. Still, they came, the three figures pursuing them.

Finally the mysterious figures came to a halt just twenty-five yards from the men.

Thaylus drew his horse to a walk, puzzling as he turned the animal to face them. The sense they emitted instilled fear, but not like the presence of the Realm Dwellers he'd felt in his dream.

"Wait!" Thaylus called to Brythan.

Brythan reared his horse, the old man clutching his waist tightly.

"Why are you stopping, Thaylus? What mad reason fills your head to go to them for any purpose! We must retreat!"

"Give me a chance. There is something different about them!"

The sage's heart throbbed and pulsated in his chest. He knew he seemed insane, but he couldn't help it. He had to know.

Slowly, Thaylus dismounted and approached the three cloaked figures, leading his horse by the reins. A delirious fear made him drowsy and faint. Nevertheless, he took hold of his nerves.

Endure, he told himself as their evil presence overflowed his senses. His face ran with sweat and a painful knot coalesced in his gullet. With all his willpower, he endured his strong bodily reaction to flee as fast and far away as he could.

Then he stopped five yards away, his breathing shallow and his legs weak.

"Who are you?" His very words trembled.

"You may call us Realm Messengers," said one. His voice rumbled deeply and crackled like burning coals.

Slowly, the mysterious beings put their gloved hands to the edge of their shadowy hoods and pulled them back.

Their faces mimicked the appearance of gloomy clouds, and their eyes burned with orange fire. The beings resembled those in his dream decades ago, but their orange eyes gave a notable distinction.

Thaylus squeezed his eyes shut in attempt to force his fear from his consciousness, a shudder washing over him at their countenance.

Finally he could bear it no more. Mounting his horse once more, he charged off toward Brythan and the stranger.

The three figures did not pursue.

"I don't understand." He frowned when he reached his friend. "They just linger there."

Brythan's eyes were wide and his mouth hung open. "Are you mad? Fortune has favored your life that those spiritual beings did not harm you!"

Thaylus lowered his head, which throbbed and tremored from nearing the three cloaked beings. It took a few moments until he regained his composure enough to speak.

"You were right, Brythan. We have encountered some kind of Ream Dweller. They have indeed crossed to our dimension."

"Then the prophecy about the time of their attack has proved false." Brythan face was a contorted scowl.

"I do not think so. Those beings have burning orange eyes, almost like fire. The prophecies are clear that true Realm Dwellers have red ones. Did you hear them speak to me? They called themselves Realm Messengers. But it probably does not matter."

Suddenly, the adrenaline seemed to leave his body, and Thaylus all but collapsed in his saddle.

"Oh, Brythan, it was terrifying. I was scared enough to die."

"But why didn't they harm you?" said Brythan.

They watched in silence as the dark beings hovered a moment, then flew back to the Western Kingdom.

What had happened? Brythan had a point—they did not hurt him. Perhaps these orange-eyed Realm Messengers held significant difference from the Realm Dwellers. Was it a warning?

Thaylus's mind froze then, dreading who now controlled the Western Kingdom.

Now out of danger, he knew: He needed to tell Brythan his dream.

"Brythan, I need to share something with you."

Brythan tilted his head. "Of course, my friend. Now?"

"Soon."

Thaylus felt his body and mind relax at Brythan's gracious word and sensible mind. Finally, someone might receive his dream! Thaylus hoped his friend's eyes could be opened to the truth.

They continued to stare in the direction of the red light.

"What if the sorcerer holds the power of the Realm Dwellers?" Brythan murmured. "His power would be great, even more powerful than King Vyprus. But how could we get in the castle of the Western Kingdom without detection?"

"Perhaps he knows." Thaylus nodded at the man who was still clinging to Brythan.

The man's head had sagged, as if all his energy was spent.

"Do you know any secret way into the castle?" asked Brythan.

The man swallowed visibly.

"Ye—yes. At the eastern side of the kingdom boundaries, a route through a cave system leads to the dungeon into the castle."

The man began expounding the direction of the route when Brythan stopped him. "These instructions should be written down."

"No need, my friend. Despite my age, my memory is quite keen."

Brythan nodded as he motioned for the stranger to continue.

When the stranger had finished, he took a deep, trembling breath. "Legends tell of a monster inhabiting the dungeon. Few have knowledge of the passageway. If you are going there, it appears you will find out if the monster exists."

"We have no choice, friend," Brythan said to the stranger.

Twilight would come soon. The three headed back toward Solace.

Leaving the stranger with a male steward and their horses in the stable, they strode into the royal hall.

"My lord, I have dire news," said Thaylus as they knelt before King Trophimus.

"That much is obvious, man. What did you find?"

"It is as Brythan suspected. King Nephaal has been subdued, and a sorcerer now resides there."

"Then it is not a Realm Dweller?"

"I am afraid they are also involved. Brythan and I have seen them."

The king put a fist to his lips. "You have seen these beings? Then the worst has happened. I hope all kingdoms will be here soon to meet tonight in the war hall. Tell me more—how did you learn about the sorcerer?"

"We encountered a man fleeing the Western Kingdom who observed the incident when the sorcerer conquered it."

"Where is this man who told of this?"

"We brought him back with us and questioned him thoroughly," Thaylus said. "He came under the possession of the sorcerer for a time."

The king sighed. "It's like the Great War the kingdoms waged on King Vyprus all those years ago."

Brythan spoke up. "Thaylus and I should infiltrate the Western Kingdom as soon as possible."

"No. Not with the new danger of Realm Dwellers and this sorcerer who has made himself king. You two are too valuable to risk harm or worse."

"The man we brought from the Western Kingdom told us a secret cave route to the east leading into the castle. Since we know the way, Brythan and I should go," Thaylus said.

The king shook his head. "Then relay your information to our spies so they can traverse the way there."

"Nay, my Lord. The way through the cavern is erratic and designated by landmarks only a keen eye can navigate. With due respect to our spies, they do not possess the acute senses I have."

Trophimus stopped short and looked down pulling his beard. "Hmm … I see. You make a good point." He looked to Thaylus and nodded. "Very well. You may bring Brythan as well. I know he is in good hands with you."

"Thank you, my Lord. Penetrating the Western Kingdom at night would be best," Thaylus added.

"That much I surmised. How long do you think it will take to get inside their citadel?"

"According to the complicated and numerous directions from the stranger, it could be some time," said Thaylus.

The king appeared to be deep in thought for a long moment. Finally, he nodded.

"It appears you have an extensive journey ahead of you. Though I do wish you could attend the meeting of the kingdoms tonight."

Thaylus shook his head. "The sooner we infiltrate the castle the better."

The king nodded. "Do as you have planned."

With that, he rose and disappeared toward the throne room, his attendants following close behind.

"He may be right that nothing can be done," Brythan said when they were alone.

"It may appear so, but things are not always what they seem."

Brythan yawed. "I will take a brief rest until it is time."

As they walked off, Thaylus caught his sleeve. "Brythan, let us converse privately. Perhaps in my chamber if it was not ruined from the quake. I must share something with you. Something important."

One of the things Thaylus had long admired about Brythan was his ability receive anything honestly and without deterrence.

Brythan and Thaylus found his quarters intact. Once inside, Thaylus spoke bluntly about his dream.

After, Brythan sat a moment, absorbing the news. "Your dream cannot be a coincidence."

Thaylus nodded. "But there is the detail of the Realm Dwellers having red eyes not orange, like the Realm Messengers we encountered."

Brythan's eyebrows raised and he nodded slowly. "I see. This dream you believe to be prophetic is the main reason for your disbelief."

"Precisely, and the prophecies about the Realm Dwellers and their red eyes." Thaylus took a breath. "But it's not just that, Brythan. I also dreamed of the unreality of the 'gods,' for in my dream, none came to rescue Khrine."

Brythan waited as if he knew what Thaylus was about to admit.

Thaylus closed his eyes. "They have never been seen and have never proved themselves, Brythan. Neither do I feel any presence or peace of them."

He opened his eyes to see Brythan appear almost defeated, as though his breath left him.

Brythan blinked, then lowered his head.

"I've always thought the gods existed in a state too high to dwell amidst men or interact with us," Brythan admitted in a low voice. "Moreover, I have believed spiritual longing is just a part of life, like suffering. But is there a way to be spiritually fulfilled?"

"Perhaps a higher power exists we do not know of."

Brythan frowned. "I don't understand. If you do not believe in the gods, why did you choose to become Arch Sage?"

Thaylus sighed. "My father wanted it. I jumped for joy at first, but as the years progressed, I developed the stance I do now. I studied night and day with fervency concerning the lineage of the kings, the noblemen, and the founding and development of Solace. I learned the dialects of many places and kingdoms. I versed myself in a few of the ancient, dead languages. Soon after, a sage named Euricle took me as an apprentice."

Brythan nodded for him to continue.

"In my hope of a real deity, I busied myself with searching for the answer in all the texts of the kingdom," Thaylus said. "Scroll after scroll, book after book, I searched for peace. It drove me on, and because of my desperation, I excelled in knowledge above all my equals. And that, my friend, is where I am today."

Brythan's eyes were glassy, and a tear spilled down his cheek.

Thaylus's heart leaped. Finally, someone to confide in. But would his young friend share his belief? Could he have the heart to completely forsake the gods the whole realm had embraced for so long?

# Chapter 4

## THAYLUS'S SECRET

THAYLUS PINCHED his brows, then got to his feet. "I would feel better if we walked in the sage's private garden. No one is there, and the flowers give me peace, especially after all that has happened. It will not take long."

In the sage's gardens, they walked shoulder to shoulder down a stone path with both sides lined with flowers. Torches at every corner of the garden illuminated the flowers with a lucid dimness amidst the darkness of night.

Thaylus felt the tension melt from his shoulders. "I am happy that I can trust you. I have always feared others knowing how I believe. Up to this time it has been a secret. It saddens me the people believe in their gods when they have never given a sign or proof they are real."

Brythan slowed to a stop and looked down, troubled. "I have heard your words and taken it to heart, my friend. Nevertheless, the situation remains difficult."

The two approached the statue of Thron, god of power, a scorpion with the head of a sea serpent who towered eight feet tall. Vines grew over the marble surface of the statue, and its eyes glistened with emeralds.

"What do you see when you look at this image?" Thaylus asked quietly.

"I see … something that gives hope and protection to all who believe. Something that quells our fears."

"What if something happened to it?"

"To the statue? The statue is a physical reflection and homage of the god himself. I would still hold to my beliefs."

"But how do you know that is what Thron looks like?"

Brythan frowned. "I have no evidence, but that is what I was taught to believe. And my teachers—including you, Thaylus—excelled in ways of wisdom."

"But what do you believe?"

Brythan was silent before speaking. "The knowledge I have is limited compared to that of the priests and sages."

"You've already said that, Brythan," Thaylus said gently.

"I—I need time to think. I cannot disavow centuries of faith so easily, but neither can I deny your reason."

Thaylus understood. He could see the pain in Brythan's eyes, the questions.

"I suggest we rest a few hours," Brythan said.

"I think you are right to do so."

As he watched Brythan retire to his chambers, Thaylus could almost feel the tension trail after his friend.

Sorrow consumed Thaylus. Had he pried too far into Brythan's feelings, even caused slight friction between them? Was there any way to criticize the gods of another man without offending him?

Full darkness descended and, with it, a sense of looming danger. The full moon gave a lurid, ominous glow that drenched the ground with a pale sheen.

Thaylus spent the next few hours seated upon a bench, gazing at the garden, stilling his mind and his heart for what was to come.

Finally, the hour arrived.

Brythan returned, and the men prepared themselves with meager supplies and two swords, but more importantly, the firmest sense of fortitude they could muster.

Just outside the castle gates, Thaylus held onto one of the wooden stakes lining the outside wall, a torch gripped in his other hand. His eyes were fixed on the pillar of light shooting down through the sky's entire starry marvel.

Brythan came from behind Thaylus and gazed, too.

"I feel something strange, Brythan. I cannot explain it—it's in the air, and it scares me.

Brythan shuddered. "I would be lying to say I am not frightened."

"The Realm Dwellers have chosen their base to invade from. I am grateful you are here beside me, whatever we face."

"Now I think I know how my father must have felt when he faced Vyprus's enchanted army." Brythan looked away, but not before Thaylus saw his tears. "It grieves me I seldom had contact with him. I was so young when he perished at the hands of that vile sorcerer."

Brythan wiped his eyes. Then the two walked in silence along the castle wall toward the stables.

"Your father was a brave soldier even when he realized he had to give his life to win against King Vyprus. You're just like him." Thaylus put an encouraging hand on Brythan's shoulder.

From a place hidden deep inside the sage's mind, the notion of the destruction of the Realm Dwellers, and at the hands of this "Lord and His Emissary" stirred his curiosity to know more of the Pyrithian prophecy.

Pyrithian remained the oldest dialect on the planet of Khrine; few knew it. Perhaps Thaylus's idea of a real God came from a desire for hope.

Yet could even hope stand against what they would meet?

"We go to discover the light and the magical being. We face great power, much greater than ours. Yet we must be brave. It is for our beloved family, our friends—for the whole realm."

Brythan looked down. "Your words give me courage. I think my father would have agreed."

"Brythan, you've always held me in high regard, and I esteem you in the same manner. I know whatever the wise choice is, you will choose. Therefore, I implore you to bear any impertinence on my part. Has doubt of the gods ever passed through your mind?"

Brythan closed his eyes a moment. "I see you are choosing a gentler tactic to convince me of your opinion of the fallacy of the gods."

He turned away, but Thaylus stopped him with a gentle hand.

"Look inside your heart and really see what you know to be true. I beg you, my young friend. Think for yourself."

Brythan ran his hands through his hair. "I ... Thaylus. How could I forsake the wisdom of the priests?" A short silence followed. "It is a hard thing, Thaylus."

Thaylus could not agree more.

They mounted their horses and departed Solace in the light of their torches, galloping hard toward the Western Kingdom with their cloaks trailing behind them.

They rode without speaking, the upset nobleman staring ahead with a stiff frown.

The sage felt sorry for Brythan, yet along with sympathy, Thaylus felt another emotion rise in his heart—frustration. Why couldn't Brythan see?

"I wonder how complicated the cave is." Brythan's words broke the long silence after they slowed at the top of a hill and stopped. It was time to give their horses a rest.

"From what I gathered; it is a labyrinth." Thaylus mused. "The old man gave intricate directions. What do you think about the monster he spoke of?"

"It's probably a rare animal, perhaps a big snake or wolf," answered Brythan, "if that at all."

Their silence was more companionable now, and they chatted quietly about insignificant things.

As they approached the base of the hill, Brythan suddenly turned to him with a warm smile, extending his arm.

"We will discover the truth together."

Thaylus shook his friend's forearm, smiling in return. "Forgive me for offending you."

"It is my fault. I should have not lost control."

"It is good to know we can still exist as friends."

They guided the horses to a slow gallop again as they rode south, where they planned to circle around and go north to the cave.

The ground inclined and declined, and they passed a river with trees growing out of it. A deer drank from the water, serene.

Then suddenly came a splash as an immense crocodile burst out onto the riverbank and trapped the animal in its jaws.

The unwary prey fell victim to the crocodile's power, thrashing around until its movements slowed and then stopped.

"I almost feel sorry for the deer," Brythan reflected as they passed by.

"It's a sad situation, but that's how things are. We live in a fallen world."

"Indeed. A person must be ever-vigilant in this life, regardless of a higher power."

The sage and the nobleman rode at a steady pace. Soon thick-trunked trees appeared. The torchlight cast upon them brought a feeling of euphoric peace. An owl looked down at them from a branch, its eyes glowing in the waning moonlight. Within minutes, the trees around them grew fuller and closer together.

Thaylus halted. "We should rest and make camp."

Small twigs perfect for kindling were spread across the forest floor. The young nobleman gathered a modest bundle and set them in a circle of rocks. With two flint stones he quickly made a fire, and they sat on either side, gazing at the flames.

Brythan's hands folded, and his expression reminded Thaylus of a child, waiting expectantly.

"Something is on your mind," Thaylus said.

Brythan nodded. "Yes. Tell me more of the Great War, specifically about what caused Vyprus to start the war."

Thaylus took a deep breath and put his hands together. "The start of the war with Vyprus occurred over twenty years ago. At first he showed himself to be a benevolent king, giving, merciful, moral, wise."

"What course of events led to his change of heart?"

"He found a map to a strange magical book under a boulder at the bottom of a cave. After he brought the book back home, he locked himself for in his chamber for a week, going without food entirely. At the end he emerged with yellow eyes and a sunken, pale face. His choice to embrace dark magic appears to have manifested then."

Thaylus tensed his jaw. "It makes my stomach knot at his great power of fire and ice, and his ability to cause people and objects to levitate. He enchanted his forces with some of that magic. Ultimately, he sought world domination."

Brythan frowned. "How could a man overcome Vyprus when he commanded elements of nature?"

Thaylus raised his finger. "His army's strength waned the farther they came from his stronghold."

The import of what he'd just uttered seemed to settle on the arch sage. Abruptly, he rose.

"Brythan! Maybe that is why the three Realm Messengers we met stopped following us. Perhaps the light gives them their power, and they came to the very edge of its reach."

Brythan blinked. "You could well be right."

They sat in silence a moment, considering.

"What about my father?" the young nobleman asked. "You were there. I know he was killed in the attack, but what happened? How did he die?"

Thaylus closed his eyes as he remembered.

"Your father, General Knaddues, led the last fighting battalion, which defeated Vyprus. Indeed, King Vyprus was almost fatally wounded by Knaddues. But after the near-deadly blow, Vyprus had a spurt of energy. With a wave of his hand, Vyprus consumed him with a fire attack. Then he fled and vowed to avenge himself on Solace and its allies." Thaylus sighed, shaking his head. "Of course, in the end, everyone gave credit to the gods—except me."

Thaylus paused, remembering that awful day. So many had died in the wrath of King Vyprus—good men. Honorable men.

"Wait," Thaylus began, as an idea struck. "Brythan, your father. While he never openly rejected the gods, I don't recall him ever giving them glory."

"What are you implying?" Brythan squinted.

"Perhaps like me, your brave father secretly disavowed their existence. Did he ever instill the homage of the gods in you?"

"Like I said, I was small, and my father had little conversation with me. My mother delivered me to the temple priests, but she never quite abided by their teachings."

A tingle, of life amidst the shadows, began to come over the sage as he reflected. A gentle gale sent leaves fluttering past Thaylus and Brythan's face.

Thaylus's body tingled. He sensed movement—something, or someone, lurked among the dark trees and brooding animals.

"Brythan, do you feel something strange?" Thaylus's voice was soft.

Brythan paused. "Yes. I feel ... observed."

Thaylus looked around. "Whoever it is, it does not feel human. Something else is out there." He cupped his hands to his mouth. "Hello?" he called.

"Whatever it is, I do not think it wishes to show itself," Brythan said.

"Something tells me this is important. We must find out who is watching us."

"It could be a Realm Dweller, or a messenger."

Thaylus shook his head. "I bet my life there is something we are to meet. It can't be my imagination."

He called out a few more times, scanning the forest as he did.

A golden light began to shimmer, then fully shine from behind a tree. Soon the light shifted to the left.

There, it revealed a woman's likeness.

They both gasped. Before them, she stood: a short, shining woman with silver hair.

Thaylus's heart thrummed with anticipation. Who is this woman?

# Chapter 5

## THE MESSAGE AND THE GIFT

BOTH MEN CLIMBED to their feet, in awe at what they were seeing.

Before them, the woman's shape shone brightly in the dark night, as if the moon itself were inside her.

Thaylus's senses were overwhelmed by the glorious creature. He dropped to his knees and covered his eyes, as if the sight—her otherworldly beauty—were too much to bear. Catching a glimpse at his friend, he saw Brythan had his face covered, too.

"Fear not, righteous ones," the woman said.

She had what appeared to be stork's wings folded on each side of her, and her voice was like a trickling stream that echoed throughout the trees.

"You are about to embark on a journey that will free the world from the Realm Dwellers and establish a new age in the world of Khrine," she said, her voice reverberating off the rocks and the forest itself.

Between deep rapid breaths, Brythan spoke to the shining woman, his eyes still covered.

"Are you a god?"

Thaylus managed a peek through his fingers.

"I am not," she said, seeming to smile. "I am Ithia, a Vessel Bearer commissioned by the One who lives in the Gate of Vessels."

The One. Somewhere in his raging thoughts, the prophecy Brythan had found came to Thaylus's mind.

"I only know this Gate of Vessels by name alone, Great One." Thaylus was in awe of the woman.

Her brilliant shine abated to a soft golden glow.

"Come. You may look at me."

Thaylus and Brythan slowly uncovered their eyes. The sage's head spun with questions. Surely this supernatural being must know things—things beyond the comprehension of these two humans. But Thaylus did know what or how he should ask, if anything at all.

Brythan's eyes were glassy as he gazed. "Forgive us, but we only know the things you speak of by a vague prophecy."

"Everything in the prophecy—including the Gate of Vessels—will be revealed within your quest," she pronounced.

Although her voice was soft, it seemed to boom with power.

Something within the silver-haired woman was mysterious and compelling to Thaylus. He burned to understand the meaning behind her words, but his mind raved in a frenzy.

Ithia spoke on. "Soon you will defeat the evil within the castle."

"How do we defeat a being of such power?" Brythan asked.

She smiled again, her whole presence filled with a deep and righteous benevolence.

"That is why I am here, to give you a message and blessing," Ithia explained. "You two have been chosen by Lord within the Gate of Vessels to free the realm from the Realm Dwellers and the false gods, and to convert the souls to the rightful ruler of planet Khrine."

What? It was one thing when Thaylus suspected the truth. Hearing it now, he wanted to cry or laugh—or both.

Ithia raised her hands. As she did, her brilliant light filled the bodies of the two friends. Thaylus could only describe it as a rushing effervescent cloud. His head and his arms were pushed behind him with the force of the light.

The two men remained on their knees. The overpowering feeling abated, but Thaylus felt ... changed somehow.

"The purity of faith over comes any evil force," Ithia proclaimed. "I have given you some of my master's faith that will be over you for a time. You will understand as each situation calls for it. And always remember to fear not, no matter how hopeless things may seem. Now I leave you, but we will meet again. Farewell in the name of Him who dwells inside the Gate."

As they watched, transfixed, she vanished. The two men were alone once more in the dim light of the crackling fire.

Thaylus looked around. Had he experienced a dream, or gone mad?

"What could it mean, Brythan? And what did she mean by 'Him?'"

"Maybe this means there is hope against the Realm Dwellers. She said we will defeat the evil inside the castle." Brythan said.

They both sucked in long breaths, trying to process what had just occurred.

"Thaylus, I am starting to believe in the prophecy. But it requires abandoning the gods and despising their reality. Doesn't it?"

Brythan looked like he wanted to cry or rage—or both.

"My friend, you can't disregard what just happened to us. This 'faith' that she gave us—can you sense its power?" asked Thaylus.

Brythan nodded. "I do feel different since we were touched by Ithia's light."

Thaylus looked skyward. "I feel more hopeful myself. I feel … protected and at peace." He looked at Brythan and shook his head.

Brythan rubbed his eyes and put his palm to his forehead. "Everything is happening too fast. Please—let us move on."

Time progressed in silence except for the branches and leaves swaying in the wind. Finally, they reached their objective.

"The cave entrance, at last," Thaylus said.

"We should be on our guard. We may encounter danger."

"The monster?"

"It's just a feeling, though it may just be my fear running away with me." Brythan swallowed, as if trying to compose himself. "Let us go."

The cave opening was ten feet tall and lined with stalactites, giving it the look of a gaping mouth with large upper teeth. As they walked, tiny rocks with shiny speckles jutted out of the cave walls. The cave branched out into more tunnels. Thaylus navigated through the complex cavern with ease, his mental recognition of rocks and the various tunnel turns and twists aiding him. Soon the passage they were walking through fell to a sudden steep decline.

"We're going down. We must be close to the dungeon," Brythan said.

Beyond, they could hear falling water. Ten minutes later, the ground leveled out into a wide area. A waterfall coming from an open channel on the right wall poured into a lake.

They took in the scene standing on a ledge of the lake. On the other side of the lake they saw what was unmistakable: a door.

It could only lead one place: the Western Kingdom, their ultimate destination.

"Look, that wooden door at the other side of the lake! That must lead to the dungeon. How do we cross over to it with all that water?" Brythan asked. "Surely we cannot swim, and my torch is going out."

"Mine is burning low too. What do we do?" Thaylus stepped to the edge and looked at the water. "I think I saw something move."

Brythan went to the sage's side. "I do not see anything."

Their torches reflected in the lake looking like two good spirits in a sea of evil.

Thaylus peered below. "It must have been a trick of the water."

He stepped away from the lake edge.

"No, wait!" Brythan pointed. "I see something!"

Both observed the lake. The water became wavy and disturbed. It sloshed around and bubbled momentarily.

Then, as they watched, a creature of some sort emerged from the surface and went back under. Surely a creature lurked beneath the water! Thaylus dreaded to think of its size.

The lake swayed and congealed. Both men stepped back and pulled out their swords.

"The monster is real!" exclaimed Thaylus.

Suddenly, there came a cascade of water as a long, green, scaly figure emerged and towered over them with glowing eyes. Its eyes were red—just like the red light.

"A sea serpent! What do we do!? We cannot possibly hurt it! It is immense!" Thaylus cried out, his sword at the ready.

"We must retreat!"

"No." Thaylus adjusted his grip on the sword, his hands damp with sweat and fear. "Ithia told us of our task—we must destroy the foe in the castle! Ithia had to have known of the sea serpent. There must be a way, Brythan. There must!"

The monster cried out, sounding like the scream of a hawk and the roar of a lion in unison.

"Why isn't it striking?" asked Brythan.

Thaylus looked down in feverish thought, breathing rapidly.

"I've read of many mythical beasts. Let me think." He squeezed his eyes shut, trying to recall what he had read about sea serpents. Beads of sweat flooded down his face. "Fire! It is afraid of our torches! It is the opposite of water. But our dwindling torches will not repel the beast for long."

"Look! The wall to the right has coal deposits!" Brythan shouted. "If I loosen enough of it, we could set it on fire. That will give us time to plan something."

Brythan ran to the wall, gripped his sword tightly, and struck the block of coal. His face contorted as small pebbles tumbled onto the ground.

"Curses! Only bits are coming out. We need more light. Our torches will fade in minutes!"

Thaylus pointed at the wall. "Wait, look! The place where you struck. Oil is leaking!"

Thaylus sprinted to the wall, running his hand over the surface.

"From the color and smoothness, the oil is compressed," Thaylus observed. "It should not take long to pry off enough coal for a strong burst of oil to come out."

"Then what? We will not get such a strong eruption of oil that will travel far enough to sear it," said Brythan.

"We'll have to lure it in."

"That is not a problem. It's coming for us!" cried Brythan, prying at the leaking oil cavity.

"Hurry, the torch will die in minutes!"

Moments later, the torchlight had faded to the glow of a match. The sound of the giant serpent's breathing loomed ever-closer as its beady red eyes sent chills down Thaylus's spine.

Quickly, the firelight dimmed to the size of a beach pebble. Brythan struck the wall, and black liquid burst out. Thaylus put the dwindling flame in front of the jet of liquid.

A long stream of fire burst forth, searing the face of the water monster and jabbing through its eye.

The sea serpent reeled and cried out, swerving and writhing in every direction. A large burnt mark marred its slippery skin.

The monster struggled, bashing its head against the cave walls as it continued to scream in pain. Its head slammed onto the rock surface as its head scraped along the ground from left to right.

Brythan brandished his sword, ready to pierce its eye as the side of the monster's head dragged towards him.

Rocks and pebbles hopped. Brythan gripped the hilt of his sword with white knuckles as, with a battle cry, he thrust his blade through its left eye into its brain.

But the force of the blow caught Brythan, the head of the monster sending him flying against the wall.

The creature swayed once, blood spurting hot and fast as the monster slammed to the ground. It lay on its side, halfway on the dry surface, its mouth open.

The raging waters abated and stilled.

Thaylus ran to the fallen Brythan. "Are you hurt?"

Red-faced with exertion, Brythan struggled to breathe. Just as he seemed he would pass out, he caught a deep, full breath.

"I'm okay." Brythan took a few more deep breaths, then swallowed. "I just got the wind knocked out of me."

"Can you walk?"

"I think so. Help me up."

Thaylus took Brythan's arm and lifted him.

"We killed the monster," Brythan said slowly, the import of what they'd done sinking in. "But how do we get to the door?"

As he spoke, the channel from the right wall suddenly stopped pouring water. In minutes, the lake completely dried up, exposing the serpent's lower half. Then two braziers on each side of the door on the other ledge ignited.

"Amazing! The draining and the burning braziers must be a magical reaction!" Brythan exclaimed.

The stream of fire shortened. Thaylus got a tight knot in his stomach.

"Give me a moment," said Thaylus as he approached the wall spewing fire. He took his sword and cut off a strip of his cloak, wrapped it around the torch, and placed it in front of the fire stream. Brythan did the same.

Then he and Thaylus returned to the edge of the dry cave lake bed.

Thaylus plunged his torch into the dark drop-off. Relief washed over him to see it hit the bottom, only about twenty feet below. There was just enough light to make out rows of small crevices that ran down the cliff face, ideal for climbing.

"Footholds!" Thaylus exclaimed. "Can you climb down?"

"It hurts a little, but I can make it," Brythan said.

Brythan inserted his foot into one of the grooves and climbed down to the second. Thaylus followed slightly slower. Below them, the sea serpent's body was pale, and a foul stench floated in the air. A good portion of its body was coiled at the bottom of the drained lake bed.

At the bottom, Brythan scanned the footholds on the other wall.

"It looks like we will have to climb up this time."

Brythan and Thaylus prepared to ascend. Thaylus was poised, about to grasp the first hand-groove, when the grinding sound of wet hide sliding over rock sent a tense jolt through his body.

They watched in horror as the sea serpent slowly began to shift on the dry lake bed. Soon its head scraped off the cliff at the rim and began to reel back.

Catching sight of the men, it uttered a low, gargling growl.

"It's alive! How? I stuck my sword through its skull!"

"I don't know! But surely our torches will keep it from nearing us."

The monster's coiled body slithered about as it raised to its full height. Its head loomed over them thirty feet above the ground.

To their astonishment, its wound had almost completely healed.

"Sorcery!" Thaylus muttered.

Without a word, Brythan brought his torch near the serpent's body.

The monster gave a sharp cry, shifting away from the heat.

Boldness anew seized him, and now Brythan touched the firebrand itself to the sea serpent.

Its deafening scream caused Thaylus and Brythan to grasp their ears. The serpent's narrow tail swung around to lash out at its tormentor. Brythan was flung, skidding across the ground as his grip on his torch was lost.

The beast lunged for him in the darkness.

Then, with a mighty yell, Brythan hollered, "Stop!"

Thaylus watched in awe and wonder as the sea serpent halted, its strong jaws inches away from Brythan.

A strange power—Ithia's power—began to radiate from Brythan. Thaylus could feel the energy of her power from where he clung to the side of the lake bed.

"Brythan! You're using Ithia's faith!"

"I feel her essence!" Brythan shouted back. "My mind feels like it could do anything!"

Thaylus gaped as Brythan glared at the beast.

"Sleep!" Brythan bellowed.

The serpent seemed to be drunk as it boggled to and fro. Its head hit the ground with a thundering crash, causing a clatter of falling rocks.

Brythan dashed to his place next to Thaylus, sheathing his sword. "We cannot hold the torches and climb too. Fortunately, the brazier lights are bright enough light our way."

The two men left their torches on the ground and climbed; their way lightened by the two braziers at the top ledge.

They made it to the top, panting in relief.

But at the door, they were baffled—there was no keyhole, only a handle.

Brythan looked at the other side of the lake bed where the stream of fire barely burned. He turned to Thaylus.

"Your age proves your cleverness," Brythan chuckled. "The idea of yours to unleash the burst of oil and ignite it to sear the beast worked splendidly."

"Wisdom comes with age young friend," Thaylus said with narrowed eyes and a pointed finger.

Thaylus put his hand on the cold handle, then paused. "Let us hope none occupy what's beyond the door."

With those words, the sage turned the handle and pulled.

A cold draft blew past them, and they stepped into the corridor.

Burning torches, lit by some force, lined the walls as they walked. Just as Thaylus hoped, the walkway remained empty.

But why? And how had they been lit? What purpose would there to be anyone going through this hall? It must have been a magical reaction.

Thaylus stepped cautiously, listening for any footsteps or voices. Nothing.

They trudged on, breathing shallowly.

Brythan spoke softly. "With all that has happened, I am beginning to believe the validity of the prophecy."

Thaylus's heart warmed at his friend's unwary comment.

"Do you then think it is man's destiny to abandon the gods as it says?"

Brythan frowned then shook his head. "That I do not know. Surely there is something odd afoot. But what?"

They walked the corridor in silence.

At the end, a metal ladder led up to a hatch. Men shouting from above echoed faintly.

"Their shouting sends chills down my spine—so violent," Thaylus whispered.

Brythan gritted his teeth. "Who knows what kind of ruffians are kept in the dungeon?"

Thaylus motioned for Brythan to climb.

"After you."

Brythan climbed the ladder, his friend following close behind. At the hatch, Brythan lifted it just enough to peer around.

"It's another corridor, but it ends with a staircase. I cannot see anything beyond that. Let us proceed."

With that, Brythan pushed the hatch open and climbed up, Thaylus at his heels.

# Chapter 6

## Inside the Castle

The metal corridor had a ceiling, walls and ground made of rusted, red metal. Parts of the metal at the corners was eroded, leaving a rough, black blotch. The stairs at the end must have led to the dungeon. The dank smell of metal rust made Thaylus cough.

"The stench is overwhelming," he said, covering his mouth.

"Who knows how old this passageway is," Brythan said.

They walked softly as they crept toward the steps Brythan had seen from the hatch. Above them came the shouts and curses of what sounded like a dozen men indicated the unruly presence of prisoners.

At the top of the stairs, a thick door with a small, barred window greeted them.

They peered through. On the other side, they could see two guards walk up and down two rows of cages. Inside the cages, prisoners in torn rags cursed and clawed at the guards.

"How do we get past the guards?" Brythan whispered.

"I have an idea," Thaylus said.

Thaylus scampered up the stairs and pounded on the door. Minutes passed—nothing.

He pounded again. No response.

Finally, he grabbed his sword, raised it above his head, and with all his strength, struck the metal door. A loud clash echoed.

Thaylus darted down the stairs. "Quickly! Hide behind the corner."

A low clinking came as a guard turned a key in the lock.

"Get ready," Thaylus mouthed.

The grinding of metal hinges put a knot in Thaylus's gut.

"Who's down there?" yelled a deep voice.

Thaylus tightened his grip on the hilt of his sword as a set of boots clanked down the metal staircase.

The footsteps stopped. They heard a singing slice as the sword was unsheathed.

Thaylus's heart beat like a drum. He glanced across at Brythan, who looked to be even more nervous.

Another footstep, and the guard was upon them.

"Don't struggle!" Thaylus seized him by the neck, pressing his sword tight. "Keep silent!"

The guard gasped, his sword clattering to the damp dungeon floor.

"Don't kill me!" He breathed heavily.

"Up the stairs. Now!" Thaylus ordered.

Roughly, they shoved him toward the staircase. But before they could ascend, the other guard sprinted down the steps, sword in hand.

"Put it away or I'll kill him!" Thaylus yelled when the guard was halfway to them. His own sword trembled in his hand.

"Thaylus!" Brythan's eyes were wide.

The free guard wavered.

Thaylus tightened his grip on the first man's throat. "I mean it!"

"Just listen, Galgion," the seized guard begged.

Thaylus felt sick at the thought of harming the captive.

Galgion sneered as he noticed at the crest on their cloaks.

"Jasper, they're just weak-minded Solace royalty. They'd never kill."

Galgion narrowed his eyes and continued down the stairs.

The sage's mouth was dry. He had to act.

Before he could lose his nerve, Thaylus made a quick slice in the Jasper's arm.

"Ack!" Jasper gasped.

"I'll do more harm if you don't drop your weapon!" Thaylus barked.

Galgion made a hand sign to Jasper, who immediately elbowed Thaylus in the stomach.

Thaylus dropped his sword.

Brythan picked up the blade.

In seconds, Jasper had a smaller hidden blade, this time pressed against the arch sage.

"Drop it," Jasper said to Brythan. "Or I'll slice him!"

Brythan released Thaylus's sword, stunned.

It was over.

"I should have remembered that. Cowardly Solace. Thanks for letting me know, Galgion." Jasper retrieved his own sword from the ground as well as Thaylus's, still holding the blade at the sage's neck. "I'm going to gut you like a fish!"

Galgion put up a hand. "Wait, Jasper, look. They're Solace dignitaries. We may get a reward for turning them in."

Jasper shook his head. "I'd rather cut them down right now. That cut he gave me hurts!"

Galgion narrowed his eyes, studying the two intruders.

"If we turn them in, we'd get a reward, and I'm sure they'll be killed anyway. If we're lucky, we may even get to disembowel them ourselves."

Jasper scowled but nodded.

Just then, the metal hold began to vibrate. Galgion and Jasper stumbled, releasing the men as they tried to regain their footing.

"An earthquake!" Jasper yelled.

The vibrating escalated to a violent rumble.

Thaylus plummeted to the floor. The guards' swords tumbled out of their trembling hands.

Jasper fumbled with his blade as Thaylus lay prone on the ground.

"No!" Brythan gasped.

In an instant, Brythan rammed Jasper to the ground, pinning him even as the walls around them quaked.

The shaking ebbed to a light rumble.

As Galgion gained his balance, he saw Brythan had Jasper pegged.

Galgion scuffled for a sword and made for Brythan.

"Brythan, behind you!" Thaylus cried.

Brythan rose suddenly, then pushed Jasper hard, right into Galgion.

Jasper clutched at his throat, coughing for air, as Galgion pulled him to his feet.

While they were occupied, Brythan scooped up one of the two remaining swords on the ground and yanked Thaylus up.

Jasper picked up the last blade at his feet.

Now it was two swords against one.

"What now?" Brythan asked Thaylus.

An understanding washed over Thaylus. He didn't know where it came from—he just acted.

Lowering his head, Thaylus closed his eyes. His fists tightened, and his breathing got heavy. He could feel his face grow hot as anger rose within him.

"What's he doing?" one of the guards said.

It was faith manifesting itself once again.

Thaylus's head shot up and his eyes opened.

Brythan jerked away from Thaylus, as did the guards.

Thaylus didn't know what he looked like, but he could only imagine their terror. What felt like burning white light shot from his eyes like daggers.

"Wh—what is happening to you?" Jasper cried.

"Let us flee! His eyes—they're flickering with madness! It's inhuman!" Galgion trembled in horror.

"Don't move." Even Thaylus's voice sounded different, as if thousands of tiny metallic shards of lightning had taken over his vocal cords.

He took the sword from Brythan's shaking hand.

"I could cut you both down in seconds," Thaylus said. "Drop your swords, now, and get on your knees!"

The guards obeyed.

With what felt like superhuman strength, Thaylus tore off the guard's tunics, then ripped them into long strips.

Brythan helped him tightly bind the guard's hands behind their backs, then gagged them. Gone was the guards' former bravado. Instead, they'd become quivering, sniveling fools.

Once the guards were tied up tight, Thaylus head began to teeter left, then right. His eyes blinked and then closed, and he stumbled, toppling to the ground in a daze.

Brythan knelt over Thaylus.

"It happened again, my friend!" Brythan grinned at him.

Thaylus inched his eyes open and smiled weakly. He let out a sigh. "Thanks be to Ithia for her faith."

Ithia had said the faith came from her god. While Thaylus did not believe in her deity, or whoever it was who existed in this holy Gate of Vessels, Ithia's belief made him yearn for a real god all the more. Surely there had to be someone, some true god, out there. A real deity, worthy of worship.

This time, Thaylus and Brythan didn't hesitate. They ascended the steps and barged down the metal hold.

"Release us!" Caged prisoners shouted from either side of the door.

An entrance to the left led Thaylus and Brythan to a huge, vaulted hall filled with soldiers standing against walls. Royalty strolled about in gold embroidered capes and robes decked with jewels.

Thaylus and Brythan watched from the darkened metal passage out of sight.

"The quake came so suddenly," Brythan reflected as they caught their breath. "Things would have gone rougher if it had not happened."

"It was an uncanny coincidence," Thaylus said.

Thaylus peered around the corner.

"Strange—there is no damage to the rest of the castle. They are so casual, so relaxed. See? There is no fear of the light in them, or of the sorcerer. And it's like the quake didn't happen at all."

"Could they and the castle be under a spell?" Brythan frowned.

"Maybe, but they also could have willingly allied themselves with this man in power."

"What now?"

Thaylus considered. "We'll need disguises."

"And I think we could reuse our previous trick," Brythan said.

Brythan peered from the corridor. Just when a man in rich attire was in arm's length, Brythan pulled him into the shadows, covering his mouth.

Brythan brandished the sword. "Take off your outer robe. Now!"

Without hesitation, the man stripped to his white undergarments. Brythan put the robe on in place of his cloak then ripped strips from it and tied and gagged the man.

Thaylus repeated Brythan's method.

They dragged the two men deeper into the corridor, where it would take some time for them to be discovered.

When they had immobilized the captives, they stepped out into the open. Thaylus whispered, looking straight ahead.

"Stay calm and make a slight smile, just like most of the royalty in Solace." He paused, then swallowed. "And hope no one recognizes us."

"Where are we going?"

"We must find out about that light and the Realm Dwellers. I surmise that we will learn the source of their relation."

"Then we are headed to the throne room?" Brythan asked.

"Indeed."

With a fair swagger, they smiled and made their way through the inner thoroughfare. People walked past them, traveling up and down the hall.

Thaylus felt something in the air—a familiar evil, one he had felt a long time ago, but it was not the same as with the Realm Messengers from before. This was a different sense of evil. He peered around nervously, doing his best to ignore the overwhelming essence that plagued his mind.

At the end of the vast main hall, two immense soldiers guarded golden double doors.

"That is where the throne room is," Thaylus said under his breath—where they would meet the terrible sorcerer.

They casually approached the entry, stopping about twenty feet from the door.

"Don't worry. I have an idea," Brythan said, then addressed the guards in a loud, confident voice. "We have business with the king."

"And who are you?" replied the burly guard on the left.

"We are wealthy merchants come to trade with the king directly. As for our apparel, it was gift from his majesty."

Thaylus worried how far Brythan's quick mind could go. What if the man did not believe him?

The other soldier folded his arms and squinted his left eye. "Do you have proof?"

A deep, guttural tightness filled Brythan's voice. "How dare you speak to us this way! It is an insult how you question us! I shall tell the highest authority about your treatment of two of the richest merchants in the land. Come, Cronus. Let us go inform those in charge of this man's outrage!"

Brythan made like he would storm off.

"Wait, stop! I'm sorry!" The second guard stumbled over his words. "Please forget I spoke as I did. I believe you. I welcome you both. May your business with the king bode well."

Slowly, the two soldiers heaved the doors open.

Thaylus and Brythan entered.

The room was empty, save for a man on a throne with a hood covering his face.

Thaylus felt a familiar, vile essence emanating from the dark figure. He reeled back, eyes wide.

Brythan stared at him. "Thaylus, what is wrong?"

Thaylus narrowed his eyes at the man on the throne. "Who is it? It feels like him, but it is not."

"Him?"

The man on the throne looked almost exactly like Vyprus, the wizard. Could he be a son or a brother? The sorcerer Vyprus was long dead. Who was this before him?

"Who are you?" Thaylus said in a sweat.

"You're right to fear me. You obviously feel my brother Vyprus's essence from all those years ago. But I am more powerful than him. I am Kyrious. I have destroyed Nephaal, king of the Western Kingdom with my power. I am the new king of the Western Kingdom!"

Kyrious slid the hood back and gazed at them hard. His eyes were a deep, devilish yellow, and his face narrow and snakelike.

"My older brother failed because he didn't have the needed prowess to rule. It was a shame I had to kill him to gain the magic from the book." Kyrious chuckled. "I can still see the look on his face as I plunged my dagger in his stomach."

He rose with a vile grin.

Thaylus abhorred him.

Kyrious opened his arms wide in a false show of welcome, bowing deeply. "It's been decades. I apologize you have never met Vyprus or me in person, but I already know you. I sensed your identity before you even entered my castle. In fact, I've known you ever since the Realm Messengers encountered you."

His deep raspy voice made Thaylus twitch.

A thick book rested on the throne.

Open-mouthed, Brythan took a step back, tugging at Thaylus's arm.

"You obviously intend on spying on my new home and my plans for the future in just two days," Kyrious said, his nonchalant tone laced with dark humor. "What would you like to see?"

"Haven't you learned anything?" Thaylus said boldly. "Your brother was defeated even with his power."

Kyrious snickered. "Oh, dear Thaylus. With the abilities bestowed on me by the dark ones, who send their power through the red light, my former magic has grown ten-fold than that of Vyprus's! I will be invincible after the Realm Dwellers cross over to our dimension—when I realize their full power."

"You do not know what you're doing." Thaylus's hands were in fists. "The Realm Dwellers only want destruction! They don't want to rule the world. They want to destroy it!"

"Our only hope is the faith Ithia gave," Brythan said in a low, trembling voice.

A sliver of hope rose in Thaylus's heart as Ithia's words echoed in his mind. The purity of faith overcomes any evil force.

Thaylus tried to use Ithia's faith in the same way with the guards. Yet he could not speak from the knot in his stomach and the horror before him. He opened his mouth but nothing came out.

Brythan choked on his words, shuddering as he shook his head.

Kyrious took his seat again and slowly crossed his legs.

"You're prudent to fear me. I could destroy you with a wave of my hand. But I want you to witness the conquering of Solace before you die. You, there!" Kyrious nodded to the guards they could now see lurking near the throne curtain. "Put them in the dungeon with all the others—those who have not sworn allegiance to me."

Defeat settled over Thaylus as guards in blue chain mail took them by the arms.

The guards escorted them through the castle and into a different dungeon from the one where they'd come in, hurling them into a large cell with a number of other people inside.

Some were in old royal raiment, some were in modest clothes. Teenagers and children were among them. Unlike the former cells, filled with wild, screaming men, these prisoners were silent, in a hopeless gaze.

The two new prisoners sat against the cold back wall, coarse with rust.

Defeat held dominant sway in Thaylus mind. This was all his fault—fear had overwhelmed them.

"It seems like it is hopeless," Brythan said with a somber tone. "Yet strangely, I feel our quest is just beginning."

"That is what Ithia said. But how can we possibly survive?"

As they spoke, a middle-aged man in a tattered blue robe took a seat next to them.

"At last, you have come." His jovial tone was a stark contrast to the hopeless, silent prison cell.

The man's eyes were completely white.

Thaylus thought him a blind, mentally degraded man.

"There now, sir. What is your name?"

"Elim. And you—you are Thaylus and Brythan, of Solace."

A stinging surge of fear ran through Thaylus.

He and Brythan jolted to their feet. Certainly, this man meant ill against them.

"What do you want with us?" asked Thaylus.

"I come in peace. And as you have, I too have met the Lady Ithia."

Thaylus and Brythan glanced at each other, than at the man.

Thaylus mind exploded with questions. "Who … are you?"

"As I said, I am Elim, a sojourner of time. I wield the ability to travel to different ages. I've waited many, many years to meet you. Now listen to me closely. I know things you must be made aware of."

Clearly the man was delusional. The sage doubted that this man could transcend time. Why would a person with such power be trapped in a prison? Yet he knew their names.

Part of Thaylus was curious. Slowly, he and Brythan sat back down and awaited the man's words.

# Chapter 7

## THE TIME TRAVELER

CROSS-LEGGED, the man took a deep breath and folded his hands.

"I'm sure much fear and confusion grips you. To ease your curiosity, I will explain more about the Gate of Vessels."

Thaylus was enthralled as Brythan's wide eyes reflected a sense of awe. The whole situation seemed to converge at this moment. What important and fantastic things did this man know?

"My whole adult life I versed myself in knowledge through much traveling and studying," Elim began. "I did not realize the scope of what I would one day discover in my life."

Thaylus could only stare and listen.

The time traveler clasped his hands together. "What if I said climbing the White Mountains was possible?"

Thaylus tilted his head. "Why do you ask such a question?"

"I have a relevant point to make."

Brythan chuckled. "No one has ever even attempted that and lived. They are unclimbable. Such a thing is foolish."

Elim smiled and waved a pointed finger. "Ah, but I would soon find out the true answer." He rubbed his hands together. "For Ithia, the Vessel Bearer whom you know, confirmed I would."

"Truly! What else did she say?" Brythan said.

"She said I would encounter a magnificent wonder at the top of the White Mountains."

"And what did you find?" asked Brythan.

"An ancient cathedral."

Thaylus and Brythan were speechless as they scooted closer.

"As I explored the cathedral, I came to room with a book." Elim took a deep breath. "Of course, I did not know it entailed more than just pages with writing."

"What do you mean?" Thaylus asked.

"The book's cover revealed its true nature. An engraved message said: 'To he who reads this, one of two powers are offered: the power of necromancy or the power of time.'"

"And is this how you gained time travel, then? Did you read from the book like speaking an incantation?" Thaylus asked.

"On the back of the book were two gems, a black onyx and a white diamond."

"Magical Talismans?"

"Somewhat, I would say. Under the onyx I found necromancy engraved, and under the diamond, time."

"What was written inside the book?" asked Brythan.

"Within the book, almost all the writing was scribbled over—except for a line of text on the bottom of the very last page."

"Who would desecrate such unprecedented knowledge and leave the most significant thing intact?" asked Brythan.

"I wondered the same thing," said the man, "unless the obscured text had more value. I cannot imagine."

"What did the last part of the book say?"

"That is how I gained time travel. The last part of the book spoke of the two gems. It read: touch what you desire and it will be granted you." The man held up a hand. "Now, it was not just as easy as touching either gem. I had a strong urge to touch the onyx. I sensed the tremendous dark power within it. As I was compelled by the power of both gems, I felt a battle wage within my heart."

"How did you manage to choose time over necromancy?" Brythan asked.

"A sliver of goodness convicted me. It was small, but in my heart I felt the power of the diamond gently warn me and help me resist."

"And what happened? What exactly did you experience when you received the power of time?"

Elim closed his eyes and stretched forth his hands. "I felt a feeling of freedom—like I was instantly pure spirit. A strong essence like a cloud filled me, and then I had it. The power to traverse time."

Brythan's eyes sparkled like a child's. "What time do you come from?"

"I lived when the Realm Dwellers inhabited the world."

"Inhabited the world!" Thaylus was shocked. "You have seen them? They lived on Khrine? Why do they exist in the Abyss now?"

"That matter is what I sought. I arrived on Khrine the very day they were prophesied to be cast into the Abyss. It happened mysteriously—one moment they were besieging the world, and the next they vanished." Elim smiled. "Only the Great Lord who dwells in the Gate of Vessels could cause this."

The great Lord. Oh, how badly Thaylus wanted to belief in one true deity. He envied this man.

"You're blind. How did you recognize us?" Brythan asked.

"I had another vision where Ithia told me I would meet two men named Thaylus and Brythan who had been given the power and essence of faith. I sensed this within you."

"Were you born blind?"

"No. It was that wicked wizard Kyrious who took my vision."

"And why did you come to this time?" Thaylus asked.

"You well can guess. The prophecy. I was sent here to this time to stop King Kyrious with the rebuke of my faith." Elim shook his head. "But I failed. I doubted. When I saw Kyrious's power it overwhelmed me."

Thaylus nodded in sorrow. "It appears I and my companion gave into the same ... lack of faith ... only minutes ago."

"Is that why Thaylus and I were sent on this same mission, to expunge Kyrious?" Brythan asked.

"Perhaps Ithia sent me on the same task for us to meet so I could tell you these things. The Lord may use our shortcomings to accomplish His will."

The Lord... Thaylus shook his head.

"What was the first place you visited after you traveled to this time?" he asked.

Elim stood and began to pace. "Let me think." He paused then snapped his fingers. "Ah, yes. I first appeared at the same cathedral that still stands atop the White Mountains. I knew if someone found the book they might touch the onyx stone and gain this great evil power. So I took the book and searched for a place where none would find it. There, hidden under the base of the White Mountains, I found a complex cave system, and I put it under a boulder to remain for all time.

"But I made a grave mistake. I traced where I walked on a scroll. But I lost that scroll shortly after I left the cave. That is when the once-noble King Vyprus found it and—"

"The rest we know." Thaylus tightened his jaw. "He gained his power from the book and was corrupted."

"When you confronted Kyrious, why didn't you escape to another time?" Brythan asked.

Elim sighed. "Traversing time taxes human vitality and strength. The more I travel, the weaker I become. I've been to many times."

"And the Gate of Vessels?" Thaylus asked. "What is it, exactly?"

"Rather than tell you, I will show you."

Elim placed his hand on Thaylus's forehead.

Instantly, Thaylus felt a bright light shine all around him. Thaylus could no longer feel or see his body. It was as if he floated high in the clouds in an endless sky.

When the light abated, he saw a grassy plain that stretched far to the horizon. Different vessels of all kinds of materials lay across the surface—iron lamps, golden ewers, bronze cauldrons, golden urns, silver chalices, platinum kettles, copper bowls, and more.

Over the breadth of the grassy ground, beings like Ithia, each possessing a bright shine and the wings of a stork, brought these terrestrial vessels to something far off, shimmering bright in the sky. It shone like a white sun.

And upon it stood an open gate.

Elim's voice echoed around him. "Before you is the Plains of Eternity, which exists in the spiritual realm. Each vessel represents the body and soul of a man."

A young Vessel Bearer in a shimmering white robe grasped a small golden urn and ascended into the sky to the bright gate. He, with other Vessel Bearers, placed them before it.

"The burning gate in the firmament above you, that is what we know as the holy Gate of Vessels."

"I've never seen such beautiful sights," Thaylus said.

"Those of mankind worthy of living with the Great Lord, who dwells inside the Gate of Vessels, will live forever within the paradise beyond." Elim's voice rang all around him.

Thaylus burned to live inside the Gate of Vessels. It brought a calm stillness to his heart and mind. Thaylus needed to see this "Great Lord" who was within the burning Gate of Vessels. What thing proved that any supreme deity dwelt inside it? The true inhabitance could be spiritual beings with great power, but not god-like.

"Ithia told me you will understand the rest as you go," Elim's words resonated around Thaylus.

"What of the Realm Dwellers? The Pyrithian prophecy mentioned them."

"Ah, the prophecies from your time that referenced their release. It came to pass by the instruction of a Celestial Servant."

"What is a Celestial Servant?" Thaylus asked.

Another flash of light obscured Thaylus's vision. When his sight returned, he found himself observing the holy Gate of Vessels as he floated high in the firmament.

Beings in golden flowing robes stood at the Gate. As the Vessel Bearers bore the wares from the Plains of Eternity up to the Gate in the sky, the golden-robed entities took the vessels and brought them inside into the brilliant place beyond the Gate.

"These ones in gold robes are Celestial Servants. They receive the objects from the Vessel Bearers and present them to the Great Lord and serve Him within."

"What happens to the vessels that get taken inside the gate?"

"These vessels are transformed into spiritual bodies." Elim's voice echoed.

"Let me see inside." Thaylus had never wanted something so badly.

"It takes complete faith to go beyond the Gate of Vessels and to see the Great Lord. For He is omnipotent, omniscient, and omnipresent."

"Only if I see your Lord and his power will I believe."

"Without faith it is impossible to see God," Elim said.

A flicker of anger rose within Thaylus. "Faith! I'm sick of faith!"

With that, the vision faded, and Thaylus opened his eyes.

Brythan stared at him. "Thaylus! What happened?"

"Elim gave me a vision."

"You must tell me!"

Footsteps sounded as a guard neared the cell.

"Chow time, vermin." One with an insolent smirk glared at them. "Guess what's on today's menu? That's right, gruel!"

The man held a large bowl with a white, chunky, pasty substance. He opened the cell door and slid it inside. "Food fit for a king."

Brythan made a face. "It smells vile."

"Once hunger sets in, you'll think differently," Elim said.

"Explain your vision the best you can, Thaylus," Brythan asked when they'd all sat down again.

Thaylus described the vision.

When he'd finished, Brythan put a hand to his brow and shook his head.

"Such a thing would prove hard to believe without witnessing other supernatural things."

Elim raised his tone. "Until one has faith to know of the Gate of Vessels, the truth of the Emissary and His Lord will be kept from that individual."

Thaylus lowered his head and put his hands over his face.

"When you came to this era, what did you think of the scarlet pillar of light?" Brythan asked.

"I believed it to be the place from which where the Realm Dwellers would invade."

"So what happens now?" Thaylus asked.

"Now, you must go to the cathedral."

Thaylus blinked. "How do we do that? We're in prison."

Elim stood and felt his way to the bars. "Do you remember the strong faith passed to me and to you from Ithia?"

Brythan nodded. "Yes. I used that faith to subdue a sea serpent Thaylus and I encountered."

"And I used it to help us escape the prison guards below," Thaylus added.

Elim smiled. "Even mountains can be moved by faith, no matter how big the obstacle. Now watch."

Elim closed his eyes. To their surprise, the cell bars before them appeared to ripple, like when a stone is thrown into a pond. The rippling continued until the bars became transparent—and eventually vanished.

All the eyes in the cell lit up. "We're free!" a boy shouted.

The two guards noticed the commotion. "That man! He has magical power!" exclaimed one.

"We must contain the prisoners!" yelled the other.

But the prisoners greatly outnumbered the guards, and they were swiftly overcome with a wave of people.

Elim just stayed where he was, unmoving.

"You freed us all!" Thaylus said. "But why have you waited until now to make a way out?"

A faint smile lit Elim's face.

"Our combined faith has given me strength to do this last act. Now you must go. Soon I will leave this world, and my spiritual vessel will be filled with the white flame of purity. I'll be taken to live forever inside the Gate of Vessels and live with the great Lord Himself."

"Come with us, Elim. We'll guide you out of the castle!" Brythan tried to tug the man to his feet.

Elim shook his head and put a firm hand on Brythan's chest.

"I am weary and tired with dwindling strength. I have told you all I know."

Thaylus felt overwhelmed with indecision. "But… what do we do when we get there? Are we to travel through time? Don't we need the book? What did Ithia say?"

"I have said to you all that she told me. I can help you no more. Go!"

Heavy boots sounded, and they knew more guards were coming. They had to go now or risk being captured again.

With the others, Thaylus and Brythan ran out and down the metal corridor following the loosed prisoners flooding into the main hall.

"We have to find a way out of the castle," Brythan shouted.

Thaylus huffed and puffed. "We can't leave the way we came. Our only hope is the front gate."

Pandemonium weaved throughout the huge main hall as the prisoners poured through the room. Royalty screamed.

"Run for the entry gate!" yelled Thaylus. "We can make it!"

The mass of prisoners barged through the gate, Thaylus and Brythan among them.

Above them, the sun shone bright and pleasant. Relief washed over them, and they smiled with relief.

But suddenly, three guards blocked their way, swords drawn. The one at the left had a shallow cut on his arm—Jasper.

"We meet again, Solace scum." Jasper's words were like a growl. "You'll pay for cutting me!"

He raised his sword over his head.

"Stop!" The guard in the middle spoke up. "Lord Kyrious may want them alive."

Jasper looked furious.

"They're inferior beings who will be destroyed in two days. I'll bet the king would see them hanged. These pitiful worms have no purpose. Please, Captain Grale, allow me the privilege of cutting their heads off."

"Remember your place, guard!" Captain Grale ordered. "I will decide if they are useless. Now stand down."

"Yes, commander."

"Both of you, help round up the loose prisoners," Captain Grale instructed, seizing Thaylus and Brythan each by an arm.

When two other guards had gone, the captain muttered in a low voice, "It's okay. Follow me."

The two looked at each other confused.

"Now. Hurry!"

Thaylus and Brythan trailed after the captain into a secluded hall, where he opened a door with a key.

Within, weapons hung against three walls. A forging pit about two-dozen yards away burned with a white flame.

"Don't worry," Grale said. "You're safe. I have one of the only few keys to the armory. It is good I caught you two when I did."

"Why did you help us? Who are you?" Brythan asked.

"I am leader of a coup of defectors against Kyrious stationed throughout the Western Kingdom. Ever since he made his presence known, I have been recruiting people. You are from Solace. Why are you here?"

"Our mission is to investigate the pillar of light and discover who has taken over the Western Kingdom," Thaylus said.

"And I gather you know who it is who is responsible?"

"Indeed. What does your circle of confidants hope to achieve?" Thaylus asked.

"I and a few others have seen him in his chambers with a book. The book has two gemstones on it." Grale pursed his lips, his words solemn. "We believe it to be a magical book. Our plan is to destroy it. We've already come up with a scheme to obtain it."

"We would love to join you, but we on a mission to go to the White Mountains promptly," Brythan said. "We have been sent on an urgent quest."

"I see. I will help you. I have a few horses tethered in a hold right around the corner. But first you must change clothes."

Grale left the room. Five minutes later, he returned with two sets of messenger's apparel and a bag of gold.

"Dress quickly. You don't have much time."

The two men hurriedly disguised themselves, and Thaylus stuffed the gold deep in his pocket.

Captain Grale went to the desk, picked up an inked quill, and scribbled a message on a piece of parchment. He rolled it and sealed it with wax and his signet ring.

"This will get you past any guards. May the gods be with you. I bid you good luck on your mission."

Thaylus and Brythan quickly headed to an open stable and mounted the two of the horses.

In the courtyard, guards milled about, patrolling. Despite Thaylus's disguise and the parchment, he felt a tightness in his stomach.

And sure enough, they were stopped by a soldier.

"Halt! Where are you going?"

Thaylus showed him the scroll without a word.

"A mission from Captain Grale." The man tipped his head and raised his eyebrow. "I've never seen you and I don't forget a face. What are your names?"

Adrenaline shot through Thaylus's body, and he froze.

"We're new messengers." Brythan lifted his chin. "And our mission is a secret."

"I don't believe you." The tall, grizzly guard unsheathed his sword. "Dismount and come this way."

"You're making a mistake. The captain will hear of this."

"This way!"

The soldier led them back into the castle, down a long corridor, and to a man in a red cape wearing golden chain mail.

"General Bainforth, I found these two imposters calling themselves messengers. I have never seen them. They may be spies."

General Bainforth glared behind dark, deep-set eyes. Slick black hair ran to his shoulders.

His presence made Thaylus squeamish.

The general stepped forward until he was inches from Thaylus's face.

"You're familiar. My guard speaks rightly. And you are not from the Western Kingdom. I see the temper of wisdom in your eyes—more than just a simple spy or guard."

Bainforth faced Brythan. "And you. The glisten of your eyes speaks of nobility as well. Who are you?"

Thaylus's heart felt like it was in his throat. He had never met such a perceptive man in his life.

Brythan stood like a statue.

Bainforth shrugged and turned to the guard. "Fine. Execute them."

"Wait, we will tell you!" pleaded Thaylus. "I am Thaylus, Arch Sage of Solace. And this is Brythan, a nobleman."

Bainforth raised a brow. "I am surprised you infiltrated the Western Kingdom so effectively. I will give you a choice: pledge allegiance to King Kyrious and become royalty, or die."

A hot surge rose from Thaylus's gullet. "I'd sooner die!"

Thaylus was surprised at himself. He would have declined the general's offer but where did this adamant anger come from? He knew it must come from somewhere sacred, deep within him. It was not Ithia's supernatural faith, he knew that much.

"Is this how you feel too, nobleman?" Bainforth asked Brythan.

Brythan stumbled over his words as gasps came out.

Bainforth raised his tone. "I see your heart is at a strait. If your decision is not complete fealty, you will die with your companion."

Brythan shook himself. "Thaylus's wisdom and choices has always been right. I stand with him. I will not relent."

"Very well. Guard, get these vermin out of my sight. And kill them!"

The guard giggled with glee as he led the two captives out to kill them.

Thaylus's hands shook, but he managed to walk upright. He would not cower even if he were walking to his death, he resolved.

The guard shoved them toward a wall.

"Stand there, faces against the wall," the guard sneered. "Time to die."

But as they turned their faces to the wall, a cry rang out behind them, along with an ear-piercing metallic slice through flesh.

They whirled to see a teenage boy in old tattered clothes—and a sword.

"One less brute to deal with," said the boy.

"You ... you killed him!" Thaylus's mouth hung open. "How?"

"I have been hiding outside by a hole in the wall that surrounds the castle courtyard. It is the only passage outside, save for the front gate. My friends and I use it to sneak out into the wilderness."

"But how did you kill this guard so easily?" Brythan looked stunned.

"He has sworn his life to Kyrious no matter how indirectly. He deserved it," the boy said carelessly. "His intention to kill you must have meant you are defiant of Kyrious. Anyone who defies Kyrious is a friend of mine. I saw you trying to escape through the courtyard gates. I can show you where my secret escape is, though it is not big enough for a horse. There is a settlement east of here. You can walk there in a day."

Thaylus and Brythan glanced at each other then back at the boy.

"Thank you. What is your name, youngling?" asked Thaylus.

"Saress."

"Saress, I wish you luck. But my companion and I must go to Ravencroft."

The boy looked surprised. "That's north, near the White Mountains. Treacherous weather I hear."

"Show us your secret passage."

Saress's face lit up as he led them along the castle wall. A steep dip formed a hole at the base of the wall.

All three went through.

They said their farewells, then Saress crawled back inside.

But moments later, the boy slipped back out.

"I've been spotted! What will I do now? They know my secret escape!"

Thaylus pulled out the gold bag Grale had given them, portioning out a third to Saress.

"Retreat to the settlement you mentioned, and use this to buy a horse. Then ride south to Solace."

"Solace? What do I do there?" Saress asked.

"Tell a nobleman that Thaylus and Brythan sent you, that they have told you of the Realm Dwellers and request asylum in the castle."

Fear gleamed in his eyes. "Will I ever see my parents or friends again?"

Thaylus looked at the boy hard. "I believe in my heart that Kyrious will fall and the Western Kingdom freed."

Saress nodded at his words. "I hope that time comes soon."

\* \* \*

THAYLUS AND BRYTHAN'S VISIT to Ravencroft was brief, just long enough to gather supplies and two horses with the gold from Captain Grale.

"Blessed travels, sirs," said the stable keeper. "May the gods protect you."

They rode off.

Once in the wilderness, Brythan frowned.

"What challenges do you suppose await us on the White Mountains?"

Thaylus considered the question. "Ithia said Elim would conquer it. Remember Ithia's instructions to us, to have faith no matter what?"

They rode north as the sun set. The sky was beautiful, with layers of yellow, orange, and purple shining through anvil-shaped clouds. The dreaded pillar of red light cast its horrid hue and red lighting amidst the firmament, tainting the joyful day with the burning column. Once again, Thaylus's mind filled with fear and restlessness. A warm breeze washed over their faces and ruffled their cloaks.

As darkness fell, the temperature dropped. Soon pine trees began to appear in great clusters.

They stopped at a large hill and glimpsed the snowy peaks with misty clouds enshrining their tops.

"The White Mountains," Thaylus said. "They tower like a giant beast. We will reach the cathedral, Brythan. We must."

Their excursion up the mountain began.

# Chapter 8

## THE WHITE MOUNTAINS

THE FIRST TWO HOURS OF THEIR ASCENT WENT SLOWLY, and the bitter coldness grew as the steepness increased. Patches of snow gathered on shrubs and barren trees.

"I truly hope our task will easily reveal itself when we reach the cathedral," Brythan said. "It is inconceivable to imagine if it does not."

"We will. We must have faith, my friend."

The snow grew thicker.

Finally, Thaylus stopped his horse. "We're nearing an incline too steep for the horses."

"We can tie them to that tree."

"No. Who knows what will happen to us on our way to the cathedral, or when we reach it. We should let them go."

Brythan took the saddles and bags off the steeds.

"Let us take only enough food and sleeping material to get to the top," Thaylus said.

The snow got deeper as they trudged up the mountain, and frost built on their cloaks and faces. They tucked their arms tight against their chests, shivering.

The frigid cold combined with the endless ascent caused a heavy blanket of despair upon Thaylus. The despair only deepened as the wind began to blow harder. Dizzy, they stumbled with the harsh gale, hands sinking into the freezing snow and ice as they caught their fall.

A jolt of shuddering pain went up Thaylus's spine. He pulled his hands from the snow and rubbed and breathed on them to achieve a semblance of warmth.

"Brythan, I'm not sure I can go on. I am too old. My body can't take this."

Brythan came to his side. "I know you can do this. You must. I can't succeed if you don't come with me."

Thaylus breathed heavily as he looked down. "I'll try." He walked slowly to a tree and leaned against it. "Give me a moment."

After a brief rest, they strove onward. The cold pushed them to their limit the higher they got.

They peered upward only to see more snow—endless snow. It looked like there was no end to their climbing.

Thaylus grabbed a ledge, elated to feel the tip of even ground. "Brythan, I think I've found a cliff!"

"Are you sure?"

Thaylus grunted as he used all his strength to pull on the ledge and get his arm over it.

"It's a cave! Finally, shelter!"

His heart soared as he hoisted himself on the flat surface then laid his bag on the ground.

Brythan climbed onto the rocky bluff and relieved himself of his burden. Both laughed while embracing each other tightly.

Thaylus felt his heart leap, and a stem of hope grew amidst their obstacle.

They walked several yards into their refuge and collapsed in gratitude and exhaustion. With a sigh of happiness, Thaylus put his back against the hard wall of the cave and slid to sit on the ground.

"Now that we are sitting, I can feel how tired I am," Brythan admitted. "I just feel like sleeping."

"So do I. A little nap may take time but it will rejuvenate us."

They wrapped themselves tighter in their cloaks and fell fast asleep to the faint sound of the storm.

But within what seemed like minutes, Thaylus and Brythan were jarred awake.

"What was that sound?" Brythan, still groggy, forced himself to come alert.

"I—think it was a footstep."

Both stood. They heard it again—footsteps. A deep growl followed from further within the cave. The footsteps became louder.

Moments later, a tall, white-haired, man-shaped creature emerged.

"Time to leave!" Thaylus shouted.

His body seemed to jump up and begin to race off on its own accord, too filled with fear to consider his young friend.

Brythan followed Thaylus into the blustering wind and snow. The wind stung as it whipped against their faces, feeling like tiny shards of glass. Quickly, they began to crawl up the incline by the cave mouth.

Thaylus peered over, heart racing. Fear coursed through his body as the creature emerged from the cave. The creature roared with rage, its eyes fierce and unlike anything he'd seen before.

"Thaylus, make haste! The creature is pursuing us!"

Thaylus clawed at the incline as he tried to go faster. Brythan followed on his heels.

Just as they reached the summit of the small hill, Brythan let out a cry and disappeared over the ledge.

The creature had grabbed his foot and yanked him off the incline onto the ground.

"Brythan!"

The towering beast looked down at its prey and began to move in.

"No! Over here!" Thaylus pitched a large rock, then another, at the beast. Anything he could find he threw, one after the other at the beast. "Leave him be!"

The beast growled his wrath, forgetting Brythan for a moment. He turned and lunged toward Thaylus on the incline.

Brythan dashed away from the snow monster and tore a long, thin shred of cloth from his cloak.

"Keep distracting it! I have an idea!"

The beast faced Thaylus, exposing the back of its head to Brythan.

Brythan felt around for a good-sized stone to fit into the cloth sling. He put the stone in the cloth and began swinging it in a circle.

Then with a flick of his wrist, the stone went flying into the back of the snow monster's head.

Blood spurted. The creature whirled in anger, ignoring the rocks from Thaylus.

With a deep growl it began stalking the younger man, forcing Brythan to the edge of the cliff. It staggered as it lunged for him, thick bands of drool oozing as it did.

"Thaylus, help!"

The creature slammed to the ground, collapsing on its chest. The momentum nearly knocked Brythan off the cliff.

Only Brythan's quick grip on the edge prevented him from falling to his death.

"Hold on!" Thaylus slid down the incline and ran to Brythan, grasping his wrists.

But Brythan was too heavy. The sage's grip on his wrists was slipping.

A look of terror plastered Brythan's face. "Please, Thaylus. Don't let go!"

"I'm trying! I'm just not strong enough!"

"Don't you give up on me. Give it everything you have!"

Thaylus's hold was failing. Their grasp slipped to their palms.

Help me. Thaylus closed his eyes.

Instantly, a surging strength flowed through Thaylus's arms. He squeezed tightly, and with a titan's grip, slowly began pulling Brythan up.

Little by little, Thaylus hoisted Brythan to the surface.

"Thaylus, how?" Brythan panted, catching his breath. "I was sure I had met my demise."

"I think it was Ithia's faith once again! Something inside me just … came out."

"Astounding! It never ceases to amaze me. I still wonder how simple faith can accomplish so much."

They looked upon the monster's large unmoving body. Whether it was dead or unconscious, they didn't know, nor did they want to stick around long enough to find out.

"What was that creature?" Brythan asked.

"A Yeti, I'm certain. I never thought they were real."

"Do you think there are any more?"

"If there are, they would be in caves like this."

They caught their breath a few minutes more, then Thaylus slowly slid to his knees.

"We should keep climbing."

Once more, they took up their sacks and began their ascent.

Snow and ice stung their faces. Their limbs ached and began to go numb, and it took every bit of willpower to go on.

Comfort came as the sun broke through the thick, grey clouds. Its warmth and light gave them hope. They climbed with their eyes fixed on the sun.

As the incline leveled out, Thaylus thought he could make out the top of a large structure.

"I think I see it!"

Soon, the whole cathedral came into view. They'd made it.

The face of it was decorated with many spires, with arches lined along it. A half-dome was built into the face of the cathedral with a colonnade circling below. Three large steeple-like towers rose majestically, with one in the center that rose magnificently. Two smaller steeples flanked each side. Statues lined the edifice—unicorns, phoenixes, dragons, sphinxes, griffins, and other mythical creatures Thaylus had never seen before.

"It's wondrous!" Brythan exclaimed.

"I've never seen something so beautiful! And to think, it's been here since Elim's time."

Both approached the half-dome supported by a semi-circle of columns.

"With snow all over the cathedral, it looks enchanted, like from a fairy tale," Thaylus murmured.

Once under the colonnade, they came to a spearhead-shaped door with a stained-glass window.

Brythan pulled on a handle, and it opened easily. The tired companions fell to their knees with a deep sigh.

"Finally! Sweet relief!"

Brythan grinned. "How good it is to be in here."

"I wonder what we do next."

"I suppose we just look until we find something."

Three indoor balconies with curved stairwells led from the base floor up three levels. Every level was lined with three doors.

"It will take considerable time to search all levels. We must consider this," Brythan said.

Two stuffed leather chairs faced each other. Thaylus and Brythan took a seat and drifted into thought.

Brythan cocked his head. "Do you hear anything?"

"No."

"I do. It sounds like humming ... a female voice. I can barely make it out, but it's there."

Thaylus listened but heard nothing.

Brythan paced, trying to find the source. "Yes, I hear singing! It's beautiful. It's coming from above somewhere."

He followed the singing to the staircase and up to the second floor.

"It is getting louder. I believe it is coming from the door in the center of the first balcony. Thaylus, come up here."

The sage was mystified. He rushed up to meet Brythan. "Are you sure? I hear nothing at all."

"I'm certain of it. My sense of hearing is excellent."

Brythan opened the door.

Before them was a large indoor garden with an arched ceiling. On the other side of the garden, a waterfall about ten feet tall poured from a pool with a fountain.

Now Thaylus could hear the singing. Brythan was right—it was perhaps the most lovely, luminous sound he'd ever experienced.

The serene voice was coming from a transparent form of a woman, standing by the waterfall. She wore a blue gown, and a rainbow shimmered over and all around her.

She sang with her eyes closed as she brushed her long blonde hair, and when she opened her eyes she appeared startled.

"Oh! Who are you?" The mysterious being asked.

Thaylus and Brythan gazed at the glorious creature, too in awe to speak.

After several moments, the beautiful, ghostly figure frowned.

"Did you not hear me, strangers? Don't be timid."

Both men were jolted out of their mesmerized daze.

"Oh … um … we don't mean to intrude," Brythan offered. "Please forgive us."

Who was this glorious woman? Thaylus had never seen someone more stunningly beautiful.

"I am pleased to meet you. How did you find this place?"

"We were sent by a man named Elim…"

"Elim!" The transparent woman smiled warmly. "I know him as well—years ago in his time, and I next saw him when he arrived back in the cathedral in this time." The woman stopped short. "You do know he can time travel, right?"

"Elim told us all about it—how he touched the white diamond and got his power," Brythan said. "But I find it odd he did not mention you."

She smiled almost shyly. "Well, we never really spoke. I just observed him."

"Who are you?" asked Thaylus.

"I am Clara, a spirit who guards this place against evil intruders. I was not alerted when you entered. I used to be a priestess of the Lord within the Gate of Vessels along with many others who served here thousands of years ago."

"This Lord within the Gate of Vessels once received open worship by men? When?" Thaylus asked. "Elim never mentioned this."

Clara smiled. "It commenced at the creation of the planet of Khrine."

"What happened to everyone else who lived here?" Thaylus asked.

Her face took on an expression of sorrow.

"Many millennia ago, when I served in this place, dark and nebulous beings with swords of black fire slaughtered everyone here—including me. As I lay on the floor dying, a female Vessel Bearer asked if I would guard this place. She gave me a power called faith, so that none like the intruders would ever come again."

"Realm Dwellers," Thaylus said bleakly. "That is the name of the beings that attacked your cathedral."

"How do you know this? You've never been to my time."

"It involves a dream I had—let that suffice."

"Very well," said Clara. "I trust you."

"When they wandered the planet of Khrine thousands of years ago, somehow they were sealed in a place called the Abyss. Do you know how, and by whom?" asked Brythan.

"I do not know. I've only encountered these beings once."

Thaylus stepped forward. "This Vessel Bearer, was her name Ithia?"

"Yes, it was!" Clara widened her eyes. "Would your names be Thaylus and Brythan?"

The two companions looked at each other in surprise.

"Yes, that is who we are," Thaylus said. "How do you know us?"

"Ithia instructed me to help you both. You are to receive the power of time travel."

Brythan blinked and shook his head.

"Ithia also sent Elim to speak to us as well. He saved our lives. But how will we obtain the power to traverse time? We don't have the book."

"We don't need Elim's book. Even if we had his book with us, only one person at a time can wield its power; when Elim dies, the power of time travel will return back to the book. But we cannot wait for that to happen. We need to act fast."

"How will we gain time travel?" Thaylus asked.

Slowly, Clara rose into the air. Her transparent form settled upon a large, grey, stone pillar.

She waved her hand. A square brick emerged from the pillar with a thin rectangle object wrapped in a red cloth.

She unwrapped the rectangle.

"This is called the Book of Realms. With it, I can send humans to different worlds."

Thaylus was mystified and excited by her words.

"You mean a different planet?"

"The place you are going to is more like another universe. It is indeed another world you will be going to, though."

"What are these other universes like?"

"Each world has subtle differences, but is also the same in many ways. The world you are going to is called Earth, where another cathedral stands with another book. That book contains the power to send one through time. You must find it and touch the stone of time, then return."

"Earth?" The word sounded awkward on Brythan's tongue. "Will we be in another time, as well?"

"I don't know. Now you two must depart, but beware—there may be danger where you are going."

Clara opened the book and mumbled a few words. A spiraling circle of blue light appeared to their left.

"There is your portal. When you have touched the diamond on the other book, the portal will reappear. May the One in the Gate of Vessels be with you," Clara said.

Both men hesitated and looked at each other.

"The portal will make you feel a little weak. Now please go," Clara said.

Faith.

Thaylus and Brythan closed their eyes, held their breath, and stepped through.

# Chapter 9

## The Dark Cathedral

Thaylus and Brythan crossed over to the other cathedral—the cathedral on the world known as Earth.

This new cathedral remained much darker inside than the one in the White Mountains. The only way they could glimpse anything was from a full moon, which glowed through several long windows on the left wall. No snow fell outside as they looked out the windows at trees swaying in the wind. The ceiling was high and vaulted.

To their right were paintings of people with evil eyes that seemed to watch them. The wall was lined with statues of gargoyles, grotesque bat–like creatures, dragons, harpies, and other vile creatures Thaylus could not name.

"What a bleak place. It feels eerie," Brythan said.

"I wonder if anyone is here."

A large iron door with a single handle stood at the far side of the hall.

Brythan touched it and jerked back.

"There is a presence on the other side. I can tell just by touching the handle," Brythan said.

Thaylus touched it and pulled away, backing off. "I feel it too!"

"It is the only way to go. If supernatural evil is on the other side, we must remember what Ithia gave us."

Thaylus nodded. "I know—faith. I only hope it will manifest itself as it has before in dangerous situations."

Thaylus pulled the door open and a loud, metal grind stung his ears.

Brythan looked around a wide room with torches fixed to the walls. "Someone must dwell here. The torches are lit."

Thaylus narrowed his eyes. "Or this place is enchanted."

"Do you think Realm Dwellers live in this dimension, too?" Brythan asked with a shudder.

"Perhaps so. But if we do encounter any, it may take more faith than we have ever experienced."

Although Thaylus lacked total persuasion in his mind, he spoke the words naturally. But Thaylus was a doubtful man when it came to any claim of deity, despite his vision from Elim. Perhaps this great Lord of the Gate of Vessels was merely a spiritual being of some sort, like Ithia. Perhaps he didn't have the love, spiritual fulfillment, and true divine wisdom the sage craved. He required definitive proof, just as the appearance of Ithia and the giving of her faith convinced him.

Thaylus remained unsure where Brythan stood on the matter of the Gate of Vessels. After all, Brythan didn't witness the spiritual things Elim showed Thaylus.

Suddenly a cold wind blew past them, ruffling their cloaks and wisping over their heads.

"Something just passed by us!" Brythan said. "I think we are in the presence of ghostly beings."

"Even so, we must continue." Thaylus stepped forward.

Soon a gust started to blow all around them. It increased to the power of a whirlwind, and they began to see transparent, human figures flying in slow circles overhead. The figures moaned and cried, filling Brythan and Thaylus's minds with a cold, resonating pain.

They grabbed their heads and fell to their knees.

"What are you doing here, mortals?" the spirits wailed in unison.

"Please, stop whatever you're doing to us," cried Thaylus. "We will tell you!"

The spirits slowed their torrent of spinning around the two. They ceased screaming and halted flying through the air.

They descended to hover over the ground.

"Now tell us. What realm do you come from and what is your intent?"

Thaylus was breathing heavily and bent over with his hands on his knees.

Brythan spoke, out of breath as well. "We come seeking knowledge. We simply want to explore your cathedral."

Thaylus kept their mission to himself, aware that the spirits would surely guard against taking the book. He glanced at Brythan, who must have realized the same thing.

The spirits looked at each other for several moments.

"We know you come from another world. All of us saw the portal you came from."

"It is true," said Brythan. "We come from a world called Khrine."

"If you intend to look throughout this cathedral, you must promise to let us go back with you. Our souls have been trapped in this dark place for hundreds of years, and your world may be our only freedom."

"Why are you trapped here?" Thaylus asked.

"We are the spirits of kings who once ruled a realm called Nephiro, in a valley east of here. Generations upon generations ago, we were cursed by evil beings with swords of black fire. Our souls were condemned to live in this brazen prison."

Realm Dwellers. "So they do exist here," Brythan murmured.

"We will let you stay if you take us with you through this portal," said one of the spirits, a transparent red-haired man in a decadent blue robe.

Brythan whispered into Thaylus's ear. "I know you may think it cruel, but it would be trouble to unleash spirits into our realm. We must beguile them. If they know of the book and its power, they will surely oppose us."

The nobleman turned and addressed the ghostly beings. "Very well, we will bring you with us."

"We thank you. You are free to browse through our abode. But beware—hostile creatures roam these halls we have no control over."

The transparent beings vanished completely as a fading voice echoed. Remember our pact.

"What shall we do now?" Thaylus whispered.

"I don't know. I wonder how the spirit Clara expects us to find the book."

"I suppose we look."

Thaylus and Brythan walked to the only other door in the room. They entered an enclosure with a single set of stairs that led up to the middle of a balcony. From there were three doors lining a wall.

"This place is not as complex as the cathedral on our side," Thaylus said.

"Indeed. We may find the book quicker than we thought."

They walked up the staircase and stopped, glancing at the three doors.

"Why don't we take the one in the center?" Brythan suggested.

"It is just as good as any."

When they had entered, a large blazing fire pit burned in the center of the room. The fire pit was circled by six black stone pillars.

"Well, we already know this place is enchanted."

"Haunted is more like it. What could this room be for?" Thaylus asked.

The door slammed shut behind them, and a loud hissing followed farther inside. Thaylus and Brythan looked all around.

An enormous black form slowly descended from the ceiling in the shadows at the other end of the room. There was another hiss, this one coming from the figure.

The figure crept forward—it was a hideous immense spider.

Thaylus was wide-eyed in fear as he backed away and ran to the door.

But it would not open. He pounded on it in panic.

Brythan simply froze.

"We're trapped! Confound it!" Thaylus spewed.

He closed his eyes and focused his thoughts while he gained control of his sporadic breathing.

"We must stay calm and make a plan."

"You're right. We shouldn't fear." Brythan ran a palm down his face and shook himself.

"We have to coax it into falling inside the fire pit!" Thaylus said.

"But how?"

"I have a plan, Brythan, but you have to trust me."

"All right. What is your plan?"

Thaylus crossed his arms. "Stand in front of the fire pit and let the spider come at you."

"You're crazy. That's a death wish!"

"Trust me."

Brythan considered.

"Let the spider come to you. When I cry 'slide,' then you slide forward," Thaylus instructed.

Brythan took an anxious, trembling breath. He ran a palm down his sweaty face. Then he peered at Thaylus with pursed lips.

"If you were any other man, I would refuse your proposal. Very well."

Thaylus hid behind a pillar as Brythan ran for the fire pit and stood there.

The spider turned to the vulnerable nobleman, creeping ever closer.

Behind the creature was Thaylus, matching every step the spider made, just a few feet behind. Brythan cringed as the creature's mouth came closer and closer.

It opened it mandibles wide to engulf him.

"Slide!" Thaylus cried.

Brythan slid, slipping under the spider's gruesome body.

With a swift motion, Thaylus bashed the spider from behind, sending it toppling into the fire pit. A hideous screech came from the burning spider. It struggled out of the pit, running around like a tumbling piece of burning coal, writhing and aimlessly hitting the walls and pillars.

Moments later, it stopped moving, aflame on its back with curled up legs.

Brythan lay on the ground in disbelief. "The crazy plan worked! Thaylus, I know you were wise, but this plan was simply clever!"

"Where there is a will, there is a way. Thank you for trusting me."

Thaylus helped Brythan up, and they shook each other's forearms.

Thaylus went to the door, and this time it opened easily.

"Just as I thought—another benefit of slaying the spider."

They shut the door behind them.

"I'm glad to be out of there," Thaylus said. "There are two doors left. One of them must lead to the book."

"Keep your voice down. Which door do we take?"

"Let's try the right door."

Nervous tension gripped Thaylus about what would be on the other side. Brythan opened the door and saw another room with no other passages.

But elation overtook them at what they saw in the center of the room: a podium-like stone structure with a book in a glass casing.

"That book! It must be it!"

"Not so loud, Thaylus!"

Thaylus cleared his throat. "Forgive me," he whispered. "What if the ghosts come back if we touch the book? They may be watching us."

"I'm surprised the ghosts have not reappeared from your outburst when you saw it," Brythan said with slight derision.

Both stepped forward. Nothing happened.

They walked farther in. The door did not close behind them.

Relaxing a little, the two continued to advance with no sign of danger.

Just as they did, three spirits appeared directly in front of them.

Both men jolted backwards and froze like two thieves caught in the act. They were speechless—trapped.

"Indeed, we are aware of your conversation." The spirits intoned. "We are curious about the book, but we cannot touch it—probably because we are spirits."

"So the book is useless to you," Thaylus said.

"Yes. Whatever power or knowledge that it has is yours. Only take us with you to your dimension."

Thaylus took Brythan by the arm, steering him to a corner of the room.

"We just can't leave them here," Thaylus said in a low voice. "They're victims of the Realm Dwellers."

"There is nothing we can do. Unfortunately, their fate is sealed."

"How can you be so heartless?"

"Bringing them with us is out of the question, Thaylus. There is nothing else we can do."

Thaylus shook his head. "Despite your knowledge and keen sense of things, young noblemen, the final word is mine."

Brythan blushed and looked at his feet. "Yes, Arch Sage."

Thaylus put his hand to his chin. "It may indeed be unwise as you say. Allowing foreign beings to live in another dimension may have repercussions. Blast it! If only Ithia's power could help them in some way."

"I remember how her faith helped us to…"

As Brythan spoke, Thaylus felt a hot feeling like lightning course through his veins and focus his mind to a crystal-clear sense. His breathing steadied as, and he poised himself. Lowering his head, he closed his eyes.

Then his head snapped up and his eyes opened.

"Thaylus, your eyes! They are like Ithia's! Her presence resonates from your body!"

Empowered, Thaylus walked over to the three ghosts.

"What is happening to you? What power is this?" exclaimed the spirits.

"In the name of the One within the Gate of Vessels, I loose you from the curse that keeps you from the next realm of existence," Thaylus announced.

The rest of the spirits appeared in the room one by one. Slowly, they started to glow with a golden hue. The shimmering light brightened and lit up everything around them.

The ghosts smiled with beaming faces; their eyes twinkled. The freed beings lifted their arms up as they all spoke in unison.

"We thank you for this freedom that we may pass on. May you be blessed exceedingly by whatever power that is."

In a flash of white light, they were gone.

Thaylus fell to his knees then toppled to his side.

Brythan rushed to Thaylus's body and held his head up.

Thaylus blinked as he came to his senses. "How strange. I have never used the name of—"

"The one within the Gate of Vessels. I know."

"It just came out of me! The power I possessed felt exhilarating. I did not know the things I spoke. Never in my right mind would I show any regard to this deity I spoke of. Why would a true God show himself so obscurely? All these riddles and teasing sounds like an entity that is skittish to be made known or be worshipped. And why would he keep himself kept secret from the world and leave the planet to the mercy of the Realm Dwellers?"

Brythan looked down and sighed. "I don't know. But there must at least be a slim possibility… wait, the book!"

Thaylus spun to look in the direction Brythan pointed.

The book was gone.

"Who could have taken it?" Thaylus exclaimed.

"It may be Realm Dweller," Brythan said. "Can't you sense them?"

"Yes, I sense it too, now—there is no denying it. But why didn't they try stealing it sooner?"

"The ghosts being here must have repelled them. The moment we freed them, the Realm Dweller snatched it from under our noses." Brythan sighed and put his head in his hands. "Now what?"

"It was stolen only minutes ago. Why would a Realm Dweller want the book?"

"We will ponder that later. We must get it back!"

They ran out of the room just in time to see a hovering figure in a black cloak headed for a large door to the outside. Thaylus and Brythan sprinted down the staircase.

As the sage neared the dark being, he started to get an anxious knot in his stomach.

Nevertheless, he suppressed his emotions and caught the edge of the dark entity as it stepped through the door and into the cold, dark night of a forest.

The being fell back and hit the ground, jarring the book from his grip.

Brythan froze with wide eyes, terrified of the dark being.

Thaylus grabbed the book. Its back cover showed the two gems: the onyx of magic and the diamond of time.

Simply touching the right one would give him the power to time travel, and the portal to Khrine would appear.

But it wasn't easy. Growing from the onyx, a subtle alluring essence manifested.

The dark figure got up, its orange glowing eyes glaring hard at Thaylus.

"It calls to you, Thaylus. Don't resist it. Think of the power that awaits you. The greatness of evil gives you strength beyond imagining. With it, you could rival Kyrious's army and rule the seven kingdoms. There will be peace."

Thaylus's hands were shaking as he held the book. He breathed shallowly as his eyes darted back and forth from the onyx to the diamond. There was no longer any fear from the entity, but the onyx overflowed him with something tremendously beyond the phantom-like being. Maybe if he absorbed magic power, he could overcome the tyrannical Kyrious.

Thaylus's fingers were inches from the onyx. Closer and closer they came to it. It was as if he could breathe in the potent power from the gem.

But a familiar voice spoke into his mind. No, Thaylus, don't give in! Remember who you are and what you are striving for.

"Ithia, I must possess the magic power. I … ahhh! I can't resist!"

Use the faith I gave to you. It is still there.

Thaylus closed his eyes and calmed. He took in a deep, steady breath. The onyx brought a tinge of power lust, yet he resisted.

Soon he sensed a small shred of righteous light shine in his darkening heart. He slowly came to reality and out of the mesmerizing trickery of the evil object.

The dark being sought to sway him. "Thaylus, no!"

The sage blinked his eyes and frowned angrily at the evil messenger. Gathering his wits, Thaylus touched the diamond.

Suddenly it shone with the brilliance of lightning. Illumination surged through him.

It was like a great rushing wind passed by him. Thaylus's body pulsed, like lightning was shooting through every limb. His head tilted back, taking in the knowledge that infused him with time travel. Thaylus felt his heart throb as he smiled with a gleaming face.

The light abated, and the evil figure retreaded into the blackness of the forest wilderness.

Brythan ran to his friend. "Thaylus, you're safe! How did you manage to overcome him?"

"It was Ithia. She helped me."

"How?"

"I heard her voice in my head. It was very calming, and it gave me the strength to choose righteousness."

"I apologize—for not coming to your aid. I was overwhelmed by the terror the being brought upon me."

"I hold no judgment." Thaylus frowned and pulled on his beard. "There is something else. The dark being called me by my name. It knew who I was."

Brythan looked down and put a hand to his chin. "Either the Realm Dweller being somehow heard me mention your name, or—"

"It wasn't a Realm Dweller. The one I just saw had orange eyes like the three we met coming from the Western Kingdom. We encountered a Realm Messenger. I am certain."

"What's inside the book?" asked Brythan.

"The book contains uncovered writing. It's in Pyrithian. I wonder what it says about the Realm Dwellers."

Thaylus thumbed through the book.

"Fascinating—it describes the nature of the Realm Messengers, too. It says their thinner, lighter spiritual essence allows them to slip through the light from the Western Kingdom." Thaylus blinked. "This book must be full of endless wisdom and knowledge!"

"Let's go back to the cathedral," said Thaylus.

The two walked to the entrance. When they had passed through, a blue sphere of light appeared. Soon it grew into a disk of spiraling illumination.

"Let's leave this place," Thaylus said.

Thaylus stepped toward the portal and stopped. "It's like someone is tugging the book out of my hand! I can't pull it through!"

"The portal is closing! Leave it!" Brythan said.

"But the knowledge, it's at our fingertips! It could help us!"

Brythan wrenched the book from Thaylus's hands and tossed it away. "We got what we came for! The portal has diminished to half its size! Leave the book!"

Thaylus raked his hands through his hair. "Confound it!"

Brythan rushed through the portal and Thaylus followed.

# Chapter 10

## The Seal to The Abyss

Clara was waiting for them when Thaylus and Brythan returned through the portal.

"Did you succeed?"

Thaylus's face was dark. "Yes, but I came close to ruining everything. Strong temptation almost persuaded me to choose the book's magic. And there is more—we encountered a Realm Messenger."

"The ones you said destroyed all who dwelled in my cathedral thousands of years ago?"

"No, these were different. Realm Messengers do not have power to inflict harm, only speak and create fearful projections. The ones you met we know as Realm Dwellers. Those are the ones that will cross over into our dimension within days."

Clara absorbed the information without words.

Thaylus lowered his head. "If only I had that book."

Thaylus felt like his fortitude was being teased with. Probably the most priceless knowledge had literally been in his grasp. Then it escaped him. What kind of deity would toy with one's aspirations?

Brythan put a gentle hand on his shoulder. "It feels unfair. But the book had to stay in the other dimension for a good reason."

Thaylus felt the hand but pushed it off. He walked to the pool and kneeled by its edge. A rainbow dazzled the small waterfall.

He stirred the water with his hand and sighed. The coolness traveled up his arm to his shoulder and then to his neck. It soothed his bitterness somewhat.

"You speak the truth, of course," Thaylus said softly. The reflection in the water showed a wrinkled face with a short grey beard and dark, deep eyes.

He stood, then approached Clara.

"I believe what I see, hear, and touch," Thaylus said, defeated. "I've seen the Gate of Vessels. But the god you worship has not proven himself. At least, not to me."

Clara raised her tone. "You must believe in Him and have faith."

Thaylus jutted his chin, his voice hard. "Enough with this faith! So far faith has only proved to be a power, albeit a spiritual one, that sometimes manifests itself!"

Clara cupped Thaylus's cheek with her hand.

"Thaylus, it is more. Faith is the evidence of things not seen and of things hoped for. These words come from the great God Himself."

Thaylus pinched his brows. "I just feel so utterly exhausted. I cannot go on like this. I ache for a god of goodness and wisdom."

At that, he turned away and wept.

When he collected himself, he faced Brythan and Clara once more.

Clara smiled with glistening eyes.

"Wait here."

She floated over the pool, her gown flowing behind her, and careened through the curtain of falling water.

A few moments later she emerged, holding a small polished, wooden box.

"I want you to have this."

She opened it in front of Thaylus to reveal a blue pearl.

He looked at the pearl, puzzled. "Why do you give me this?"

"Let this serve as a reminder of the words of God that I told you."

With a soft sigh, Thaylus took the pearl in his fingers. "Very well."

Thaylus felt at the end of himself. What could accepting this insignificant object hurt?

Clara led them to a long bench near the pool.

Thaylus ran his palms down his face and took a deep breath, composing himself.

"Something else that was odd happened in the other realm. The Realm Messenger we saw? It tried to steal the book from us. What is more, it knew my name."

"Perhaps this being could identify you because he is spiritual," Clara offered.

"The spiritual realm is like the Gate of Vessels—it transcends all time and space."

"That is what I surmised," Thaylus said.

"It also explains why the Realm Messengers knew our intentions," Brythan said.

Thaylus paused, reflecting. "I feel the power to time travel but I do not sense how to use it."

"Ithia told me you must focus on a time in your mind, then say '*tempus itinerantur*,' and a time portal will appear," Clara said. "You are to travel about four thousand years into the past. That is the last thing she told me."

"What precisely are we to accomplish?" Brythan asked.

"Ithia did not say. But I believe she will tell you the next time you meet her." Clara tilted her head and smiled. "I shall deeply miss you two. Without a doubt I sincerely believe you will succeed and defeat the evil that seeks to destroy us. Perhaps we will meet again."

"I trust we will," Thaylus said.

The sage shut his eyes and took in a few deep breaths.

Then he thought of the point in time.

"*Tempus itinerantur*," Thaylus said.

A bright spiraling portal appeared.

Clara put her hand up in farewell, then Brythan and Thaylus walked through.

Instantly they found themselves flying through a vast heavenly display. All around them were celestial bodies—nebulae, comets, and colorful stars. Spiraling galaxies spun. Colors burst everywhere, red, green, blue, yellow.

It was like a dream yet real at the same time.

"Brythan, where are we?"

"I don't know. Perhaps a spiritual realm of some sort."

Thaylus pointed to a glowing object above them. "What is that?"

"It feels familiar. It's peaceful and ... something else."

"It feels ... alive."

As the glowing light neared them, they saw it had a female shape.

"I think it's Ithia," Thaylus said.

"Is it really?"

Ithia drifted in the air toward them with her stork's wings spread and her arms reaching outward. When the two humans were a few feet from her, they became stationary in the dazzling expanse. The same golden hue enveloped her form. This time her eyes illuminated with a white light.

"Greetings, once again."

"Oh, Ithia, I'm glad to see you!" Brythan said.

Thaylus's mind flooded with curiosity and questions. He wished she could explain everything to him at once. Foremost were proof and clarity about his ultimate question: Is there a true deity, and how does one have fellowship with such a being?

"It is good to see you both as well. You are probably wondering where you are," Ithia gestured to the swirling heavens around them. "This is the Realm Rift, the ultimate time dimension where all times and realms are connected."

"This wondrous place is where Elim goes when he time travels?" Brythan asked.

"No. You are here in this space between times so I might speak with you. But before I tell you, you must know some things."

Thaylus's heart jumped at her words.

Ithia placed a hand on each of their heads.

Immediately, a flash of light came, and they found themselves on a mound in a valley. As they watched, a battle of thousands raged over the vast landscape. Above them in the sky, thick dark rumbling clouds like sackcloth obscured the sun. A flowing grey mist entwined the land like jungle vines.

Below, a young man in armor with a shimmering blade fought a dark, shadowy being with a sword of black fire.

The young man breathed heavily, gripping his sword with white knuckles.

"Die, cursed Realm Dweller!" he yelled and charged.

The Realm Dweller swiped its burning blade against the young warrior's weapon, sending it flying. The warrior held up his shield as the Realm Dweller brought its flaming blade down upon it with a crackling clash.

The warrior grunted as he held his ground.

But the fiery blade bit into the shield as sparks flew. With a grinding, clenching, guttural sound that chilled Thaylus's heart, the dark being seared through the shield.

The black blazing weapon dug into the young warrior's chest.

"Where are we?" Thaylus asked. "Is this a vision, Ithia?"

Ithia shook her head. "No. We have traveled back in time four thousand years ago, when the Realm Dwellers first crossed to this dimension."

"Are we in danger?" Brythan asked.

"No. I have obscured the sight of them that dwell in this time from seeing us."

Thaylus frowned. "I do not feel the fear that I understand comes with their presence."

"My holy presence shields the Realm Dwellers' effects. Come, I will show you things from a different vantage point."

In another flash, the three stood amid a burning village. Women screamed in terror as they fled the Realm Dwellers. Smoke and ash filled Thaylus's lungs, and he coughed.

Thaylus looked at Ithia, then gasped.

Tears gathered in her eyes, and her lips trembled as she stared at something nearby. He turned to see a burning cathedral about a dozen yards away from them, people locked inside.

Ithia pointed, her voice husky with unshed tears. "That is the most tragic thing here—the death and torment of the worshippers of God."

"How could such a god allow this?" Thaylus asked.

"His ways are higher than ours. He has His reasons." Her voice trailed off.

She took their hands. "Now, let us go—one thousand years into the future."

Another flash of azure sent the three onto the top of a battlement. They could see Realm Dwellers creeping up its grey stone surface. Far off, the same foul red pillar of light reached to the sky.

"The scarlet light!" Brythan said.

"As you know, it is the portal from the Abyss to Khrine," Ithia said.

Around Thaylus, Ithia, and Brythan, men in armor shot flaming arrows upon the invaders below.

"Stay vigilant, men! Ready the catapults!" ordered a man in a green cloak. A golden phoenix clasped his cloak together.

"That phoenix crest is from the old kingdom of Nimithar," Ithia said. "During this battle, the Battle of Nimithar, the Realm Dwellers will be cast into the Abyss. Behold."

Among the Realm Dweller throng, spread across the stretch of ground below the wall, a surge of golden light erupted from a spot near the scarlet beam.

The red light flickered and dimmed. Rays of sunlight broke through the evil dark clouds as the red light shrank from its height in the sky.

The Realm Dwellers shrieked. Some on the wall fell.

The vertical beam of light narrowed and dimmed until the last dwindling illumination was quenched. A cataclysmic explosion of golden light filled the battlefield.

When it abated, all the Realm Dwellers had vanished like a snuffed candle flame.

"The bright golden light came from a holy object that sealed the Realm Dwellers back into the Abyss," Ithia said. "You can call it the 'Seal to the Abyss.'"

"Did the seal work on its own? Did anyone have a part in its use?" Thaylus asked.

"The Lord in the Gate of Vessels chose a man rich in wisdom to use the seal. Only he had the faith to wield it."

"Why not let the Vessel Bearers use the seal?" Brythan asked.

"It is forbidden for us to directly reveal ourselves to the world, for it would distract them from the great Lord and even tempt some people to worship us as gods. Instead, the great God shows people things secretly in dreams and visions."

"What does this seal look like?" Thaylus asked.

"It is a golden shield that glows with the power of the One within the Gate."

"Why do we need to know all this?"

"Because you have a mission: You must find the seal in the past."

"Find the seal?" Brythan asked. "How?"

"Yes. The reason you must find it is because it was lost, shortly after the wise man sealed the Realm Dwellers in the Abyss, a thousand years after they first appeared. This seal must be retrieved wherever it lay. You two will look for it."

"I surmise we are intended to use it to seal the Realm Dwellers in our time when they are freed," Brythan said.

"Very perceptive. That is indeed what must be done."

Thaylus took a breath. "What happens now?"

"You will be transported to a time shortly after the Realm Dwellers were banished to the Abyss, three thousand years ago. There, you will meet a guide who will lead you to the shield."

Ithia turned to face them. "Now I leave you. You both are in the middle of your journey, and soon you will understand the full mysteries of the Gate of Vessels and the gift of He who lives within it. And henceforth, you will have no need to travel through the Realm Rift. Instead, the transference will happen in a simple flash of light."

She took their hands and smiled kindly. "Farewell until I see you again. When you emerge, you will be three thousand years before your own time."

With that, Ithia vanished.

Thaylus and Brythan found themselves floating in the direction of a blue vortex. A few moments later, they passed through it.

When they emerged, they were in bright sunlight, standing upon a mountain with tall blades of grass, growing among blooming red flowers and tall trees with elongated, deep green leaves. The charming sound of small, brown birds completed the cheerfulness of the setting. A little hill overlooked a small town below.

A wave of weariness swept over them.

"I feel a weakened effect on my mind and body. It is very potent, just like Elim said," Brythan said.

"Indeed. I'm sure my old body wears worse than yours."

Thaylus shook his head until it cleared. Soon the effects subsided, though Thaylus still felt a subtle drain.

"I suppose we might as well begin looking for our guide in that town," Thaylus said.

"But will we find him or vice versa?"

"It will work out as always. Besides, I hope to rest awhile before we set off with him."

Brythan yawned. "I could do for some sleep, too."

The two went down the steady decline full of weeds and rocks.

At the bottom, the terrain leveled out onto the smooth dirt path, and soon they could hear the town. The commotion of people filled the air.

The braying of horses and the neighs of donkeys mixed with the sounds of other animals in a lively atmosphere. Soon they could see stone buildings and people dressed in odd, but clean clothes.

When Thaylus and Brythan were near enough, they saw a sign, written in their own language of Berinth: Tarken Town.

They entered the busy abode. Everywhere they looked, people were decorating trees and houses with long ribbons and selling small cakes, hard candy, and other sweets in colorful booths and tents. Archery contests, apple bobbing, horseshoe throwing, chess games, and other manner of celebration filled the air.

"I've never seen such joy in my life!" Brythan grinned.

"Yes, it's wonderful."

A man neared the two and peered at them with a raised eyebrow. The man was dressed in layer of blue nylon from head to toe with only his face bare. A broad hood-like protrusion lined the back of his head and neck. His shoulders had pads that curled up of each side and his knee pads curled up from the front. His shirt piece had hanging layers of silk with many colors overlapping each other from chest to stomach. His clothes contrasted from Brythan and Thaylus's blue shirt, long grey tunic and wool cloaks.

"Um, where do you come from? You are dressed strangely." The stranger tilted his head as he looked the companions up and down.

"We live in a rural dwelling place that is very remote," Brythan said, inclining his head to the man in greeting. "We don't know what you are celebrating."

"So you've not heard of the demise of the dark ones?"

Thaylus's heart jumped.

"Who are these dark ones?" Thaylus asked hesitantly.

"They're called Realm Dwellers. Fifty years ago, all who lived witnessed their dark forms disappear in a flash of golden light. Soon it was known abroad that this same mysterious thing had happened everywhere. Then it was recorded in a book."

"Where is this book?"

"It is kept in a vault somewhere in the Tower of Brea, to the North."

"The Tower of Brea!" Thaylus took Brythan aside, keeping his voice low. "I've read of the Lost Tower of Brea. It was said to have housed one of the most expensive sources of written knowledge ever built."

"It is a shame we cannot go there. We must find the guide," Brythan whispered back.

"What is it you two are so secretive about?" asked the man good-naturedly.

Thaylus bowed politely. "It is best it is not disclosed, good sir."

"Very well then. Welcome, friends. I am Gealin. Enjoy Tarken Town and the celebration."

Gealin smiled and walked off.

Thaylus peered around. "Now then, what course of action do we take to find this guide?"

"Perhaps he might approach us. Let us continue exploring."

They walked off, taking in the sights. People said hello as they passed, and smiles were plenty.

"In a way, I wish we could stay here in this time," Thaylus said. "There is no need to fear the Realm Dwellers' invasion."

"I agree, but alas, we will have to leave when we find the seal."

They reached a building, and Thaylus put a hand against the exterior, sagging slightly.

"I'm sorry, but I am very weak from traveling. Could we find an inn to rest and eat some food? These old bones are not as strong as your young body."

"I am famished myself. Only, we do not have any money."

Then they heard a voice behind them.

"Excuse me, but I couldn't help but follow you two strangers, what with you being completely oblivious to common knowledge."

It was Gealin.

"And I admit, I have been listening to your odd conversation," Gealin added.

Thaylus drew to his full height. "As it is, it would be unwise for us to elaborate on whatever you overheard."

Gealin inclined his head. "I'd be willing to pay for a stay in an inn, and for you to eat some food."

Thaylus knew their story would seem lunacy to anyone, but his physical needs overcame his caution. Surely there would be no danger in telling just a little of their quest, he told himself. How much harm could a single man do?

He exchanged a look with Brythan, who sighed in concurrence.

Thaylus gave a scant explanation, simply saying they had come from the future seeking an object of great importance.

"From the future!" Gealin chuckled in delight. "Well, I've heard of stranger things. It would explain why you are so uninformed and strangely dressed."

Thaylus shook Gealin's forearm with a smile. "I am Thaylus, and this is my companion, Brythan."

"Come."

Gealin led them. As they went, he told them a bit about the town.

"Oh, and there is an odd rumor floating around," Gealin added.

"What is this rumor?" Thaylus asked.

"While little have claimed to have seen it, there have been reported of sightings of a ghost around town."

"A ghost?"

"Those who have claimed to have seen it say it wears a grey hooded cloak and has white eyes. I don't believe the claims, but you'll likely hear more at the inn."

Gealin led them to a building of ashy stonework. A hanging sign read "Providence Inn."

A pleasant enough name, Thaylus thought.

Inside, they could hear hearty laughing, and people were bustling about.

Behind the counter stood the innkeeper, a clean-shaven man with neat blond hair. His eyes were wide and bright.

"Hello, Gealin! What brings you here?"

"Enix, these two travelers here would like some food and the most hospitable room you have. I'll be handling the payment."

"As you wish! Sit anywhere, and the waitress will attend to you as quickly as possible."

"We are much obliged for your courtesy," said Brythan.

He and Thaylus took a seat at a table by a wall.

"I suppose we should be on the lookout for our guide. Though in this throng of people, it is doubtful," Brythan said, scanning the room of boisterous celebrators.

Thaylus also began to look around the room. In a corner, two fellows caught his attention. They sat alone, as if separated from everyone, staring at their food plates gloomily.

A jovial female voice interrupted his thoughts.

"What will it be, gentlemen?" asked a young woman with thick reddish-brown braids. "Today the house special is grilled steak. To drink we have three kinds of ales: weak ale, pale ale, and Clare Household Strong."

"Thank you, miss," Thaylus said. "If I may ask, who are those gloomy individuals by themselves over in that corner?"

"Oh, those men. They say they've seen a ghost around these parts, if you believe those things."

"I see. Would you give us a few more minutes to decide what we want?" asked Thaylus.

The woman nodded and walked away.

"I have a thought, Brythan. Could this ghost be a being like a Realm Messenger?"

"I've surmised the same possibility. However, they have an evil presence that causes great fear to anyone around. A lot of people would have sensed it. Although, this ghost's appearance does not match with what we know about any Realm being."

Thaylus and Brythan approached the two lonely souls and bowed slightly.

"Greetings, sirs. May we join you?"

The men looked up in surprise. They glanced at each other.

One of them, a plump, balding man, shook his head. "Have you come here to laugh at us or to be entertained?"

Brythan frowned. "No, we genuinely want to hear of your sighting. We understand you saw a ghost. Would you permit us to sit along with you?"

The man glared at him. "What game are you playing? No soul has ever believed us. Kindly depart."

Thaylus pulled up a chair and sat. He leaned in and looked squarely at both individuals, one after the other.

"Look at my face."

Widening their eyes, they looked at him, then peered at each other.

"I know the eyes of an insane person or a charlatan. You two do not look like madmen or liars," Thaylus said seriously. "Do I appear to be a man intent on getting mocking jollies?"

"You genuinely want to know?" the second, much younger man said. "None has ever believed us."

"Trust me. We two are not normal men." Brythan took a seat next to his friend.

"I'm Nithose, and this is Doren," the younger man said.

"A pleasure to meet you both," Thaylus replied. "Now please, tell us your tale."

Doren, the older, peered around, as if still making sure they were not the butt of some joke.

Finally, Doren took a heavy breath. "I'll begin by telling my first encounter."

# Chapter 11

## The Guide

In the dark space in a corner of the loud inn, Doren looked all around him once more, then began.

"The first time I saw it, it was night. I was drawing some water from the town square well. That's I felt something cold and eerie pass my back."

Thaylus and Brythan listened, rapt.

"But when I turned around, there was … nothing," Doren said. "I took my bucket of water and walked away. The next time, I had the same feeling. I was at the well once more, and when I sensed it, I spun around. This time I saw the presence. It wore a grey cloak and had a deathly pale face with a gem in the center of its forehead.

"I was terrified. I dropped my bucket and ran without looking back. A few minutes later, I chanced a quick glance behind me. Just as the ghost had appeared out of nowhere, it had vanished."

Brythan looked at Nithose. "And when and where did you first see it?"

"I was in bed inside my home," Nithose began. "It was early morning, and I shivered as I lay on my bed, so I went to put more logs in the hearth. As I passed by the window I saw something out there among the flowers and bushes. It was a human figure, standing erect. I looked closer and saw just what Doren described—a grey-cloaked figure with a pale human face. I was scared to death as it hovered there over the garden. It just stayed there, for no reason except maybe to frighten me."

"What followed?" Thaylus asked.

Nithose rubbed his eyes. His voice trembled as he spoke. "Then it rose up higher into the air. I did not know what it intended. I thought it was about to attack me and come breaking through the glass. I was so frightened. It continued to elevate slowly, up and up. I was about to run, but instead of attacking me, it just floated up into the sky and out of sight."

Brythan looked thoughtful. "Well, it hasn't attempted to harm anyone. Could it simply desire to frighten people?"

"Perhaps we should try interacting with it," Thaylus said.

Doren, Nithose, and Brythan all stared at him, eyebrows raised.

"Well, what do we have to lose? Like Brythan pointed out, it could have harmed you if it wanted."

"Absolutely not!" Doren exclaimed. "It could be toying with us before it goes for an attack."

Nithose shook his head at Doren and grabbed his sleeve. "Just listen to the man. What Thaylus says may be true."

Doren scowled. "If it is so friendly, why does it leave every time we see it?"

"Maybe it leaves simply because we're so frightened," Nithose said. "Think about it. If you wanted to speak to people who were petrified of you, how would you react?"

"The thought never crossed my mind." Doren put a hand to his chin. "Still, the idea of talking with the ghost makes me queasy, even if it does not intend harm."

"I'm not completely comfortable about this, either, but I think Thaylus is right. We have to try," Brythan said. "I wonder what that gem on its forehead is."

"It is curious," Thaylus said. "I think we'll learn about that once we've spoken with the ghost. So, are we all in agreement to speak to the ghost when it appears next?"

All the men conceded with a nod, Doren the most reluctant.

"Very good," Thaylus said. "Well, I don't know about the rest of you fellows, but I am bone weary. I think I will retire early."

"The journey has wearied me as well. I will do the same." Brythan stood.

"Remember to act peaceably if you encounter the ghost," Thaylus said. "Farewell until the time comes."

Thaylus and Brythan headed toward the stairs leading to the guest rooms, and the two witnesses went home, with a plan to return and meet at breakfast.

A cold chill awoke Thaylus in the middle of the night. He rose from bed to retrieve an extra blanket.

As he passed the window, something caught his eye below. It was hard to see, but movement stirred among the trees.

He waited for a few minutes. Nothing.

Then he saw something stir again. Slowly it came from behind the trees into an open clearing.

There it was! A grey-cloaked figure floated just above the ground.

I can't show fear, Thaylus thought. I must welcome it.

He opened the window. Cold wind blew inside as the trees swayed.

Thaylus made eye contact with the ghost. As it came closer, he could see it possessed no pupils or irises—its eyes were entirely white.

Swallowing hard, Thaylus beckoned for it to come to him.

The ghost floated slowly to Thaylus's window. As it neared him, not a hint of danger came from its presence. Its face looked sad, somehow lost.

At last, it approached the window. It looked like a man, with white wiry hair and a strange jewel on his forehead that glistened.

Mesmerized silence overtook Thaylus. Being in the presence of the ghost proved peculiarly peaceful—nothing like he'd expected from typical ghost tales. The sage saw that a distraught emptiness filled its eyes.

Any inhibitions that might have been in Thaylus dissolved.

"Who are you?" Thaylus asked.

"I have no name."

"What do you want?"

"To be … accepted. You are the first human who has not shunned me. Why?"

"I deduced you were not hostile because of your manner of interaction with people. You seemed to intend no harm." Thaylus took a step closer to the window. "How did you come to be this way?"

"I'm here not by choice. I am trapped to wander the mortal plain."

"Did anyone do this to you?"

The lonely soul raised his white eyebrows and lowered his head.

"Say you will not reject me if I tell you."

"I swear."

The ghost opened his mouth, but he seemed to have trouble speaking.

Finally, he admitted, "I … used to be a Realm Dweller."

"You? How could such a thing even happen?"

"It was because of a choice I made. When we were still in the world, I observed the pain and anguish we caused. For some mysterious reason I began to feel pity those we killed. I am the only outcast from their ranks."

"I never thought it possible. Beings, so tremendously evil, could turn good?"

"I was marked with this jewel on my forehead and this alternate form as my punishment. Soon after, all the Realm Dwellers were sealed in the Abyss with a magical shield. I somehow remained."

At a sound, Thaylus turned to see Brythan standing in the doorway.

The sage addressed his friend. "How long have you been listening?"

"Enough to hear all that was spoken." Brythan slowly walked toward Thaylus, and the ghost. "You spoke of the shield that trapped the Realm Dwellers. We need to find it. Do you know where it is?"

"I do. And I could lead you to it," the spirit said as he moved eagerly closer.

"I think we may have met our guide, Brythan," Thaylus said.

"A former Realm Dweller? Do you really think so?"

"It is ironic, but it would appear so."

Brythan ran a hand through his hair. "This is … a little disturbing." He looked at the ghost. "You say you were once a Realm Dweller. How can we trust you?"

Thaylus took an exasperated breath. "Brythan, please. Who else could know where the seal lay?"

"You can trust me. I give you my word," the ghost said.

Brythan looked at the ghost a moment, considering. "Despite any risk, I suppose I will accept this odd situation."

"Thank you, Brythan. I do believe his word is true," the sage said.

He addressed the ghost. "Where is the shield?"

"It lies on an uncharted island northwest from here. It is not far, but some perils await any who wish to go there."

"What kind of perils?" Thaylus asked.

"The water you will cross is very tumultuous. Even more heinous is the sea monster that dwells beneath the surface. It would be wise to obtain a sea vessel armed with a harpoon in case we encounter it. Harming it would require such a strong weapon."

"Where is the nearest seaport?" Brythan asked.

"About a mile east of here."

Thaylus pulled his beard and squinted in thought. "Horses would speed our journey to the sea border. We'll also require provisions and a boat. How will we get them?"

"Doren has a boat and a harpoon," said the spirit. "I have been watching him. He is a good man."

"If we inform him of the circumstances, he may be willing to provide the boat and necessary things," Brythan said.

Thaylus tilted his head. "Us vouching for the spirit will hold more weight on Doren and Nithose than anything."

"I agree. But they may still be fearful of him," Brythan said. "We should show him to Doren and Nithose in a private place. I see no more convenient or private place than this very room."

"Very well," said the spirit. "I will be here in the morning."

Brythan looked out the window into the breezy night. "We should sleep. We'll need the rest."

It seemed like only minutes of slumber when they awoke at the joyful crowing of a rooster introducing the new day.

Downstairs, Thaylus found Brythan sipping frothy white milk and eating poached eggs. The whole area smelt of maple sausage, buttered corn, salted pecans, and other savory breakfast items.

"Let's explore the town. It is still early. If nothing, the walk will be pleasurable enough to enjoy our surroundings," Thaylus said.

The two strolled down the cobblestone street. Trees lined the path, and they could hear birds singing happily over dawn.

Thaylus noticed Brythan's soft smile and glistening eyes as he observed swaying trees and the muted colors of the morning sky. Affection swelled in his heart for his young friend.

They came to a crossroad with the left path leading to a beautiful garden, and they followed it.

"It is a thing of wonder to see the work of the gods …." Brythan stopped abruptly. "I am sorry I said that, Thaylus. It is just that years of homage are not so quickly disavowed. I do indeed question my beliefs, and it is not just your words and reasoning. It's all we have gone through. Besides that, I am contemplating more and more of this Gate of Vessels, and the 'One Great Lord' within it. Could this being be a god, as Ithia says? A god more powerful than all the other gods combined?"

Thaylus nodded. "I believe in the Vessel Bearers because I have seen and spoke with Ithia. But I do require proof of this 'One' as a god. He may be just a strong spirit and not the all-powerful deity I seek."

"Ithia said that everything, including the Gate of Vessels, would be revealed," Brythan pointed out. "It is my burning desire that your—our—question will be answered, and that the true nature of this 'One' will be unfurled."

Thaylus felt a jolt of energy rush through his body at Brythan's words. He blinked, smiling.

"If only something like that would happen, my friend." Thaylus felt his stomach relax and a gentle wave passed through his body. "I would not hesitate to forsake my tittle of Arch Sage to find out the truth."

Brythan tilted his head and his chest rose with a deep solemn breath. "Your passion is exceptional. I've never known anyone so dedicated to a purpose as you."

Thaylus looked down, both heartened and embarrassed at Brythan's kind words. "I am proud to have your admiration."

They followed the path to a grove inside an autumn garden. Fallen leaves crunched beneath their feet like wet broom bristles.

They came upon a wooden bench and sat.

"What do you think the world was like all those years ago when the Realm Dwellers were in the world?" Brythan asked.

Thaylus shut his eyes and shuddered. "It pains me to try to imagine such a thing."

Brythan looked away to the ground and cleared his throat. "I'm sorry. I forgot … your dream."

"My nightmare from my earlier days was just as real as our very heartbeats." Thaylus exhaled. "Let us return to the inn."

"Why do you wish to leave so soon? We just sat."

"I am not in the mood to talk of my deepest pain and longing. It would ruin the morning joy. Come, Doren and Nithose will be arriving soon."

Doren and Nithose were eating at the inn when Thaylus and Brythan returned and joined them.

"We've done it," Thaylus began, smiling at their new friends. "We've made peaceful contact with the spirit."

"Truly? Where did this take place?" Nithose asked.

Thaylus chuckled. "It happened upstairs in my very room."

Doren and Nithose were speechless.

"I spoke to him, too," Brythan said. "He means us no harm. And he said he will reveal himself to you in the same way."

Doren trembled, but Nithose's eyes sparkled.

"When do we see him?" Nithose asked.

"Whenever you're ready. Just come up to my room."

"What are we waiting for? Let's go!" Nithose jumped up with a smile.

Doren stood slowly. "All right. If I am to be part of this … endeavor, I would prefer to get it over with as soon as possible."

The four ascended the stairs and into Thaylus's room.

Brythan shut the door.

A few minutes later the spirit appeared.

Nithose and Doren's eyes widened, and they stepped back.

"Don't be afraid. Talk to him," Thaylus said.

Nithose licked his lips. "What are you, and what do you want?"

"I simply want companionship and not to be shunned or feared. As for what I am, that will require trust." The spirit looked down, sorrow and repentance emanating from his presence. "I used to be a Realm Dweller, but I rejected their tyrannical ways. Because of this, I was cursed to be like this forever."

"I could hardly believe it myself, but just look into his eyes," Thaylus said to Doren and Nithose. "See how gentle they are?"

Nithose and Doren inched closer to the spirit and peered at his face.

His white eyes were unsettling, but behind them was a steady stillness.

"They're filled with a desperate complacency—nothing at all like I would imagine a Realm Dweller to be," Nithose said.

"What is the reason you are showing us all this?" Doren looked at Brythan and Thaylus.

"We are on a special mission," Thaylus said seriously.

"We require the use of your ship to travel to an island," Brythan added. "We are in search of a seal, in the form of a magical shield, to help us finish our task."

"That is no small request." Doren frowned. "What do you have to recompense this act?"

"I think we should help them, Doren." Nithose put a hand on his friend's shoulder. "They have gone through so much trouble to get this far."

Doren considered. "Very well. At the word of my young friend, we will go together to this island on my boat. When do we leave?"

"As soon as possible," Brythan said.

An hour later, they all gathered at the dock, the spirit among them.

Doren's vessel looked seaworthy enough, and its harpoon was sharp with retractable hooks. The whole ship was about twenty feet long, with a lower deck and two beds.

At full light, they boarded, the spirit at the helm.

The voyage began.

# Chapter 12

## THE QUEST FOR THE SEAL

THE WEATHER WAS PERFECT for sailing. The clouds were a purple-red hue from the rising sun.

Doren steered the boat northwest.

Thaylus leaned against the deck railing, his arms wide and his head back, smiling as he took in the salty air.

"Have you ever been out to sea?" Thaylus asked Brythan.

"Never. Have you?" said Brythan.

"I have been on two water excursions—first as an ambassador to a small island province, and a second time on a simple fishing trip farther out to sea. This search is like no other, though. Despite the reason for our trip, I feel a stillness within me, like a placid pond. I have no racing thoughts, not even the slightest tension in my stomach."

"I feel the same, despite the danger we may face," Brythan said.

"Do you think this comes from Ithia's faith?"

"Perhaps, though nothing threatening is around us to bring her essence."

Nithose approached. "Who are you two? And what in the gods are you talking about?"

"Eavesdropping, are you, lad?" Brythan grinned.

"I'm sorry. Our small town hasn't had any visitors before."

Thaylus tilted his head. "I see no reason to keep them in the dark, Brythan."

Brythan nodded.

"We come from the future, Nithose," Thaylus said. "Although this sounds like an absurd notion, it is true. There is something on that island we must take back to our future to save us from the Realm Dwellers."

"But … the Realm Dwellers are gone."

"In our time they will return."

Nithose gave them an odd look. "Are you teasing me? All this seems truly unbelievable."

Brythan only smiled. "When the moment arrives, you'll believe," he said with a chuckle.

Doren called out to them.

"The spirit directs me at the helm. He says we will be entering turbulent waters soon."

"How long will we be at sea?" Brythan asked.

"He said the island is very close."

"What is our likelihood of encountering the sea monster?" Brythan asked.

"Sea monster?" Doren said. "You certainly do not believe that myth, do you?"

Doren and Brythan were approached by the spirit. "It is no myth. I have seen it when I went to the island where I discovered the seal."

"You would have us go on a journey and not tell us of a sea monster?"

"I thought everyone knew of it. It is common knowledge."

Doren put a finger in the spirit's face, his other hand in a fist. "Well, I thought it was a myth! You listen here! You are risking our lives and my ship, along with my provisions. And you thought not to tell us?"

"Doren, do not blame him." Nithose said softly. "I went along with this quest believing in the monster. Most do. You never told me you thought it a myth."

"I thought it was vein to try to convince fools who are set in their dumb beliefs!" Doren spewed. "No offense, Nithose."

"Wait, Doren, please." Thaylus put a hand on Doren's shoulder. "I beg your forgiveness. But you must know something. Our mission is far more dire than we let on."

"What do you mean?"

Thaylus took a deep breath and poised himself. "We are sojourners from the future—a future doomed at the hands of the Realm Dwellers."

"Absurd! Prove it!"

The sage closed his eyes. "*Tempus itinerantur!*"

At his words, beads of blue light coalesced into a sphere above the waters. It pulsated until formed a spiraling portal.

"This is a time portal," Thaylus said. "We traverse time through these portals.

We come three-thousand from the future, where the Realm Dwellers will besiege the physical world of Khrine. We need the seal on the island to trap keep them bound in the abyss."

Doren's mouth was gaping as he stared.

"Does this validate our claim?" Brythan asked.

"My word! This proves it!" Doren said. "But why did you not show us before?"

The sage lowered his arm, and the vortex closed.

"Only because of the people around us did we not show you before."

"I understand," Doren said. "I am more than willing to aid you with my boat."

Suddenly, the ship tottered to one side, then to the other.

The men stumbled.

"Troubled waters are nearing us," yelled the spirit from the wheel.

Doren joined the ghost at the helm, and Thaylus went below to rest.

Brythan and Nithose stood at the bow observing the ever-mounting waves. The waters were darkening, frothing with white bubbles.

A moderate squall began to form as winds battered the sails like giant leaves.

"If this gets any worse, I fear we will start to take in water," Doren said. "Spirit, how long will we have to bear this violent sea before we arrive at the island?"

"Harsh waters should not last much longer."

"What exactly is this monster?" Brythan asked.

"It is a large creature impervious to small weapons," said the ghost. "The abomination resembles a mythical sea serpent with three heads, and it spews seething hot water. That is another reason for your boat—it has a harpoon."

"Do you think we will meet the sea beast?" Doren asked.

"Chance alone will determine that."

Tempestuous waters splashed high, washing over and onto the deck.

"Thaylus and Brythan's presence ensures me we will succeed," the spirit told Doren. "There is something about those two that gives me hope—even beyond the time travel."

"I just hope we avoid the monster." Doren paused. "Are there any other things that you know? Like the future?"

The spirit shook his head. "No. But when I was a Realm Dweller, I knew all the thoughts of the whole company of my former kind."

"It's good that you forsook the Realm Dwellers. You'd be gone with the rest of them," Doren said.

"I would. And though I am cursed, I am quite glad for it."

Thaylus emerged from the hold a little more refreshed. The men stood, looking out to sea in silence.

Then Thaylus saw something far beyond the waves.

"Look, do you see that?" Thaylus pointed. "There is something splashing in the water."

As they watched, they began to see what appeared to be three giant whips slashing and writhing about.

"The three-headed serpent has found us!" Doren yelled. "I'll ready the harpoon!"

The monster rushed for the boat.

Nithose gripped the boat, fear washing over him. The beast had scythe-like incisors and three horns on each head.

"It is getting closer!" he cried.

Finally, just yards away, the sea serpent stopped. It reared to what appeared to be its full height, swaying and writhing before them. It raised its heads above them like jade pillars, flaring its necks like a frog.

Doren aimed right below its head. "Take this, you big ugly beast!"

He pulled a lever, and the cannon jostled as the pronged harpoon flew. It stuck into the monster's bulged neck, spilling out hot water and blood.

The prongs expanded, snagging it fully.

The harpoon chain grew taut as Doren pulled a lever.

"It is bigger than anything we have encountered. This thing could swallow half the ship!" Thaylus cried.

One of the beast's three heads was violently yanked onto the edge of the bow. It was still as rotting meat. The other two heads were motionless.

"Please, let it be dead!" Brythan pleaded.

"I think it is. It's not struggling," Nithose said.

All four men took hold of the heavy harpoon and heaved. With a tremendous thrust, they managed to rip the harpoon out of the creature's head, dark blood spilling onto the deck.

"We have to push it off the bow!" Doren yelled. "It'll sink us!"

Grabbing a spear, Doren got to work prying it off the ship.

Nithose, Thaylus, and Brythan each took spears and began to do the same.

At first it did not budge even a little. But they pressed on, and it began to slide off. Inch by inch, it edged off the boat and finally toppled into the water.

But the salt water appeared to revive the creature. As they watched, its necks began to expand in the bizarrely frog-like motion.

"All of you, take cover!" yelled the spirit.

All four hid behind the mast as seething hot water shot in a straight stream toward them. Thaylus felt the heat, thankful the mast took the brunt of the spray.

The spirit hovered near the stern, floating there without a word.

The remaining monster heads plunged beneath the waves, blood bubbling and surfacing from its wounds.

"Are they dead?" Brythan asked.

"Maybe." Thaylus looked all around, waiting for anything to stir.

The wood of the boat creaked eerily in the silence.

Suddenly, an explosion of water broke through the surface. The two remaining heads reared up over the stern.

"No!" Nithose shouted.

Doren swung the harpoon around and pointed it up, almost vertical.

He fired a shot directly at the monster's right head.

The head smacked the water with a giant crash.

But as it did, the impaled head reeled backwards, causing the harpoon winch to rip off the boat, sending pieces of plank and metal clamps sputtering into the air.

"The harpoon—we've lost it!" Brythan cried.

"How do we kill the last head?" Doren shouted. "We've lost our only defense!"

But the agonized creature appeared to have been bested. Its sporadic movements slowed until, gradually, all three heads lowered lifelessly into the sea.

"Yes!" Doren cheered.

"That is all it took! We've won!" Nithose hugged him.

The onlookers shouted in victory.

But their cheering came too soon. For just as the final head was about to submerge, it spit a fiery line of water that hit Doren squarely in face.

Doren screamed in pain, clutching at his bloody and seared face. He tottered and then toppled into the water. In its dying act, the sea serpent snagged Doren in its jaws and dragged him beneath the water.

It was done.

"Doren!" Nithose wailed.

Thaylus and Brythan stood stock-still, horrified.

Nithose screamed in grief and fell to his knees.

"This is your fault, Thaylus!" Nithose cried out. "If you had not come, this would not have happened. I was wrong to trust you!"

Clenching his fists, the younger man staggered to his feet, as if he wanted to pummel the arch sage. Then he stopped, darted past them in the direction of the hold hatch and down below.

Thaylus wept. "I fear he is right. I am to blame."

Brythan went to his side. "None are to blame, my friend. Doren knew the risks. I believe he would have given his life for our cause if he had to choose. Imagine all the lives that will be spared when we retrieve the shield and seal the Realm Dwellers into the Abyss. Forever."

"Still, I wish we could have saved him." Thaylus wiped his face.

They stood and watched the now-calm sea, chunks of battered wood the only evidence of their battle.

"Thaylus, do you remember the prophecy of the Gate of Vessels?" Brythan asked.

"What of it?"

"We've both seen the red pillar of light. Do you believe it substantiates the Gate of Vessels?

Thaylus shrugged, dejected. "I just want to know who and what this Great Lord and His Emissary are. They are said to live inside the Gate of Vessels. Are they gods? Spiritual beings?"

"Thaylus, what if we do find a true deity along our quest? Ithia said everything will be revealed."

Thaylus looked at Brythan with a frown. "What exactly does 'everything' include? Surely even Ithia has her limits of knowledge"

With Brythan and the spirit at the helm, the sun was high in the sky by the time they made out a land mass far in the distance.

At the sight, Thaylus and Brythan laughed and jumped like children.

Nithose came out of the hold.

"I heard laughing," he said flatly.

"Look, there." Brythan pointed to the sliver of land in the distance.

All three watched the land draw closer. Thaylus's heart swelled the nearer they got.

"At last! The island where we will find the seal," Thaylus said. "The very sight of the trees brings a … a feeling of enchantment."

Nithose sighed. "If this proves successful, if this mission truly is meant to save the world, Doren's life will not have been lost in vain."

Brythan dropped anchor into waters that reflected the sky like a mirror.

The three stepped into a skiff to be lowered onto the water.

But the spirit did not board with them.

"Aren't you coming?" Brythan asked.

"No. Such a thing may harm me. I will wait here," answered the spirit.

"But—you're not what you once were," Thaylus said.

"Nevertheless."

"I am sorry for this," Thaylus said. "I feel great sadness for you. This might be the last time we speak to you."

"Do what you must. I will live on in this perpetual state. Perhaps we will see each other in the future."

Thaylus bowed and boarded the skiff with the other two.

They lowered themselves upon the surf and rowed to shore.

As Brythan had said, there was something mysterious and wonderful about the forest. Tiny brown birds sung and hopped from tree to tree while a single deer chewed on grass.

Even Nithose began to bask in the glorious scene all around them. The fresh scent of pine tantalized Thaylus's nose, and the moisture from the bark filled the air.

"I still feel an indescribable peace," Thaylus said.

"Indeed. Certain complacency fills the air," Brythan said.

Nithose watched a cheerful squirrel gnaw an acorn.

"I've never seen this kind of animal before. This place is wonderful. I could live in this forest."

"Everything here is quite tranquil. But how much longer must we go on aimlessly before we find the shield?" Brythan asked.

"We simply must have faith," Thaylus said. "It will guide us as it always has."

Brythan sighed deeply. "You're right. You seem to have a keener resolve when it comes to faith."

As they went on, a light came from deeper within the forest.

"What could that be?" Nithose asked.

"Ithia said the seal had a golden shine," Thaylus said.

The golden shine put them in what felt like a blissful trance as they got closer. They were still conscious, but they walked with no fear, no sense of hunger, not even sore muscles from their sea battle.

As they approached, they began to see the light was emanating from an inverted triangular-like core.

At last they came to an open grove. There, a golden, blazing shield hovered six feet above the ground.

"Amazing!" Nithose said with wide eyes.

"If this astounds you, you would faint at what we've seen," Thaylus said with a chuckle.

But as he approached the shield, a wall of green fire burst forth, surrounded it. Thaylus lurched back.

Brythan frowned. "It appears something intends to impede our possession of the shield."

Thaylus narrowed his eyes and stroked his beard in thought. "Why would Ithia not tell us about a barrier of fire?"

"She must have known. There has to be a way to reach the shield," Brythan said.

They surveyed the flames in silence. Nithose took a seat, mesmerized.

Finally, Brythan spoke. "When we encountered problems before, we relied on faith."

Thaylus's eyes widened. "You're right! And the answer may be right in front of us."

"What do you mean?"

"Think—in what way would faith aid us in this situation?"

Brythan looked down in thought. "Perhaps ... we command the flames to go away?"

"I don't think so. I have sense that Ithia wants us to do something that requires greater faith—one that would truly test us."

"What course of action do you propose she wants?"

"She may want our very lives to be tested."

Brythan's face grew pale. "You can't possibly mean for us to pass through the fire?"

"That is precisely what I mean."

Brythan turned to Thaylus. "What if you're wrong? What if the flames devour you the moment you set foot in it?"

"Reach down and gather all the faith you can. Trust me!"

Brythan closed his eyes. "I feel something. It is small, but it is there."

Without a further word, Thaylus neared the green flames. The heat was almost unbearable.

He clenched his fists and took a deep breath.

Then, with gritted teeth, Thaylus barged forward and disappeared into the fire.

# Chapter 13

## A Special Visit

Brythan and Nithose were like petrified statues as they listened for any word or sound from Thaylus. But nothing except the loud crackling of the green flames filled the moonlit grove.

They waited.

"I hear no sound of screaming or struggle," Brythan said. "Perhaps he has done it!"

"Will he come out? Are you supposed to follow him?" asked Nithose.

"I ... do not know." Brythan paused.

The fire roared as a shining object poked out of the flames. As it emerged, Thaylus's body appeared behind it.

Thaylus's face gleamed with the golden illumination of the shield.

Brythan and Nithose backed away.

"It's me." Thaylus frowned. "Why are you so scared?"

"Your face, it shines!" Brythan exclaimed. "Your countenance is like Ithia's. How do you feel?"

"It's hard to describe it. I feel—powerful, like fire is coursing through me. Yet my heart and mind are calm and relaxed."

"Now I know you are without a doubt from the future! I've never seen such a thing!" Nithose said.

Thaylus knelt to place the golden shield on the ground, but as he released it, the shield vanished and the illumination of Thaylus's face faded.

"It's gone! How do I get it back?"

"Perhaps it is just like opening time portals," Brythan offered. "Just imagine the shield."

Thaylus closed his eyes and stretched forth his arm.

The shield appeared in his hand.

"Very astute, Brythan!"

Brythan tilted his head. "Hmm…your face has stopped glowing."

"I see. It must be a transient effect like the rushing wind feeling when Ithia gave us the gift of faith. I assume this shield is spiritual like she is."

"That makes sense." Brythan shifted his attention to the present situation. "Now that we have the shield, we must return to our time so we can keep the Realm Dwellers in the Abyss," Brythan said.

He turned to Nithose.

"With the spirit's help, I think you should be able to navigate back to Tarken Town."

But Nithose looked filled with sorrow.

"Why are you so sad?" asked Thaylus.

The young man wiped a tear off his face.

"I have no living kin left in Tarken Town. My father and mother died a few years ago. Doren was their best friend. To me, he was my only family."

Thaylus and Brythan were silent a few moments.

"Could we simply go back in time and save Doren?" Brythan asked.

Just then, a burst of blinding light appeared in the air above them. As the light dimmed, they began to recognize a familiar form.

Ithia.

Frightened, Nithose poised to run.

But Ithia called to him. "Do not fear, young one. There is no need to flee."

Nithose froze. "Who are you?"

Brythan placed a hand on his shoulder. "She is our friend and guide."

"Why are you here, Ithia?" Thaylus asked.

"I have been told by the One within the Gate of Vessels to bring you courage for your next task. I have also come for Nithose … to bring him to his brother."

"My brother?" Nithose's face went from somber to hopeful. "You know where he is? My parents searched everywhere for him. Where is he? What happened to him?"

"It was a slave trader who stole him, but he escaped when he was sixteen and has been living in a village north of here. Returning you to him is partly why I am here. Come, and stand before me."

The young man was wide eyed as he approached.

Ithia descended and touched his shoulder.

"By the authority given to me by the Great One, I now return you to your brother."

A golden cloud spun like a whirlwind starting from his feet, to his waist, and eventually to his head, obscuring his body.

The cloud shot up and flitted in a northerly direction. They could see it far off, drifting over the trees.

Nithose was gone.

Ithia smiled warmly at Thaylus and Brythan.

"You both have made good use of the faith I gave you against mighty foes. Now you must return to your time to seal the Realm Dwellers in the Abyss before they are freed."

But Thaylus hesitated, his face darkening.

"Ithia, wait. We need some explanation—what does the Pyrithian prophecy mean? When will we see this Lord and His Emissary? All these cryptic quests and notions about the Gate of Vessels… we need some proof! I have seen the holy Gate of Vessels, but there is no proof of a spiritual God who is truly omnipotent."

Ithia shook her head sadly. "The time will come when your mind will understand all you desire, including the Lord and His Emissary, who are in essence one entity."

Brythan stepped forward. "You said we would find a guide, and it ended up being a ghost of sorts, who was once a Realm Dweller. He helped us a great deal. Is there any way to free him?"

"Only the Lord within the Gate of Vessels can condemn or liberate a being. But I will bring your petition to my master."

Ithia drifted toward Thaylus and gently placed her hands on his temples. She looked deeply into his eyes.

"Soon, righteous one, very soon."

Thaylus nodded. For now, he would trust and wait. But his impatience was growing, as was his anger.

Ithia continued, "Before you go, He within the Gate has a gift to bestow upon Brythan."

Brythan blinked in surprise. "Me? What is it?"

"For you to see your father."

Brythan's jaw gaped. "My … father? You'll let me see him?"

"Yes, but you must not reveal your identity."

Ithia turned to Thaylus. "Picture a time in Knaddues's life before the war with King Vyprus. In this way, Brythan may meet his father."

Thaylus closed his eyes as he recalled the image of the lush green land, untainted by war.

He spoke the words, and a spiraling portal appeared.

When Thaylus and Brythan walked through, they found themselves in the highest tower in Solace in the darkness of early morning.

Thaylus felt dizzy and weak for a few moments and stumbled after stepping though.

"The damage from time traveling never lessens," he said.

Brythan was bent over, rubbing his temples. "I know. I feel eventually we will be so afflicted by the wearing, we will not be able to traverse time."

After a few moments, Brythan shook his head. "So where is he?"

"Your father will be getting up soon. Knaddues patrols the main perimeters of the kingdom in the morning after he breaks fast in the knight's banquet quarters. That is where you will be, disguised as a guard so you may meet him. Speak for however long it will take for him to finish his meal his food, and then disembark."

"What shall we speak of? I would not know what to say."

Thaylus put a hand on Brythan's shoulder. "Then don't speak. Ask him things pertaining to his life as a warrior or…"

Thaylus pursed his lips, considering. He stepped close to Brythan. "Would you ask your father something for me?"

"Of course. What do you wish to know?"

"Do you recall me telling you in the forest that your father never openly denied or accepted the existence of the gods?"

"I do."

"When you speak with him, will you ask if he believes in the gods? You would be doing something most important to me."

"Very well."

They descended a spiraling staircase. When they reached the bottom, they entered the main hall with its high vaulted ceiling.

"Are the banquet quarters still in the west wing of the castle?" Brythan asked.

"They are."

"I shall proceed there now."

"You are not disguised yet. Wait, I'll bring you a guard's outfit."

When Thaylus reappeared, he carried a folded tunic, chain mail, helmet, and a glistening spear.

Brythan dressed in the guard's attire, uncharacteristically quiet.

Then he walked through the hall toward the west wing and came to the double oak doors of the eating hall.

There he waited for what felt like an hour. At last he saw a figure come his way with a torch.

Instantly, he realized he didn't really know his father's face. He'd been so young when his father had been killed. Was this him? Would he recognize his own father?

Brythan recalled the general from his own time. That man always wore distinguished apparel, specifically a notable golden brooch with the seal of Solace clasped to a scarlet cloak.

Brythan stood at attention, as though he were guarding the door to the banquet hall. From the corner of his eye, he inspected every soldier who passed near him.

The first soldier stopped in front of Brythan and nodded to him before he entered. No golden brooch. Three minutes later, two more soldiers entered side by side, laughing and speaking loudly, then more.

Finally, Brythan saw a muscular man with slicked-back blond hair and blue eyes in a red cape come down the hall. Brythan got a tightness in his stomach. The man wore a golden brooch— the same one Brythan knew to be a general's trademark.

Brythan stood speechless, mouth slightly ajar, as his father approached. What would he say? Would he have any words at all?

He did not realize his expression until his father, General Knaddues, stopped right in front of him, examining his son with concern.

"Are you all right, guard?" Knaddues tilted his head. "Who sent you to guard the banquet hall?"

Brythan shook his head and quickly bowed, fighting the urge to embrace the man who stood before him.

"Forgive me. I have completed my guard duties for the next hour and I…" Brythan felt like crying. He rubbed his eyes. "I'm sorry, I'm just very tired."

"You should be resting then. Why are you here?"

Brythan flushed. "I, ah, know the general eats here, and I wanted to see what it was like to be around him. I hold him in the highest esteem. Is he indeed you? You are General Knaddues?"

"Indeed." Knaddues inclined his head.

"W—would you allow me to join you inside?"

Knaddues chuckled warmly. "Very well."

An involuntary grin spread over Brythan's face as Knaddues guided his son into the chamber.

He took his seat at the head of a table and gestured for Brythan to sit next to him.

"What is your name, young guard?"

"My name is … Doren." Brythan blurted the first name that popped into his head.

"So, what would you like me to share with you?"

Brythan didn't know what to ask.

"Ah, when did you fight your first battle?" It was a general question, not a more personal one he would have wished to ask, but it would have to do.

Knaddues began to speak, describing a war with the kingdom of Rune and its destruction when he was a soldier right out of training. He explained the fear and violence, how it took everything within him to muster up the valor to oppose the enemy.

Brythan listened raptly, asking questions here and there. He did not absorb a word his father was saying, only his mood and demeanor.

Knaddues was an animated speaker, serious at times then laughing at others. His laughter was infectious, and Brythan smiled, wishing this moment would go on and on.

But before he knew it, the meal was over.

Knaddues wiped his face, then stood.

"Thank you, Doren. I have enjoyed this time to reminisce about the old days."

They walked toward the doorway.

"Doren, who are your parents?" Knaddues asked at the exit. "Do they live?"

"I have always been an orphan, sir."

"There is something oddly peculiar about you."

Brythan's chest thrummed. "What do you mean, General Knaddues?"

"You seem … like someone I've met in my past, someone I feel a strange kinship with. Perhaps we could do this again."

"Certainly." Brythan smiled, though inside his heart fell.

There would never be another time. It was a one-way ordeal.

He watched his father's back as he walked off and out of Brythan's life forever.

As Brythan walked in the direction of where he had last seen Thaylus, at the foot of the tower staircase, he wept. But at the same time, he clung to joy—this was a memory he knew he would always cherish.

He wiped his tears. Then he realized what he forgot to do.

"Oh, Thaylus. I forgot to ask about his beliefs concerning the gods."

The arch sage shrugged. "It is all right. My curiosity will have to wait." He straightened and spoke in a louder voice. "Are you ready to leave?"

"I'm ready. Let us depart."

"Very well. I think we should return to when the red pillar of light first appeared. Then we can travel to the Western Kingdom and vanquish the light, keeping the Realm Dwellers in before they are even released."

Brythan considered this. "What exact spot will we appear at when step through the time portal?"

"That is a good question. I surmise we will arrive where we last were when I first saw the red light."

"Where was that?"

"I was in a tower with King Trophimus," Thaylus said.

Brythan's eyes widened. "Won't that frighten him?"

"I am certain it will. But we have no choice. And perhaps it will substantiate what we are to do."

They prepared themselves, then grasped arms.

"*Tempus itinerantur*," Thaylus said. "See you on the other side."

# Chapter 14

## The Return to The Present

In a flash of light, Thaylus was on the tower next to King Trophimus.

The king reeled back. "What magic is this? You look like my sage. Who are you?"

"It is I, your Arch Sage, my Lord!" Thaylus said. "Do not fear!"

"Thaylus, what happened? One moment you were next to me, then you vanished. Now in a flash of light you've reappeared. But you're in different clothes!"

Suddenly the terrible beam of red light shot up from the Western Kingdom. It reached to the clouds, causing them to flicker with red lighting.

Trophimus shuddered with wide eyes. "Thaylus, what is that light? It fills me with a vile dread!"

"My Lord, please listen. I know what the light is. I will explain everything. But I must depart immediately to go there. Also, I request the nobleman Brythan to accompany me. We have something that will keep the Realm Dwellers in the Abyss, but we must leave now."

"The Realm Dwellers? Where did you obtain this magic, Thaylus?"

"Your Majesty, I assure you—my appearance in that flash of light you saw was not sorcerer's work. I promise you I will divulge everything. But first I must go the Western Kingdom. Please, trust me."

"But what—"

"Please, my Lord. I must go."

King Trophimus breathed heavily. "Do what you must."

Thaylus sprinted down the tower stairs.

At the base of the steps, a small group of noblemen stood pale and wide eyed just like before. This time, everyone was gathered around Brythan.

"Arch Sage Thaylus, something unbelievable just happened!" A trembling man in a rich azure robe was pointing at Brythan. "Brythan was with us, then in a flash of light he appeared in entirely different attire! Is he a—a sorcerer?"

"Don't panic!" Brythan interjected. "I am still the Brythan you know. I have simply gone through a supernatural experience. And I am no sorcerer."

"It is true, my good sirs," Thaylus said. "Please accept his words and go about your business. Brythan, you must come with me."

Everyone in the small crowd glanced at each other before most nodded and stepped aside for them to pass.

But one man in a white robe with a white beard came forward.

"What of the pillar of light? Is it the Realm Dwellers! By the gods, Arch Sage, what is happening!"

The man's words made people murmur and bicker anew.

"Silence!" Thaylus shouted. "Do not concern yourself. I am going to the Western Kingdom this moment to investigate with permission of our king. Do not panic or make rash conclusions."

"Forgive us, Arch Sage," the white-bearded man said. "May the gods be with you."

Thaylus and Brythan rushed through the hall and outside to the stable. They acquired two horses highly praised by the stable hand and sped off to their destination.

As they neared the Western Kingdom, the three Realm Messengers in their black, shadowy cloaks were hovering at the two men just as before.

"I have an idea," Thaylus said.

He visualized the shield and held out his hand, and it appeared.

The Realm Messengers backed away, then retreated to the keep of the Western Kingdom.

"It repels them!" Brythan shouted with a grin.

"Indeed! And look!" Thaylus pointed at the pillar of red light. "The light, it weakens in intensity!"

Brythan gave a triumphant laugh and flicked his reigns. His horse galloped faster.

"Come, Thaylus, you can ride faster than that!"

Thaylus returned the smile and rode to catch up with his young companion as they rode for the Western Kingdom gates.

At the gate, the guards seemed transfixed by the shining shield. Then they began to close the gates.

"We must ride faster!" Brythan shouted. "It will be a narrow fit if we make it. Get behind me."

Thaylus fell in line behind Brythan.

The gates were shutting. They pushed their horses to their limits.

As the gate was about to close, Brythan took out a bronze dagger and hurled it at a guard in his chest, diverting the attention of the other guards trying to close the gate.

Thaylus and Brythan zoomed past the gates, past scores of people all running from the Arch Sage's shining shield.

But at the dead guard, Thaylus stopped, and the shield vanished.

Thaylus's face contorted.

"There was no other way, Thaylus. I'm sorry."

Thaylus sighed. "He opposes us as the enemy. Still, I wish it could have been gone differently. All life is precious."

"I took no pleasure in his death. Summon the shield. We have a job to do."

Thaylus nodded.

He extended his arm, and the shield reappeared. Its golden luster filled the hall. Even the soldiers fled the burning light.

In the center of the main hall, almost everyone vacated the immense space.

Thaylus released his grip on the shield, and it vanished.

Turning, Thaylus saw a familiar face. It was Captain Grale, the spy who'd helped him and Brythan escape.

At the disappearance of the shining shield, Grale unsheathed his sword and glared at Thaylus.

"I will not relent even in the threat of a sorcerer!"

Grale rushed at him, sword pointed.

"Halt, Captain Grale. We know you!" Thaylus yelled. "We mean no harm."

The captain stopped, his sword still brandished.

"Who … who are you? And what was that a magical object you wielded?"

They dismounted, and Thaylus put his hands in the air as he approached Captain Grale.

"I know you lead a sect of secret defectors intending to overthrow the evil Kyrious."

Captain Grale shook his head . "I demand to know your identities and what your intentions entail."

Thaylus sighed. "We are of Solace. The bright shield you just witnessed is an object we intend to use to keep the Realm Dwellers from being released from the Abyss."

"I thought only the gods could do such a thing!" Hope lit the captain's face. "Ones with such an object must have power to do so. Follow me!"

Thaylus and Brythan followed Grale and soon came to a door. The seal of the Western Kingdom was engraved upon it.

They entered and walked through a long corridor. At the end was a set of steps that led to a large platform. The whole surface was aglow with the illumination of the red light.

Thaylus extended his arm, and the shield appeared in his hand. It shone brighter than ever.

The red beam of light kept dimming.

"It's working!" Brythan shouted.

But as victory seemed nigh, Thaylus felt something huge and burning hot strike him from behind.

He fell forward, and the shield disappeared.

Brythan and Captain Grale turned to see King Kyrious chuckle maniacally, his outstretched palm smoking that had to have dispersed some magical fire attack.

"It seems as though I underestimated your power, Thaylus. I had no idea you've concealed such magic from so many people. Where did you get your power? It even thwarts the evil light of the Realm Dwellers."

Kyrious stepped closer, his walk a swagger.

"However," he continued, "it looks like harnessing that powerful magical object of yours takes will and concentration. And I have disabled you from doing so."

Thaylus grunted from where he lay.

Kyrious tilted his head at Brythan. "There is something familiar about you, young man."

Brythan rushed to where his friend had fallen. He was still on his face, and he had a large scorch mark on his right shoulder.

"Thaylus, speak," Brythan pleaded. "Are you all right?"

"As for you." Kyrious turned to Captain Grale. "I am disappointed at your treachery. You did a foolish thing. Now you will share the demise of this Solace filth."

With a wave of Kyrious's hand, Grale was encased in a pillar of ice.

Brythan helped Thaylus to his feet. His eyes were unfocused and his head was limp.

"Summon the seal, Thaylus!" Brythan urged.

"I cannot. I am too weak. You must do it."

"What?"

Thaylus put a hand on Brythan's forehead.

Brythan's eyes snapped shut.

Thaylus raised his arms and felt energy flow from his own body into his friend's.

The nobleman's eyes glistened. "I understand," he murmured.

Kyrious howled in rage and lifted his arm.

But as he did, Brythan extended his own arm.

The shield appeared in his hand just as a bolt of lightning from Kyrious's palm struck the shield, pushing Brythan back.

Kyrious gaped, his face a twisted mask as the shield's bright gleam caused him to grab his head and stagger backwards.

"Whatever power you have, you cannot overcome me!" Kyrious roared.

Then, in a plume of smoke, Kyrious vanished.

Brythan turned to Thaylus as the shield disappeared once more. "Can you walk?"

"I'm in considerable pain."

Thaylus tried to stand but could barely get to his knees.

"Did we destroy him?

"I'm not sure," Brythan said.

The pillar of red light was beginning to revive. Moments passed with no sign of Kyrious.

Thaylus throbbing heart slowed as calmness overcame him once more.

"But what of Grale?" Brythan motioned to the solid block of ice, the captain trapped within. "Is there any way to help him?"

Thaylus felt a tinge of strength return as he struggled to his feet with Brythan's help.

"I can think of nothing. Perhaps when the beam of light fades, something may happen."

"You're right," Brythan said. "The light held a link with Kyrious's power. Let us finish our task and see. But I must understand. How did you even know how to pass the power of the seal to me?"

"I don't know. It just came to me, like how Ithia's faith comes over us at certain situations."

Brythan scratched his chin. "Strange. Things like this never cease to amaze me. Now, let's do away with this evil concoction.

Once more, Brythan summoned the shield in his hand, facing the beam of light.

The beam of light flickered and became transparent at random points.

"It's working!" Thaylus's heart surged with hope.

But they didn't expect what happened next. One moment Brythan held the shield, afire with blazing and brilliant light.

The next the shield had dissolved, and Brythan had tumbled forward onto his chest. With a knife in his back.

"Pity, pity," came a sneering voice.

Thaylus whirled.

Kyrious.

"I can stay invisible for as long as I want without any sound," Kyrious said. "If only you had chosen my side, you would have been my right-hand commander and chief lord.".

"I would rather perish!"

Thaylus fell to his knees beside Brythan. "Brythan! I'm here. I've got you."

But Brythan's skin had turned a dull color, and his eyes were rolling back, as if into his skull.

"Thaylus...I..."

"Brythan, you're strong! You can't go. I need you!"

But the wound pierced almost straight to his chest. His death was imminent. Thaylus realized Brythan's fate.

Tears welled in Thaylus's eyes. Clenching his fists, he turned to Kyrious once more.

"You monster! You'll get what's coming to you!"

But Brythan could barely draw his final breath, much less return the power of the shield.

Thaylus had one option—escape to another time.

The Arch Sage gathered all his strength and will to summon another time portal. Sweat ran down his temples.

"*Tempus itinerantur*," he breathed.

The spiraling vortex of light appeared.

"What magic is this?" Kyrious raged. "You won't escape me!"

Kyrious's words echoed as Thaylus went through the portal.

He looked behind him, only to see the form of the wicked sorcerer fade out of view as he passed through a tunnel of azure light. The portal closed as he fell upon a grassy surface, struck by grief, on his knees not looking up to see where he was.

Never, since he realized the doomed world at the threat of the Realm Dwellers, had Thaylus felt such grief.

Then he suddenly turned bitter.

Raising a fist at the sky, Thaylus shouted, "Whatever deity you be, I curse you for doing this! You don't deserve my allegiance wherever you are!"

A thought occurred even as he spoke these words. If there was a possibility of no true god, then why did he say what he said?

But his anger burned hot. He refused to acknowledge the existence of such a being.

"That is it, then," Thaylus growled. "There is no higher power or omniscient being. How could there be? Ithia lies!"

Thaylus wiped his tears.

He would hide in the past, he resolved. There was nothing more he could do—someone else could save the world, if it was even worth saving.

# Chapter 15

## Lost

THAYLUS FOUND HIMSELF on a grassy hill. The weather was mild, and a gentle midday sun cast beams of light all around.

He lay there a long while, letting his anger and despair surround him until finally a restlessness forced him to his feet.

From the top of the grassy hill, he surveyed the landscape. He saw it overlooked a large town. What looked like a great number of stone cut buildings in vertical rows, next to small, open huts with wooden beams holding up wicker roofs housing horses, pigs, and cows. A knot formed in his stomach. He had no idea of their ways or even what language they spoke.

Nevertheless, he made for the town. It was his only choice.

He trekked forward.

Soon he came to a wooden gate with what he recognized to be Pyrithian writing on a wooden post. He surmised it was the name of the town.

Inside was a bustle. People bartered at kiosks and tents. Children played and ran in and out of the tents among adults carrying wares of wheat grain, beans, and other produce. As he listened to the commotion, he was curious at the language. It seemed the people were speaking in the ancient tongue of the Pyrithians. But he could barely read it, let alone speak it.

A tall man with red hair approached him and raised his hand in greeting. He spoke something in the Pyrithian language that Thaylus assumed was a customary greeting.

Thaylus mimicked the motion, then patted his chest, indicating himself.

"Thaylus," he said.

The stranger returned the motion. "Kiroff."

Thaylus cleared his throat and tried his best to say "I am a traveler" from the few Pyrithian texts he'd read. He worried if Kiroff understood.

Kiroff just smiled and beckoned for Thaylus to follow.

All buildings were decked with ornately designed edifices.

Kiroff led the sage into an inn. There, the kind man pulled out some coins and placed it on a wooden counter for the innkeeper. The innkeeper smiled and gave Kiroff a key.

Kiroff led Thaylus to a room with a bed and a stand with a large candle. Then the man put his hands together and pressed them both to a temple.

"You want me to sleep?" Thaylus returned the motion.

"Sleep." The host repeated Thaylus's word.

Then Kiroff made a slight bow and left the room, shutting the door.

I might as well. I am tired, Thaylus said to himself.

He lay on the bed wondering what the next day would bring until sleep finally took him.

Morning came early, and Thaylus woke to a knock on the door.

It swung open it to reveal Kiroff, beckoning, again with that kind smile.

The sage got out of bed and followed Kiroff to a table downstairs with sumptuous breakfast foods: sausage, eggs, bacon, grapefruit, cake, and a few other foods. He could smell the smoky, rich aroma of the sausage and the freshly baked bread.

Thaylus sat down and found he was quite hungry. He plunged into the food before him. The cake was sweet and fluffy, and the sausage tender with the scent of fresh spicy sauce.

When he had eaten his fill, once again Kiroff beckoned Thaylus to follow.

He was led outside and across the way, into a large building with about fifty children siting on the ground with opened books. The children faced a single old man who sat on a chair. Next to the old man was a long, wide parchment that hung almost to the floor.

Kiroff pulled a book from a shelf. He pointed to Thaylus and then at the book.

Ah, you want me to learn what is in the book, Thaylus thought.

Looking around, he realized he was in a school for young children learning the basics of the language.

Kiroff approached the man on the chair and conversed.

Then he returned to the sage, giving Thaylus the book.

Thaylus sat among the children.

The first thing he learned was the name of objects and shapes. The teacher pointed to a picture of a house depicted on the parchment and spoke a word. Thaylus repeated it in unison with the children. He felt quite silly at first, but eventually it became a joy.

They gave all the children food at lunch, and he took a meal with them.

That evening, he made his way back to the inn. The innkeeper bowed slightly and motioned for Thaylus to return to his room.

The next day Thaylus did not wait for Kiroff to escort him to the school but made his way there on his own.

Thaylus sat on the ground with the children. On the large parchment were five objects: a house, a tree, a river, a donkey, and a castle.

The teacher pointed to each thing individually, speaking its name. The parchment was rolled around a metal rod attached to the wall. The teacher pulled down on it as the day progressed, showing more objects.

The next few months passed in this fashion. Soon Thaylus could name more than two hundred objects.

During these first months, he continued to sleep and eat at the inn with no cost to himself at the kindness of the owner. Eventually Thaylus took it upon himself to be a serving hand for the innkeeper, Theophilus. At first it was hard for Theophilus to understand Thaylus's desire to be a server, but after a few crude gestures and words, Theophilus comprehended the offer.

At school they began to learn small phrases and sentences. Soon Thaylus came to understand things like "please," "thank you," "goodbye," and "do not." He learned the name of the town was Bailise.

Soon the learned sage gathered enough skill to compose his first complex conversation, which he directed at Kiroff.

"Thank you for welcoming me to Bailise. And for showing around and introducing me."

Kiroff nodded. "I was just showing common courtesy, my friend. If there is anything else I can help you with, just ask."

"There is. I was curious how old this town is and what gods you worship?"

"I'm not sure how old Bailise is. We only worship one God."

"Does this God live inside something called the Gate of Vessels?"

"Yes! You know Him?"

Thaylus shook his head. "In a way. But I do not worship him. Who is he?"

"If you seek clarification, you could ask priest Ferin," Kiroff said.

"Where do I find him?"

"Follow the main road until you see a cobblestone path to your left. It will lead you to a meadow where a small cathedral is. He is always there."

"I thank you, friend."

Thaylus followed Kiroff's directions and came to the small cathedral. It had two small spires coming from the edifice. The quaint but articulate structure reminded him of the temples of one of the lower gods from his own time.

Inside, a man in a brown wool mantle kneeled with his back to Thaylus. He looked to be in some sort of a vigil or trance.

The priest roused from his vigil when Thaylus touched his shoulder.

"How may I serve you, sir?" the priest asked.

"Are you Ferin?"

"I am." Ferin gazed at him closely. "You are the stranger who arrived some months ago. I was wondering when you would come here."

"Forgive me for being blunt, but I do not believe in your God."

"Ah, I see. May I ask why?"

"I do not understand such a god. How could one so powerful allow such suffering? What god would allow his name to be forgotten and replaced by false gods and stand by while Realm Dwellers inevitably destroy the world?"

"I am curious. What do you mean by false gods, and what are Realm Dwellers?"

Thaylus sighed deeply, knowing this priest was clueless of his situation. He was venting more than actually expecting an answer to his questions.

But he decided to be honest with the priest.

"I must share everything with you, but it will likely shock you. I ask you to prepare yourself."

Ferin nodded. A few moments of silence passed as the priest waited.

Thaylus finally spoke. "I come from the future. I must be over four-thousand years in the past from my time because the Realm Dwellers enter Khrine exactly four-thousand years from my era. And you may be interested to know in my time, our planet of Khrine has no knowledge of your God, and it worships false gods—many false gods."

The priest just listened.

"And these Realm Dwellers I mentioned," Thaylus added. "They are evil spiritual beings that will decimate the world in my time. I fled here from them."

# Chapter 16

## Origins of The Realm Dwellers

Priest Ferin put a gentle hand on Thaylus shoulder and smiled. "I believe you."

Thaylus shook his head. "Why do you believe me so easily?"

"Your body resonates with the power of He within the Gate of Vessels."

Thaylus felt like his very heart was being exposed. Indeed, there was something uncanny about this individual. Did this priest sense Ithia's essence like Elim the time traveler did?

But the man who stood before him seemed to have no special powers or supernatural experience.

"How did you sense this? Have you ever met a Vessel Bearer?"

Ferin continued to smile. "No. Recognizing the spirit of a man is a gift of the Great God. It does not have to come through a Vessel Bearer."

"How did you receive this ability?"

Ferin patted Thaylus on the back. "Everyone who believes in the Great God has direct communion with Him."

"Do you imply you … you speak to this god of the Gate of Vessels?"

"Yes, but usually He speaks to us in our souls and hearts, not through words. It is like how your conscience speaks to you."

"Your god never speaks to me."

Ferin sighed. "That is because you do not believe in Him. My hope is that someday you will come to understand."

"It would take a miracle. But if your god is as powerful as you make him to be,

I suppose he will give me one. My thanks for your time."

Thaylus turned and left the cathedral.

He walked the main path with his head down.

As he walked, he noticed vines crawling up a wooden fence enclosing a garden of yellow and purple flowers. The garden stood in front of a small ash-colored stone house with a timber door braced with metal latches.

Thaylus approached the fence and picked a purple flower, smelling it. The scent relaxed his mind and brought a satisfying but temporary pleasure, for his mind soon returned to his bitterness and despair. Brythan's death. This supposed "true god." Everything.

He tossed the flower on the ground and trudged over the flower.

When he found the inn, he walked through the rowdy guests, all drinking ale and laughing heartily. He walked up the steps to the upper rooms and collapsed on his bed. All the things he'd discussed wearied him, and he quickly fell asleep.

The next morning was cloudy. Thaylus descended the stairs at the inn, rays of red-orange casting speckles as he walked.

The inn was empty, and Thaylus realized he'd slept past breakfast. Only a few items were still out, left for others who had not been early risers.

In the corner of the room, Thaylus spotted a man in a priest's mantle sitting alone at a table. Thaylus recognized his attire.

The man beckoned to Thaylus.

"To what do I owe the pleasure, sir priest?" Thaylus asked.

"It seems the pleasure is mine," said the priest. "Sit with me. My name is Mordecai, the head priest of this region."

Thaylus sat next to him. "What do you wish of me, head priest?"

"I spoke with Ferin yesterday. He mentioned something most profound about you."

Thaylus froze.

"Do not worry," Mordecai said. "I can be confided in. And don't blame Ferin. He knew it would be good for you if he told me."

Thaylus relaxed some but was still leery of what this would entail.

"I see. And why have you come to me?"

"I have the knowledge of when the Realm Dwellers will come to Khrine," Mordecai said.

The sage's mouth dropped. "You know of them? But how?"

"Four years ago, I received a vision from a Vessel Bearer calling himself Cortan."

"You've seen a Vessel Bearer! Besides myself, I know of only three others who have seen one. One was called Elim. The other was Brythan, who used to be my companion. And the last was a woman, a spirit named Clara."

"What is the name of the Vessel Bearer you encountered?"

"Ithia," Thaylus said with a level tone. "Describe your vision to me."

Mordecai gave a slow nod. "Cortan showed me something amazing. He touched my forehead, and instantly I witnessed the appearance of the Realm Dwellers, as well as their arrival, in a vision."

Mordecai tilted his head. "I am an artist, and I illustrated everything I witnessed. Let me show you. My home is close."

Thaylus followed Mordecai outside and walked to a small round stone building.

"Sit," Mordecai said. "I will bring my book to you."

The high priest brought a large, thick book and opened it on the table before them.

"In the vision, I saw many days pass in a few fleeting moments. I was told by Cortan I had traveled seventy years in the future. This is what I saw."

Mordecai's skill proved exceptional. On the first page, a large green star, like a lighthouse in a sea of darkness, shone in a cloudless sky. The star outshined all stars.

The priest pointed to the next page.

"Once again, in two blinks of an eye, I was brought seven years further in the future, and the star fell to Khrine with a trail of fiery thunderbolts as it plummeted. But what appeared to be a star happened to be an immense spherical emerald."

The portrayal was so intricate and gifted it was as though Thaylus saw the celestial occurrence himself.

Mordecai turned the page. He cleared his throat and hunched his shoulders.

There, an immense crater with burning green ridges showed on the page. In the center was the spherical glowing emerald-colored object. Cracks covered the emerald.

"What I saw within the crater was the most glorious thing I have ever witnessed. I was brought down the side of the crater, and I approached the object."

"A magnificent being, like a Celestial Servant with a golden sash, shone from within the emerald. Also, in the emerald sphere were seven smaller beings that looked like Cortan. I imagined they also were Vessel Bearers."

The Mordecai pointed to the next page. The being with the golden sash was frozen, but its open eyes burned with a white flame.

"The being with the golden sash had a presence many times greater than a Vessel Bearer. Things became even more fantastic. As I stared at the beings inside, the glowing object moved, and it cracked more."

On the next page, the vast sphere illustrated glinting cracks of light, like rods of lightning. The next picture showed the beings within the emerald breaking free as vivid green shards flitted everywhere.

"After the beings broke free of the emerald, they rose into the sky claiming to be gods."

Mordecai turned the page. There, the eight beings stood with their arms raised, their faces twisted with pride. Balls of fire like giant pieces of burning coal lay in their hands.

"They exercised miraculous power, calling fire from the sky to devour those who did not follow them as gods—even apparently raising people from the dead. I couldn't believe my eyes. They had power to transform into whatever physical form they wanted.

"Then I was told they were to be worshiped for seven years. At that time the True God took these eight shining beings, these false gods, and cast them into a spiritual prison. Cortan told me it was called the Abyss. This next page shows near the end of my portrayal—the doorway to the Abyss."

The next illustration showed a pit on the top of a tall mountain like the mouth of a volcano. Thick, bellowing smoke from it obscured the sky.

An immense tornado from within it caught the eight beings. Their expressions were no longer benevolent or beautiful. Some raged with clenched teeth, and others looked to be screaming.

Mordecai closed the book.

Thaylus's face contorted. "It sounds like you speak of the Realm Dwellers, but that's not how they appear. They look like dark—"

"—yes, like dark shadow-like beings with burning red eyes with swords of black fire."

"Precisely!"

Mordecai folded his hands to his chin.

"Thaylus, the true God took these doomed beings to be eternally cursed, to remain in a dark, ominous form in the Abyss. Hence, the first Realm Dwellers came into being. There within the Abyss, they possessed the knowledge to spawn spiritual entities like themselves."

Thaylus leaned in. "These beings had power to create life?"

Mordecai rubbed his temples and was silent a moment. "No. Only the Great Lord within the Gate can create life. These eight abominations, they made entities without souls of their own. These are Realm Dwellers as well. In the future there will be hundreds of them."

"You did not illustrate this in your book."

"This I did not see. Cortan simply told me of the soulless nature of the Realm Dwellers, and that they would be released in the future."

Thaylus frowned. "That is strange. So Cortan did not say when they were later released, or that they were resealed in the Abyss by a holy object wielded by a wise man?"

Mordecai looked surprised. "I do not know what you speak of. What do you mean?"

"The Vessel Bearer Ithia also showed me a vision. In my vision, she brought me to a time, a little after these eight spiritual beings were first cast into the Abyss. It was the first time they came from the Abyss in their dark forms. Ithia brought me to the future, when a holy object in the form of a shining golden shield banished them into the Abyss once more."

"A seal? I am curious."

"Stand back," Thaylus said.

Thaylus closed his eyes. "*Tempus itinerantur!*" A blue, spiraling time portal appeared.

Mordecai stumbled back.

"What ... what power is this?"

"It is the power of the Vessel Bearers," Thaylus said.

Mordecai stood speechless.

Thaylus did not know how to close the portal. But about twenty seconds later portal vanished on its own.

"Why were you chosen for such a task when you do not believe in God?" Mordecai asked.

"I do not know. Perhaps it is because I do not worship the idols that exist in my time like all others. My mind is not so narrow minded as theirs."

Thaylus blinked. Suddenly, he felt like crying.

"Forgive me." He sniffed, took a deep breath and sat straight. "I mentally witnessed something disturbingly otherworldly as a teenager concerning the Realm Dwellers."

"What happened to you?" asked Mordecai.

"I had a vivid, lifelike dream—really, a prophetic dream—about the world being destroyed by them. My dream was brief, but I saw the destruction of the planet at their hands. I've never been able to forget it."

Mordecai's eyes widened.

"You honestly believe the world will one day be consumed by the Realm Dwellers? Could this dream have sprung from some deep fear inside you?"

"I am certain it did not. Did this Vessel Bearer say anything else?"

"No." Mordecai was silent a moment. "If the Realm Dwellers are trapped in the Abyss, how do they destroy the world?"

"A powerful sorcerer is responsible for their return to the world. I was told by the Vessel Bearer, Ithia, what I was to go back in time and obtain a spiritual object to stop their return." Thaylus pinched his brows. "But traveling through time takes a toll on human health. I do not think I can make it through any more trips through time."

Thaylus looked down. "If only Brythan were here," he murmured.

Mordecai took Thaylus by the shoulders. "I may not know the full extent of your grief, my friend. But the Great God who dwells inside the Gate works all things for good, even pain and catastrophe."

"I have yet to witness something good from all the meaningless effort and trouble I've experienced—nothing! I've failed my mission, the future is doomed, and I am helpless to do anything."

"You must have faith, Thaylus."

"Don't speak to me of faith! That liar Ithia said I must have faith. It seemed like it was proving true. But the culmination was nothing but defeat."

Mordecai let a few minutes pass before he spoke again.

"Would you consent to going with me to a special place while it is still morning?"

Thaylus shrugged. All was lost, as he saw it, so he saw no harm in whatever the head priest wanted to show him.

The day was bright, the morning's clouds now gone as Mordecai led him outside.

Black sparrows chirped joyfully, flying from tree branch to tree branch as butterflies fluttered about in rich gardens of tulips, daisies, and sunflowers.

The townspeople were smiling as they set up tents and kiosks, stocking them with watermelons, oranges, grapes, shining red apples, and more. Others were selling carrots, potatoes, tomatoes, and other kinds of produce.

Thaylus and Mordecai walked along a straight cobblestone path with grey, stone buildings spaced out on either side. A light breeze ruffled Thaylus's beard, and he blinked in the sunlight.

Thaylus still marveled at the unusual joy and happiness that pervaded the townspeople. He had never seen anything like it. And he was amazed at the generosity, kind attitudes, and honesty of the town of Bailise.

The broken sage followed Mordecai into what appeared to be a cathedral like Ferin's, but this one was much larger. At its top, a hollowed-out square in a spire housed a bronze bell. An arched opening with no door revealed people inside, bowing and murmuring.

As they entered, a strong, mental clarity washed over Thaylus. It was like Ithia's essence but more powerful.

"What are they doing?"

"They are saying their morning prayers."

Thaylus saw a woman in tears with a glistening shine in her eyes and a beaming smile.

"Why was that woman like that? Crying yet smiling?"

"Her name is Ember. She has been praying for the healing of her son, who was afflicted with a disease, and her prayers were answered. She was expressing her joy and thanks."

"Why have you brought me here?"

"So that you may present your requests before the Lord within the Gate."

Thaylus was cynical, but part of him had an overwhelming urge to do as the great priest suggested.

Yet why should he prostrate himself and surrender his deepest wish to this alien being?

Finally, Thaylus surrendered. He murmured, eyes closed, "Pray for me that all that I have spoken will turn for the better. It feels foolish, but I cannot deny the essence in this place."

"Very well." Mordecai kneeled and closed his eyes, mumbled something for a few minutes.

Then Mordecai stood up. "Now we wait for the Master of the Vessel Bearers to act."

"I hope he does."

Thaylus left the temple and Mordecai half in doubt, half in consideration.

He returned to the inn and sat at a table, brooding until dusk. As Thaylus was cleaning the tables with a white cloth, washing dishes and mopping the floor, he felt fatigued and ready for sleep.

"Good work, Thaylus," Theophilus said. "I'll see you in the morning."

The innkeeper went to his room, and Thaylus retired to his.

That night Thaylus had a familiar dream-like experience. He was on a flat grassy plain with vessels of every kind, shape, and size. Some were urns, others like lamps, chalices, and ewers. The plains went on for hundreds of miles in all directions.

Then he heard a voice.

"Thaylus, Thaylus."

It was Brythan's voice!

The voice was loud and resonating. It came from a silver urn about two feet high and two feet in diameter.

Thaylus ran to the urn.

"Brythan, is that really you?!"

"Indeed. This container is the spiritual manifestation of my body and soul."

"Why am I here again?"

"You're here so I may exhort and encourage you— and to help cast away your doubt and bitterness."

Thaylus was distraught and disturbed his thoughts were so transparent.

"If this is a 'vision' and you are truly Brythan, then tell me what purpose there was in your death? And do not say that I must have faith or that all things will work out. I am weary of all this obscurity."

"Thaylus, if you abandon faith, then failure is certain. You must look beyond the circumstances… look to what has been promised in the Pyrithian Prophecy."

"This is pointless. Just hollow conjecture."

Brythan raised his voice. "You must leave your skepticism and take hold of the truth. Khrine's future depends on your work, and it calls for faith. I beg you to heed my words."

The vision began to dissolve.

When Thaylus awoke, he was in his room once more.

He sat up and rubbed his temples, hoping he was not losing his mind.

He stood and walked toward a window, peering up at the sky.

"If you are real, God within the Gate of Vessels, prove yourself."

Nothing happened.

With a sigh, Thaylus got dressed and went down the stairs. He greeted Theophilus and unlocked the entrance door.

People came in and sat at tables, and Thaylus served them beef and other kinds of meats and ale.

As he was doing his duties, a man sat at a table in the corner of the establishment looking at a scroll. A candle lit the scroll so he could see better.

Thaylus approached him. "May I serve you something?"

"A plate of dates, please," the man said and returned to the scroll.

In the candlelight, Thaylus could see a map on the scroll. A burlap traveling sack sat on the table.

Thaylus peered closer. "If I may ask, where do you from?"

The man glanced up. "Why do you ask?"

Thaylus shrugged. "Only curious."

The man stared at Thaylus for a few moments as though he were harboring a great secret.

"I'm a traveler."

"I see you're looking at a map."

"Indeed. It is an outline of the greater lands of Pyrithia. I am looking for something."

Thaylus was even more curious now. "Might I enquire what you are searching for?"

The man frowned and looked down at the map.

"I've never told anyone what I seek. Few would believe it."

"I must say, you have driven a spike of curiosity into my mind." Thaylus sat next to the man and leaned in. "I believe in things most would call absurd. I'll seriously consider your matter."

The stranger's face lit. He pursed his lips and narrowed his eyes.

"What I am searching for is a thing of wonder. I have spent two years scouring the land for it. And I think I am close. I recently acquired this map."

The man licked his lips. "It is called the Pool of Healing. Every year, a Vessel Bearer travels from the realm of the Plains of Eternity and enchants its waters. All who drink of it are given complete wholeness."

The man's eyes lit with a sparkle, and his mouth stretched with a beaming smile.

Thaylus thought for a few moments. Why should he care about being "made whole?" The Arch Sage was old, and certainly such a pool could not make one immortal—or could it?

And yet the traveler's mention of Vessel Bearers and the Plains of Eternity could not be ignored.

Then something came to mind. Perhaps this Pool of Healing could repair the physical fatigue and wear afflicted upon him from time travel. Perhaps ... perhaps he could sojourn to the time when he first found the shield seal, then forward in time to save Brythan. If he did that, he could maybe even kill Kyrious and then keep the Realm Dwellers in the Abyss…

Thaylus took a breath, reigning in his exploding thoughts.

"My name is Thaylus."

"I'm Varian."

"Do you have an infirmity?"

"No."

"Then why are you looking for this Pool of Healing? Surely there is much danger and painstaking toil and risk?"

Varian exhaled. "It's my sister. She is deathly sick with a strange and baffling disease. My family has prayed to the Great God, but my sister remains afflicted."

His remark only reinforced the idea that this "great god" was nonexistent. The only supernatural forces Thaylus knew to be real were the Vessel Bearers, the Realm Dwellers, and the Celestial Servants, and they were not gods.

"How long has she been sick?"

"When she first got the disease, the physicians said there was no hope. She has only gotten worse as the years have passed. But I know if I can only bring a cask of the water from the Pool of Healing to her, she will be well."

"How do you know this Pool of Healing is real?" said Thaylus.

"I am desperate, Thaylus. I've heard other travelers speak of it. Moreover, this map I got in the Kingdom of Rune attests to its reality."

Thaylus turned the matter in his head. With all the supernatural things he had witnessed, an enchanted pool would not be farfetched. The only thing he had to lose by going with Varian was the risk of running out of provisions or encountering hostiles along the way. But for some reason Thaylus felt compelled to go and so, he would accompany the man.

"Forgive my bluntness, but I have a reason to go there that presses me." Thaylus looked Varian squarely in the eyes. "Would you allow me to come with you?"

Varian nodded. "It would be pleasant to have a companion. I must admit, I do get lonely—especially being one of the only persons who knows of the enchanted waters let alone believe it. To have another who keeps me company and agrees with my goal would be welcoming. Very well, we will go together!"

Varian extended a hand that Thaylus promptly shook.

"When will we be leaving?"

"We will leave as soon as the shops open tomorrow morning to buy victuals." answered Varian. "I just arrived here from hours of traveling and I need a night of rest. The reason I am not sleeping in a room now is the excitement this map has caused. But I feel my tiredness will overcome me by late afternoon."

"Thank you. I promise to be a delightful partner."

Thaylus looked over at Theophilus with sadness. "It will be a little hard to leave my friend the innkeeper." He paused. "I shall also miss this wonderful town that I have come to adore for the last several months."

Thaylus promptly went to Theophilus first to tell of Thaylus's plans and say goodbye. It was a sad moment and no less somber when he went to Kiroff, the man who welcomed Thaylus. With a heavy heart, he said his two last goodbyes to Priest Ferin and High Priest Mordecai who wished him favor and protection from God for Thaylus, something he accepted with reluctance but thankfulness.

He would spend his last night at the inn when he would depart in the morning for his new destination.

# Chapter 17

## LEGEND OF THE POOL OF HEALING

THAYLUS AWOKE at the sound of a rooster. He sat up, stretched, stood and dressed himself and exited the inn.

As Thaylus walked out of the inn Theophilus came up from behind him. "I think you may need this just in case." The inn keeper said as he held out a straight double edge sword. "There may be bandits afoot in the wilderness. You had best be prepared."

Thaylus was handed the blade and he took it with a slight bow. "Thank you, my friend. We've known each other for many months. You've always looked out for me. This sword will be a reminder."

With those words the sage and his companion led Fervent, the horse Thaylus bought, outside the city gate with victuals and supplies packed in three burlap sacks laid over the steed.

Thaylus looked back to admire his former home one last time.

"I'll miss you all," he uttered.

"All right, here is how the situation is," said Varian.

He called Thaylus's attention to the map that was dotted with small shapes with writings under each one.

The traveler pointed to a square in the upper right corner of the map with Bailise written below, the town they were now in.

Then he moved his finger to an outline of three small trees.

"From where we are now, we will head northeast to the Forest Plains." Varian pointed diagonally left to a far-off sliver of green, marking the forest border.

"After we pass through the Forest Plains, it is a straight, short ride to the Shrine Lands. Then we go north and cross the Crescent Lake on a ferry. Finally, we reach the very place where the Pool of Healing is—Durath's Keep!"

They passed the hill on the left where Thaylus had stepped through the time portal. Slowly, Bailise appeared smaller as they rode away.

The rolling, grass-covered land gradually began to display coniferous trees. Small bushes dotted the surroundings, and the ground was covered in dry leaves that crunched under Fervent's hooves. The ground started to lose its rolling hills and small reliefs and level out.

"We will be entering the Forest Plains soon," Varian said.

"I can tell. I've never seen the floor of a forest be so flat. This truly is a plain full of trees."

"Indeed. It is as I remember it. Can you feel its peace?"

Thaylus nodded, captivated by the forest. He was silent for a time as he took in the effervescent euphoria.

After a time, the sage broke the silence. "What was the last place you visited before coming to Bailise?"

"It was a small town situated east of Bailise. But that was months ago."

"I imagine being a nomad entails potential dangers."

Varian chuckled. "It does. I used to sojourn on a horse of my own before my sister fell ill." His tone became somber. "But a year ago I met bandits who took my horse and all I had. Good fortune let me escape with my life. I thank the Master of the Vessel Bearers for that."

Thaylus sighed at Varian's last words. In his heart, he desired to speak with Ithia. Did nothing but illusions and supernatural power fill the god she served?

Thaylus pushed these thoughts aside. "Your home city, what is it like and what is it called?"

"My city is called Rithmoore. It is a large city with one of the biggest temples dedicated to the God of the Vessel Bearers. The people there do not possess the unusual kindness of Bailise. I've never been to such a city that compared to it. Nevertheless, my fellow citizens were generally thoughtful. Rithmoore possesses some of the most knowledgeable people in the realm."

Varian looked at Thaylus. "Where do you come from?"

Thaylus saw no harm in disclosing the truth. After all, all others who he told believed him. He looked with a relaxed face to Varian.

"I come from a kingdom called Solace years in the future. I assume it to be many years."

Varian became still. "I see. And why have you gone back in time?"

Thaylus frowned. "That is complicated. It is because of an attempt to save Khrine itself, and something else."

Varian reeled back. "If you are to save the world, you are quite blessed by the great God."

Varian's words reinforced Ithia's message that he would deliver the world from the Realm Dwellers. It was pleasant and encouraging to hear a mortal like Thaylus declare it.

At nightfall, moonlight began to illuminate through the trees. Then the forest was filled with the sounds of nocturnal creatures. An owl stared at the men with the moon's nightglow reflecting in its eyes. It perched high on a tree branch to their right and began to serenade the air with a haunting hoot. Thaylus looked up and saw the fluttering silhouette of large moths in the moon's gentle shine.

After two more hours of riding, Thaylus and Varian dismounted, spent.

"Look there." Thaylus pointed to a large hawk.

"It's searching for prey, no doubt," Varian replied.

Thaylus studied it as it circled closer and closer to the open grove below. Finally, the sage smiled.

"It's a Merlin."

"What?"

"It is also a called a Pigeon Hawk," Thaylus said. "There is a legend it is a magical bird that can turn into a spirit and soar through the night sky and see through anything, even into the spiritual place where a man's soul lives."

Thaylus stretched. "Let's make camp."

Varian and Thaylus collected twigs and small branches together from the surrounding trees to make a fire.

Thaylus broke off a long thin branch. "Tell me of the Shrine Lands. The name makes me curious."

Varian spoke with his body turned away, gathering a pile of sticks.

"They say the dead ghosts of those who live there still inhabit the place. I wonder if there are."

Immediately, Thaylus recalled where he and Brythan encountered the ghosts of the Dark Cathedral in the other dimension. He tilted his head and shrugged as he broke of another small branch. "I think it is possible, but the myth may or may not be true. Either way I would not worry."

Thaylus felt there was no reason to worry about ghosts at the Shrine Lands although ghosts were real.

Varian faced Thaylus and twitched. "Well, the thought nevertheless turns my stomach."

"Do not worry, my friend. Something tells me there will be no ghosts," Thaylus said lightly.

"Have you ever seen a ghost?"

It seemed Varian was open to the idea of ghosts but Thaylus didn't know if this man would believe Thaylus's claim to have seen them himself in the cathedral in Earth's dimension. Thus, he would give a stiff, stilted answer. "It is just that I have heard of people who say they have seen ghosts. And they were all sensible people."

After gathering adequate kindling, the two walked back to where they left the horse and made a small circle of stones where they put the wood and ignited it with flint stones they brought.

After eating dried mutton and hazelnuts, they coiled up in their sleeping sacks and fell asleep.

# Chapter 18

## THE BANDIT'S HIDEOUT

THE NEXT MORNING, they rose, folded up their sleep sacks, and loaded them on their horse.

"What direction?" asked Thaylus.

Varian pulled out the map and a compass. "We go northeast, toward the Shrine Lands."

The Forest Plains did not extend far, and soon they met its edge.

The Shrine Lands expanded through a low valley they could see from their vantage point. The valley was too steep for the horse to simply go down, but a natural trail skirted down to the left around it and into the valley.

The shrine ruins were old and weather-marred. Great statues and pagodas varied in width and shape, with cracks and chips that attested to an era long ago. A whitewashed statue of a coiled cobra with a single carved ruby eye dwelled in a hollowed pillar.

Thaylus looked at all the great carved images made to look like anthropomorphic gods, confused.

"I heard in Bailise that all the lands only worship the God of the Gate of Vessels."

"Haven't any of the books and scrolls you've read spoken of the ancient people who built this place?"

"Not a one, though I must say I am most enthralled by these works of art."

Varian looked at the ruins and sighed. "I too wish to know this mystery. However, it comes second to the Pool of Healing."

Thaylus stopped. "Someone is watching us."

"Who?"

Thaylus's head snapped to the left. "There! I saw a head peak out from behind that shrine. Show yourself!" he yelled.

"Get a hold of yourself, man," Varian said. "We're alone."

The sage brought the horse to the corner of the shrine. His eyes searched every nook and cranny.

"This is foolhardy. Now please—"

But Varian stopped speaking as he realized there was indeed a human figure crouched beneath the statue of a fallen scorpion.

A staircase of eroded jade led up to an altar where another man looked at them with glaring eyes and a malicious smile.

"Now why would an old man and his friend be all the way out here alone in the Shrine Lands?" came a raspy voice.

"We're … artifact seekers." Varian lied. "We mean no harm. We want to collect some parts of these ruins and study them."

The man walked down the stairs slowly, his hands clasped behind him.

Suddenly men in black clothes came from behind corners, carved crevices, and statues. There must have been fifteen men surrounding Varian and Thaylus.

"I am Kaldourn, leader of the Havoc Wolves," said the man descending the steps, sliding out a crude dagger made from carved bone, its hilt wrapped in leather. "Unfortunately, you two are at the wrong place at the wrong time. Now be cooperative fellows and give us all your goods and your horse."

The men began closing in on them. Each possessed knives, spears, or other sharp weapons as well as blunt clubs.

Varian looked panicked. "Thaylus, we must do what they say!"

At his words, Thaylus's own fear dissolved. His heart quickened, and his mind sparked with electrifying focus.

Brandishing Theophilus's sword, Thaylus leaped from the saddle.

Something had taken over. It was like a warrior's spirit had possessed Thaylus.

Two tall, strong, sword-wielding giants on both sides of Thaylus backed away.

"Take your men and retreat, or I'll slaughter you all!" the sage said in a loud stern tone, twirling his blade with the skill of a sword master.

He stared at the bandit's leader.

"Thaylus, what has come over you?" cried Varian from the horse.

"Men, attack!" Kaldourn yelled.

Two bandits closed in on Thaylus, one in front of him and one behind. He parried the sword stroke of the man front of him, then pierced him in the stomach. Then he kicked at the bandit behind, breaking his sternum with a loud crack.

Next, a bandit came from the left with a knife.

The warrior sage dashed out, flipped over the horse, and came down upon the foe with the sword.

Three more attackers came from three sides with raised spears.

When they were in arm's length, Thaylus tossed his sword into the air and rolled on his back. He spun in a circle with his leg out, hitting their ankles.

They fell to the ground.

The mighty sage got to his feet and caught the sword he had tossed into the air, then impaled the three men one by one.

Only seven men now remained, including the leader who looked like he had seen Death itself bearing down on his men.

Varian was awestruck at this old man performing such acrobatic, offensive fighting moves.

The bandits backed away.

"A warrior spirit of the shrines possesses his body," the burly band chief cried. "We cannot overcome such power!"

It was indeed as though a warrior's soul had possessed Thaylus, who fought with fearlessness and passion.

"Leave this place and halt your assault, and I will let you live!" Thaylus bellowed in an almost-otherworldly voice.

The bandits ran for their lives.

It was over.

Varian watched as Thaylus collapsed on his side.

Sliding off the saddle, he went to the sage on the ground.

"Thaylus! Are you hurt?"

Thaylus looked up at Varian, dazed. "I'm ... all right."

"Who and what are you?" Varian looked utterly amazed.

Thaylus chuckled. "That is a long story. But I assure you I am mortal like you."

Varian helped his comrade to his feet. "How did you do that?"

"It was because of something that happened a while ago. It involved a Vessel Bearer."

"You've actually seen a Vessel Bearer?"

"I've seen such a being on a few occasions."

Varian peered at his friend like he was a holy relic to be revered.

"I'll explain on the way," Thaylus said. "How far are we to the Pool of Healing?

"Maybe an hour or two at most."

Thaylus took a deep breath. "Her name is Ithia. She had stork's wings and shone brilliantly. She gave me a power called faith. That power is what allowed me to assault the bandits. Now, come. The rest I will tell you as we travel to the pool."

Thaylus told Varian everything related to Ithia, from where the quest began with Brythan through all they had gone through together. He expounded upon the fear of the scarlet light, his prophetic dream, encountering the sea serpent, the shield seal, losing Brythan, the Realm Dwellers, leading up to meeting Varian himself.

When the sage had finished, Varian didn't know what to think.

"I'm sorry about your friend, and for your unfortunate experience. Nevertheless, you prove a man to be reckoned with. To be blessed by a servant of the Master of The Gate of Vessels is quite exceptional."

"Indeed, I am very grateful for the gift from Ithia. But I can no longer have this faith with all that has happened and what will happen. I'm afraid the gift is wasted."

Varian raised an eyebrow. "How could one who experienced such things not realize His existence?"

"I'll only believe that which I can see and hear. And I still cannot believe an all-powerful deity would suffer people to forget Him and worship stone and metal, then let evil beings destroy life on Khrine."

"How do you know your dream was prophetic?" asked Varian softly.

"It would seem farce to you if I told you. It was simply real, and I could just tell it was."

Varian shook his head. "It must be so much for one to bear."

Thaylus felt something warm in his tunic. He felt for it and withdrew Clara's blue pearl that he wore as a necklace—it glowed a soft azure hue.

"How astounding! I forgot all about it. I wonder why it glows," Thaylus said gazing deeply at the pearl.

Thaylus recalled how it acted like a reminder of Clara's words from her God: Faith is the evidence of things not seen and of things hoped for. However, he did not comprehend the saying, nor the truth of it coming from a true deity.

"Thaylus, you baffle me. You said this Vessel Bearer gave you faith. How is it that you do not trust that your quest is true? Only you can believe the God of the Gate of Vessels and His guiding hand-no one can force you."

Thaylus sighed with aggravation. "Very well, I shall keep an open mind. We will see what will become of our situation. And if it ends in death or shortcoming from the Vessel Bearers and their Lord, so be it."

They slid from the saddle and ascended a set of stone stairs that led to a domed tower with lookout openings. Below they saw the layout of the shrine paths. Thaylus looked down at the ground to a rectangular tile that was loose. He plucked it from the ground. Next, he picked up a sharp rock and began scratching on the tile.

"I am going to plot a path out of this labyrinth from this viewpoint."

Thaylus slowly and meticulously started to chart a way through the shrines.

"You are very prudent. I never would have thought of this," said Varian.

"Yes, but I must be precise. One wrong turn and we are lost."

When he'd finished, both men descended the tower steps with Thaylus holding out the tile. Both hopped on the horse and followed the directions indicated by the markings on the tile. The sage would stop at points to ensure their progress.

Navigating through the maze was relatively easy but it took some time before they left the Shrine Lands. Thaylus's calculations proved perfect.

They eventually entered a long corridor leading to open wilderness. As they emerged, they beheld the lush trees and blooming flowers around them.

"Ah, I am glad to be rid of those ceaseless walls and insufferable paths," said Varian as he inhaled the clean, potent wind carrying the scent of pine trees and grass.

"Indeed." Thaylus flicked the reigns and Fervent charged forward.

The air rushing past Thaylus was invigorating. He looked up and inhaled deeply.

Soon they approached the top of the incline and looked down on a grassy plain.

"Look, I can see Crescent Lake," Varian said, blocking the sun with his hand.

"It's quite a serene sight."

Despite the beauty of the lake, an eeriness about it filled his heart. What was the source of Thaylus's suspicion?

"Varian, what do you know of this lake?"

"Just what you and I see with our own eyes. It speaks for itself like you said—serene."

"I sense a peculiarity about it."

"What do you mean?" asked Varian.

The sage didn't answer.

Thaylus and Varian neared the bank of the lake. When they were close enough, the two saw a small hut-like cabin close to the edge of the lake. Next to it was a small ferry that was still as a stone on the placid lake surface. Two metal chimneys with smoke stains on the rims rose six feet into the air.

They came to a door of the wooden structure and knocked.

Seconds later, a slender man in worn trousers and a thick brown shawl came out.

"Hello sirs. Good day to you."

"Likewise, friend," returned Thaylus. "I'm Thaylus, and this is my travel companion Varian."

Both men slid off the horse.

"You can call me Amalek. Do you desire a ride to the other side of the lake?"

"Yes, we do," Varian said.

They paid Amalek, who guided them to the water.

"How long do you estimate it will take to traverse the lake?" asked Thaylus.

"It will be an hour. But Crescent Lake has a way of entrancing boaters with its beauty. We'll be so occupied enjoying it, time will pass quickly," Amalek said. "Climb aboard."

"I hope Fervent likes boat rides," said Thaylus as he patted the horse on the back and led him onto the craft.

Thaylus and Varian stepped onto the ferry. It bobbed a little with their weight. Thaylus tied Fervent to a slat of wooden railing.

Amalek excused himself to put coal into the engine.

The metal exhaust chimneys began pushing off smoke as the paddle wheel turned, and off they went.

# Chapter 19

## The Shadow Squall

THAYLUS AND VARIAN LOOKED OUT over the lake's enchanting waters.

"It is curious as to why this lake does not exist in my time. Even after so long, there should at least be a trace of it," Thaylus said.

"Perhaps it has to do with those evil beings you mentioned yet to come."

"But I don't think even the Realm Dwellers have the power to displace or destroy a lake this size."

A silence fell.

Varian glanced over at Thaylus. "Why do you want to travel to the Pool of Healing?"

The question was like an arrow that shot out of nowhere, pricking Thaylus's resolve.

"Truly, what is the reason? Do you have an indiscernible sickness?"

Thaylus frowned. "When I time travel, my health is depleted with each trip. I need to be healed of the damage done to my body, if for some reason I choose to time travel, though it would be to just explore time periods for discovery. I know of several times where lost or damaged relics from my time still exist, such as the Tower of Brea. But I do not think I can survive another excursion through time in my present state."

"What about your mission?"

"Bah! It is fool's errand! I shun the so-called Gate of Vessels and all that relates to it!"

Varian looked down in silence. Thaylus frowned as he looked away from Varian.

A long silence followed until Thaylus's eyes shifted to the waters. He looked at the deep lake waters around them. They were dark and still. Not even the sun reflected off the lake surface.

A heavy sensation dropped in Thaylus's stomach, but he did not know why.

Thaylus scanned the waters. "How strange," he called to them. "These waters are lifeless. A lake like this should be full of ducks, swans, and geese. There are none, and barely any fish."

Amalek's eyes darted to Thaylus. "Hmm ... that is a little odd," Amalek said as he shrugged and gave a sparse smile.

Thaylus had a nervous build up of tension in his stomach that further added to his sense something was wrong.

"It feels like ... no, it can't be," Thaylus stared at the dark surface of the water.

"What are you talking about? What are you feeling?" Varian said with a trembling voice and a flushed face.

"It's the same kind of fearful grip whenever I encounter Realm Dwellers." Thaylus shook his head. "It's too early, though. Calculating from the first vision, Mordecai said the six spiritual beings would not be loosed yet!"

"What do you mean?"

"The beings that fell to Khrine will deceive the people for seven years. Then they will be cast into the Abyss. Then they will emerge from the Abyss as Realm Dwellers."

Thaylus knew it would make no sense to Varian, or Amalek for that matter.

The three men stared at the water. It was darker now and becoming turbulent. The ferry began to totter and take in water.

The water began to turn tar-like as bubbles formed and gave off a sulfuric smell.

As Thaylus watched, a figure rose from the quagmire. It was like a tree trunk. As it rose, it grew two protrusions on each side, each sprouting arms and hands, with a sword of black fire in one of them.

Then red fiery eyes appeared.

"This can't be!" A surge of tension rushed through Thaylus faster than his racing heart.

Amalek fell against the wooden rails as the ship teetered. "What is happening?"

"Your quest is over, Thaylus," said the Realm Dweller with a gargling, crackling voice. "You will die here."

The ferry tipped to the front.

Amalek hit the wooden railing and toppled into the water.

"Help me!"

But Amalek was pulled under the waves.

Gone.

"His life is mine, and yours will follow," the miry figure said with a laugh.

"Thaylus, what do we do?"

"Ithia! Help me with your faith!" Thaylus cried at the sky.

The dark being laughed again, filling Thaylus's head with a stinging echo.

"I followed you through the portal from Khrine when Kyrious killed your companion, and I've been waiting until you came far enough from the Spirit of God within the priests of Bailise. I will enjoy killing you."

Varian gasped. "Do something!"

Thaylus's heart raced. Never had he more desired Ithia's faith to manifest itself.

The Realm Dweller raised its arms.

"Now that you are here, I will show you just how powerful I am."

The mucky figure sank into the lake. The water began to slush around.

The ship teetered, and more waves began to spill into the boat. A large rolling wave lifted their vessel and dropped it hard on the surface in a cascade of water, spilling more in.

The squall worsened. The boat heaved up and down, left and right.

"Your attempt to stop the Realm Dwellers is futile," the creature's deep voice resonated.

Waters continued to thrash the craft in every direction as the lake around them spiraled into a whirlpool. It increased in speed.

Soon the boat began to sink in the middle of the wide eddy.

"Ithia, where are you? I need your faith!"

Why was he not receiving power?

Just as they were being pulled into the eye of the whirlpool, a very large boat about a hundred yards away came toward them.

"Ah, no! Go away!" said the Realm Dweller.

As the boat drew closer, the lake storm started to subside.

The Realm Dweller cried out once more.

The spinning water slowed, and the waves shrank in size.

"This is not done," the dark being choked and shrieked as it returned to its watery form. "You are marked for death. It will come."

Then the watery form sunk into the depths as the craft approached the other boat in the stillness.

In an instant, the thick darkness broke apart and fizzled away. The tumultuous waters leveled, and the putrid smell faded.

The two men stood drenched to the bone, looking wildly around them.

"What just happened?" Varian gasped. "I've never been so scared. What if there are more?"

Thaylus shook his head and wrung the water out of his shirt. "I do not sense any more. The danger is over."

Both men watched the boat as it came closer.

Those aboard waved.

"You there, are you all right?" a man called out.

"We're fine, except for our captain. We just need time to dry and a little rest," Varian called in return.

"That you shall have. Come aboard."

A ladder lowered from the larger boat, and they climbed onto the boat.

Thaylus saw there were three men, all dressed in grey mantles with a kind of green fringe at the edges.

"I'm Bram," said the youngest man, who'd helped them aboard. "We are servants of the God of the Gate of Vessels. I must say, that storm you two were amid was very unusual. It centered on your boat entirely. The moment we saw you were within it, we all prayed to the Lord that you would be saved and that the squall would cease."

Thaylus studied them. "Who are you people? We were under attack by an evil spiritual being, and it was distressed the moment you neared us."

Bram raised a pointed finger. "Well, however strong this being was, every evil essence must flee in the presence of the Holy God."

"Hmm, so that is what drove the evil being away from us," Varian said.

Thaylus turned his attention to the three men. "What are your names?"

A plump bald one spoke. "You've met Bram, I am Elveon, and this is Fabian," he said, patting the arm of a tall man with long hair.

"I am Thaylus, and this is my companion Varian."

"Now if you will suffer some curiosity, these evil beings. Do you know what they were?"

"The answer to that is quite an unbelievable ordeal and would take time to explain," said Thaylus.

Elveon's eyes sparkled. "Fortunately, we have all the time in the world. Your eyes show you are neither a deceiver nor a madman. In our travels we have learned how to discern the hearts of men."

"Please," Bram added. "We are most curious and we will not upbraid you for anything."

Thaylus took a deep breath. "As you wish."

He gave them a brief but honest description of both where he came from and what they were doing there now.

"Now, there is a matter quite pressing. My companion and I are headed to Durath's Keep."

"Then we will take you to the bank of the lake leading to it," Bram said. "Would you be seeking the Pool of Healing?"

"We are!" Varian blurted. "Have you been there?"

"Indeed," Bram said. "Elveon here caught leprosy when we passed through an old, dilapidated town where we hoped to build a temple to the Lord of the Gate of Vessels. That was many years ago."

"Where did you learn of the Pool of Healing?" inquired Varian.

Elveon clapped his hands together. "We learned through a night vision of a Vessel Bearer telling us of it."

Bram spoke in a low tone. "However, I must warn you. There is an individual with magic who keeps the Pool of Healing. Only our faith and trust in God protected us against the magic user."

Thaylus's gullet knotted, and he looked away. He did not believe in the God that Bram spoke of. How could he stand against this sorcerer who guards the Pool of Healing?

Instead, he said, "I saw a woman, a Vessel Bearer, in physical form in a forest rather than a vision. Her name is Ithia."

The three priests gaped.

"First, we were petrified. We did not know at to think. It could have been a ghost for all we knew," Thaylus said.

Fabian tripped over his words. "D—did she say anything else?"

Varian was still, staring like the priests. "Tell us, Thaylus."

"She said she would give us a power called faith. To go further would be too arduous to explain—and too painful."

"I understand." Elveon looked as though he did. He gave Thaylus a kind look.

Varian yawned. "Are there clothes we can change into? We are soaked to the bone."

Thaylus and Varian dressed in priest's mantles, which was all the men had, and rested for the rest of the trip.

When they were close, Elveon roused the men, Bram and Fabian at his side.

"We are nearing the bank. I will say a prayer for your safe journey," Elveon said.

He bowed his head and closed his eyes. "To the Great King who dwells within the Gate of Vessels, we beseech You to guide these two souls and give them a speedy journey. Keep them from evil and those who wish them harm."

It was the first time anyone had so clearly evoked the name of this god in front of Thaylus. His mind cleared and his heart calmed, like a placid lake. It was an essence like the presence of Ithia, but different, grander.

The Arch Sage closed his eyes as his breathing slowed and his heart beat with a steady pace.

"I've never felt this way before," Thaylus said softly. "I will be honest with you all. Before and after the death of my friend, I spurned the idea of your God."

"Are things so different in your time?" Bram asked.

Thaylus nodded. "Yes. No one even believes in your god where I am from."

"What do the people of your time believe in?" Elveon asked.

Thaylus cringed. "That is something that has haunted my days and nights. My people are fools. They worship dumb idols."

Fabian wrinkled his brows in sadness. "What could cause the whole world to forget the King of the Gate of Vessels?"

"Apparently, it is because of a great deception of a Celestial Servant."

Bram gasped. "How can a Celestial Servant, one who lives in the presence of God, turn deceptive? How do you know this?"

"A high priest called Mordecai told me."

"We know Mordecai!"

"He said he had a vision of the future."

"And what happened in his vision?" Elveon asked.

"Seventy years from now, a celestial object having the appearance of an emerald-green star will appear. It will fall to Khrine seven years later. Within it, there will be eight spiritual beings. In the same year, they break free and demand people to worship them as gods."

"How horrid!" exclaimed Fabian.

Thaylus looked out into the expanse of the waters. "Indeed."

He peered down and folded his hands, then looked at the three priests, one at a time.

"In my era, there is a prophecy in the Pyrithian language about the Gate of Vessels and the being living within it. It is quite beguiling."

"Is that so?" Bram asked. "Tell us this prophecy. We may be able to clarify it."

"I don't remember it word-for-word, but it mentioned something about a Lord and His Emissary who would save all whose swear fealty to them."

"I believe this 'Lord' is none other than He who dwells within the Gate of Vessels." Elveon pulled on his beard.

"I feel the same way, my friend," Bram said.

"I sense likewise," Fabian added.

Bram fixed his eyes on land fifty yards away.

"We will part ways shortly, Varian and Thaylus." He put his hand on the sage's shoulder. "As I said, my partners and I have come to perceive the human spirit quite accurately in our years. The bitterness and disbelief you have will very soon give way to a revelation that will vindicate your heart and mind."

"What will happen to me?" Thaylus felt like a forlorn child.

"I cannot say I know, but I believe God is with you. And the fulfillment of the prophecy you mentioned, and its secrecy, will shortly come to pass. My intuition tells me this."

Thaylus locked eyes with Bram, then looked at the approaching bank.

"I do feel ... different. As I said, it is beguiling, but the notion of your deity who lives in the Gate of Vessels, he does not quite seem so..."

A small tear ran down his cheek, and Thaylus caught his breath.

"...I feel there is hope."

"That hope will not disappoint you," Elveon said.

Everyone held silence all the way to the bank.

Varian and Thaylus stepped off the craft and onto the grassy land.

"May the blessings from within the Holy Gate keep you both," said Bram with a bow.

"Thank you all, friends," Thaylus said. "Perhaps we will meet again."

The boat pulled away from the water's edge, and the three priests waved as Thaylus and Varian walked further onto the shore.

"I had no idea you possessed such knowledge," Varian said, then paused. "You know, you do have a different demeanor than when I first met you. That prayer of theirs has changed you."

"It has." Thaylus did not speak for a few moments. "I feel my anxiety subside a little. It's like a new path has been opened to me."

Varian put a hand on Thaylus's shoulder.

"I'm happy for you, friend. Let's get moving."

The two men walked through a small line of trees before passing onto a broad rocky plain. Below them in the distance, a large ruinous structure lay before them.

"It's Durath's Keep!" Varian exclaimed.

"It shouldn't take long to reach it."

They sprinted forward. As Varian and Thaylus neared their destination, both saw the keep was situated on a piece of land surrounded by a dark precipice.

The bridge that was supposed to reach it was broken off in the center.

Varian fell to his knees. "It can't be."

"No, there must be a way. Something tells me."

They looked around and noticed a large bird high in the air, flying in their direction.

Then it began to descend.

When it was close enough, the two saw it was covered in golden feathers with a long tail.

"A phoenix!" breathed Thaylus. "They have long been extinct in my time."

"It is considered good fortune to be met by a phoenix," Varian said.

The full enormity of the magic bird became apparent as it descended.

"Such an amazing creature!" Thaylus exclaimed.

The phoenix swooped around them, then finally landed in front of them with a delicate lilt. The two stared at the bird's stature.

"Greetings, travelers," the bird spoke, gazing at the with wide, intelligent eyes.

The two men gaped.

"It appears you have never met a creature such as me," said the phoenix.

Thaylus composed himself and bowed.

"It is an honor to be in your presence. I am Thaylus, and this is my companion, Varian."

"Do you seek to reach the keep on the other side of the precipice?"

"We do," Thaylus answered.

"I will fly you both over to it. But first, I must ask you to do something for me."

"What do you wish?" Thaylus asked.

"My two hatchlings have been stolen by thieves. I would recover them myself, but their den is in a deep cave with an entrance too small for me to enter. I saw how you warded off the bandits in the Shrine Lands. Bring them back to me, and I will transport you to the other side."

Thaylus cast his eyes down. "What you witnessed me perform is not something I can summon at will, I fear."

Thaylus dreaded such a dangerous task, unsure that the power of Ithia may not manifest itself. Besides, one sword could not prevail against several thieves, all most likely armed.

"I do have one idea, but it requires trust on your part, great phoenix."

"In what way?" the tall creature said he cocked his head.

"We both seek something called the Pool of Healing in the keep. I need it to restore my health. In that way, I may retrieve an object that will work against the thieves."

"Thaylus, what is this object and where is it?" Varian narrowed his eyes.

Thaylus ran his palm down his face. He exhaled deeply before he looked back up.

"The object is magical, and I first found it on a remote island, many, many years ago."

"What do you mean?" asked the phoenix.

"He is a time traveler, good phoenix, as unbelievable as it may sound," Varian said.

"I don't think you're mad, Thaylus," the phoenix said. "On the contrary, you have the demeanor and benevolence of a wise soul. Call me Grithin. What do you require of me?"

"You must first carry us to Durath's Keep. Once I am healed, I will retrieve the object. I give you my word. I will return with it, and then I will overwhelm the thieves with its great power."

"Very well, then. I trust your word. Let us not wait a moment longer! Climb on my back," said Grithin as he extended his wing to the ground so both could climb up. "Hold on."

With that, Grithin ascended into the skies in a burst of flight.

# Chapter 20

## Durath's Keep

Varian clutched Grithin's feathers as he buried his head in them.

"Let me know when we land!" Varian yelled through the rushing wind.

Thaylus laughed with a broad smile, and his heart throbbed as he took in the dew-filled clouds.

"This is wonderful! I have never felt such freedom and joy!"

Below Thaylus, the lake he and Varian had crossed stretched far and wide. In the distance, he could barely make out Bailise, with one of its grand cathedrals towering into the sky.

Far off, the White Mountains rose like frozen behemoths that touched the clouds.

"What is this magical item you seek?" Grithin asked.

"That would require some tedious explanation. Let us just say it has power to subdue spiritual evil."

"Hmm. That is still vague, but it will suffice."

When they crossed the precipice, Grithin careened down.

"Hold on, we're almost there."

Thaylus could feel the rising of his innards as they descended to the threshold of Durath's Keep.

When they landed, Varian and Thaylus slid off Grithin's wing. Thaylus scanned the keep, his eyes sharp.

Durath's Keep could contain the Castle of Solace several times over. Its collapsed walls and immense green pillars exposed to open air gave off a feeling of grandeur Thaylus had never experienced.

Durath must have lived a wealthy life and possessed much power, whoever he was.

"I will wait here," Grithin said.

"Very well."

Thaylus and Varian walked through an archway with hanging vines. Trees grew in the heap of ruins.

But after twenty minutes of walking in what felt like circles, Varian stamped his foot.

"How will we find the pool this way! At this rate, it could take months to find."

"What did you expect? Markers telling us where to go?"

They reached a clearing, where a tall obelisk with a broken pinnacle lay in a circle of stones. A large dove perched on top.

Varian frowned. "Doves do not dwell in places like this."

"Indeed. What could it want?"

The two reached the obelisk, and the dove fluttered to a stone door frame several yards away.

The two stepped over pieces of fallen roof tiles with murals of strange creatures.

They climbed up a heap of stone where the dove was perched. Five adjacent archways lay a dozen feet from them.

The dove darted through the one on the very left.

"It's almost like it's guiding us," Thaylus said.

"It is acting strangely."

Thaylus and Varian passed under the archway. It led to a cracked, white-stoned stairway.

The dove flew to the top.

When they reached it, the bird perched on a partly standing balcony.

They walked to it.

Next the dove flew inside a corridor close by.

They entered the corridor and passed a narrow bridge without railings.

The dove landed on the other side.

This time, when they reached it, the dove did not fly away. It simply looked up at them.

Before Thaylus and Brythan, a white marble staircase led down to a rectangular pool with pillars around it.

"Could that be it?" Varian clutched Thaylus's arm.

"There is no way to know," Thaylus said. "That is, unless we drink it and see how we feel."

They took a step, then Thaylus halted.

"Wait. The priests said a hostile wizard dwelled in the keep."

Varian looked around. "I do not see anyone."

"Perhaps we have managed to avoid him in this ruinous labyrinth."

They raced down the steps to kneel at the edge of the pool.

But as their knees hit the stone, they felt an invisible force push them away. With a crash, they went skidding against the stone ground, landing a few yards from the pool.

A man in a robe of azure with golden hems and emeralds on each shoulder hovered over the water.

"I am Durath the immortal. Have you come to my keep to drink of the Pool of Healing?"

Varian struggled to his knees. "Please, great one. That is what we desire."

"Only I may drink of its waters," Durath said.

"We have come so far, King Durath. Please, let us! I beg you!"

"Silence! None who dare come to my stronghold shall leave."

Varian scrambled to his feet. "Thaylus, we must flee. Get up!"

The mighty Durath spread his arms, and a ball of blue light glowing like a small star appeared before him.

Thaylus and Varian ran.

They hid behind a pillar as the blue sphere burst forth and struck the pillar, encasing it in ice.

They ducked around a corner.

But Durath floated like a drifting mist toward them.

"There!" Varian said.

They walked along a sun-bleached wall to a portico and ran through the shaded space.

"Such sport! Few have evaded me as long as you have except for those blasted priests and their God who actually subdued me."

Durath had a coy grin as he floated to the portico entrance.

Thaylus and Varian stepped through a hole in a wall at the far side of the enclosure.

Durath sneered. "You two fools think you're worthy of the gift of the Pool of Healing. I will have fun slaying you!"

With that, Durath volleyed lightning bolts that blasted the stonework into falling pieces.

"He's mad! He'll cause a cave-in right over all our heads!" Varian said.

"We have to get out of here," Thaylus said.

The two ran to the end of the portico. A broken bridge separated them from the other side.

"The only option we have remains to jump from here to the other side," Thaylus said.

"The gap must have a six-foot span!"

"It's the only thing to do! Durath is coming."

Both men backed from the edge of the broken bridge. Thaylus barged forth in a mad dash. He leapt over the drop off and planted his feet on the other side.

"It's simple, see? Come on!" Thaylus said.

Varian looked behind him. Durath followed, closer and closer.

With a deep breath, Varian dashed forward. With a loud yell, he jumped to the other side.

"We have to keep running!" Thaylus said.

"Will we run until we drop? This is pointless!"

"What else can we do?"

In pile of rubble a little way off, something glowed. Thaylus thought it was his imagination or a trick of the light on a golden object, but as they ran, it grew even brighter.

He narrowed his eyes.

"Varian, do you see something glowing over there?" Thaylus pointed.

"It looks like shimmering gold!" Varian ran ever closer.

"Look," he said. "It's a lance, and it does glow. It must be magical!"

Thaylus went to Varian. "Let me see."

Thaylus held the object. A feeling like rushing water coursed through his body. His mind filled with a mental resonation like he had stepped in a placid lake. "I know how to use this. I can't explain it."

Thaylus made out an inscription in the Pyrithian language. The Bane of Durath. This proves we have our weapon to defend ourselves, he thought.

Thaylus glanced behind him.

Durath stood on the other side of the drop off.

"The golden lance!" Durath cried. "How did you find it?"

"We have discovered your weakness. Let us drink from the pool, and we will not harm you."

"I will never surrender! Curse you!"

Durath made a fist, and a fireball formed around it. He hurled the fireball like a stone at the two men.

Thaylus braced himself.

As he did, the glow of the lance grew to a shine, and the illumination engulfed the fire attack.

Durath scowled and pulled out a glinting sword. He dashed forward, his blade pointed at Thaylus.

Thaylus held up the lance in defense, and sparks erupted from the weapon clash.

"If I must go, I will go fighting!" Durath said through clenched teeth.

Thaylus gripped the lance tighter and pushed his opponent back.

Durath sent a lightning bolt that struck the base of where Thaylus stood.

The edge crumbled to debris and fell into the precipice, along with Varian and Thaylus.

Six yards from the bottom, the lance flashed! Their fall halted, and they floated to the ground, safe.

Durath appeared in front of them. "Die!"

He twirled his blade, and a strong gust of wind pushed Thaylus and Varian back.

But when Thaylus held the lance up, a shield-like barrier resisted the wind attack.

He ebbed closer.

Durath's red face burned with anger. "Cretins, you'll pay for this!"

But as Durath came down with his sword, Thaylus swiped it from the side and knocked it out of his opponent's hand.

Then Thaylus pointed the lance at Durath's neck.

"Lead us back to the pool."

"Never!" Durath roared.

"Do it. Now!"

Thaylus touched Durath on the neck with the lance. A searing sound, like a branding bar, came from it.

His stinging cry could have rattled the mind of the bravest warrior.

"I relent!" Durath panted.

Minutes later, they were all at the pool.

Thaylus held the sword at Durath as Varian knelt at the water's edge.

"Durath, do you know when the Vessel Bearer enchants the water?"

Durath was silent.

"Speak," Thaylus commanded, "or there will be more pain!"

Durath gritted his teeth. "As long as the Vessel Bearer is faithful to bless the water, its effects are continuous."

Varian drank from the pool.

"I have never been more refreshed," Varian cried. "I feel like I am a youth again! I have such clarity of mind— such vibrancy."

"Is the Pool of Healing the secret of your immortality?" Thaylus asked Durath.

"Yes. But one must drink directly from the pool daily to sustain everlasting life."

Thaylus continued to brandish the lance. "Where did you get your magic from? I know it's not the pool."

"From the Dragon of the Abyss."

"How did you go to the Abyss? And what is the Dragon of the Abyss?" Thaylus asked. "No mortal can go to a spiritual realm on his own. Answer me!"

"Very well," Durath said, his face dark. "I used a magical object called the Book of Realms."

"The Book of Realms." Thaylus turned to Varian. "I am familiar with its power. A spirit named Clara sent me to a realm called Earth with it. I did not know it could send beings to the Abyss."

"Show us where the book is," Thaylus said, holding the lance tip at Durath's neck.

Durath walked to his throne and pulled a book from a groove at the base.

Thaylus took the book and opened it. It contained countless realm names, along with descriptions and the incantations to reach each one.

Thaylus flipped through the pages. "Remarkable!"

Varian grasped his friend's arm. "Remember why we are here."

Thaylus jerked and closed the book. "Of course, forgive me."

Stepping to the edge of the pool, he knelt, cupped some water, and drank. His muscles strengthened, his vision became clearer, and a youthful curiosity filled his mind. He felt even his bones click into proper place and thicken as his frame became straighter.

Indeed, he felt born anew, like a fresh body had budded.

"It is done," Thaylus said. "Now I will go forward in time and retrieve the Seal to the Abyss. Then I will return and fulfill my word to Grithin."

"Wait." Varian turned to Durath. "Does the water's property work if it is transported?"

"I don't know." Durath stood stoically with folded arms.

Thaylus took Varian by the shoulders.

"This does not mean it will not work. There is still a chance. Now, I will return shortly—"

Just then, the ground beneath them jostled.

All three men fell to their knees as the stone beneath them cracked and trembled.

Pillars, walls, and staircases broke up, and holes swallowed the debris.

"Where did this quake come from?" Varian cried. "What can we do?"

Durath sneered. "At least I will have the pleasure of taking you to the grave with me!"

"You! You're causing it!" Thaylus said.

"All I had was to think this quake and it occurred." Durath laughed maniacally. "We'll all perish together."

"Look!" Thaylus pointed above.

It was Grithin, soaring above them in circles, lowering in his flight.

"Grithin! Save us!"

The phoenix landed on the top of a tottering staircase. "Climb onto me!"

"Wait!" cried Varian. He dashed to the water's edge and dipped a leather flask in it and returned to Thaylus side.

Thaylus climbed onto Grithin's back with the golden lance in hand, and Varian climbed on behind him.

"Hold tightly!" said the phoenix as he darted almost vertically into the air.

What was left of the keep became a ruinous heap. The rubble sank into the precipice that circled it.

When Grithin had climbed a good height, the tightness that afflicted Thaylus's stomach released.

Varian smiled. "I have done it! My sister will be healed!"

Anvil-shaped clouds rumbled and darkened. A bellowing wind blew across Grithin, Varian, and Thaylus.

"What could cause clouds to act that way?" Varian asked.

"I sense the power of magic afoot," Thaylus said.

"I will have to fly over it," Grithin said.

The phoenix angled upwards, and Thaylus felt the air thin and turn colder. The top of the cloud cluster crackled and flashed with a hideous red glow. It felt like the essence of the red beam of light that Thaylus encountered at the Solace tower.

If only he had the shield seal!

A knot formed in Thaylus's stomach, and a tremble filled his body. "Let us hope nothing comes from the clouds to harm us."

Below them, a dark figure emerged from the clouds and then slithered back within.

"Below!" Varian pointed.

Thaylus and Varian looked as an immense black hump rose from the clouds and delved back into them like before. A loud roar, like a burning fire, emanated from the darkness.

"What evil have we aroused?"

The black figure rose.

Thaylus gasped. "It looks like a head."

The head rose with the rest of the figure's extremities to reveal an enormous black dragon. The dragon opened its mouth, and a smoldering ball of red fire swelled in its throat.

"Grithin! It is preparing to attack us with fire. Get ready to dodge!"

"All right!" said the phoenix.

The evil beast breathed a ball of fire and Grithin dove, skimming the cloud tops.

The dragon trailed them and neared closer.

"I have an idea!" said Grithin.

His long tail straightened, and its feathers burned like candles. The flames grew to that of torch lights. His whole tail flared into a streaming flame.

The flame seared the center of the dragon's eyes.

"Blasted phoenix!" the dragon cried.

"It speaks!" Grithin said.

Thaylus addressed the dragon. "Why do you attack us?"

"I know you, Thaylus," the beast roared. "If you fulfill your quest and vanquish all evil, I will perish!"

This must be the Dragon of The Abyss.

If only his supernatural faith would manifest and save them, but it had not yet happened. Would it ever, or was Ithia's gift of faith now lost?

As the doubt zipped through his mind, Thaylus's golden glowing lance suddenly became like a lightning rod. It flashed and flickered.

Thaylus instinctively knew what to do.

He raised the lance. Instantly, it dispersed golden lightning that struck the dragon's left wing.

The dragon cried out and teetered to the side, then disappeared into the dark clouds.

"It could come from anywhere!" Varian shouted.

Thaylus closed his eyes. His mind became like an all-penetrating eye in every direction. He could feel an intuition at work.

The dragon burst from below, and Thaylus sent another lightning bolt that struck its neck.

"Wretched creatures!" the dragon bellowed.

"He can't go on for much longer!" Thaylus said.

The dragon prepared to spew another fire attack, but Thaylus countered it. With a swift flame volley from the dragon, Thaylus dispersed a lightning bolt that shot into the dragon's mouth—and through the rest of its body.

A deafening cry pierced Thaylus's ears.

The dragon fell back, plummeting into the clouds.

"We've won!" Grithin said.

"You did it, Thaylus!" Varian cried.

But they spoke too soon.

A long tail swiped through the clouds like a whip and hit Grithin's side.

Grithin shrieked and shifted to his left wing.

"The pain!" Grithin wailed.

He plummeted into the smoldering clouds. Darkness covered their vision.

I can't breathe, Thaylus thought in a panic as he coughed.

He clutched Grithin's feathers tighter, he and Varian holding onto Grithin as he spiraled down and down to the land below.

Thaylus felt the onrushing wind push him back and he and Varian held on for their lives. They broke through the dark clouds.

But the dragon did not appear anywhere.

"I'll do my best to slow our descent, but it will be a rough landing," Grithin managed.

The flapping of his wings barely slowed their fall. Below them a forest stretched on for miles.

The phoenix flapped harder and the speed of their fall decreased.

They went tumbling through the canopy and crashed to the ground.

They fell to a leafy forest floor in a thickly shadowed area.

Thaylus moaned. Getting up sent a sharp pain running through his body.

Varian kneeled over him. "Can you move?" Varian asked.

"It hurts. What's wrong with your arm?"

"It's dislocated," Varian said. "I need you to put it back in place. But first you must get up."

"What about Grithin?"

But the phoenix was dead.

"I think he snapped his neck on a tree," Varian said somberly.

Both men wept.

"I feel sorry for him." Thaylus sighed. "He deserved our thanks."

"Can't you go back in time and save him?"

"Yes, yes I can. Let us not waste time! Stand back!"

Before Thaylus uttered the incantation, he saw a bright source of light amidst the trees. Perhaps it was Ithia.

The light remained stationary for several minutes.

"What could that light be?" Varian asked.

The two men walked between trees and bushes as more of the light became exposed. It hypnotized Thaylus.

When they got to the center of a large grove, his eyes widened and he opened his mouth.

There stood a domed structure with a pillar of white light shooting into the air.

It reminded Thaylus of the scarlet light in his time. But instead of fear, this light brought a peace and stillness.

An archway led inside.

Without a doubt, something of great importance lay within.

# Chapter 21

## The Wastelands of Brea

Thaylus went before Varian. He inched to the entrance, overwhelmed with a feeling of calmness and joy emanating from the place.

The feeling increased as they entered. Even the air felt like it had changed somehow. It smelled clean and fresh, like after a spring rain.

Inside, they discovered the bright light rose from a circular altar of gold. Three statues, looking like Vessel Bearers lifting urns, stood around the altar.

Thaylus neared it. With a slow hand, he reached out and touched the light.

Instantly, he was transported to another place, this one with a white light shining all around him. A loud voice echoed like it came from within a vast cave.

"I am a Celestial Servant who serves the One who lives in the Gate of Vessels."

Thaylus could now make out the form of a being of light. Its presence and brightness overwhelmed him.

"Why am I here? What is this place?" Thaylus trembled.

"This is the Temple of The Crown, the first building made to worship the Lord of the Gate of Vessels." The being took out a long object. "Stretch forth your hand."

Thaylus obeyed.

As he did, the light became the figure of a man in golden shining robes. The man walked to him.

"This is the Sword of the Spirit forged by the word of the Great Lord."

The man put the hilt of a flashing blade in Thaylus's hand. It felt like lighting coursed through his veins.

"Why do you give me this object when I do not believe in your God?"

The being looked at him gently. "God has guided you every step of the way, from Ithia's interventions to the dove that led to the Pool of Healing and the golden lance. Most importantly, you have been given the faith of the Lord."

"What do I do with this?" Thaylus looked at the flashing sword.

"Someone is stealing vessels from the Plains of Eternity. You will need the sword of the Spirit to defend yourself where you are going."

Slowly, Thaylus brandished the shining sword. It sounded like embers as its blade sliced through the air.

"What challenge awaits me?"

"I do not know. That is all My Master told me. Travel north past the kingdom of Evercrest to the land of Brea. The same dove that guided you in Durath's Keep will indicate the way. His word is true."

The being backed away and put up his hand in farewell.

"Rest assured. Have faith."

With that, the light abated, and Thaylus found himself back where he had been, with Varian.

He pulled his hand away from the pillar of light.

"What happened?" Varian asked. "You disappeared, and moments later you reappeared!"

Thaylus held up his right arm. The flashing, flaming sword materialized in his hand. He held it high above him as though in triumph.

Varian stumbled back. "You are a wizard! Who are you, really?

"I am no wizard, and I do not have magic. I stood before a shining man just moments ago who gave me this sword." Thaylus stared at the sword, baffled. "He said he was a Celestial Servant who comes from your god."

"The Lord who dwells in the paradise inside the Gate of Vessels?"

Varian's smile was so wide it could have lit the room.

But Thaylus stood stoically, his expression brazen.

Varian's smile fell.

"You have seen a celestial being and you still do not believe in God?"

"The god you believe in plays games and tricks people. He speaks things in riddles and obscurity that confuse me! The future inhabitance of Khrine will abandon this God you speak of, and now I know why. He has allowed so much suffering and death, and for what?"

Thaylus felt his hands close into fists even around the sword. "I believe in Vessel Bearers and Celestial Servants because I have seen them and experienced their power and glory. But not your god. I still do not believe."

"You must have f—"

"Faith?" Thaylus gave a mocking laugh. "That is what everyone says."

"Why are you so bitter?"

"I don't know," Thaylus sank to the ground.

Hot tears overcame him, and he sobbed.

"Part of me wants to believe." It was like another man spoke from him. "But another side has nothing but disdain."

Varian took Thaylus by the shoulders. "You will find what you seek. Be patient."

Thaylus wiped his face and stood. "I must go north from here."

He pushed past Varian and trudged out of the building.

Varian followed.

"If we go north, we will meet the kingdom of Evercrest. You may stay there."

"But … what about my sister? I must return to my kingdom to give her the water."

Thaylus extended his forearm to shake. "I give you my word I will find a way. If your god is truly benevolent, we will reach her."

Varian nodded solemnly as he shook his arm in return.

"Thank you. I believe you. But Thaylus, what do you want in Evercrest?"

"It is on the way to the land of Brea."

Varian gasped. "What about the legends?"

"If monsters and evil spirits dwell there, I will face them."

Thaylus explored around the dome. On the other side, he saw the dove in a tree.

His guide.

He left the dome and walked in the direction of the bird, Varian following. Neither spoke along the way. The dove always stayed just ahead of them.

Sunlight broke forth as they emerged from the forest. Far off, the castle of Evercrest gleamed in the setting sun. It sat gallantly on the pinnacle of a hill.

"It's nearing twilight. We will not make it there before dark."

As they gazed toward the castle, a rider on horseback crested over a hill and stopped, looking their way.

"Who is that rider?" Varian asked.

"We have grown lucky. I think that is a messenger or scout."

The rider trotted down the hill and toward them.

Thaylus raised a hand in welcome. "Greetings, sir."

"Hello, travelers. Why are you alone near dark at the edge of the Emerald Forest?"

"We intend to go north, to Evercrest."

"Where do you come from?" The rider cocked his head.

"We live on the other side of the forest."

The rider looked surprised. "You come from Nepheseer. You have sojourned a long way."

"We have," Thaylus said.

Another rider crested the hill. "Is everything in order, Anithen?"

"These travelers come from Nepheseer," Anithen replied.

"I see. If your goal is Evercrest, you may come with us. My name is Relik."

"I am Thaylus and this is Varian. A ride would be wonderful."

Thaylus was helped onto Relik's horse and Varian onto Anithen's.

They rode toward Evercrest.

Thaylus felt jittery inside. He was about to see an ancient kingdom long gone in his time. Thaylus had some knowledge of it from some rare texts, but to actually lay eyes upon it felt surreal.

Thaylus felt a serenity and a benevolent feeling from the land. Birds flew in formation, and in the distance, wild buffalo thundered across the rolling hills. Pools of water appeared everywhere.

And the clouds, oh the clouds! They looked like a spiritual realm all on their own.

As they approached a cluster of buildings, the horses stopped, and the two strangers dismounted.

"Welcome to the outer kingdom of Evercrest. Now we must bid you farewell," Anithen said.

Then they trotted off the way they had come.

Thaylus and Varian looked around. Huge buildings lined the sides of a polished stone concourse. Each house stood like a small castle, with stained glass windows and beautiful architecture. Almost every house had decadent statues and sculpted hedges in the form of animals or shapes.

The townspeople waved and smiled at each other in the evening light, and children ran to and fro in laughter. All looked to be dressed in clean, well-made tunics and cloaks. It resembled the mood of Tarken Town or Bailise, so content and jubilant.

At dusk, men lit torches and fire pits.

A loud bell rang, and everyone stopped and began to make their way up a stone concourse to an immense colonnade with porcelain fountains.

"This must be a place of worship," Varian said. "I will join them."

They walked with the others to the colonnade. There, everyone kneeled and bowed their heads, Varian included.

Thaylus stood on the outskirts, feeling a force telling him to pray with the others.

But most likely, no real and all-powerful deity listened, Thaylus thought. Prove yourself if you are real, he whispered.

Nothing.

Bitterness swarmed his heart. He wanted to believe in this "great god" of the Gate of Vessels, but another part abhorred such a being—any being who would toy with his people.

Varian rose and approached Thaylus.

"If only you believed." Varian's eyes glistened with a childlike luster.

"I believe in what I see and hear, what offers proof."

Thaylus felt a warm sensation within his cloak. He withdrew Clara's blue pearl. It glowed a hypnotizing blue like a clear, deep ocean.

He recalled her words: Faith is the evidence of things not seen and of things hoped for.

Thaylus felt he understood more of her words than at first. A kernel of hope tugged at him.

What if this was a true god? The slightest chance appealed.

Thaylus shook himself. "We need a place to sleep. Let us see how kind this city is."

They found a lush garden in front of an immaculate house. A tall young man with a water bucket stood there over a large well.

"Excuse me, lad. My friend and I have traveled far and have no supplies or money for an inn. Could you help us?" Thaylus asked.

"Certainly. As you can see, the city's people enjoy great wealth and dwell quite fairly. Come with me. I am sure my father will agree."

Thaylus and Varian trailed the young man to the tall, wide house with columns. An oak door contained a small stained-glass window. Grey smoke puffed from two chimneys.

Inside, tall, vaulted ceilings loomed over a lush rug of woven designs.

"Father, I must speak to you."

A mid-sized man in a green and scarlet tunic came out of a door against the back wall.

"What is it, Son?"

"These two travelers have come a long way. May they stay with us?"

The man approached. His brown eyes were warm.

"I see. What is the nature of your travels?"

"I am passing through on my journey north, but my friend will be staying indefinitely."

"Very well. Please, join us for dinner. You may stay here this night." The man offered an arm. "My name is Berinth."

At dinner, Thaylus and Varian sat at a long table. Berinth sat on the other side with his son. A black-haired woman came to the table and joined them, holding the hand of a small child.

"What kingdom do you come from?" Berinth asked.

"Past Nepheseer."

"My, you have traveled a great distance, and through a treacherous forest. Now, I will say the meal prayer."

The family clasped their hands and bowed, as did Varian.

Thaylus merely folded his arms with a scowl.

Berinth looked up. "In Evercrest, we bow when we pray."

Thaylus placed his palms on the table. "I do not pray."

"What do you mean?" Berinth looked horrified. "Everyone does. Who do you pray to?"

"I pray to no god."

Berinth frowned. "Where do you put your faith if not in God?"

Thaylus felt hotness rise in his face. "Your god is nothing but a spiritual being, like any other!"

Berinth jumped from his seat, his eyes flashing.

"How dare you! You are lucky God does not strike you dead!"

Thaylus stood to meet him. "Just because a being has great power does not mean it is a deity."

Berinth pounded his fists on the table. "I'll see you hanged for this spiritual treason. I could tell everyone now, and they would stone you to death!"

"Thaylus, please!" Varian tugged at his friend's sleeve.

"Would your god kill me for not knowing about him?" Thaylus roared.

Berinth circled the table toward him. "I should pummel you right now."

"Berinth, you're losing control" said the woman.

"He deserves it!"

Thaylus neared the man. "Strike me!"

Berinth made a fist.

But Varian jumped between the two men. "Stop!"

"You both should leave," the woman said quietly as her husband stalked to the other side of the table. "I am sure someone else will shelter you."

"Thank you for the brief pleasure, ma'am," Varian said, ushering Thaylus toward the door. "I am sorry for the disruption."

Thaylus strolled outside with a swagger. "What a spiritual soul that one was."

"Thaylus, you could have faked it!"

"I shouldn't have to. Berinth's reaction showed he was a brute."

Varian turned away. "For the love of heaven!"

"Don't get emotional on me, too."

Varian huffed out a breath. "Thaylus, you infuriate me. I cannot stand your stubbornness. You acted like a child." He paused. "Perhaps this is where we should part ways."

"What will you do?" Thaylus asked, disarmed and shocked into a receptive qualm.

"I do not know. I do not know the way back to my sister in the kingdom of Wrethmire. What if I am stuck here? And even if I did know the way, she would die before could reach her."

They looked at each other a long moment.

Finally, Thaylus extended an arm.

"I understand. I promise I will bring your sister the water from the Pool of Healing. You have my word. Just tell me where to find her and her name."

"With someone so blessed and guided by God, I can know you will reach her," said Varian. "She is in the physician's lodge, made of white stone, just inside the city gate. Her name is Nara." Varian gave Thaylus the water flask and shook him by the forearm one more time.

"Goodbye, friend," said Thaylus.

Then the two separated as they walked from each other.

\* \* \*

A MIDDLE-AGED WIDOW NAMED ABIGAIL TOOK Thaylus in for the night. She had a quiet spirit, and they spoke little.

In the morning, she told him the quickest way north out of Evercrest.

As Thaylus walking along a bridge that led out of the kingdom, he heard Varian's voice from behind him.

Thaylus turned and Varian's face was lit up with a broad smile. "Thaylus I have great news! I know where Wrethmire is! I found a library here where, upon asking, a man told me of a map this region of Khrine. It took some time but I found it. My sister is only but three days away on horseback!"

Thaylus smiled too and grabbed Varian by the shoulders. "That is wonderful news!"

"Indeed. God must have guided us here."

Thaylus overlooked Varian's last words. "I am happy we can part glad terms. You should get what you need for your journey. I wish you the best, my friend. Here you are," he said as he gave Varian the water flask.

"And I, you." Varian embraced Thaylus and turned and ran off.

Thaylus crossed the bridge and passed into the wilderness. It was stunning. It abounded with hills and valleys with full spreading trees, lakes, and palms. He found himself smiling as he walked. He missed Varian's company, but the silence was welcome.

He wondered whether monsters and spirits really did fill Brea, not to mention what the terrain looked like or whether any people lived there. Maybe the myths about Brea were just myths after all.

After a time, the luscious vegetation became sparse. Animal life appeared less and less. The scent of the air turned slightly odorous, like a dead tree. Paleness covered the sun that scorched Thaylus's head.

He came to the edge of a valley. It had brown, short grass and gnarled trees.

Thaylus descended the weed-covered decline. His shins brushed past tumbleweeds and small rotting trees. He stumbled at points and skidded down.

Tar pits and swamps covered the ground. The smell made Thaylus's stomach turn. He inched around the many obstacles.

An exploding bubble from a tar pit spewed the black muck onto Thaylus's cloak.

"Ack!"

He cast the ruined clothing off and traveled on.

A fallen log crossed above a sloshing swamp pit. Thaylus sought a way around it, but tall intertwining trees blocked his path, like a wall of wood.

He stepped onto the log, testing its balance.

It did not move.

The swamp bubbled and stirred. The log remained steady, and the knot in Thaylus's gullet released as he almost reached the other side.

But just as he reached the end, a long creature burst from the quagmire in a great splash.

It looked like a giant lamprey and loomed over Thaylus like a serpent. Green saliva dripped from its circular mouth.

The creature lashed at the log, and it split.

Thaylus slid into the muddy slosh.

He grasped a loose vine.

The creature constricted his legs, pulling him down.

"No!" Thaylus cried.

He gripped the vine with all his might.

But his hold slipped. Now the swamp was at his neck. A groan slipped from his lips.

With a final burst of energy, Thaylus reached for a sharp stick and jabbed it at the giant lamprey-like monster. The stick pierced its skin, jostling the creature so that it loosened its hold.

Again and again, Thaylus stabbed its body.

"Take that, you filthy creature!" he yelled.

Finally, the monster let go.

Thaylus dragged himself onto a dry patch of dead grass.

He stumbled to his feet.

But just as he did, the monster burst forth over the edge of the swamp and wrapped around Thaylus's torso.

With a violent yank, it pulled him beneath the swamp waters.

Thaylus struggled and writhed. But every move pulled him deeper.

He felt his lungs would explode.

Then, Thaylus remembered.

Tensing his hand, he felt the Sword of the Spirit in his grasp.

He stabbed the monster near its mouth. A muffled scream came from it.

Then with a mighty swipe, Thaylus sliced the creature in half.

Thaylus flailed his limbs as he swam for the surface.

He emerged, gulping a breath of air.

Grabbing a vine, pulled his way onto the ground, coughing.

An exhausted smile covered his face. He had slain the monster.

Giant vultures circled in the sky. They screeched.

The sound sent a chill down Thaylus's spine.

"Well, that is encouraging," he said, "but I am not dead yet."

He rose and wiped off as much muck as he could and walked on.

The terrain remained the same as he went. The putrid smell made him cover his face with his collar, and the blazing sun beat down upon him.

Thaylus came to a ruinous dome. A chimney gave off smoke.

Another person! He would be glad for any human company. But was this individual friendly?

Thaylus would risk it. He would be a formidable foe with his flashing weapon if the person was hostile.

"Hello? Is anyone here?"

A tall man in dirt-blotched armor that had a tinge of rust dashed out. He smiled and ran towards Thaylus.

"Thank God! I thought I would die all alone here!" said the man.

"Who are you?"

"I am Crom, a knight of the kingdom of Nephelous. I have been searching for the legendary Tower of Brea."

Thaylus's heart jumped. The Tower of Brea had passed from existence by Thaylus's time. The wisest men to have lived were said to have built it to house the largest collection of texts ever constructed. It was said to hold books and scrolls that were one of a kind.

"How far away is it?" asked Thaylus.

"If I knew, I would tell you. I have been wondering the land of Brea for ... I do not know how long. Why are you here?"

What else could he do? He would be blunt.

"I have been sent on a quest north from Evercrest. "I have been sent by a Celestial Servant. I believe I am meant to go to the Tower of Brea."

Thaylus brandished the burning blade of the Spirit.

Crom's eyes widened and he stepped back.

The sword vanished.

"My word! How can I not believe you!"

"Will you accompany me?"

Crom lifted his chain mail, and a deep gash showed a green tint.

"I have a sore infection after a harpy attacked me. It was a grievous fight, but I slayed it at the end."

If only the faith that Ithia passed on would empower him to heal Crom's lethal gash. But a miracle had not happened in a while. Had the Vessel Bearer abandoned him?

It did not matter.

Thaylus looked down. "I am sorry my, friend. I cannot stay with you, but how can I leave you, either?"

"Don't concern yourself with me. Go to the tower on your own. I can barely go a few meters without stopping to rest. And I am in so much pain. Every day it gets worse."

"I wish could do something."

"There is something. My desire was to not to die alone. Please, put me out of my misery."

"I ... I can't."

Crom's eyes filled with tears.

"I am in terrible pain, and I am dead as it is. I beg you!"

Crom walked into the dome and retrieved a long double-edged sword.

He held out the blade for Thaylus to take.

Thaylus took a deep breath. "Is this what you truly want?"

"It is."

Thaylus trembled. He raised the sword, but then stopped.

"I can't do it. I—I can't strike a man down."

"Then I will die a slow and unbearable demise."

Thaylus inched his hand to the hilt. As he grasped it, a cold feeling went through his body. He didn't know the man, but Thaylus felt deeply for him.

Crom fell to his knees and closed his eyes, breathing heavily.

Thaylus raised the sword in a sweat. He clenched his teeth.

The thought of Crom's blood being poured onto the ground made him nauseous. He had killed before, but not like this. Would this make him a murderer? Was this morally wrong?

Thaylus dropped the sword with a clatter. "I cannot!"

Crom picked up his blade and held it pointed at his stomach. He stood.

"No!" Thaylus cried.

Crom fell forward and pierced his gut.

Blood spilled out, and Thaylus reeled back, covering his mouth.

The wounded man toppled to his side. He gasped, then breathed his last.

Crom had acted bravely, Thaylus understood. He seemed to hold no fear of death.

Thaylus wished he'd known him better.

The gore sickened him, but he slid the sword out of Crom's corpse and dragged his body inside the dome. Finding a stone shelf about six feet long, Thaylus heaved the body upon it.

Thaylus shed a tear when he finished. He closed Crom's eyes and rose.

"May whatever god that might be receive you."

Thaylus walked on, not knowing where the Tower of Brea lay.

With every step the terrain offered nothing but the same decrepit state.

Finally up ahead, something large and black stirred on top of a tall hill. It felt familiar. The figure evoked a fearful, heart-racing tension.

As he climbed, Thaylus stopped, a bead of sweat trickling down his temple.

More sweat came as the black figure reared a dragon's head.

"We meet again, Thaylus." It was the Dragon of the Abyss. "I am surprised you risked so much to come here. Have you come to slay me?"

"I seek the Tower Brea. I did not know you were here."

"I cannot allow you to go there." The dragon crouched and bared his scythe-like teeth.

It leapt forth with an open mouth.

Thaylus jumped to the right, landing on his side.

The beast turned its head and roared.

"You are helpless without your magic lance!"

"Not quite, wretched beast." Thaylus stretched forth his hand, and the Sword of the Spirit appeared.

The dragon reeled back, shrieking at the brightens of the holy weapon.

It backed away and clenched its teeth. "What manner of power is this?"

"Power enough to kill you where you stand. Yield, and I will spare you."

"Never!"

A spiky tail swung around to hit Thaylus, but he cut it off with a swift swipe. Blood sprayed everywhere as the tail writhed to and fro.

"I will not be overcome by a mere human!" the dragon bellowed.

The dragon charged at Thaylus and made a pounce to crush him with his enormous, clawed foot.

The sage pierced it as it came over him.

The dragon lurched back and sneered. "Blasted fool!"

But the dragon was losing blood and teetered like a drunkard. Its huge body fell over.

Thaylus darted close and pointed the sword at its belly. "Why are you here? Has someone sent you?"

"Kill me! I will say nothing."

"Then you shall face torture."

The blood disturbed Thaylus, but he had no pity for this evil creature. Thaylus touched the stomach with the fiery blade.

Finally, the dragon conceded. "A Celestial Servant sent me to keep you from the Book of Realms at the top of the tower," he said, panting.

"It cannot be a Celestial Servant. I have seen them. They are righteous beings who are benevolent. And how did the Book of Realms get to the tower? How are these two things so!"

"So that you do not go to his secret realm."

"What is this realm called? Why does he keep it secret?"

But the dragon's eyes rolled up, and his body stilled.

Thaylus's mind raced. The Book of Realms had been destroyed in the collapse of Durath's Keep, along with Durath himself. So how did the book get to the tower?

Thaylus knew why he had been told to go north—he knew he needed to go to the Tower of Brea.

Beyond the dragon, at the top of tall hill, Thaylus could now see what looked to be a white tower. The Tower of Brea, surely.

He walked on, wondering what his new quest had in store.

# Chapter 22

## The Tower of Brea

The walk to the Tower of Brea proved simpler than the travel so far. The land surrounding the tower was a circle of dry, cracked plain. Heat from the sun and the terrain caused a dreary, faintness within Thaylus, and he realized he not had not eaten or drank in many hours.

Thaylus drooped over as he breathed through his mouth. His face dripped with sweat. Time slowed to a crawl in the inferno. Loneliness afflicted his heart.

At last, Thaylus stepped into the shadow of the tower. It was near twilight. The height of it made him hesitate. For a moment, he thought of forsaking the mission he had been sent on.

Thaylus felt relief when he reached the wall; the long walk had ended. But relief turned to dejection as he realized the only way to the top would be stairs.

The tower stood like a stone giant. Yet Thaylus felt faint and sleepy.

He circled the tower and found double doors.

He went in, and the doors slammed shut. He jerked around but saw no one.

Thaylus trembled—the place was enchanted or cursed.

He saw no stairs. He fell to his knees and sighed at the coolness of the tower.

He wondered what to do next.

Turning around, Thaylus saw a fountain lay before him.

The fact that it had appeared from nowhere did not faze him. He did not consider whether the fountain was a magical illusion or a mirage.

His only thought was of a thirst that overwhelmed him.

Thaylus went to the edge of the fountain and gulped down water so fast he coughed.

"It is the best water I have ever tasted," Thaylus murmured to himself.

A shriek echoed in the chamber. It sounded like the scream of a man getting a limb cut off.

The cry came again.

Thaylus jumped up, his eyes darting everywhere. A chill passed through his body as something invisible brushed by him.

He turned.

Nothing.

"Where are you?"

Yet he knew some entity lurked with him in this room.

Spirits were said to inhabit Brea. From what he was experiencing, it appeared it was true.

With no stairs and the doors seemingly barred to his exit, Thaylus paced the room. He ran his fingers along the wall, feeling the coolness, and pulled at his beard.

"What do I do next?" he whispered.

With a thundering crash, a block of stone fell inches from him.

Above, a transparent, haggardly female figure stood.

"Who drinks from the Waters of the Abyssal Fountain?" she screamed.

Thaylus covered his ears.

"I am Thaylus. I have traveled far, and I was desperate in my thirst."

The ghost-like figure glared at him from above, bearing fingernails three inches long.

"The water you have drunk has made your body and soul vulnerable to the power of the Abyss."

At her words, Thaylus narrowed his eyes and summoned his flaming sword.

"Yield. You have no chance."

"I am spirit of the Tower of Brea," the ghostly woman shrieked again. "I will do you no harm. Hostile beings await you. It is them you must fight."

"How do I ascend the tower? There are no stairs."

The spirit laughed with a high-pitched rasp that sounded like a taunt. It echoed then faded.

Thaylus paced the room with his head down.

In the center of the chamber, a round insignia of a three-headed dragon caught Thaylus's eye. It was the emblem of Kyrious, the sorcerer king of the Western Kingdom.

Thaylus stepped closer and examined it.

As he did, the round platform vibrated, jostling Thaylus. Then it began to rise, higher and higher, through an opening in the ceiling.

The platform stopped. Thaylus froze—would it fall or rise higher?

But it seemed to hold steady.

Thaylus peered around. The platform had brought him to a new level of the tower.

Shelves filled with books lay everywhere.

If he'd had the energy, Thaylus would have run to them, but his fatigue and dejection allowed a slow trudge. He walked to the books, kneeling.

Thaylus picked out a book, forgetting himself.

How amazing, he thought. It tells of the first wars of Khrine.

Nothing in all the realm of his time went back in history as far as the book in his hands.

After a few minutes, his thinking cleared. Where could the Book of Realms be?

A tall bookshelf to his left interested him. It was secluded behind an entire section of the curved wall.

Thaylus slid a book from the shelf. It referred to the Gate of Vessels.

"The Emissary shall rule on behalf of the Lord of the Gate of Vessels," he read, opening a page at random.

Who could this "emissary" be? He'd heard the term before, but he still had no idea what it meant or who it might refer to. Thaylus knew only of Vessel Bearers, Celestial Servants, and the lord within the Gate of Vessels.

His body tensed.

Suddenly, he sensed a fearful presence in the room.

The presence became stronger as he saw something like smoke and fog gathering into standing pillars.

Three dark, man-like figures took form before him. Their burning red eyes looked like smoldering coals. Each figure bore a sword of black fire.

Realm Dwellers! But how did they get to the realm of Khrine?

Thaylus swallowed. Of course—he had drunk from the water from the fountain, as the ghostly woman had said. Now he was susceptible to them.

Thaylus remained stalwart and coy. He had the Sword of the Spirit. Perhaps this was the reason he'd been given the holy weapon.

With a flash of light, the sword appeared in his hand.

The three figures backed away.

Thaylus heart swelled—they feared him!

He lunged at the one in the center with his blade over his head and came down hard upon the Realm Dweller. It blocked the attack, making a deadlock.

Thaylus could feel the burning in his muscles as he bore his sword against the other.

"You wield the weapon of light. But the power of darkness is greater," said the one holding his sword against Thaylus's own.

"Your manipulations will do nothing. Darkness flees in the presence of light!" He did not know where his words came from, but he believed them.

Thaylus shoved his foe back.

The dark being's eyes burned stronger. It cried out and swung its sword to the right.

This time, Thaylus ducked and thrust his shining blade into the Realm Dweller's chest.

The punctured Realm Dweller fell to the ground, howling. Its body blew away like a pile of ash being carried off in the wind.

Thaylus took a deep breath and took a steady stance. One Realm Dweller remained in front while the other circled behind Thaylus.

Thaylus attacked the one in front with a diagonal sword strike.

His foe matched his move.

Thaylus glanced behind to see the dark being twirl its blade, making a whirlpool. It ebbed closer from behind.

The one in front fought to push Thaylus into the spinning attack at his back.

"Despite what you are, you fight two against one—cowards!" he taunted.

"Honor means nothing," said the one before Thaylus. "Victory is the only thing."

Thaylus ducked and made a three-hundred-and-sixty-degree swing, knocking the being's sword out of its hand.

It backed off.

Then Thaylus turned to face the spinning blade behind him. "Come at me, abomination!"

A wave of tension shot through Thaylus's body.

As he watched in horror, four more Realm Dwellers took shape, spaced evenly side-by-side in front of Thaylus.

They closed in on him.

He jolted to the right, into a row of bookshelves. Stumbling over his feet, he went right and then right again, reaching a dead end.

At least he could not be surrounded.

Thaylus fell to his knees, trying to catch his breath. Despite the Sword of the Spirit, he was one man. How could he win? What if more kept coming? If he didn't die from the Realm Dwellers, fatigue would subdue him.

He collapsed against a shelf behind him.

As he fell, a book fell with him, opening.

A passage in Pyrithian jumped out at him: Greater is He who is in us is than he who is in the world.

Thaylus wondered at that. And suddenly, it was like a light had been lit. He understood what it meant. How could it be anyone else?

It was the spiritual being in the Gate of Vessels. And perhaps "he who is in the world" could be the Realm Dwellers.

While Thaylus still remained unconvinced the former was a deity, he felt a spiritual power and a peace inside, nonetheless.

He rose and grasped the sword. Its brightness grew three-fold. Thaylus felt like the flame of the sword flowed through his body.

"You come at me with the power of darkness, but I come with the power of celestial light," he said to the Realm Dwellers.

He strode forth and struck down a Realm Dweller. Its body dissipated like the previous one.

Thaylus swung his sword again with a war cry as he charged for the group of foes.

They scattered. The six remaining Realm Dwellers kept away.

Thaylus selected one and sprinted to it, sword pointing. When he was inches from the Realm Dweller, the creature vanished.

One after another, so did the rest. The enemy had retreated.

Thaylus stood still and firm, with not so much as a tremble or a racing heart. His body was relaxed and his mind clear of any menacing thoughts. Never had he felt such power.

Thaylus lifted the shining, fiery blade above him in triumph. He released his grip, and the sword vanished.

Lifting his chin, Thaylus stepped onto the platform, and it lifted him into the air, bearing him up to the next floor.

There, a pillar of fire rose before him. Thaylus backed away and held his arm up to his eyes.

The pillar of fire burned as Thaylus summoned the Sword of the Spirit.

Then it spun like a tornado. The pillar turned purple and dwindled to a thin funnel of light and disappeared, revealing a cloaked figure in a mantle.

Thaylus widened his eyes and shook his head. What he saw made him shiver—he stared at an apparition of himself!

It appeared like a living mirror.

Thaylus lunged at it with his bright weapon.

The evil rendition of the sage called forth a duplicate weapon. A sound like thunder came with the sword clash.

The doppelganger sneered.

"My master's power rivals yours now. Stop struggling, sage, and give up!"

"Never!"

How could evil conjure a weapon like the Sword of the Spirit? Who was this person? He had to be a sorcerer.

"Who are you?" Thaylus cried.

"I am a being of great power and a messenger of doom."

"Who sent you?"

The shapeshifter disappeared.

Thaylus turned about, looking everywhere, but none filled the chamber.

The being laughed, its voice echoing around the room.

"The master of Aderath is superior to you!"

The changeling swung for Thaylus's neck, grazing his skin.

Thaylus jabbed with a return stroke to its torso, but it stepped back just in time.

"What is Aderath?" Thaylus demanded.

"Silence!"

The assailant thrust his palm forward.

Thaylus flew back against the wall.

"Ack!" he uttered.

With a leap, his foe torpedoed through the air with sword tip pointed at Thaylus, fully intent on impaling him against the wall.

Thaylus struck sideways against the foe's sword, sending him reeling.

Thaylus came down on his foe, but he put up his blade to block the attack. Another deadlock came.

This time, Thaylus had the upper hand as he bore his blade against the wizard, who was forced to his knees.

"Enough!" said the shapeshifter.

His body erupted with a blinding white flash of light. In place of the doppelganger, a Vessel Bearer-like being manifested.

"I do not care if my true nature and identity is revealed," the creature howled. "I will now summon my true power!"

"In fighting me you have betrayed your fellow Vessel Bearers, and the being you serve!" Thaylus said, his sword raised.

"I now serve the Celestial Baron."

Celestial Baron? Thaylus never heard of this kind of spiritual being. He also did not know what or where Aderath was. Thaylus wondered if this being knew of the Book of Realms. He had to.

"Where is the Book of Realms?" Thaylus asked.

"I will never let you reach it!"

The hostile Vessel Bearer took out a golden bow next and shot a flaming arrow at Thaylus.

Thaylus held up the sword and parried away the aerial attack. But the force of the attack drained him. If only the faith of Ithia would come upon him.

The shining entity shot another a flaming arrow, then another. This one struck Thaylus's sword.

Thaylus stumbled back and fell to one knee. He groaned as his aching body struggled to rise.

He could not.

"I will enjoy taking your spiritual vessel from the Plains of Eternity!"

"You are the one! The Celestial Servant Atrophies told me about someone stealing them. Why?"

"No more talking!"

The shining being stretched forth his hand and grabbed Thaylus, clutching his forehead.

It felt like his whole being was being grasped and lifted into the air.

Thaylus saw he was now in the Plains of Eternity. Up and up he went, the clutch around his forehead like a vice.

But his struggle was fierce. The foe's grasp abated, and Thaylus found himself once more back in the Tower of Brea.

Beside him, he saw the nefarious Vessel Bearer wrestle with another, a glowing spirit who appeared suddenly and was now pinned to the floor.

"Thaylus, take out your sword!" cried the glowing spirit.

The spirit took a silver chain and bound the evil being's torso.

"Strike him, now!" he begged Thaylus.

Thaylus brought down his sword upon the immobilized foe.

The foe shrieked, and his body faded like a dying star.

"Well done, Thaylus." The spirit rose before him. "I am the Vessel Bearer Cortan."

"I know of you! You gave a vision of the future to a man named Mordecai."

"Yes. From the words of that being you just destroyed, we now know about the being that calls himself a Celestial Baron. Aderath is one spiritual realm among hundreds."

"What was this being?" Thaylus gestured to where his evil foe had just faded away.

"He was a Celestial Acolyte. They are former Vessel Bearers, and they have been seen escaping through portals with the stolen vessels."

"What do I do now? And how do I find the Book of Realms?"

"To get to the top, you must battle a magical beast of evil more powerful than the Dragon of the Abyss."

Thaylus quivered at Cortan's words. What kind of beast could rival the dragon?

Then he remembered the newfound strength from the words of the book that had fallen beside him. Greater is He who is in us is than he who is in the world.

Cortan grabbed Thaylus's hand.

They flew upwards through the ceiling like ghosts and reached an open-air pinnacle.

There they stood in physical form.

Cortan put a hand on Thaylus.

"I leave you now. When you find the Book of Realms, go to Aderath. God is with you, even if you feel you are not with Him."

With that, Cortan ascended into the air and disappeared.

Thaylus heart thudded hot and thick. When would this terrible beast appear? And how hard would the battle be?

Thaylus summoned the sword, but no sign of any creature appeared on the tower top.

The floor beneath his feet began to vibrate with a low rumble. Thaylus felt like the tower would fall.

Then with a terrible clash, a gigantic dragon-like claw gripped the tower ledge. Another followed.

The beast's appearance came into full view as it planted six dragon's legs on the tower surface.

Unlike the Dragon of the Abyss, this beast did not possess all the extremities of a dragon. Its legs joined to a scorpion's back, supporting three long hairy necks, each ending with a different head. The center head resembled that of a hawk. The one on its left looked like a serpent, and the one to the right was like a spider's head with long, curved mandibles.

On its chest a small, bonelike protrusion glowed like an emerald. A long tail like a centipede was at its rear.

The abomination spoke, the three heads all in unison.

"Why have you come here, man creature?"

"I have come to slay you and take the Book of Realms!"

"None can slay me. I am the great Dracmire, and I have killed many brave warriors from the period of my conception all over the realm of Khrine," it cried. "Your blazing weapon must be powerful, but I will crush you like all the rest."

The Dracmire screamed with its hawk head, causing a stinging pain in Thaylus's ears.

The creature stood up on its back legs and came down on its front four with a mighty thwack.

The ground trembled and cracked.

Venom dripped from the mandibles of its spider head. The head hissed and lunged for Thaylus.

Thaylus held up the sword to block the attack, but the mandibles gripped the Sword of the Spirit and flung it away, toward the edge of the tower, where it teetered.

"You are at my mercy," the spider-head said. "I could kill you now, but I will have sport with you."

Thaylus's heart beat like the steps of a rampaging buffalo. Surely his end had come. He had failed his mission.

Khrine was doomed.

The Dracmire swung his tail around, this time grasping Thaylus with his pinchers. He lifted Thaylus up to his serpentine head.

The head licked the sage's face with its tongue, then slowly wrapped the tongue around his torso.

The center hawk reared its head point-blank in front of Thaylus.

"I could peck off your head, but that would end the fun." Dracmire laughed.

In a flash, the serpent's head loosed its tongue on Thaylus, and he fell twelve feet, flat on his back.

Thaylus longed for his weapon. How could he reach it?

"Your god has been stopped," the Dracmire kept taunting. "Soon this whole world will be overrun by the Celestial Baron's forces."

A sharp blow to Thaylus's right hip came from the side of the hawk's beak.

Thaylus felt one of his ribs snap.

The Dracmire pierced his shoulder with his sharp claw and twisted it around.

"Just finish me off!" Thaylus cried out.

"There will be a time for that. First I want you to curse the god of the Gate of Vessels."

Thaylus spoke though grunts and cringed teeth.

"I believe in no god. I only acknowledge that this is just a powerful spiritual being."

"A wise surmising. He might as well be."

Thaylus lay dying. As his spirit ebbed, he wondered what would ensue after his death. Would his spiritual vessel be brought inside the Gate of Vessels? Would he see and somehow know this great lord?

He felt the essence of faith begin to glow in his heart. It was not a power, knowledge, or a holy object.

It just … was.

He felt his wounds heal and his broken bones click together.

An idea filled his head. He closed his eyes and held his breath, playing dead.

The beast nudged Thaylus. His body slumped over.

"A pity. I was having fun." The Dracmire chuckled, and he turned away.

Thaylus cracked his eyes. The Sword of the Spirit lay twelve feet away from him.

Drawing a breath, he inched to his feet and to the edge of the tower, picking up the sword. He planned to attack from the beast's rear than go for the jewel in its chest.

With a wild swing, Thaylus severed the pincher appendage.

The monster turned around, all eyes glowing red.

Thaylus knew he had to hit the emerald before the beast healed.

The Dracmire struck with its serpentine head. But its fangs missed its target and the monster's snout merely bumped Thaylus, knocking the wind out of him.

Thaylus stumbled but stood firm with his flaming sword.

He gathered all his might and charged at the emerald in the chest. He sprinted like lightning below the beast's line of sight.

With a swift, deep thrust of Thaylus's flaming sword, the emerald cracked.

He thrust the sword, boring farther inside the jewel.

The beast fell to its side, writhing and screaming.

"If I die, you will die with me!" said the beast.

With its front legs, the Dracmire gripped the cracked jewel in its chest and ripped it out. From its front torso, an eruption of green fire sent Thaylus flying back, sliding towards the edge.

Thaylus grasped the sword as he slid and staked it into the stone surface, dangling over the edge. He hung from the sword as the massive green flames passed above him.

He felt the heat, and his arms were aching. He hoped it would stop within seconds—that was all he could hold on for.

A burst of fire came, then stopped. The creature shrieked in agony and a loud explosion ensued as flaming parts of its body parts went flying.

Thaylus gasped. He could not pull himself up from the ledge.

He grunted as his grip slid from the hilt.

He lost hold of the sword handle.

But as he fell, a flash of light burst around him, and a shining arm caught him.

The arm pulled him up.

Before him stood a male being like a Vessel Bearer, but he had no wings. The shining man felt familiar. Who could he be?

Thaylus prostrated himself before the being. "Thank you for saving me."

The shining man pulled Thaylus up to his feet. "I am not to be worshiped. I am a created being like you. Instead, we worship the God of the Gate of Vessels."

"Who are you?"

"It is I, your companion Brythan."

"Brythan? How can this be?"

"My spiritual urn has been accepted into the Gate of Vessels, and my body has been transformed."

Thaylus wanted to laugh out loud. "By far this is most exceptional thing I have seen! Brythan, what is inside the Gate of Vessels? What does the ruling being look like? Your face is like Brythan but more childlike ... and your eyes! They glisten like a sun-struck lake! And your hair is white. Will I have a body like yours when I die?"

Thaylus's mind was racing with questions.

"I do not know. I have been sent back to the Realm of Khrine to aid you as you go to the realm of Aderath."

Thaylus caught his breath, staggered at what he was experiencing.

"Where is the Book of Realms?" Thaylus finally asked.

The metamorphosed Brythan walked to a golden platform in the center of the tower surface.

"Come here, Thaylus."

Thaylus did so and looked at the platform at his feet. A long groove with illustrated flames surrounded it.

In an instant, he knew what had to be done.

Thaylus plunged his sword into the slit, and a golden pedestal rose from the ground.

On it, a large book with a golden dove on the cover lay on the pedestal.

"Is this it?"

Brythan nodded.

Thaylus opened the book. A plethora of strange names were on its pages. They had to be names of realms.

Thaylus looked at the book in his hands.

"How do I go to Aderath?"

Brythan nodded. "Speak the incantation under where Aderath is written."

The pages turned to the place bearing the name Aderath.

Thaylus had a strange inclination to touch the page. It felt something was calling to him from within the book, like how the diamond of time travel in the realm of Earth had beckoned to him.

The sage inched his hand over the book and touched it.

As he did, his mind was filled with images and odd words. It felt like he was in a dream, both peaceful and mystifying.

Aloud, Thaylus recited the words in the book.

A blue portal appeared.

Thaylus grinned at his friend, tears welling. "This reminds me of the good old days, Brythan."

Brythan laughed. "We have been through our share of portals."

Thaylus looked down then, his shoulders drooping with sorrow.

"Is this where we part?"

But Brythan smiled broadly and put his hands on Thaylus's arms.

"You will be happy to know I will tarry with you for a further mission."

Thaylus's eyes and face lit up, and he lifted his arms to embrace Brythan.

Brythan put up his palm. "Do not touch me," he warned. "My spiritual body would harm you."

Thaylus backed away. "I see. Brythan, why did you leave me?"

"There is a time to live and a time to die, Thaylus. My time came. It is that simple."

Thaylus put a hand to his head.

"I do not understand but I will take your word for it."

Then he shook himself and broke into a smile. "Shall we go?"

Brythan nodded, and he and his friend walked side-by-side into the portal.

# Chapter 23

## The Realm of Aderath

Thaylus and Brythan stood on the wall of a small partially collapsed castle. A precipice lay behind them. Instead of darkness, ribbons of red and blue shone out of it.

Thaylus was awestruck. "This place is more amazing than the Plains of Eternity!"

Aderath did not have any sun. It was lit by a dim, soft, glow from three blue stars.

"It is strange that an evil being, who has opposed a supreme being of light lives in such a heavenly place."

Brythan nodded. "Every realm and being is given all power and appearance form God, although the Celestial Baron abuses it."

Thaylus peered out. "What are all these Vessel Bearers doing here?"

"These are servants of the Celestial Baron. They have abandoned their role in the Plains of Eternity and are no longer worthy of the title."

"Then what are they?"

"They are called Celestial Acolytes. They are named after their rebellious master."

Dozens of Celestial Acolytes entered in and out of portals located touching the ground or suspended high in the air. Castle-like structures stretched across the terrain, while others appeared to float in the sky. Networks of bridges and stairs connected them together.

Far off, an immense castle stronghold rose above a mammoth wall taller than the Tower of Brea.

A plain filled with cracks and fissures that emitted a blue glow stretched for miles.

"Is the Celestial Baron behind that huge wall?" asked Thaylus.

"I'm not sure. I have never been to this realm. But I believe we will find him there."

In a flash, light erupted around Brythan and he reverted to his original body. "My spiritual form would attract attention."

Thaylus eyed Brythan carefully. "What other abilities do you have? I wonder if you could summon fire from the sky!"

"I am not that powerful." Brythan laughed. "Only God could do that."

Thaylus frowned. "Why do you glorify this 'god?' How do you know he is truly supreme?"

"Oh, Thaylus. When you step into the Lord's presence, you will know."

Thaylus did not know how to respond so he stayed quiet.

The two walked along the top of the wall to a set of cracked steps going down, the wall to their left. They reached the ground and found the terrain was soft soil.

They walked on, and two portals opened, one Acolyte coming out of each. Both held vessels.

"How did you man creatures get here!" asked the one on the right.

Brythan turned to Thaylus. "We must destroy them before they alert more!"

Thaylus brandished his shining, fiery sword.

Alongside him, Brythan produced one much like it.

"I should have expected as much." Thaylus eyed Brythan's blade.

Rather than brandishing weapons, the Celestial Acolytes clasped their hand together. Lightning resonated around them.

"Thaylus, hold up your sword!" Brythan cried.

A blast of lightening from the hands of the Acolyte struck Thaylus's sword, pushing him a few feet back.

Brythan gripped his sword with both hands. A beam of light shot from his sword point at the evil being's chest, but it blocked it with a right palm.

The Celestial Acolyte continued to resist the steady stream of light.

"They should not be this strong," Brythan said. "Something has increased their power!"

The Acolyte chuckled.

"Our mighty ruler has granted us with abilities unimagined."

The being rushed at Brythan, breaking off the beam lock. It grasped Brythan's neck and lifted him up. The sword tumbled to the ground.

"Brythan!" Thaylus cried. "Use your other form!"

Brythan kicked his legs and his face turned red as he dangled in the air.

Why didn't Brythan transform? Desperate, Thaylus threw his sword at the Acolyte.

It jarred him, and the being dropped Brythan.

Thaylus ran to his friend. "What happened? Are you all right?"

Brythan struggled to breathe as he coughed and clutched his neck.

"I … couldn't … change form. I don't know how to beat them!"

The Celestial Acolytes laughed. "See how your God is so weak?"

They fluttered towards the two men.

"I fear for you, Thaylus. If I die in this form, my vessel will be brought back into the Gate of Vessels. But yours…"

"What will happen to mine?" Thaylus swallowed.

"Yours will stay on the Plains of Eternity for all time."

The evil beings ebbed closer, putting their arms up. A ball of red fire coalesced between them.

Thaylus could feel the heat. "How do I change that? Is there any way?"

"Believe who He is!"

"I … I can't! I can't change what is!"

"You must!"

The heat from the sphere increased, and the Acolytes cornered them against a wall.

Thaylus dug deep within his soul and grappled for any faith he might possess. He could not ignore his disbelief, but he knew there had to be a real God. Was this great spiritual being inside the Gate of Vessels a real deity all along?

The possibility roused him.

Thaylus looked to the sky and prayed aloud.

"I put my trust in the God that be!" Thaylus shouted. "If it is He within the Gate of Vessels, so be it!"

He'd never felt such desperation and anguish. The core of his grand dilemma, a real God, had been ripped free and lay before him, raw and open. He stood on the edge—of either epiphany or madness, he did not know.

But what else could he do? He would believe.

Thaylus's back pressed against the wall as the ball of fire drew nearer.

Forgive me, Great God. I have failed completely. His head sank as the magnitude of all of it snaked over him.

The thought had barely formed when Thaylus body released a thrust of fiery wind. It was like a hurricane or a cyclone of heat, pushing back the Celestial Acolytes.

Their sphere of fire flickered and dissipated like a snuffed candle flame.

And in its place, a warm, steady glow of something new—true faith—burned within Thaylus's heart.

"Thaylus, you did it! I feel the power of true faith about you!"

Thaylus fell to his knees and smiled, tears flowing down his cheeks.

He knew a God existed—and that God dwelled inside the Gate of Vessels. Contentment filled his heart.

He tucked it all aside. There was something else there, some other thought or doubt, but he pushed it away for now.

They had a task to complete.

Before them, the Celestial Acolytes took out swords.

With a mighty roar, they rushed at Thaylus.

But Thaylus stood strong. He took out his spiritual weapon, the powerful Sword of the Spirit. It flickered like lightning. For a moment, Thaylus felt like he had an impervious, mighty body, as if his body were one with the sword.

Thaylus charged at the two foes as they came at him. Their swords clashed against Thaylus's. A thunderclap echoed as sparks and smoke came from the collision of weapons.

"Your treachery will end in death!" Thaylus gritted his teeth and drove back the Acolytes.

Breaking free, Thaylus whirled and struck down the one to his left. It wound erupted with a white light that consumed the Acolyte in an instant.

The remaining one dropped his sword and fell to his knees in terror.

"Please! Spare me!" it begged.

"How do we get inside the stronghold?" Thaylus demanded, his blade at the being's neck.

It stretched forth its hands, cupped them, and opened them to reveal an orb, much like a large pearl. It was larger than Clara's, and it glowed a blood-crimson.

"This orb will point the way," the Acolyte said.

Thaylus took it.

Then he paused. "Brythan, what do we do with him? We cannot tie him up and hide him, and it would be inhuman to kill a living soul who has surrendered. He asked us for mercy and has given us the orb."

"Celestial beings exist under different law than men. Destroying him would transgress no moral code, even for you."

Brythan had to know more about mercy and justice than he did, Thaylus reasoned, being a spiritual being himself.

Brythan brandished his sword above his head.

"Please! I will tell no one about your presence!" the Acolyte cried.

The nobleman refused to listen. He slashed a vertical slice down the Acolyte's chest, creating a strip of glowing white light.

He cried out once more, and the wound widened until it consumed his body.

The Acolyte was gone.

Thaylus blinked a few times and looked at his hands. "That power and peace I felt. I cannot believe what happened. I feel so … different."

"Your heart is changed."

"How?"

Brythan chuckled and put a hand on Thaylus's shoulder. "Deep down, I think you know."

Thaylus did not know how it had happened. But something was altered within him. His dying thoughts saved him.

He could not recall the state of mind that had come over him as he'd made that last thought. But Thaylus knew he had made a spiritual stride. He wished he could relive the moment and retain it.

"Come, we have a mission," Brythan said.

Thaylus took a deep breath. "Let us go."

He held up the orb, and a glistening, diamond edge in the orb pointed the way.

The two ran quietly across the soft soil.

Soon they came to a green, marble bridge that arched over a dark pool. Its still, placid water shined like a smooth onyx stone.

On the other side, they came to a tall wall.

They went left along the wall and rounded the side.

There, two portals appeared.

"Hide!" Brythan breathed.

Thaylus and Brythan jerked behind the wall, peering just enough to avoid notice.

"Two Celestial Acolytes have emerged, both with vessels," Brythan whispered.

"Can you tell their direction?" said Thaylus.

"They approach our position coming from overhead. We must hide!"

"Hide where?"

Brythan pointed to the pool. "Into the water. But leave the orb on the ground."

"It could be freezing!"

Brythan put a hand on Thaylus's shoulder. "It will only be seconds. We must go."

Thaylus set the orb at the water's edge.

Then they plunged into icy water.

A shock wave ripped through Thaylus. The water stung like he'd been rolled over a cactus grove.

Thaylus looked through the water's surface at the two Acolytes above him. They'd stopped in the middle of their flight. Why?

Thaylus's lungs were burning. He had to breathe. He ached for them to pass over them.

Why did they float in midair?

Any longer and he'd faint. He had to have air now!

Thaylus swam up to the surface, but Brythan grabbed Thaylus's arm. He turned Thaylus around, clutching him by the neck.

Thaylus kicked and flailed his arms. He exhaled, and a bubble went to the surface.

This time, he elbowed Brythan in his stomach, and Brythan released him.

Thaylus swam up farther, but Brythan held his feet.

With his last effort, Thaylus exhaled the rest of his air, gulping in a measure of water on reflex. His insides trembled and grew cold and still.

A moment later, the Acolytes moved on past the pool.

Thaylus was limp as Brythan dragged him beneath his arms to the surface. Brythan pulled him to the edge of the pool and onto the soft ground.

Thaylus's eyes were still as death.

Brythan yanked him upright and turned his body to the side, draining out the water in his lungs. He smacked Thaylus on the back to force the rest of the water out.

Thaylus slumped against him.

"Thaylus, stay with me! Spit it up!"

Brythan held his head against his friend's chest. He had no heartbeat.

"Thaylus, no!" Brythan sobbed, his arms cradling Thaylus's head.

Brythan closed his eyes. "Oh, Creator of my Soul, the One Who dwells inside the Gate of Vessels, spare this man, though he has not fully come to you."

Brythan gazed up at the sky fervently, as though he looked at the Gate of Vessels itself, pleading with God to save Thaylus.

Minutes passed, and no sign of life occurred.

Brythan wiped his eyes and stood.

"Oh great One, Your will be done whatever the situation," he murmured.

Brythan swam to the edge of the pool, where he retrieved the orb. Gathering his legs beneath him, he stood on the damp ground.

He looked at Thaylus's body for a long moment, and finally turned around to leave.

Then, a sound!

A gargling cough!

He jerked around to see Thaylus, coughing hard and leaning on his side. Water came out of him, and his body trembled with cold.

"Thaylus!"

Brythan wept as he helped Thaylus to his knees. More water gushed from his mouth.

"Brythan, I was there," Thaylus gasped. "The Plains of Eternity! I beheld my spiritual vessel. It sat on a rocky plain. Others retained a dull, rusty appearance. They must have been there for hundreds of years. I felt so alone. But then a Vessel Bearer came from the sky and touched my vessel. Suddenly I found myself back in Aderath."

Brythan held his friends until his sobs stopped.

"You have been shown great mercy, Thaylus. Count yourself blessed."

There was no denying it—Thaylus had been helped. Brythan was certain it had been the supreme being inside the Gate of Vessels working through a Vessel Bearer.

For his part, Thaylus did not know who or what had happened. Things were still confusing and obscure. He would wait longer to make a final judgement.

And they had a job to do.

Thaylus and Brythan crept along walls and under domes, arches, and any kind of roofed structure to avoid being seen from the Celestial Acolytes above.

Eventually, they came to a green marbled corridor lined with torches.

A silver door lay at the other end.

The two stopped in front of it.

"What could be on the other side?" Brythan asked.

"I do not see any lock."

Thaylus pulled the door open by a handle, and a bright azure light glowed in the doorway. "I think this is an entryway to another realm."

Thaylus put his hand in the light.

"It's warm."

Brythan furrowed his brows. "It would be wise to be leery of danger like we have with all portals. Summon your sword, Thaylus."

Brythan now donned his spiritual form of shining light.

"This form should give ample defense against any foe we may confront."

Thaylus stretched forth his hand, and the Sword of the Spirit appeared in his grasp. He and Brythan went through with their weapons drawn.

On the other side of the portal, they found themselves at the base of a stone staircase in a tunnel of golden clouds.

"This is another realm!" said Brythan. "But I do not recognize it. It is nothing like Baron's realm of Aderath."

At the top, two men with lances and eyes of pure black stood on either side of a shining Celestial Acolyte sitting on a throne.

Brythan addressed the Acolyte. "I command you in the Name of God to explain why you are stealing vessels and what these two beings are!"

"The answer to both questions is one in the same. We are taking the mortal vessels from the Plains of Eternity to make slaves of them. I only tell you this because I offer you this great opportunity, Brythan. Submit to the Celestial Baron, and you will have your own Spirit Spawns to rule over—and your own realm."

"Is that what you call your human slaves? I would rather waste away in the Plains of Eternity forever." Brythan's words were a growl.

"Then you shall perish!" said the Acolyte. "Destroy them, my Spirit Spawns!"

The slaves walked down the stairs toward Thaylus and Brythan.

Brythan lunged for them, his sword pointed at one of the Spirit Spawns, but it struck down the attack, sending Brythan jarring to the side.

"These beings are so powerful," Brythan said. "They match the Vessel Bearers!"

"How do we defeat them?"

"Stay behind me!"

The Spirit Spawns approached.

"There is only one way to survive and to enjoy prosperity," they said. "Join us, Brythan."

"I will not!" Brythan came at the same Spawn again.

He put all the strength into his attack, and his sword clashed with the foe's lance. But the Spirit Spawn bore down on Brythan's weapon, pushing Brythan back.

The Spawn kicked Brythan in the chest, and he reeled back. He gritted his teeth, breathing heavily.

With a louder cry, Brythan again charged at the Spawn.

This time, the Spawn smiled.

Thaylus gasped to see a lance point jut out of Brythan's back.

Brythan fell to his knees, holding his wound, then toppled to his side.

Thaylus gasped and backed away.

Now the two Spirit Spawns neared Thaylus. The portal behind the silver door Thaylus and Brythan had come through vanished.

Thaylus tightened his grip on the fiery blade. If his fate came to death, he would go down fighting.

Just then, a shining figure with stork's wings emerged from the clouds.

"Ithia! Thank goodness you are here. Please, save us!"

"Thaylus, look away," Ithia said.

Thaylus turned. A bright light strobed from behind him.

When he faced Ithia again, the two Spirit Spawns were groping around aimlessly.

Ithia placed her hand on Brythan's wound, and it sealed. He jerked, then blinked his eyes.

He stood and frowned. "Ithia?"

"I have blinded the Spirit Spawns. Destroy them!" Ithia commanded.

The two sprinted at their foes.

Moments later, the Spirit Spawns died with a sword thrust into the chest. Their bodies melted on the stairs.

Ithia glared at the Celestial Acolyte watching from the throne.

"How could you, Arem? Your existence began at the dawn of the creation of Khrine's universe."

Ithia faced Thaylus and Brythan and held out two fiery swords much brighter than the ones they already had.

"These two blades come from Celestial Servants who stand in the presence of God within the Gate of Vessels. Take them," Ithia said.

She extended her arm and another shining fiery sword like theirs appeared. "I wield one as well."

Arem jumped from his throne.

"You do not know the power you defy. I will give you three a final chance to join me or this battle will be your last."

"Our God is more powerful than your corrupted master! Any power you wield comes from the will of our God!"

"Enough!" said Arem.

The Celestial Acolyte took out a double-edged spear that gleamed orange like it was in a forging fire. Then he rose into the air with his wings and sneered.

"My power granted me by the Celestial Baron trumps yours."

"Believe what you will," Ithia said. "Brythan, Thaylus, we will take him together."

The two nodded. Thaylus felt a resonating tension pulse through his body. It came from their combined power—himself, Ithia, and Brythan.

Arem raised his spear. Red lightning dispersed from his weapon in all directions.

Ithia and her two friends absorbed the barrage of lightning with their spiritual weapons.

Next Arem charged at them from above, blade pointed straight at them.

Again the three held up their swords, and a pillar of fire rose between them and Arem.

Arem backed away.

"Meddling fools! You're no match for me!"

The Celestial Acolyte pierced the staircase with his spear. It cracked like shards of glass.

Thaylus and Brythan stumbled. Pieces of the staircase broke off into the clouds below.

Ithia put her right hand on Thaylus's shoulder, then on Brythan's. Their bodies began to glow a light azure, and they ascended into the air.

The staircase crumbled to pieces.

Ithia sheathed her sword. "We must pray for strength," she said to Thaylus and Brythan.

Thaylus hesitated.

Ithia gazed at him, her eyes soft but filled with strength. "Thaylus, even if you merely acknowledge Him for all He is, it is better than nothing," she said. "Pray. Just bow your head and assert our petition to He who dwells inside the Gate of Vessels."

Thaylus bowed his head, unsure of what he did or what it meant.

Ithia bowed her head. "Oh, great God, grant us power to overcome this evil foe, so you may be glorified."

Thaylus felt no change until Arem lunged for him.

With supernatural might, Thaylus blocked the attack, and the two were in a clash. Thaylus shoved Arem away, sending him back through the air.

Arem gasped.

Ithia, Thaylus, and Brythan moved through the air, surrounding Arem.

"You're outmaneuvered. Surrender!" Ithia said.

Arem glared at them in turn. "The one I serve is a hundred times more powerful than I am. I may perish, but he will thwart you."

With that, the conquered Celestial Acolyte pierced himself with his burning spear.

He gave a howling cry and burst like an exploding star.

Thaylus, Brythan, and Ithia flew backwards, spinning with the force of the blast.

They landed on a lower part of the staircase, dazed.

Thaylus got to his knees and shook his head. "That was amazing! We beat him Ithia, thanks to you!" Thaylus said.

"It was God. The Great God sent me to this realm. I did not know why. He is to be thanked."

Brythan got to his feet. He folded his arms, his expression turning somber.

"Ithia, we now know the vessels are being stolen from the Plains of Eternity to be made into Spirit Spawn slaves. But why?"

"That is the other reason I came. Take these." Ithia held out two green cubes. "These are Aratos stones. They will make you fully undetectable in any way, including your presence, the sounds you make, and your appearance."

"What are we to do?" Thaylus asked.

"You are to return to Aderath and get close to any Acolytes—enough to hear why the Celestial Baron is amassing Spirit Spawns. You may have to do some scouting. But try to stay on the path the orb leads you as much as possible."

"Then let us depart with all speed," Thaylus said. "I trust you will make a portal."

"Brythan will transport you back."

Brythan touched Thaylus's arm, and in a flash of light, they stood on a roofed colonnade with the four blue suns of Aderath shining their lurid glow.

A Celestial Acolyte with a jade lamp stepped out of a portal several feet away. He walked in Thaylus and Brythan's direction.

Thaylus froze.

"Don't worry. We have the Aratos stones," Brythan said.

The Acolyte retained a relaxed face and a slow walk. Thaylus and Brythan parted, and he strolled between them.

"For a moment, I thought he saw us."

Brythan nodded. "Indeed. Let's try following him."

The companions trailed the Acolyte to the edge of the colonnade as he went down steps and met another Acolyte with a golden rod.

"Inform the master we will have enough souls from the Plains of Eternity within two weeks," the first Acolyte said.

The one with the golden rod took the lamp from the first Acolyte and turned to a wall, passing through it. The wall must have been the one surrounding the fortress. It rose high into the air and stretched along the ground for a long distance.

"If only we could get inside," Thaylus said.

"We should follow the orb."

"Very good."

They followed the diamond pointer to another staircase. Ascending, they came to a wide circular balcony suspended in midair high above the ground.

Celestial Acolytes flew past them in many directions.

Fixed several yards away, on the immense wall, a door with a small balcony was there. On the door was the symbol of a dragon.

"Brythan, what could that be?" Thaylus pointed.

"Perhaps it is an entry point of some sort."

"That is a good surmising. How do we reach it?"

"Unless we sprout wings like Celestial Acolytes, we cannot." Brythan stroked his chin and narrowed his eyes. "The orb does not point in that direction. There must be another route to it."

The orb pointed to an arch to their left at the edge of the balcony.

Thaylus and Brythan glanced at each other, then back at the arch.

"It is a drop-off. I am confused," Thaylus said.

"That is where the orb points. Maybe something will happen."

Brythan led Thaylus to the archway, and the piece of stone surface they stood on floated horizontally to another platform with a doorway of a dim passage.

"Doubtless this will lead to more danger," Thaylus said.

"Ithia told us to follow the orb."

Both men entered the dark doorway. They found themselves on a stone platform supported by a pillar rising above dark water. In the center of the platform where they stood, a small pyramid sat. It glowed with a mystical hazel hue.

"I am the Spirit of the Realm of Heth. I hold the power to enter Baron Erebus's keep," said a woman's voice coming from the pyramid.

Thaylus and Brythan froze.

"First you must put your hand upon me to test your worthiness."

Thaylus and Brythan looked at each other.

"What choice do we have?" Brythan asked.

The two men placed their hand on the pyramid.

A shock raced through Thaylus. He convulsed and cried out. A surging twinge permeated his consciousness. It seemed like a dream or an outer-body experience.

Brythan convulsed and cried out as well. Images flashed through his mind like revelations.

The experience abated, and Thaylus and Brythan fell to their knees breathing heavily.

"What just happened?" Brythan asked.

"Your worthiness has been tested, and you have passed. Had you not been worthy, you would have died," the spirit said.

The ground vibrated, and a bridge began to extend from the small platform to another platform, this one with an archway.

"I'm certain that archway leads to a portal," Brythan said. "It must lead inside the keep."

The two men walked across the bridge to the other side. When they neared the archway, a blue portal appeared.

"You were right," Thaylus said.

Brythan and Thaylus entered. Instantly, they were transported to a small balcony overlooking the network of buildings, stairs, bridges, and other structures. Directly behind them was the wall with the dragon insignia, shining with a red-gold gleam.

The orb shattered and the diamond point shot forth and pierced the dragon symbol.

The wall turned to sand and poured out onto the ground, making a man-sized circular entrance.

They entered and stood, still as statues.

Thaylus's stomach dropped, and he trembled at what he saw.

# Chapter 24

## The Armies of Erebus

Below them, myriads of Spirit Spawns were in an immense roofed quad with six Celestial Acolytes hovering over six enormous garrisons.

Sitting on a throne, a man-like being in a black robe held a metal rod with a glowing spherical emerald at the top.

"I, Baron Erebus, declare our time is near. Soon we will have enough Spirit Spawns to lay siege to Khrine."

The being's words echoed like a trumpet.

"So that is the Baron's ultimate scheme. What should we do?" Thaylus asked.

"We must tell Ithia."

Thaylus shook his head. "I agree, but how? We do not know how to contact her. You and I must do something."

"What can we do?"

"I have a feeling that rod with the glowing gem holds the key. The Aratos stone will allow us to get it."

"The idea makes my blood congeal even though we are invisible." Brythan shook himself. "Let us do this with haste."

To their left, a ramp led to a flat circular brick with the dragon insignia on it. They rushed to the platform.

The ground glowed, then opened, and Thaylus and Brythan were lowered to the surface, far below.

The cataclysmic shout of myriads of Spirit Spawns filled the enormous chamber. They called out the name Erebus in unison, again and again.

After long minutes of verbal worship, the Spirit Spawns ceased.

Thaylus and Brythan walked along the wall in the direction of Erebus. A staircase led to his throne.

Thaylus and Brythan approached the staircase with much trepidation.

Thaylus felt a chill run down the back of his neck. Being so close, the Baron's presence seemed greater in power than many Acolytes combined. It was as if he thrummed with dark energy.

Even with the Aratos stone, Thaylus and Brythan crept up the stairs.

But when they were six feet away, Erebus stood and turned.

"I see you two men. An Aratos stone holds no sway over a former Celestial Servant. Who sent you, and why?"

Thaylus and Brythan gasped.

Brythan transformed into his shining, spiritual form.

Erebus grinned and sat back down. "I see you come from the Gate of Vessels. No doubt you had the terrestrial body of a man and now don your heavenly body."

Erebus frowned and glared. "I ask you again—why are you here?"

"We come to stop you, Celestial Baron," said Brythan with a quivering lip.

Erebus laughed.

Thaylus knew Erebus must have more power than Brythan. It appeared they stood at the Baron's mercy.

"You amuse me. In any case, I could kill you, but that wouldn't be very fair or very sporting." Erebus considered, his eyes narrowed. "Here is what will happen: I will take back the power I have given to one of my Acolytes, and you shall battle him with his power alone. If you win, I will let you go. If not, I will turn you and your friend into Spirit Spawns."

Brythan brandished his sword.

Thaylus shuddered. Did his friend possess the power to match a Celestial Acolyte?

Erebus selected an Acolyte.

The Acolyte smiled and took out his own shining blade. He twirled it, making the appearance of a spinning galaxy, then gave a menacing grin.

"You are a fool to challenge me even if I do not have the added power of Erebus," the Acolyte said to Brythan.

"My power is a righteous one. It comes from the One in the Gate of Vessels who surpasses a Celestial Baron," Brythan said.

The two opponents charged at each other with swords over their heads. The sound of thunder resonated with the sword clash. The impact pushed the two apart. Brythan swiped at the Acolyte with a horizontal stroke and he backed off missing him by inches.

The Acolyte went for a sword thrust but Brythan parried it.

His foe used the momentum to spin around with a quick strike at Brythan's waist.

Brythan cried out as the blade sliced his hip. He fell to his knee, holding his wound.

The Celestial Acolyte made a vertical strike while Brythan was down. He lurched to the left, dodging the swipe, then rolled over and onto his feet.

The two stood six feet apart.

The Acolyte charged as before with sword over his head. Brythan struck his blade, an inch from the hilt, sending the weapon flailing away.

"Surrender!" Brythan said.

"Die, vermin!" said the Acolyte.

A beam of light shot from his palm straight toward Brythan.

Brythan blocked the attack, stumbling. He gritted his teeth as he grew brighter and resisted the force, driving it back.

The Acolyte grunted and brightened as well, growing stronger. Bolts of lightning shot through the beam, dispersing in every direction as they hit the sword.

Brythan closed his eyes. "Greater is He that is in me than he that is in the world."

He said the phrase repeatedly, growing three times brighter with every repetition.

The Acolyte covered his eyes, ceasing his light attack.

Thaylus had to shield his own eyes, as well.

The Acolyte lurched as Brythan thrust his sword at his chest.

In an instant, the Acolyte's shining form was consumed by a glowing green wound, and it disappeared like smoke.

Erebus jumped from his throne. "Impossible! Where did you get such power!"

"The words of my God gave me the power. Now keep to your word, Erebus!" Brythan said.

"Not so fast. You cheated. I withdrew my power from my servant, whereas you summoned help from your God."

Erebus beckoned with his hand to the five last Celestial Acolytes.

"You there. Take these cheating men with you. I want to see their faces when I deal my first assault on Khrine."

"Wha—?"

Before they knew what was happening, Thaylus and Brythan were seized by an Acolyte and hauled into the air.

Erebus raised his staff, and the jewel atop it glowed. A glowing green energy sphere shot forth at the end, and an immense oval-shaped fissure opened, showing a kingdom of Khrine on the other side.

"My five Acolyte generals, it is time." Erebus looked down, clenching his fist in frustration at the death of his two Acolytes. "Lead my Spirit Spawns to conquer the first of my many kingdoms!"

Innumerable Spirit Spawns marched through the portal. They stepped onto the grassy surface of the realm of Khrine. One of Erebus's Acolytes led the first wave.

"Oh, no! We are too late!" said Thaylus.

Brythan shook his head and spoke sternly. "God would not allow Erebus to win. Something will come to overcome him."

Upon a hill, across a long stretch of land, the castle of the kingdom of Rune stood proudly. Squads of human soldiers in the distance flowed out of the base of it.

But they were outnumbered three-to-one by Erebus's army.

The two armies neared, closer and closer.

Thaylus and Brythan were roughly deposited by the Celestial Acolyte upon a mound overlooking the battle clash.

The Acolyte shook his head. "Do you not see the futility of this battle? If you submit to Celestial Baron Erebus, I know he would reward you."

"You, like your Baron, are nothing but tyrants," Thaylus said.

"Even though I do not think the spiritual being you betrayed is a real God, I believe His spiritual power is greater than yours!"

"And how has he interceded through this whole ordeal?" The Acolyte snorted. "He has done nothing."

Brythan chuckled. "You think you have won? God will work all things, even this setback, for good."

As they watched, the two forces collided. Men cried out as they were cut down by Spirit Spawns. For every Spirit Spawn killed, five men fell.

Finally, the end of the fight drew near.

The army of Erebus, led by one of his Acolytes, pushed back the last of the kingdom defenses. Soon the castle would be overrun.

Just then, a blast of light erupted in the sky, illuminating the battlefield. All present looked up.

At least thirty Vessel Bearers floated in the air.

They flew across the ground with shining swords, obliterating dozens of Spirit Spawns with every stroke. The Spawns fled these righteous spiritual warriors. The Vessel Bearers would swoop down in long, quick passes, strike down Spawns, then fly around for another attack.

"No!" Enraged screams came from the lead Acolyte.

As Thaylus and Brythan watched, he opened a vast portal to retreat to Aderath.

But he was followed by the pursuing Vessel Bearers. They split and disrupted the squads of Spawns and began to assault the Acolytes.

"I told you Thaylus! God has provided our salvation!" said Brythan. "They are being forced back into Aderath! May God be praised!"

Their evil battle proved futile. With the power of God behind them, the warriors of light overwhelmed the Acolytes despite their infusion with Erebus's power.

The Great Lord from the Gate of Vessels had intervened!

The five Acolyte generals flailed, trying to ward off all the Vessel Bearers closing in on them. They fled toward Erebus for protection.

The Vessel Bearers encircled Erebus and his seven Acolyte generals.

Raising their arms high, the Vessel Bearers began to speak in a strange, beautiful language.

Beads of light revolved around the eight evil beings. A green transparent shape appeared amid them. It began to take on a solid green, spherical form.

It fully materialized with the eight beings encased in a large, round emerald.

The ground trembled, then reverberated with a boom, and all the Spirit Spawns vanished.

Thaylus gasped. This was not supposed to occur for seventy-seven years! Had Mordecai's prophecy been wrong? What had happened?

A Vessel Bearer descended to Thaylus and Brythan with a warm smile.

"It is good your presence alerted us to Erebus's position. Once you crossed over the portal to Khrine, we sensed you."

Thaylus opened his mouth to speak, but the Vessel Bearer spoke first.

"Do not concern yourself with the occurrences of the future—all is in order."

"I beg you, great Vessel Bearer! Tell me what is to become of me!"

"You still need to recover the seal to the Abyss, but like the Abyss and the space within the Gate of Vessels, it transcends time and space. When Brythan left the mortal realm, the seal left him and was lost in the Realm Rift. Now you must go retrieve it—but without Brythan."

Thaylus faced Brythan, his eyes filling.

"This last mission has been wonderful, but oh, how little time it was, Brythan."

The two friends shook each other's forearms.

Brythan put a hand on Thaylus's shoulder. "Have faith, my friend."

Thaylus's heart was pricked. "That is my wish."

The Vessel Bearer motioned with his hand and a small, blue portal appeared.

"Go," he told Thaylus. "Time is short."

Thaylus stepped into the Realm Rift.

# Chapter 25

## The Realm Rift

Thaylus found himself on a golden boat that floated through the vast space of the Realm Rift in all its heavenly glory. It was just like when he had been there with Ithia and Brythan. He gazed wide-eyed at all the celestial bodies and portals surrounding him.

At the front of the boat there was a white orb. He approached the object and put his hand on it.

An image of all the farthest boundaries of the Realm Rift appeared in his mind's eye. Somehow, he could see all the portals arrayed throughout infinite space.

He intuitively understood which time and place each portal led to. Thaylus was leery of any spiritual being, good or bad, encountering him. Was he alone?

Thaylus careened through the scape. He became aware of something immense in the Realm Rift. It did not have any solid form, but just a black, cloudy material. It disturbed him.

He released the orb, and the image vanished from his mind.

"What was that?" Thaylus shook his head and rubbed his temples.

He cupped his hands over the orb again, and the nebulous form coalesced in his mental sight. It barged through the Rift in the direction of Thaylus's craft, heading straight for him at an incredible speed.

The cloud took the shape of a winged creature.

Thaylus's heart thumped as the mass formed a cloudy tail and a long neck. A face with flaming eyes appeared.

Thaylus stepped back from the orb and brandished his shining sword. He gripped it with both hands.

He sensed the aberration charging at him was familiar.

His mind spun as he searched his memory. He gasped and his jaw dropped.

The Dragon of the Abyss.

"I killed that abomination! How is this possible?"

Thaylus ran to the edge of the bow and stared below toward the evil essence. Sweat pooled.

Finally, he saw the dragon near him with its two flaming eyes. Soon its whole body emerged in the dark backdrop of the Realm Rift.

"You think you had seen the last of me, did you?" The dragon rose over Thaylus. "You only killed my body, but my spirit lives on."

"I overcame you twice, and I will do so again."

"Fool, my spirit is more powerful than yours!"

Thaylus clenched his jaw. "As I said once, light surpasses the power of darkness no matter how much of it you bear."

The dragon spirit roared. "Silence! I will destroy your body, and your soul will waste away in the Plains of Eternity forever!"

Thaylus held his spiritual sword and focused all his will into it. It shined brightly.

"Come at me, you beast!"

The brightness of the sword obscured the dragon's sight and he shrieked, turning away from the light.

Thaylus's heart raced and as the dragon regained his strength and loomed over him.

Thaylus slashed at it from below.

The spirit cried out, thrashing around before recovering once more.

"I was careless. It will not happen again!" The spirit taunted with a coarse laugh. "Flee from me, you worm! You cannot escape me!"

Thaylus sprinted back to the orb and clutched it. The complete recesses of the Realm Rift returned to his mind.

He sensed a portal nearby and comprehended it led to Aderath. The emerald that trapped Erebus and his seven Acolyte generals shined through the portal.

Thaylus made out another open portal. He sensed it led to Khrine.

But the portal to Aderath was the closest. He pushed the craft as fast as he could imagine.

In a burst of speed, the dragon was upon Thaylus again in minutes.

Thaylus fought him off as best he could. The dragon tried to attack directly above him as Thaylus swung and thrusted his sword at the beast, keeping him at a short distance.

"Your strength will die soon," said the dragon spirit, laughing. "Then you will be mine."

Thaylus looked at the portal to Aderath with his own eyes. He was almost upon it. The emerald appeared as a green star in the distance, just as Mordecai had illustrated. But how would the shining emerald prison fall to Khrine? And who or what was responsible?

Thaylus's muscles burned. He no longer had the strength to wield the sword.

Moments later, the sword vanished. Thaylus collapsed.

With a triumphant shriek, the dragon spirit opened his jaws to devour Thaylus from above.

"No!" Thaylus cried out in panic, cringing at the open mouth closing in on him.

In an instant, he burst through the portal, safe in Aderath.

The dragon reeled back, like a strong wind pushed him away.

Thaylus fell to the soft soil rolling over a few times until he came to rest.

"I might not be able to cross into Aderath, but there is nowhere you can go," said the dragon from the other side of the portal. "Soon you will have to leave it. I just have to wait."

The emerald that encased the five Acolyte generals and Celestial Baron Erebus shined a hypnotic, green gleam.

Thaylus lay exhausted, panting on his back. He waited to regain his strength, staring at the emerald. When would a celestial event cast this immense spherical emerald to Khrine? Or had he and Brythan somehow prevented that from happening?

Thaylus sat up. "My whole body aches."

The spirit of the Dragon of the Abyss loomed in silence on the other side of the portal, but for his burning eyes that crackled like embers. Those, Thaylus could still sense.

Without the Celestial Acolytes flying about, Aderath was so different, Thaylus thought. He wondered what he was to do.

Thaylus was still mortal, so he needed food and water. Did Aderath have anything like that?

He began to explore. The ruined stronghold of Erebus looked like a quake had occurred, or like a tremendous tornado had ravished it.

Amidst the rubble, a green light glistened. Thaylus wondered what it was. He pulled at his beard and narrowed his eyes.

His body jolted as he realized—the rod that Erebus held. It was still here!

He glanced at the dragon spirit, then faced the green gleam once more. The light was about a dozen yards away.

Thaylus stumbled over the stones and debris as he went to the light.

It seemed to grow stronger as he drew closer.

When he was about twelve feet away, he stopped and gazed at it with an open mouth. He neared it slowly like it was a holy relic.

Finally, the glistening jewel at the top of the rod lay at his feet.

Thaylus was entranced and hypnotized as he was lured to bend over and grasp it.

Then he froze.

With his slight touch, the power of the jeweled rod overwhelmed him.

The feeling was stronger than the book's allure, when he chose time travel over magic.

Indeed, it felt like the very essence of Erebus—and oddly, he didn't want it to stop.

Thaylus grabbed the rod.

With that, a feeling of power like nothing he'd ever felt rushed through him. He felt as though he could rival multiple Vessel Bearers with a command from his mouth. The power he felt grew until finally was too much to contain. He shuddered and convulsed. He cried out as the rod and the jewel atop it glowed a deeper green.

Besides the power that infused Thaylus, there was something else—it was like a living essence trapped in the staff, an intelligence within.

A voice echoed in Thaylus's mind, Erebus's voice.

Summon my ally.

Thaylus could not resist the command of the voice. His will was becoming Erebus's—and he found he liked that. He wanted Erebus's will to take over, take control.

A corner of Thaylus fought it the best he could. But the mind and the power had a force he could not resist.

Zings of light erupted from the rod. Images flashed through his mind as emotions and sensations flooded his consciousness.

Thaylus felt the spirit of Erebus overcome him.

With a resounding crack, the jewel broke from the rod and shot into the sky.

The rod, now a shell without power, fell unceremoniously to the ground.

A great flash of light exploded and a being like a Celestial Servant appeared, but it was not Erebus.

The being had a voice like a hundred shouting vessel bearers. "I, Cleerious, have come."

Cleerious shone with the brightness of seven suns like a beacon of power, but his presence was filled with a vile aura.

With two hands, Cleerious took hold of the enormous, round emerald prison.

Then with a mighty thrust, he threw it through the portal directly into the Realm Rift.

The emerald prison shattered the dragon spirit as his cloud-like form burst apart into nothing.

Thaylus fell to his knees. He was why the emerald came to Khrine! The rod somehow possessed him to allow this Celestial Servant to appear in Aderath and throw the emerald prison to Thaylus's world.

Bitter guilt tore through him.

What had he been thinking? What arrogance possessed him to believe he would not be susceptible to such evil?

Obviously Cleerious had been a former Celestial Servant and was now the rogue Celestial Baron. His action would free the evil Erebus and his seven Acolyte generals from the emerald.

Thaylus put his head in his hands. What had he done?

Cleerious approached. "So, you are the chosen vessel. How does it feel to be the instrument of our plans?"

Thaylus let out a cry.

Turning, Thaylus dashed for the portal. Soon he was once again aboard the golden ship.

Thaylus touched the orb and instantly understood where the portal to Khrine was—and the time. It was now seventy-seven years in the future.

Perhaps Thaylus could reach the portal before the emerald came to Khrine. There had to be something he could do.

The emerald streaked like a shooting star toward the portal to Khrine.

Thaylus cupped the orb and pushed the ship as fast as he could imagine. He was gaining on the emerald.

Minutes later, Thaylus was flying alongside it. He decided to cut the object off its path.

"Grr!" Thaylus uttered as he clenched his teeth.

He careened his ship against the emerald; it inched to the side.

He needed more momentum. He maneuvered about two-dozen yards away from the immense, round gem.

"Take this!" Thaylus roared as he rushed the craft towards the emerald from the side.

But he missed it! It jumped in speed and evaded Thaylus's move.

Only moments remained until it would enter the portal to Khrine.

Thaylus's heart fell in desperation—there was nothing else he could do. There was no changing the time line. Despair took hold.

Seconds after the emerald entered Khrine's sky, so did Thaylus. The ship disappeared and he plummeted along with the emerald to the foot of a mountain.

A mile-wide crater opened with the emerald's crash.

Just as Thaylus was about to strike the ground, he was borne up by two Vessel Bearers. Each had an arm, and he was lighted onto the ground.

Thaylus scrambled to his knees, breathing heavily.

The Vessel Bearers smiled at him.

"My name is Nearod," one said. "Be at peace, Thaylus. You are nearing the end of your journey."

Thaylus shook his head. "But what about the shield seal? I did not sense it in the Realm Rift. Will you send me back to the Rift to get it?"

"The reason you couldn't sense it is because spiritual darkness has hidden it from your mind."

"Spiritual darkness? Can Realm Dwellers exist in the Rift? Could it be them?" Thaylus asked.

"It is possible, but they would need a Celestial Servant or a Vessel Bearer to open a portal," Nearod said.

"I have my answer," Thaylus said.

"Answer for what?"

"When I visited Aderath the second time, I accidently loosed a Celestial Servant, or a Celestial Baron as I think he has become. He threw the emerald prison through the portal into the Rift, on a course for the portal to Khrine."

"I wonder who it could be?" Nearod said to the other Vessel Bearer.

"He called himself Cleerious," Thaylus said.

"Cleerious? I cannot ponder such a thing! Cleerious is the oldest, wisest, most powerful Servant of the Lord within the Gate of Vessels."

"Then you must tell your Lord of Cleerious's treachery."

"There is no need," Nearod said. "Our God is all knowing and privy to all situations."

"How am I supposed to find the seal if Cleerious clouds my senses?"

"You must reach deep within yourself and take hold of your strongest sense of faith. The Shield Seal to the Abyss is the essence of faith. If your faith is great enough, it will connect a spiritual link to the seal and to you. But you must be in the Realm Rift."

With that, Nearod raised his arm, and a portal to the Rift appeared.

In moments, Thaylus was once again on the flying ship. He walked to the orb and cupped it, and his senses of the universal Realm Rift instantly came upon him.

All was empty. He was alone.

Thaylus feared he could not conjure enough faith to see through the darkness and sense the shield seal.

He kneeled, then closed his eyes and focused. His face contorted as his mind strained. He took a deep breath.

He waited.

"Something should have happened by now!"

Thaylus recalled how he'd evoked the name of the God within the Gate of Vessels when he was in that perfect state of faith.

Pray to Him. The thought was almost inconceivable, yet it echoed. Where did this strange thought arise from?

Thaylus felt an inner peace and power slide over him. It was not like the presence of a Vessel Bearer or even a Celestial Servant, but more of an inner anomaly that seemed to beckon him.

It was all quite baffling. Something strange but pleasant was working in his heart.

Thaylus was fearful of completely submitting to this essence. He felt something he never had in a spiritual being—love. Not fear. Not wrath. Just love.

This Being, this God, cared for him.

It was one of the aspects and qualities he had always craved from a true all-powerful God.

Was this … Him? Was this Being, this Great Lord from the Gate of Vessels the true deity he'd been seeking all along?

Thaylus came to an epiphany he had never genuinely and consciously embraced.

Yes, this being may be God.

And Thaylus would do anything to find out.

Thaylus bowed his head and folded his hands.

"If you be the true God, reveal yourself. I am listening."

Thaylus went back to the orb and held it. His mind's sight sensed the shield seal amidst a dark, evil essence far away in the Rift. It must have been the evil manifestation obscuring the shield seal.

With his hands on the orb, Thaylus mentally accelerated his ship toward the darkness—and the shield.

As he neared it, he knew what the darkness was.

Realm Dwellers.

They floated, shoulder-to-shoulder, in the shape of sphere.

Thaylus brandished the Sword of the Spirit and the Realm Dwellers shrieked. Thaylus stood at the bow as he charged at the Realm Dwellers. He slashed at the dark conglomeration, and there was a large tear in their ranks.

A brilliant golden hue shone through the tear. The shield! A joyful laugh bubbled within him. Soon he would have the shield seal.

A group of Realm Dwellers went for the base of the craft, pushing it back. Thaylus stumbled to the right.

He took hold of the orb and mentally pushed back the ship.

The Realm Dwellers matched his strength. They were in a deadlock.

"No, you will not!" Thaylus gritted his teeth and pushed his will to its limits.

The craft flailed against the dark beings' push.

One of them went straight for Thaylus. It charged with its fiery, black sword pointed.

Thaylus went to parry the attack, and the Realm Dweller's sword flung out of its hands.

Thaylus raised an eyebrow. "I barely put any strength into that," he said with a chuckle.

He closed his eyes and sensed that newfound inner strength.

"Is this ... You?" he questioned the inner presence.

The Realm Dweller backed away as Thaylus barged forward and struck it down. It dissipated like black mist being scattered in a breeze.

The remaining Realm Dwellers fell back a few yards, taking the shield seal with them.

They whirled about and coalesced over the shield, obscuring its light.

Next a giant shape took form. It began with a head and a body, then an enormous pair of wings. Last of all, a long dark lance appeared in the entity's hands.

An immense Realm Dweller took form before Thaylus.

The sound of its voice reverberated like hundreds of Realm Dwellers shouting in unison.

"I bring you word from Baron Cleerious. Join us and you will become the high king over men."

"No chance," Thaylus said.

"You have sealed your fate."

The monstrous being twirled his lance and threw it at the base of the ship. A large eruption of sparks came as the lance embedded into the ship. The being stretched forth his hand, and the lance ripped from the hull of the vessel and returned to him.

The weapon was too long for Thaylus to defend against.

He ran back to the orb and charged his craft at the dark entity. He pierced its chest as a cavity revealed the shining shield beyond.

The hole in the Realm Dweller's misty, nebulous chest closed. The being raised his weapon, preparing to impale Thaylus from above.

He shot just as Thaylus leaped to the left, and the lance stuck fast into the ship's surface.

Thaylus cut off one of the hands holding the lance.

The dark essence yanked back his arm and reeled away.

"Blasted mortal!"

The missing hand reappeared and grasped the lance. The giant Realm Dweller once more took hold of the lance and pulled it out, jarring the whole craft.

"Your pitiful weapon cannot harm me!" it bellowed.

Thaylus's heart sank and he covered his face with his hands. I need more faith, he thought.

Something small and warm in his inner garment called his attention.

Clara's pearl.

He pulled out the blue pearl from the spirit Clara, and her words sounded in his head. Faith is the evidence of things not seen and of things hoped for.

It was like he had heard the words for the first time. Suddenly, it made almost complete sense!

Thaylus closed his eyes and meditated upon the words. Not seen. Hoped for.

Tightly, he gripped the Sword of the Spirit and lifted it high. The holy weapon broke forth with a cascade of penetrating light.

This time, the giant being released his lance and covered his eyes. His body began to waste away like wind-driven ash.

Thaylus pointed his blade fully at the dark form and vanquished it with a blast of light aimed at its chest. When the blast of light abated, only the shield remained. All Realm Dwellers had been expunged by a light explosion that happened as the beam hit the apparition's chest.

He had recovered the seal to the Abyss!

"I am coming for you, Brythan! I will keep that vile wizard from killing you!"

Thaylus went back to the orb and grasped it.

He saw Ithia amidst the Realm Rift in his mind's eye. She came at him at great speed.

Thaylus went to the front of the ship and waited.

Ithia's form drew nearer and nearer. Finally, she was there with him, smiling with glistening eyes.

"I congratulate you on your victory. I recall your spite and doubt when I first met you and Brythan in the forest. Look at you now."

"How did you find where I am?"

"I came to you when the spiritual darkness disappeared, and the shield seal became discernible in the Rift."

"Ithia, I aim to return to my time and keep Brythan from being killed by Kyrious. I also mean to travel back in time to a keep a phoenix from perishing and save its younglings. With the Sword of the Spirit and the shield, I cannot fail!"

Ithia shook her head and put a hand on Thaylus's shoulder. "Rest assured. I have gone to Grithin's time to reunite with his children. Brythan also is all right."

"I thought I was supposed to do those tasks. Why was I allowed to have intentions to proceed and help Brythan and Grithin?"

"Those were just small tests to build your faith and prove your moral loyalty. God knows you would fulfil your oath to both. Presently you are needed to do something else.

"God wants you to see the things that will take place, from start to finish. You have witnessed the fall of Erebus and his five generals. But soon they will break free.

"I will show you this. But first you must see the beginning, when all worshiped the true God in the Gate of Vessels."

# Chapter 26

## TESTAMENTS OF KHRINE

A FLASH OF LIGHT FILLED the space around Thaylus. He looked below at the crater from the emerald's impact as he stood on a small mountain peak. Near the horizon, a kingdom stood with a tall castle in the middle.

Thaylus looked all around. "Where are you, Ithia?"

I am with you. You cannot see me.

"Where am I? What time is this?"

What you see in the distance is the forgotten kingdom of Hither Tor. Once again, you are three-thousand years in the past from your own time. This is when the Realm Dwellers are first cast into the abyss after they first appeared a thousand years earlier from now. I assume you remember Doren, Nithose, and the spirit, when you went to the island with Brythan to get the seal to the abyss? You are now a few years after that whole ordeal.

"Why am I here?"

Remember the things you see here.

"Why?"

The knowledge you obtain will be given to another. This transferred spiritual knowledge will be a testament in an era many years from your time.

Thaylus put his palm on his forehead and stumbled against a boulder.

"How long will this take? Will I be in danger? Won't I weaken like I do when I time travel?"

Not this time. God's great power and faith, that has built in you over time, will sustain you.

In flash of light, Thaylus appeared at the entrance to Hither Tor.

"Ithia?"

Go into the kingdom. What is meant to happen will occur.

"Ithia? Ithia!"

Only silence followed.

Thaylus frowned. "It appears I simply go as usual."

Hither Tor had houses of brick with thatched roofs. Narrow cobblestone paths with small weeds led through the outermost part of the kingdom.

It was nearing twilight as Men and women bustled up and down, back and forth in a tight crowd along the narrow streets running between two rows of houses. They appeared to be middle-class culture. The people were in long tunics that were plain and clean. The houses were quaint made of simple cut brick and mortar with a simple decorative design on the doorways and windows of smooth square glass.

Thaylus began to walk along the path until he came to something magnificent that stood out of the mediocrity of the layout.

Four dozen yards away was a small castle with an open, narrow gate, where two burly guards stood with spears. Beside it, a small cathedral was full of people going in.

A man brushed by Thaylus, and he caught the person by the arm. He spoke in Pyrithian, making his best assumption.

"Excuse me sir, what god is worshipped in that cathedral?"

The man looked confused. "What do you mean? What other God is there than He who lives in the Gate of Vessels?"

"Thank you, sir. I come from a land where He is not worshipped."

The man gasped. "How horrible! Where do you come from? I am certain one of our priests will share the message of the living God with you."

"Don't concern yourself. I know Him."

Thaylus's eyes drifted as he took in the scene as the tip of the sun's disk lowered glinting an orange red over a mountain range, and he felt a serenity wash over him, like he was relaxing in a calm lake. It was the truth—he did know Him. Indeed, he truly had come to rely on God, the One True God.

It was the truest, holiest allegiance he had yet to possess.

In the sky, a golden phoenix descended onto a large, fenced mound. The bird's feathers glistened with a golden, fiery hue. His eyes glowed emerald green with golden pupils. He had a ten-foot statue that gave him an imposing, regal appearance.

Thaylus's heart throbbed with joy at the amazing creature. He stared, wide-eyed.

The bird cocked his head. "Why do you stare at me, human?"

Thaylus shook himself. "Forgive me. Your kind is a rarity where I come from."

"Where is your home situated from here?"

"I ... live in a small settlement in a forest." Thaylus ran a palm down his sweating face. Hopefully, the phoenix would not press further.

"I am Kromious. Who are you?" asked the phoenix with a mild tone.

"I am Thaylus."

Kromious ruffled his feathers. "Welcome to Hither Tor, Thaylus."

"Thank you."

Kromious raised his voice over the crowd. "I need to speak to King Nathail. Where is he?"

"He worships in the temple," called out a man with a long white beard.

The phoenix flew off the mound and onto the ground where the people traversed.

Thaylus followed as the phoenix passed through the throng to the temple and entered. The roofing shaded Thaylus as a cool draft wafted past his face and over his bald head.

The magical bird approached King Nathail. A man in a decadent red silk robe was kneeling before an altar with his back to the phoenix.

"King Nathail, I need your aid," said Kromious.

Nathail kept quiet momentarily before standing and facing the phoenix. "What is it that you need?"

Kromious sighed. "Our king has been stolen from us by a vile necromancer with powerful magic. We need a priest with the strength and holiness of God."

"Very well. I will send priest Garen. He is young, but he is full of the presence and might of God," said King Nathail with a bow and a smile. He turned and called out, "Where is Garen?"

"I saw him walking in the market square about ten minutes ago," said a priest.

"Bring him here."

"Yes, Lord," said the priest as he bowed then ran off.

Kromious stretched out his right wing and pointed it at Thaylus. "This fellow has never seen a phoenix, King Nathail."

"That is not all," a man spoke up.

Thaylus, the king, and the bird looked at the speaker. The man Thaylus first addressed in the kingdom stood listening to them all.

"It is more. He has no knowledge of God where he lives!"

Everyone jerked a glance at Thaylus and stared with wide eyes. King Nathail frowned and looked at Thaylus up and down.

He opened his mouth to speak but a young man in a priest's clothes ran in and planted his feet in front of the king.

"You summoned me, Lord?" asked the young priest.

"A mysterious wizard has abducted Naramor, king of the Phoenixes. I have chosen you to retrieve him."

Garen gaped. "Why me, Lord?"

The king smiled at Garen. "No one so young has ever been full of such faith and wisdom."

Garen took a deep breath and looked the king in the eye. "As you wish, my Lord."

"Go to the stables for a horse and victuals," Nathail said. "I Imagine it will take at least a few days to reach the wizard."

Kromious stepped forward. "Not necessary. I will fly you where the sorcerer dwells. The quicker the better." The bird bent over and spread his wing over the ground for Garen to climb up.

"Wait! Let me go with you," Thaylus blurted.

"Why?" asked Kromious.

"I have never ventured past my settlement until now. I would like to experience all I can, and help, even if there is danger."

"Such boundless curiosity." King Nathail nodded. "I do not reject your request. The decision is yours, good phoenix."

"I do not mind," Kromious said.

He extended his wing once more, and Thaylus and Garen climbed onto the phoenix's back and they were lifted into the air.

As they set out, Thaylus recalled the attack from the Dragon of the Abyss while riding on Grithin. His death gave him a sinking feeling. He wished he could be the one to go back in time right away to save Brythan, Grithin, and any others he could possibly help. But for the moment, he had his instructions from the Vessel Bearer.

The scenery below took Thaylus's breath away. Forests with lush, rich meadows filled the landscape. Shimmering lakes and rivers glistened with the luster of the sun. Besides the primal beauty of it all, something else permeated the surface of the natural wonder. It was pure and untainted with war scars, nor did he see any kingdoms, mining colonies, or timber cutting lines.

"We are nearing the wizard's mountain. Hold on." Kromious took a dive straight for the craggy, misty mountainside.

As Thaylus was brought into the thick, dark web-like strands of mist, beads of water collected on his face. He wiped them off as the phoenix flew down and landed on a barren rock ledge.

Garen and Thaylus slid off the phoenix's back.

"His cave is not far." Kromious nodded his head toward the incline. "But what little sun we have is veiled by the mist and we cannot see but five feet ahead."

Thaylus felt warmth within his clothes and knew it was Clare's pearl. He took it out and it glowed a soft blue color. In seconds it grew in illumination so that they could see over fifteen feet in all directions."

Kromious and Garen were stunned with wide-eyes.

"That amazing thing you have." said Kromious. "I have seen my share of magic talismans in my centuries of living. That object is quite exceptional."

"It's mystifying!" said Geren.

"I received it a long time ago from a friend. But it has never done this before. I have seen it aid me in the past."

Kromious cocked his head and ruffled his feathers. "God has provided as He always does. Now, let us continue."

Thaylus peered ahead at the way before them in the pearl's light. The three walked on and made out a small cave.

"I cannot remember if this is it or not," Kromious said. "The wizard chained up our king and then transformed into red, winged manticore and flew off with him. I secretly followed the sorcerer to his cave."

"I do not think it is," said Garen. "There is no evil essence in this cave."

"I sense nothing either," said Thaylus.

Garen tilted his head. "I did not know you had spiritual training."

Thaylus opened his mouth to speak but did not have the words. "I ... yes."

Several minutes later, Garen pointed.

"Look! A staircase hewn out of stone!"

"His cave must be close," Kromious said.

The two human companions trudged up the staircase as the phoenix hopped from step to step as his talons clicked on the stone terraces.

Garen stopped. "Do you feel that?"

"Yes, a wicked presence," Thaylus said. "We are near."

At the top of the staircase, two stone gargoyles stood sentry.

"I must have followed him a different route, the phoenix said. "I did not see stairs or statues."

As they passed, they heard the distinct sound of crumpled rocks.

Turning, they froze.

The gargoyles had come to life. Their fangs and tusks were sharp as spear tips. They stretched their wings above their heads and made a course, rumbling roar that stung Thaylus's ears.

"Save us, Kromious!" Garen cried.

The gargoyles advanced toward them.

"Stand behind me!" said the phoenix.

He spread his wings as they ignited with flames.

At the blaze, the gargoyles disappeared behind the wall of mist.

Thaylus's heart beat like a fist pounding on a metal door. The humans and the phoenix glanced in every direction.

"They may come from anywhere!" Garen whispered.

Kromious grunted. "I have just enough power to even the odds. Stand back!"

Garen and Thaylus stepped away and the phoenix ignited in flames. "Now our grotesque foes will face incineration. Whatever I touch will be set ablaze. But we must hurry, my fire will last only for so long."

Thaylus poised himself. "I can sense the sorcerer. We are just upon him. Let's make a run."

They dashed ahead, the flames from the phoenix as Kromious's fire dimmed somewhat. They ran on and passed slopes and inclines filled with jutting stalagmites. They past a baron tree and a large boulder as Kromious's flame abated.

The wizard was just a few dozen yards away—Thaylus could sense him as if he still held the orb from the Realm Rift.

Just after the phoenix's flame fully expired, a shrieking, a gargoyle latched onto Kromious's back.

Thaylus still held the pearl that gave a bright gleam all around them.

Kromious screeched and fell to his side.

"We have to help him!" Garen cried.

The other gargoyle cornered the young priest.

"I have never tasted human flesh. This will be a treat," the evil beast sneered as drool dripped from his mouth.

Faith. The words settled on his heart. He raised his hand, and just like that, the Sword of the Spirit came forth in all its shining brilliance that shone, lighting up the landscape like it was day.

The gargoyle jumped back as if the light from the sword stung him.

Thaylus lunged at the creature and pierced its chest. Instantly, it turned back to stone and crumbled.

Then he turned for the beast on Kromious's back.

Thaylus waited for an opening where the gargoyle was completely exposed. Then in a flash, Thaylus slashed at the evil foe.

The second gargoyle fell to the ground, clutching his sliced torso until he, too, reverted to stone and crumbled.

Thaylus fell to his knees exhausted, the sword disappearing once more.

The wounded phoenix lay bleeding with heavy breathing.

Thaylus forced his aching body to Kromious's side. "How badly are you hurt?"

"I think that abomination broke my spine. I cannot move," Kromious said in tears.

Thaylus did not know how to help. It was obvious Kromious would surely die soon.

"Go," the phoenix said softly. "Rescue my king. Leave me here. I die knowing it was for a special purpose."

An odd notion came to Thaylus's mind. Pray. He'd asked the God in the Gate of Vessels to prove himself. This would be proof like no other.

Thaylus put a hand on Kromious, bowed his head, and closed his eyes. He felt that perfect presence—of love and inner peace.

"I beseech you, oh Great God, restore this dying creature to health."

Tentatively, Kromious moved his wing, then his back.

"Thaylus, I can feel my body. I can move!" Kromious peered his head around, inspecting his back. "My wounds are gone!"

Thaylus fell to his knees and cried. Was he on the brink of coming to know and believe in the One and Only God? All that he lacked was to see and witness this Being and feel His full presence. As he had been told, his journey surely was concluding, and he sensed it.

Kromious rolled and stood just as Garen rejoined them.

"What was that shining thing you were holding?" Garen asked. "I have never seen such amazement!"

"It is called the Sword of the Spirit. I received it from a Celestial Servant."

"How long have you had this?" Kromious looked astounded.

Thaylus shook his head. "I will tell you everything later."

They began to walk toward the cave, and Thaylus brandished the sword once more, lighting the way for dozens of yards ahead.

Then a thought came to him and he made the sword vanish. "The light could alert the wizard far before we reach him. It is best we walk in the light of the pearl."

"Nevertheless when you do use that sword, the wizard doesn't stand a chance," Kromious said.

"Beware, evil has a way of surprising you."

Thaylus sighed, unable to stop thoughts of Brythan and their unexpected encounter with Kyrious from seeping in.

They walked to a broad cave mouth. Inside they could see stalactites loom overhead. The smell of soil and rock mixed with moisture tickled Thaylus's nose.

The pearl's light illuminated the much of the cave. Stone clefts dotted the high walls. A stone bridge crossed over a precipice not even the pearl light fully exposed.

Across the bridge, they came to the carved likeness of a dragon's mouth.

As the three neared it, a door within the stone mouth opened.

Garen flinched and glanced at Kromious and Thaylus, then back at the opened passage with a gaping mouth.

"It is just an enchantment. I have been in a similar cave with my lost companion where we faced a sea serpent," Thaylus said to the stunned priest, Garen.

"If this is the wizard's work. Why would he allow the door to open for just anyone?" the phoenix said with Thaylus's same mild reaction.

"What magic! I have never seen such a thing, myself! And I sense the wizard within this door!" said Garen.

Kromious bent over and looked. "It is too small for me."

"Garen and I will enter."

"God be with you," the bird said.

The two humans entered and ascended a ramp.

At the top, they froze. Before them was a phoenix chained inside a cage. Beside the cage, a man in a crimson robe stood with a wooden staff in his hand.

"What power is this?" asked the man with a raspy voice.

"It is the divine power of God!" Garen stepped forward.

"Doubtless, you come here to save King Naramor. I will not test your power. If you do not want a dead phoenix on your hands, you will surrender."

Thaylus saw large cauldrons burning with fire and put the pearl in his inner pocket and the light vanished, leaving the chamber in the illumination of the lit flames.

The cauldrons lined the walls of the cave chamber that made shadows like chaotic spirits.

"Garen, do as he says. I have a plan," Thaylus whispered into the young man's ear. "Wait until we get closer."

"We surrender," Thaylus said.

"Come here and enter the cage," said the wizard.

The two neared the cage.

"Who are you and what are your names?"

"I am Thaylus and this is Garen."

"I am Bram, the powerful," he said with a slow bow and a coy, mocking grin.

Thaylus's plan was simple: get close, then brandish his sword and cut him down. But Thaylus did not know the extent of Bram's magic. What if he had power like the shapeshifting Celestial Acolyte in the tower of Brea? What if he had his own spiritual sword like the Acolyte?

When Thaylus was at arm's length from the wizard, he summoned his weapon. In a burst of light, the Sword of the Spirit appeared.

Thaylus went for Bram's heart, but the wizard disappeared in a plume of smoke.

"What happened?" Garen gasped.

"He is not gone, just invisible. I have seen this before. Stand back-to-back."

Where would the man reappear? Thaylus scanned the room, tightening his grip on the hilt.

Closing his eyes, Thaylus focused his senses throughout the cave. A gust of wind went by him, and his eyes flipped open.

He held up his sword just as the wizard appeared and came down with his own blade and an echoing crash.

Bram bore his unbroken staff against Thaylus, the two in a deadlock.

His arms ached.

The sorcerer sneered at him. "Is this the power of your god? Pathetic! I will have sport with you."

He lifted his staff, and Thaylus rose into the air, as if commanded by the wizard.

"No!" Garen cried. "Let him go!"

Bram gnashed his teeth and contorted his face. "Little worm!"

The young priest yanked the staff out of Bram' hands, and Thaylus fell to the ground.

"Give that back!"

Garen thrust his palm forward and the wizard went flying back.

Garen broke the staff. "Greater is God in me than any sorcery!"

The defeated wizard lunged at Garen with a mighty roar, but he wasn't fast enough.

Thaylus jumped to his feet, summoned his sword, and charged at Bram, impaling him.

"My magic! How?"

A purple glow came from the wizard's wound. He fell, thrashing around, until his whole body was engulfed into a purple haze and dissipated.

"We've won!" Garen cheered.

Thaylus slashed at the side of the cage leaving a mark like a lightning strike.

Garen opened the cage door and to find King Naramor. He unchained the phoenix king, who hopped out and spread his wings.

"I am in your debt, my friends. I could hardly believe my eyes. You two have exceptional powers."

Thaylus was prepared to explain everything. But then he heard the voice of Ithia: You have done your task in this time. It is time to move on.

# Chapter 27

## The Great Deception

In another flash of light, Thaylus stood on an open plane. The twilight gleam from the sky was outshined by the green star of Erebus, which Thaylus knew was the emerald prison.

Behold the green star. Do you recall when you went back in time four-thousand years into the past and learned of Mordecai's vision?"

The words were Ithia's.

"Yes. He said seven years from Mordecai's time the star would appear, then seven years later it would fall to Khrine. What do I do here?"

Simply take note of the star. Now we go seven years more according to Mordecai's vision.

Now, Thaylus stood at the edge of a cliff with a forest behind him. In the horizon, the emerald was shooting through the sky headed for the land below him.

The landscape was illuminated like a green sun as the star plunged into the ground making a loud crash. A crater a mile in diameter formed.

When the smoke and debris cleared, the glowing, spherical emerald gave off clouds of mist. In another flash of light, Thaylus was transported within the crater, and he noticed cracks that lined the object.

Thaylus neared the emerald peering inside. Within, he saw Erebus and his seven generals.

Thaylus knew they would soon break free. He recalled Mordecai's witness of the event.

He jolted as the emerald shook and cracked even more. The crack lines gleamed and flickered like rods of lightning. Pieces broke off, and the ground vibrated. The vibrations increased, and the cracks beamed like rays of green sunlight.

Thaylus hid behind a boulder and peeked out.

The emerald split part, sending shards into the air. It sounded like exploding coals.

"We are free!" Erebus raised his fist into the air. "And we are on Khrine. But who could have done this?"

"Baron Erebus, only a Celestial Servant could have put our prison here," said one of the Acolytes.

"No matter," Erebus said with a wicked smile. "Now that we are here, our plan has changed."

The Celestial Baron raised his hands.

"We will use our powers to seduce men to worship us as gods! Doubtless, God does not expose himself openly that frequently." Erebus laughed. "If we claim we are all-powerful, we cannot fail!"

In another flash of light, Thaylus stood at the edge of the crater.

Two winged Celestial Acolytes bore Erebus by the arms and lifted him onto the edge.

One of the Acolyte generals shot high into the air. Minutes later, he darted back to his place on the ground.

"I have scanned the land. Two large kingdoms lay north."

"Very good," Erebus said. "That will be our first place to take control."

"We should take different forms—ones that strike fear and total submission in the minds of men," said another general.

Erebus was the first to transform. His appearance mimicked a scorpion's body with the neck and head of a dragon and a pair of wings. It was Thron, god of wisdom, Thaylus knew from his own time.

The first Acolyte to change became a man-beast with two dragon's legs and feet. He had a man's torso with four arms and an eagle's wings and head. It was the god of rain, Oracle.

"Excellent! You," Erebus said to one of his Acolytes. "We will show ourselves first so we do not overwhelm them."

The two god forms shot forth in flight for the closest kingdom.

Another flash of light came, and Thaylus found himself in that very kingdom at the base of a tower, watching as the two transformed spirits zoomed closer. They stopped in midair over the populace. The people stared and murmured.

"I and my fellow god come to you so you may know us, two of the many true gods," Erebus said.

His herculean body landed on the ground with a reverberating boom.

Four guards pushed through surrounding a man in a scarlet robe and crown.

"You are deceiving beings," the king cried with a red face. "You speak blasphemy!"

Erebus replied with a voice like a trumpet that went straight through Thaylus's bones.

"You dare test us!"

He stretched his wings over his head, and burst of wind came forth. A blast of hail shot like rocks in a hurricane.

People fell back and cried out, their shouts barely audible in the torrent of air.

The king slid back on his knees and shielded his face with his arms like the others.

Erebus lowered his wings, and the gale abated.

"Do you need more proof?" he sneered with his teeth bared like broadswords.

Most fell on their face and palms. "We submit. Forgive us!"

"No, do not relent!" cried the king. "Our God is supreme and sovereign forever. You two are deceivers, false and evil gods."

"Listen to our king! There is no God but ours!" cried another.

But fear won out.

"We all give our allegiance to you!" most of the crowd shouted.

The king ran among the people. "Do not give glory to these charlatans! Even if they kill us, we have our home beyond the Gate of Vessels that awaits us!"

"There is no Gate of Vessels!" spewed the Acolyte. "And this 'god' is no more than a spirit like you are. He has no power."

Erebus raised his fist. "Die with your king or live with us."

"We bow to you great gods!" said a man on his knees.

"My subjects, bring those who oppose our rule to stand before us," Erebus ordered.

The throng took the king and others who resisted, forcing them to stand beside each other in a line.

"You have one last chance," said the Acolyte.

All were silent. The king straightened his back and narrowed his eyes.

"So be it!" said Erebus.

He opened his mouth and devoured the king in one swallow. The rest were stung by the scorpion's tail, one by one.

Thaylus tightened his fists and clenched his jaw as he watched. He'd never felt such anger.

He was about to brandish his shining sword when he heard Ithia's voice.

No, Thaylus. The time line must go untainted. God is in control.

"What am I to do now, then?"

You have witnessed the beginning of the great deception. But God will not tolerate the false gods to continue to vex the people of Khrine for long. Now we go another seven years into the future.

In another flash of light, Thaylus stood in a temple with prostrated people before a tall, muscular being with a crow's head and a pair of fiery eyes that burned blue. It was one of the oldest and most sacred false gods of the realm of Khrine. His name was Overon.

Thaylus's stomach turned in disgust.

He dashed outside, only to find statues of the false gods everywhere. He grabbed his head and wanted to cry out in anguish. He staggered against a wall and wept.

Then a loud boom resounded from a mountain in the distance. The top had exploded, and smoke like from a giant furnace rose into the clouds. It began to swirl and crack with lightning.

One of the temples burst and stone debris went flying.

As Thaylus looked on, a false god was ripped from the building by an invisible force and was carried away into the air toward the immense, dark, bellowing tornado upon the mountain.

In the distance, more of the shapeshifting Acolytes followed the first one. It was like an invisible wind sucked them spinning into the air.

Before Erebus himself was carried away, he gave a final message.

"This is a test. We leave you for a time. But stay faithful, and you will be rewarded. Farewell, my subjects!"

Then Erebus, too, went flying into the tornado and drawn into the mountain.

All the people were silent and glanced at each other.

"W—what just happened?" asked a young girl.

"It is a test, just like Thron told us," said one of priests with a stern frown.

"What does this mean for us?" asked a man.

"It means we continue to worship them until they return. It is that simple. In homage of the lost gods, let us make more images of them. As head priest of Thron, I proclaim this day as Day of the God's Oath, the day when they were taken from us with a promise to return."

All were silent, looking at the rubble.

"Don't stand there! Let us rebuild the temples to the six gods!" said the high priest.

People started to gather pieces of the temples by hand and by wagon. Time slowed to a crawl as they lowered their heads and drooped their arms while collecting debris.

"Fools!" Thaylus said himself. "It is obvious they were taken unwillingly!"

Thaylus sunk his face in his hands and shook his head. He fell to his knees and looked heavenward.

"Why did you let them be deceived?"

Ithia spoke within him once more.

Despair not, Thaylus. God has allowed this. What you have just seen is God sealing Erebus and his generals into the Abyss. But God will suffer them to escape the Abyss and dwell on Khrine for a season longer.

In a flash of light, Thaylus was on the peak of a high mountain facing another that looked like where the shaft of the Abyss opened.

Ithia spoke.

You have traveled four-thousand years from your own time.

A bright light in the shape of man drifted from the sky to the adjacent mountain. A shining golden key appeared in his hands.

The man approached a stone altar with a keyhole. He inserted his key and turned it.

Then he stepped away.

The Abyss opened as myriads of Realm Dwellers crawled out and descended the smoking mountain.

Erebus emerged from the smoke in his false form of Thron. His five generals also came out in their altered guises.

Erebus rose into the sky and looked across the breadth of the realm of Khrine. He raised his voice like a trumpet to his dark, misty, shadowy beings, all of them with burning red eyes and swords of black fire.

"My children, head east where you will find a kingdom of men. Destroy all you encounter!"

The false-god Oracle raised his eyes and spoke with a tremble. "Master, our intention was to rule them."

"No longer! I will spite God for locking us into the Abyss! The suffering of man is on His head!"

Another light, and Thaylus was at that very kingdom. He stood on a low balcony and watched as droves of Realm Dwellers spilled into the kingdom, striking down men, women, and children.

Guards and knights broke through the castle gates and charged at the dark foes. The Realm Dwellers shot forth and cut down the defenders. The defenders tried to push back the assailants, but the Realm Dwellers outnumbered the men three to one.

But even in the human soldiers' obvious defeat, they fought on.

Thaylus saw what must have been the human general dressed in chain mail and a cloak of scarlet and blue. He wore a golden crest pinned to his right shoulder and had an air of gallant pride.

His fighting style unmatched the others. He made wide strokes and struck down multiple Realm Dwellers with each blow.

"Fight on, men! The gods are with us!"

The clash of steel blades and swords of black fire sent sparks into the air that sounded like crackling embers exploding. The general's words must have inspired them as several men charged at a group of Realm Dwellers and pushed them back.

The smell of blood and sweat filled Thaylus's nostrils. It mixed with putrid smoke from the Realm Dwellers' black fiery swords.

Thaylus fought the urge to spring upon them with his shining sword.

The Realm Dwellers, the creation of Erebus, filled the outside concourse, headed for the citadel gate. Screams of men made Thaylus shudder, while the laughs of the Realm Dwellers made him cringe.

With a valiant last offensive assault, the enemy broke through.

It was over.

"Ithia! Take me from here!" he said as he looked away.

You have two more tasks to complete. You will go a thousand years from this time into the future to seal the Realm Dwellers into the Abyss.

"But ... that is three-thousand years into my own past. You told me and Brythan that the wise man full of faith seals them in. It happened during the battle of Nimithar when the great flash of light from the seal expunges the Realm Dwellers."

You are the wise man.

Thaylus gasped. Me?

He raised his hands and looked at them as if pondering his own ability. It was something he'd never considered. But now, examining the past with all that had happened, he understood.

"I am ready."

In another flash of light, he stood on a mound as droves of Realm Dwellers tried to scale the tall castle wall. The men on battlements threw down rocks and shot arrows upon the dark foes.

Like the Spirit Spawns' attack on Khrine, the Realm Dwellers' numbers trumped the soldiers atop the wall. Some were yanked down and fell to their deaths. Others were overcome by the Realm Dwellers who came over the wall and ended the men with a short sword battle.

Ithia's voice came again.

He within the Gate of Vessels has given the seal to you. Fulfil your task.

Thaylus felt it-a subtle inner fluctuation. A familiar power coursed through his body. Thaylus knew it would take surpassing will and faith to transport so many Realm Dwellers into the Abyss. But he had to have faith.

After all, as Ithia said, it had happened already.

But in his present state, he knew he could not perform his task. He wasn't strong enough on his own. Thaylus still had doubt, and his bitterness still put a twist in his gullet.

He needed total faith, and he knew what that meant—putting his trust and fealty entirely in the deity who lives in the Gate of Vessels.

He needed to admit once and for all: He is God.

Around him, the ground thumped and the smoke-like mist made Thaylus's head spin. The war cries of the dark entities were like burning coals being crushed and turned. It made his body ripple with a wave of fatigue.

The Realm Dwellers looked like leeches that crawled up the wall, grasping soldiers and casting them over to their deaths.

Soon the enemy would penetrate the castle.

The thought strained Thaylus's head, and he bent over.

"Oh, Great God, give me the power to believe in you! I cannot do it alone!"

Thaylus fell on his face and wept loudly.

As he did, he felt a peace like still waters overtake him. A perfect sense of love abided within him, too. This time, the presence had more power.

He stood and wiped his face, then poised himself, closing his eyes. He knew the time to completely trust in this Being as God had arrived.

Thaylus clenched his teeth and squeezed his eyes shut. He felt the warmness of Clara's Pearl and reflected on her words: Faith is the evidence of things not seen and of things hoped for.

It had happened—he fully understood the words she'd spoken. His belief began to wash away the corrosion and hardness in his heart. He smiled and cried tears of joy.

A bright light surrounded him, and suddenly a man-like being was there. He resonated with the power of the God of the Gate of Vessels.

"Are you God?" Thaylus asked.

"I am the Emissary—His incarnation."

Thaylus bent his knee and bowed his head. "You are God and there is no other."

The Emissary walked to Thaylus and raised him by the shoulders. The Emissary's eyes sparkled like a child's.

Thaylus's heart swelled with joy.

"You have one remaining task after today. I will see you again shortly," said the Emissary.

The light abated, and Thaylus was back on the mound. His heart beat with a slow, steady rhythm. His breathing was full and deep.

It was time.

Thaylus lifted his arm straight over his head. The shield, the Seal to the Abyss, appeared in his hand. The holy, golden shine was like the sun.

At the shine, the Realm Dwellers turned away and covered their faces, shrieking violently.

The shine increased until nothing was visible. When the shine disappeared, not a Realm Dweller remained.

A young soldier at the base of the mound gripped a shoulder wound and breathed heavily through his nose, gritting his teeth from the pain. His head jerked all around.

He looked at an older man a few yards away.

"Captain, what happened?" the young man said between breaths.

"I ... don't know," said the captain.

He ran to the young soldier and looked closely at his shoulder. "Your wound is severe."

Thaylus's heart ached with compassion. He went down the mound and neared the fallen soldier.

The captain looked at Thaylus like he was a Vessel Bearer. "Who are you, stranger?"

"I can help this young man." Thaylus felt such peace.

His encounter with the Emissary had made Thaylus believe—completely. He realized the answer to his ultimate question: There is one God, and He lives in the Gate of Vessels.

Thaylus kneeled and put his hand on the soldier's wound. At his touch, the shoulder wound closed and the bleeding stopped.

"Have the gods sent you to us?" asked the captain.

"I serve one God who is over all. Although you cannot bear my answer now, the time comes when men will worship the one true God."

Then came another flash.

This time, Thaylus was on a high tower with the scarlet light coming from far away.

He was back in his own time.

Thaylus, you are three days after the light's appearance from the period you first stepped through time.

But this time, the voice was not Ithia's. It was the voice of the Emissary. Thaylus knew the complete faith and wisdom he'd gained allowed this.

The wise sage had one more task.

# Chapter 28

## THE FINAL TASK

THAYLUS STARED at the red pillar of light with his fists tensed and his stance firmly set. His body was relaxed and mind was focused and filled with one thought: accomplishing his last task.

The Emissary spoke.

"Thaylus, the time has come to bring a complete end to Erebus, his five generals, and his dark creations, the Realm Dwellers."

"How? The shield cannot destroy them, only seal them in the Abyss, and the Sword of the Spirit cannot subdue so many."

Thaylus sensed the warmth of the presence of the Emissary draw near. He felt a hand on his shoulder.

"What is happening?" Thaylus asked with a long sigh.

Your soul is being filled with my Holy Spirit. With my power inside you, your strength will grow in ways unimagined.

Thaylus stretched forth his hand to summon the Sword of the Spirit.

But the Emissary stopped him.

Restrain the full power I gave you, or you will destroy a third of everything on the planet of Khrine.

The time of the Realm Dwellers had arrived. The red light darkened as a loud rumbling vibrated the ground.

The gates of the Western Kingdom opened, and the dark foes poured out in droves.

The six remaining kingdoms, including Solace, charged into a valley to meet the Realm Dwellers.

The battle cries resounded throughout the valley. The burning eyes of the Realm Dwellers looked like lava running down a volcano.

The first weapon clash cast sparks and smoke.

"What do I do?" asked Thaylus.

Wait until all the Realm Dwellers cross to this realm. As the sword's power has grown, so has the shield's power. With it, you will bind the Realm Dwellers deeper to a single spot in the Abyss, and they will be destroyed forever.

"Does that mean I have to go to the Abyss? What about Erebus and his five generals? Where are they?"

They hide in the Abyss. Their fear is that I will send the Vessel Bearers to destroy them.

Thaylus cringed and shuddered at the men being overwhelmed by the Realm Dwellers. One after another, the evil foes cut down the flesh and blood forces of Khrine. Blood stained the ground as more and more Realm Dwellers filed out of the Western Kingdom.

The carnage around Thaylus brought tears to his eyes. The warfare stunned him.

But he knew God allowed everything for a purpose.

The dark forces invaded the castles of Heth and Darvy, the two oldest kingdoms that had survived centuries of war without penetration. Today was different.

The red light flickered and vanished as the final group of Realm Dwellers came from the gate.

"That is the last of them," said the Emissary.

Thaylus raised his hand and the shield appeared in his grasp.

He closed his eyes and focused, and the shield shined like never before, filling the entire valley.

When the light finally faded, it was just like before, except far more were now sealed into the Abyss. A thunderous silence filled the landscape.

Thaylus was wide-eyed as he scanned the battle plain with only warrior men left. They looked everywhere for the evil foes. The defenders of Khrine blinked their eyes as though they were seeing an illusion or a dream. They approached each other murmuring and shrugging their shoulders. The smoke from the Realm Dwellers and the smell of blood blew away in a strong wind, replaced with the glorious fresh scent of grass and trees.

Large spaces among the remaining warriors on the battlefield were left from where large hordes of Realm Dwellers had disappeared.

Thaylus sat on a hilltop and watched a long while. Hope stirred within him. But he knew there was more to come. His task wasn't finished yet.

A vortex of dark clouds appeared, and Thaylus reeled back.

A portal.

"I can sense the evil within that ... thing. Will it take me to the Abyss?"

"It will," said the Emissary.

Thaylus trembled. "I must go inside?"

"Yes," said the Emissary

"Your presence will go with me?"

"Of course, but you will not feel my Spirit. It is the ultimate test of faith."

Thaylus took a breath. Then he stood and wiped the sweat off his face.

"Very well."

He stepped into the portal.

Immediately, Thaylus was in a dark place, filled with an evil essence. A rush of cold air chilled him, and beneath his feet, the stone surface felt hard and unforgiving.

Beyond that, he felt nothing. It was as if all his faith and power had vanished. He felt ... alone.

He raised hand over his head but the Sword of the Spirit did not appear. His heart raced and his breathing because uneven.

He could not hear the voice of the Emissary, but Thaylus knew what he would say...

I am with you. Fear not.

Thaylus closed his eyes and inhaled deeply. Then he kneeled and folded his hands.

"To the God who dwells inside the Gate of Vessels, hear me and guide me."

Rather than a feeling, he got a notion: I have the power to wield the sword.

He raised his arm, and the shining sword appeared.

A dark fog retreated from the sword light. How was he to find the brood of Realm Dwellers?

Thaylus recalled how he'd used the orb in the Realm Rift. If only he had it!

The ground looked like dried lava. A light breeze carried the faint smell of smoke.

Thaylus came to a boulder and sat on it to think. He put a fist to his chin and sighed.

The Emissary said Thaylus had been given insurmountable faith and power. But he felt powerless.

Yet in his head, he knew he had more power and faith than ever—the epitome of both. The Spirit of the Emissary dwelled inside him.

He closed his eyes and focused. On what, he could not say. But it was there. It was a subtle, poignant revelation barely discernible.

Thaylus recited the words from the book he'd stumbled upon in the Tower of Brea. Greater is He that is in me than he that is in the world.

He was not in the world, but the meaning rang truer than ever.

He took the sword by both hands and thought of the words of the book in the tower.

Then Thaylus's eyes shot open.

He cried out, as loud as he could, and the Sword of the Spirit instantly erupted with illumination over a hundred-fold!

The deep recesses of the Abyss were exposed. On a nearby plateau, surrounded by a gulf, he could now see an immense multilevel caged prison. It teemed with thousands of Realm Dwellers. Their red burning eyes came into view from the thick darkness.

But where were the Baron and his five?

The sword stopped shining, but the room remained lit as though it had an invisible source.

"Time to do away with you forever!" Thaylus cried.

He pointed his sword at the trapped beings and prepared to purge them from existence with a beam of light.

But suddenly, something hard knocked Thaylus to the side.

He rolled and came to rest on his back.

Looming over him was the familiar form of Thron, the false god of wisdom, along with the five other false gods.

"You were foolish to come here," said Thron, surrounded by his seven generals. "Even if you defeat us, I will not allow you to escape this place."

"Why do you stay in your fake forms?" Thaylus studied him.

"Many years in the Abyss has drained us of our glorious forms."

"Erebus—"

"I am Thron now!"

The false god raised himself on his scorpion torso and roared with his dragon head.

Thaylus shuddered. Faith, he reminded himself.

In an instant, Thron lunged for him with open mouth.

Thaylus whirled and blasted at Thron with a surge of light.

Thron went reeling back.

He seethed with wrath, his jaw dripping with blood. "Surround him!"

The five generals, each in their own anthropomorphic forms, circled Thaylus. Closer and closer, they closed in on him, snickering and cackling.

Thaylus knew he could only harm one being at a time, leaving him open to attack from the others.

Then a thought occurred: Would the generals be killed if Thron himself was vanquished? At the least they would lose the power given them by Thron, enough that Thaylus could slay them.

Thaylus faced Thron and shot him with a continuous light beam.

Thron shrieked as the light consumed him little by little.

But it was taking too long, and the others were almost upon him.

A streak of light flashed across the chest of a general, splitting him in half as his voice echoed with a loud shriek.

The six remaining generals spun around to see what had just vanquished one of their ranks with one fell slash.

Thaylus's heart throbbed with joy.

There, he beheld a shining being holding a sword of fire.

It was Brythan!

"Thaylus, let us do away with these abominations!" Brythan shouted.

Thaylus nodded with beaming face and a broad smile. He continued to blast Thron with light while Brythan protected Thaylus.

"Nooo!" yelled Thron as light consumed him. The sound like thunder echoed as the ground quaked. His cry became louder and fissures of white light opened over Thron's body until there an explosion of light erupted. When the light abated, Thron was no more.

The Baron was dead.

"Thron's absence weakens them! Don't hold back!" Brythan yelled.

With Thron gone, Thaylus charged at the false god before him. Their swords clashed as Thaylus drove him back. Thaylus bore down on his foe and soon his blade came back on him.

Five generals remained.

Brythan made a diagonal strike across the torso of one of the generals. He dropped his weapon and fell on his back, writhing and crying out until light overpowered him like the others.

Victory seemed near as the two friends cut down the rest of the Acolyte generals.

"Please spare me! I have done wrong and I relent," said the last one.

It was Siethen, god of the wind. His chest was man-like with golden and scarlet feathers. He had pair of stork's wings and a pair of bat's wings. His legs and feet were like a deer's.

But Brythan shook his head. "You are no longer fit to live."

"No!" shouted the general.

Together, Brythan and Thaylus pierced him.

Then they turned to each other with broad grins.

"Brythan! You are here!"

"I asked the Emissary if I may aid you again."

"It appears it was needed. I thought I was surely dead."

"Ah, but even if you had died, your vessel in the Plains of Eternity would be accepted into the Gate of Vessels. You finally submit and believe in God."

"It is true, I have. Something in me is now peaceful and full of power. I finally understand."

Brythan switched from his glorious form into his mortal one.

He and Thaylus clasped forearms and shook them.

"You may do the honors," said Brythan, motioning in the direction of the horde of caged Realm Dwellers.

Thaylus took the hilt of the sword by both hands and raised it over his head. The shining blade flickered and a sound of flames echoed throughout the Abyss. The Sword of the Spirit grew brighter.

Thaylus centered his thoughts on the Emissary and prepared to unleash a terrible burst of light.

But then, Thaylus was on his knees, Brythan next to him. His head shook wildly as the ground cracked, making a sound like splitting coal embers.

A shining being like a Celestial Servant stood in a crater of burnt, black terrain just feet away.

Thaylus knew this being.

Cleerious.

He was the one who'd thrown the emerald prison from Aderath to Khrine. And now he stood before them, ready to best the God of the Gate of Vessels.

"Thaylus, you are a menace," Cleerious hissed. "You have destroyed Erebus and his Celestial Acolytes. But you will go no further. The Realm Dwellers I will claim as my own!"

Thaylus's body went still.

But then he remembered the power he had received, and the truth.

Brythan stared with glossy eyes.

"Thaylus, this is no simple Celestial Baron. Cleerious was the most powerful Celestial Servant the Creator ever made."

Cleerious lacked the wings of a Vessel Bearer, yet he floated into the air and moved closer to the two humans.

Thaylus lifted his chin. "What does it matter if the Realm Dwellers live? You are trapped here!"

Cleerious smiled coyly as he descended from the air and stood before Thaylus.

"I will leave by whatever means you will leave."

Brythan looked at Thaylus. "When will we return to Khrine?"

Thaylus pulled on his short beard. "I assume when we destroy the Realm Dwellers."

"Then it appears we must vanquish Cleerious as well."

The presence of the Celestial Baron felt like a hot wind rushed past Thaylus. Only the Emissary had greater spiritual stigma.

Brythan donned his shining form once more and brandished his flaming sword. Thaylus summoned his own sword as well.

"Come at me, fools!" Cleerious cried.

The two rushed at him with their blades pointed.

But Cleerious tensed his fingers as if he were grasping an apple. As he did, both men lifted into the air, their swords tumbling to the rough ground.

"I have been observing all your exploits since the scarlet light. But without your God, you are helpless."

Cleerious relaxed his hand, and Thaylus and Brythan fell to the ground.

Thaylus rose. He stepped forward and raised a fist.

"God is with us! I have something you can't understand—faith!"

Cleerious roared. The ground of the whole Abyssal Realm shook with his anger.

"This cannot end like our encounter with Kyrious," Thaylus told Brythan. "We must have faith and not fear."

Cleerious raised his hands, and flaming rocks plummeted from the sky. He slammed the ground, and it began to crack.

"He will destroy the whole terrain of the Abyss!"

"We must attack, Brythan."

"Let us pray for victory first."

Brythan kneeled and mumbled a brief prayer.

As he prayed, Thaylus was filled with faith. He knew he could slay the Celestial Baron.

Brythan looked at his friend. "Do you sense that surge of faith?"

Thaylus nodded. "God is with us. Let us put end to this monster."

Thaylus knew he could slay the being. But there would still be a struggle.

"Get behind him. He cannot fight on opposite fronts," Brythan said.

"Have you not learned?" Cleerious raged. "Even Erebus could kill you despite any tactic you devise. My power is much greater."

Cleerious raised his hand, and the darkness of the firmament of the abyss rumbled with lightning.

"My power is unimagined!" Cleerious's voice echoed through the whole Abyss.

Thaylus felt nauseous and weak from the tremendous display of power. He worried that he would give into his fear as he had with Kyrious.

But things were different now. Thaylus possessed the Divine Spirit.

Thaylus steeled himself. "No, you will not win. My God is omnipotent!"

"Then attack me!" Cleerious taunted.

Brythan's eyes widened and he spoke in a low tone. "Thaylus, I have doubts."

Thaylus did not answer.

He closed his eyes. His face began to relax and his head lifted upward.

Finally, Thaylus opened his eyes and turned his palms up as if to take in light from a warm sun.

"Greater is He that is in me than he that is in the world," he said.

Thaylus repeated his words.

"What are you doing?" Cleerious demanded.

"Greater is He that is in me than he that is in the world," Thaylus said again.

"Cease this language!"

"Greater is He that is in me than he that is in the world."

The Celestial Baron's shine faded momentarily. "Stop! Stop, you cretin!"

Brythan began saying the words also.

Together, they said it over and over: Greater is He that is in me than he that is in the world.

Greater is He that is in me than he that is in the world.

Greater is He that is in me than he that is in the world.

"Ack!" Cleerious bellowed. He extended his arm and dispersed a bolt of lightning at Thaylus and Brythan.

They crossed their swords together, and the lightning bounced off the blades.

Together they continued to chant the words, louder and louder.

The two men pushed against the force of the lightning volley.

Finally, Cleerious withdrew his hand, stopping the lighting.

"Enough!" shouted Cleerious as he spread his arms.

Thaylus and Brythan flew backwards along with the cage that held the Realm Dwellers.

"You will trouble me no longer!" Cleerious said. "If I am to be doomed to live in this dark prison, I will turn it into a wasteland!"

The Celestial Baron made a fist. Lightning mixed with hail poured from the thick darkness above. It went on as far as the eye could see in all directions.

The ground shook and split as the sound of it echoed across the Abyss.

Rifts formed as the ground kept splitting.

Rock shelves fell into the endless depths of crevasses.

"What do we do, Brythan? He'll decimate the whole Abyss and the both of us."

"We need to get out of here."

"But we require a portal," Thaylus said.

"Then we must make one."

Thaylus believed he and Brythan were meant to overcome this obstacle like all others. The Emissary Himself had sent them.

But he could not see how.

"We should pray," Thaylus said.

Brythan's shoulders sank. "I don't know if I even have the faith to do that."

But he went to his knees and folded his hands.

Thaylus did the same. It was hard to hear his own voice in the destruction of the Abyss, but he kept his focus on God.

"To He who dwells inside the Gate of Vessels, nothing is too hard for you. And You are always with us. Make a way of escape from this place so we may glorify You."

Nothing happened.

"Ha, ha!" Cleerious cackled madly. "All of us shall perish!"

Brythan looked at his friend. "It appears I shall see you in the life beyond the Gate of Vessels."

Thaylus embraced Brythan. "So be it."

Then a beautiful voice spoke loud and clear into their hearts.

"Be of good cheer, my servants."

Thaylus and Brythan looked up at the speaker—the Emissary stood over them!

"As I have delivered you from all foes and situations, so will I now."

Thaylus and Brythan rose as the Emissary smiled.

"Let us leave this realm to its ruin."

A portal appeared, and He led Thaylus and Brythan through it.

# Chapter 29

## THE RECKONING

THAYLUS STOOD ATOP THE HIGHEST TOWER of the Kingdom of Solace with Brythan and the Emissary.

The Emissary put a hand on Thaylus's shoulder.

"You are the special servant of Mine who will tell mankind about Me."

Thaylus blinked. "Me?"

"Yes. Show them the Sword of the Spirit. That will be a witness to My existence."

The Emissary went to the tower balcony, where He hung His head and cried.

"Why are you sad?" Brythan asked.

"Many people will not believe in Me. They will die in disbelief like Thaylus was headed to. But they will not reach the truth like you did, Thaylus."

"What exactly do you want me to do?" Thaylus asked.

"Do you see that large mound there that is in the middle of the seven kingdoms?"

The Emissary pointed to a mound in the distance.

"That is where you shall brandish the Sword of the Spirit. All men will see you and you will testify about Me, so they may have faith in Me."

"What do I say?"

The Emissary touched Thaylus's forehead

"The words you are to speak are in your mind."

Thaylus's mind felt like it resonated with the Emissary's touch like a lake reflecting bright sunlight.

Brythan looked deeply into Thaylus's eyes. "Your eyes are like the Emissary's! They glisten like a child's."

"I … I feel so in touch with the Emissary's Spirit." Thaylus breathed in deeply. "It's so peaceful yet so powerful."

"It is time to begin the reconciliation," said the Emissary.

In a flash of light, Thaylus was on the mound. He looked around, then peered skyward and raised his arms.

As the remaining soldiers from all the kingdoms were tending to the wounded, gathering the dead and conversing, Thaylus stood on the mound and raised his hands into the air. The Sword of the Spirit appeared in his hands, and it shined like the sun.

So bright was the sword, all citizens, royalty, and servants of all six kingdoms could hear and see Thaylus.

All who saw fastened their eyes on the flaming, flickering sword. A strong, hot wind went out from the blade as the people shielded their faces.

Thaylus paused as he prepared to speak. His voice rang out like a thunderclap.

"To the seven kingdoms of the realm of Khrine, I speak to you a revelation of life and death, truth and lies, wisdom and foolishness, pain and healing."

The soldiers across the breadth of the battleground and kingdom inhabitants were still as statues.

"I come on behalf of the God who dwells in the Gate of Vessels—the one true God. The ones who you worship as gods are nothing more than lying spirits."

Thaylus was silent so the people could comprehend his words.

He continued. "These false gods are they who brought forth the Realm Dwellers."

"Who are you?" cried out a young soldier.

"I am the God's mortal servant."

"You lie!" said the high priest of Oracle, god of rain. He turned to all around him "This is a test to prove our allegiance to the gods! This prophet is a deceitful worker of the Realm Dwellers."

People muttered, and a commotion was arousing.

Thaylus would have marveled in disbelief at someone wielding a shining sword. But his mind had been altered by the Emissary and Thaylus. He knew men's stubbornness and lust for power. He had been told some would not receive his testimony of the Emissary.

"To all who wish to know the true God, swear your allegiance to Him and you will have peace, fulfillment, and love. And when you die, you will have eternal life in a paradise beyond a threshold called the Gate of Vessels!"

"Our priest is right. This man tells fairy tales!" yelled a tall, bulky soldier. "Stay vigilant, men!"

From a group of soldiers, King Trophimus stepped forward.

"My fellow warriors and rulers, he must speak the truth. Have the gods ever wielded a shining fiery blade or had a voice like a horn?"

Some traded glances and nods.

"Tell us more of this God and this Gate of Vessels," asked a soldier.

Thaylus smiled, and his heart throbbed with joy.

"I will explain everything. First, I ask all who want God to kneel in surrender."

A wave of people kneeling swept across the battlefield.

But Thaylus's smile faded as he saw thousands still standing with folded arms or hands on hips in defiance. He felt his face burn red with anger. He would have vaporized them immediately with his sword, but his mentality had been made anew.

In the midst of his anger, he felt compassion.

Those who opposed him, shouted obscenities and shook their fists at him.

"He is a deceiver as our priest says!" yelled one.

Thaylus descended the mound and spoke to the young soldier who'd asked about the Gate of Vessels.

"You will be the first priest of God. All I explain, I will write in a book so the following generations will have the knowledge of God. What is your name?"

The young soldier's face lit up and he smiled broadly. "My name is Harek. I will not fail you."

The shining sword dimmed in Thaylus's hands until it glowed.

King Trophimus approached Thaylus.

"Who knew my humble sage would herald the knowledge of the true living God? As soon as I bowed, I felt His presence. I know your words are true,"

Trophimus kneeled before Thaylus.

But Thaylus took his king by his shoulders and raised him up.

"Bow before God, King Trophimus. Not me."

* * *

THAYLUS TOOK HAREK to the castle of Solace by horse.

As they entered the main hall, all stared at the sword that was now a soft glow.

A nobleman bowed his head. "Hello, Arch Sage. Is there anything you … ah

… require of us?"

Thaylus put a hand on the nobleman's shoulder.

"Trust in God, my friend."

Thaylus turned to Harek. "Come, my young priest. Your instruction begins now."

In the sage's chambers, Thaylus sat at a desk piled high with books and Harek sat across from him.

Thaylus took out a blank book and quill and wrote as he taught the young priest.

Thaylus told him everything—about God, specifically the Gate of Vessels and the different spiritual creations, like Vessel Bearers and Celestial Servants. He also thought it necessary to tell of the evil spiritual beings now gone, like the Celestial Barons, Celestial Acolytes, and Spirit Spawns.

He told Harek of Ithia, the seal, the Sword of the Spirit, the Realm Rift, the Pool of Healing, and the Dragon of the Abyss.

"And when I die, my spiritual vessel will be bought into the Gate of Vessels too?" Harek asked, his attention rapt. "And I will get a spiritual body?"

"If you believe."

Thaylus rose and stretched, and they retired for the evening.

\* \* \*

THE NEXT NIGHT, Thaylus could not sleep. Restless, he got out of bed and dressed in his cloak, making his way to the sage's gardens.

The air was cold and moist as mist came from his nostrils. A full moon hung in a cloudy sky. He approached a large sunflower with dew on it. Thaylus smiled and went on.

A rustling came from a bunch of bushes behind him.

He frowned. "Hello?"

No answer came.

Thaylus neared the bushes. He spread them to look inside.

A dark figure leaped out at him and pinned him to the ground.

"False prophet!" the man spewed. "I am the instrument of the gods' wrath. For your blasphemy, you deserve death!"

The assailant pulled out a dagger.

Thaylus grabbed the man's wrist, his arms burning with exhaustion.

The attacker gritted his teeth, and his eyes bulged with madness.

"If you kill me, there will always be followers of God," Thaylus told the man. "I will die as a martyr, and my spirit will be with God inside the Gate of Vessels!"

"I will stop your lies to my dying breath! There will always be those who will strive against your lies."

Thaylus said nothing for a few minutes, his arms still holding back the dagger.

Finally, he looked deeply into the man's gaze.

"I forgive you," Thaylus said.

Thaylus's strength left his arm, and the dagger pierced him. Thaylus gasped, and felt his blood leaving him.

Thaylus turned his head to see a young woman in a blue nightgown. She covered her mouth.

"Princess Athinia! What are you doing here!" said the attacker.

"I ... I was just walking ... "

The man charged at the princess, grabbing her by the arm.

"Keep silent about this or you will be next!"

"Guard, guard!" she yelled.

"Insolent witch!"

Athinia bit the man's arm and drew blood.

With a loud cry he released her.

She fled to the garden gate a few yards away.

Thaylus lay on the ground watching as the blood flowed from his body.

But the gate was locked. Athinia pounded on the gate.

"Help! Help, someone!"

The attacker lunged at her with the weapon raised.

"Halt, you!" yelled a man in chain mail, holding a spear.

The attacker jerked the princess close and pressed his dagger against her neck.

"Stay back!" he told the guards with his back at the gate.

"Think what you are doing, sir!" said the guard.

"Sage Thaylus is a false prophet. Can't you see? He is just...ah!"

A spearpoint burst through the man's stomach. He dropped the dagger and sank against the gate.

On the other side of the gate, a guard stood.

"Are you unharmed, Princess?" he said through the gate.

"Yes, but ... Thaylus!"

Athinia gasped and ran to Thaylus's side.

The guard joined her.

Athinia held his head and cried. "We must do something!"

"The wound is too close to the heart," the guard said.

He addressed Thaylus. "I am sorry, Arch Sage."

Thaylus cupped Athinia's cheek.

"I will live on in the next life. I ask that you follow my footsteps and submit to God. And teach young Prince Romous the teaching of the Most High God. I believe he will be one of the greatest kings to live. And then we will see each other again. Go in peace, child."

With that, Thaylus breathed his last, and departed with a warm smile.

# Chapter 30

## The Emissary's Abode

Thaylus felt himself being lifted into the air, but he could not see. Up and up he went. He saw a bright light and beheld the Emissary.

Thaylus's body trembled and it felt like fire coursed through his limbs. Yet he felt no pain. His hands and body emit light, and his clothes became flowing white robes that swayed like he was floating in water.

The Emissary gestured, and Brythan came forth, also in his glorious form.

"Hello, old friend."

"Hello, Brythan. We have come a long way to get here."

Brythan smiled. "It was all the Emissary's work."

Brythan turned to the Emissary and bowed, and Thaylus did the same.

"Rise, Thaylus. There are some who wish to see you," said the Emissary.

He motioned with his hand for Thaylus to enter the Gate of Vessels.

Once he did, he beheld wonders and images he could not describe. The beauty and grandeur made him cry.

Four people in spiritual bodies neared him—before him stood Elim, Clara, Doren, and another that Thaylus knew somehow, but could not name him.

The mysterious figure stepped forth. "I was the spirit being from Tarken Town who led you to the seal to the Abyss. God was merciful to me, and He gave me a soul. Thank you for giving supplication on my behalf.

Clara, the guardian spirit, neared Thaylus.

"I am happy to have known a chosen one of God. He chose well. I am here because helping you was my last task. My spirit was free to move on."

*252*

Elim addressed Thaylus. "I hope your journeys through time were enjoyable."

"They were quite unique and sometimes dangerous, but fascinating. If only I had more time strength to go to other eras! It is good to see you."

Doren spoke to Thaylus last. "Hello, Thaylus. I wish I could have seen what happened after I died. What became of Nithose?"

Thaylus smiled. "He was sent by a Vessel Bearer named Ithia to be reunited with an older brother."

Doren sighed. "I did not know that. I am glad. I worry what would have happened to him after I left him. I took care of him after his parents died. But I know I'll see him again."

"Welcome all to my kingdom," the Emissary said with his arms wide. "Here you will have dominion over all spiritual beings I have created."

Thaylus neared the Emissary. "What will happen to the vessels of those who do not believe in you?"

"They will grow old and rusty. Eventually they will corrode to nothing."

Thaylus looked down. He thought of all those evil souls who would not submit to the Emissary and live benevolently. Thaylus forgave all those who were hostile to him, even the wizard Kyrious.

But perhaps he could change. Perhaps others could, too.

A bright winged woman in shining clothes descended from the sky.

"Ithia!"

"Greetings, Thaylus!" she said with a bow. "It was a joy to help you get this far. I welcome you."

"It was a pleasure as well."

"Now that we are acquainted let us enter my realm."

The Emissary led the small group of six individuals into the glorious celestial kingdom filled with indescribable wonder. They joined a throng of other spiritual beings, all celebrating with joy and gratitude the One True God who dwells in the Gate of Vessels.

As Thaylus entered the glorious realm, he wondered if there would ever be a day when all on Khrine would submit to God.

Perhaps another chosen one would be selected for that task.

What a joyful day that would be!

# About the Author

JACOB SUAREZ is a longtime writer who holds an Associate of Arts degree in creative writing from the College of Southern Nevada. He has embraced his debilitating mental anxiety affliction, for it enables him to delve seamlessly into the world of speculative fiction. He has produced more than eight hundred Christian/spiritual fantasy short stories and poems, many of these shared on his website, Fantasyrealm.blog, and on Writing.com.

Made in the USA
Columbia, SC
24 September 2024

42938035R00157